Artificial Culture

Routledge Research in Cultural and Media Studies

Artificial Culture

Identity, Technology, and Bodies

Tama Leaver

Routledge
Taylor & Francis Group

NEW YORK AND LONDON

First published 2012
by Routledge
711 Third Avenue, New York, NY 10017

Simultaneously published in the UK
by Routledge
2 Park Square, Milton Park, Abingdon, Oxfordshire OX14 4RN

First issued in paperback 2014

*Routledge is an imprint of the Taylor & Francis Group,
an informa business*

Typeset in Sabon by IBT Global.

Library of Congress Cataloging-in-Publication Data
Leaver, Tama.
  Artificial culture : identity, technology and bodies / Tama Leaver.
    p. cm. — (Routledge Research in cultural and media studies ; 37)
  Includes bibliographical references and index.
 1. Artificial life. 2. Artificial intelligence. 3. Virtual reality.
 4. Popular culture. 5. Technology—Social aspects. 6. Science—
Social aspects. I. Title.
  BD418.8.L43 2011
  306.4—dc23
  2011031244

ISBN13: 978-0-415-89916-1 (hbk)
ISBN13: 978-1-138-85152-8 (pbk)

For my grandparents, Joan and Fred.
True inspirations.

Contents

Figures

Acknowledgements

This book has been in the pipeline for just over a decade, so I owe a great deal of thanks to a number of people and apologise in advance to anyone whose assistance I've neglected to mention.

Artificial Culture began as my doctoral thesis, so I must express thanks to Jane Long whose guidance, patience, scholarly rigour, and intellectual breadth coaxed the earliest ancestor of this book into existence. As part of that journey, a number of people offered insightful comments on drafts of chapters and helped me refine ideas. In particular for their help I would like to thank Lorraine Sim, Marianne Hicks, Justine Milton-Smith, Kate Riley, Chantal Bourgault, Sara Buttsworth, Jennie Campbell, Tanya Dalziell, Stacey Fox, Fiona Groenhout, Natalia Lizama, and Mark Poster.

I appreciate the encouragement from colleagues in the Department of Internet Studies at Curtin University and want to particularly thank Helen Merrick, Michele Willson, Matthew Allen, and Clare Lloyd. Thanks, too, to Angela Ndalianis for her helpful advice regarding comic books and copyright. Thanks to Erica Wetter at Routledge for her initial interest in this project, and also to Felisa Salvago-Keyes and Julie Ganz for their assistance, advice, and most of all, their patience.

An earlier version of chapter 3 appeared as "Iatrogenic Permutations: From Digital Genesis to the Artificial Other" from *Comparative Literature Studies*, Vol. 41, No. 3, 2004, pp. 424–435. Copyright © 2004 by the Pennsylvania State University Press. Reprinted by permission of the Pennsylvania State University Press. An earlier version of chapter 6 was published as "Interstitial Spaces and Multiple Histories in William Gibson's *Virtual Light, Idoru* and *All Tomorrow's Parties*," *Limina: A Journal of Historical and Cultural Studies*, Vol. 9, 2003, pp. 118–130, and I thank the Limina Collective for permission to reproduce it here. Elements of chapter 7 initially appeared as "'The Infinite Plasticity of the Digital': Posthuman Possibilities, Embodiment and Technology in William Gibson's Interstitial Trilogy," *Reconstruction*, Vol. 4, No. 3, 2004. My thanks to the editors of those journals and several anonymous referees for their helpful feedback, with particular thanks to N. Katherine Hayles, Ximena Gallardo and C. Jason Smith.

This book also reproduces two comic book images featuring Spider-Man © and TM Marvel Entertainment LLC, all rights reserved and used with permission.

Finally, I would like to thank my long-suffering family who have had little choice but to put up with me and my various moments of eccentricity in dealing with the writing and the thinking behind this book. My sister, Simone, her partner Paul, and my nephews Jake and Cooper have been rocks, while my parents, Margaret and Bob, have gone out of their way to ensure I've always had every opportunity and a world of unconditional support. My wonderful wife, Emily, has inspired and supported me in ways I can never adequately describe, but suffice it to say this book would never have existed without her. To Henry, I offer an apology for stealing so many hours from your early years to finish this book, but from now on I promise I'll be there in the evening to read whatever book you like. Emily's parents, Geoff and Carrie, were particularly supportive to the three of us during the final writing stage for which I am very grateful. Lastly, I would like to thank my ever-inspiring grandparents, Joan and Fred, to whom this book is dedicated.

Tama Leaver
Curtin University
July 2011

An Artificial Introduction

In the months following the phenomenally successful release of James Cameron's blockbuster *Avatar* (2009), the news media were saturated with stories of viewers who were so enthralled and immersed that they suffered withdrawal symptoms when the 'real world' failed to live up to the film's pixel-perfect digital fantasy (for example, Connelly, 2010). On one hand the idea of withdrawal from a film, even in 3D, seems fanciful, and yet *Avatar* gripped people in a way which was at times both profound, but also complex and contradictory. It's a film which champions nature, privileges the ideal of living as part of an ecosystem rather than at odds with it, and yet the vast majority of *Avatar* was shot against blue-screen and created using hugely expensive and complex computers and digital equipment. The ecological dream of Pandora exists only as a digital simulation. However, rather than seeing the technological creation of a parable about nature simply as an unworkable and irreconcilable contradiction, I would argue that that this tension highlights a complexity in the relationship between nature, technology, and human beings. More to the point, while the stellar financial success of *Avatar* thrust questions about the boundary between people and technology into the media spotlight, these questions are far from new. Indeed, exploring the complex relationships between nature, culture, humanity, and technology has long been a common theme in many forms of popular culture and especially in what is broadly defined as science fiction. What might be new is that these questions have shifted from being somewhat novel to completely ubiquitous; from popular culture to our communication through email and social media, our relationships to, with, and mediated by technology are deepening daily and permanently under scrutiny. While measuring or even just highlighting cultural trends is an awkward and imprecise business, examining popular culture does provide one useful lens through which these changing relationships can be at least partially mapped. It will thus be the central argument of this book that by analysing certain examples of popular media, the deepening and increasingly complex relationships between people, bodies, and technology can be usefully explored. Indeed, far from being able to easily demarcate where people end and machines begin, I will argue that our culture at large has become artificial.

The artificial, if nothing else, is conventionally thought to signify objects and things outside of the realm of the natural and the realm of the human. Before delving further into the contexts driving this book, I want to begin by sharing my own *Avatar* moment, that is, the first moment I can recall being unsettled in a way I couldn't immediately express about the unclear division between our technologies and ourselves; the first time I can pinpoint where being artificial did not immediately mean being outside of what it means to be human. So either remember back, or try to imagine, a seven-year-old boy arriving home from school in 1983 to discover my father spending the afternoon of his birthday watching a movie on his brand-new Beta video cassette player. When I walked into the lounge room the tape was paused and a strange space pod was hovering on the screen with little mechanical arms outstretched; I thought the pod looked rather like the bulky 'stack hat' bicycle helmet my parents were forcing me to wear while riding, and immediately took a firm dislike to it. Later that night I sat with my father and watched the entire film from the beginning; it was Stanley Kubrick's enigmatic science fiction masterpiece *2001: A Space Odyssey*. At that age a lot of the film's plot was only vaguely accessible, but I do recall feeling far more sympathy for the emotional HAL, whose glowing red eye and exuberant voice were far more engaging than the boring astronauts who talked as though exploring outer space—my personal fantasy—was no more exciting than doing the dishes. After HAL's demise, one of the boring astronauts goes into the dark Monolith in Jupiter's orbit. While that bizarre series of special effects made a real impact on my mind, what stood out more than anything else was during the journey the camera focuses on the astronaut's eye bathed in the bright colours of the alien world outside. At one point, he blinks, and the colours shift, showing a deep red eye with blacks and yellows, an image very similar to poor lobotomised HAL. While I lacked the vocabulary to express it, this recognition of similarity between the astronaut and HAL—whom I later understood to be an Artificial Intelligence—was the first moment when I recognised that sometimes our artificial others and ourselves are confrontingly similar. In the weeks after seeing *2001* I remember vivid dreams and, indeed, nightmares in which my own eyes would change to those colours. In retrospect, I suspect at seven years old, I may have been trying to deal with the implications of connectivity between my own subjective and fleshy corporeality and the heights of digital technology which I had until then imagined *using* to fly into outer space, but never *joining* with those technologies. While a few things have occurred in the intervening decades, this book is in some ways coming to terms with the confusion and shock I first felt after watching *2001*, a confusion not dissimilar to the withdrawal experienced by some *Avatar* viewers.

The full title of this book, *Artificial Culture: Identity, Technology and Bodies*, contains a number of terms which are far from self-explanatory, and need to be situated and defined within the specifics of this monograph. Investigating and reclaiming a particular sense and meaning of 'the artificial' is at the heart of this book, so that term needs to be addressed in the first instance. According to most modern definitions and all contemporary dictionaries, the artificial is specifically outside the realm of the natural. The *Penguin Concise English Dictionary*, for example, defines artificial as: 'made by human skills, not natural; made as substitute for a natural product; insincere in manner, shallow' (Garmonsway, 1991, p. 38). From this definition it is clear that objects and things can be artificial, and that these are explicitly outside of and distinct from the natural. While they may be the product of human intellect and labour, artificial objects are also explicitly beyond the bounds of what it is to be human. However, where do recent concepts such as Artificial Intelligence or Artificial Life fit into this definition? Non-natural life or non-human intelligence certainly challenge the very terms 'life' and 'intelligence' as they have been conventionally understood in Western philosophical traditions for centuries. Taking those difficulties and challenges as a provocation, in this study the artificial is acknowledged as a boundary point against which the natural and the human have been historically defined, but it also highlights the emerging links between the artificial and both subjects—the way people conceptualise themselves—and embodiment. The link of the artificial with technology is also fundamental in the blurring of boundaries between the human and the non-human. The shift in our artificialities underpins the book's five parts, each in turn asking where the boundary between the artificial and the concepts in question—intelligence, life, space, people, and culture—lies, as well as just how flexible those boundaries may actually become in the face of examination.

The body or, more specifically, embodiment is a similarly vague term which has shifted in meaning significantly over the last century. At least from Descartes onward, liberal humanist thought feared the body and the flesh as something distracting, something other than the mind, and also something more clearly linked with the feminine. However, political changes in the twentieth century (and earlier) in both the various forms of feminism and other movements have partially reclaimed embodiment and corporeality as sites of subjectivity and identity for all people. For the purposes of this book, embodiment refers to the specific carnal and corporeal instantiation of bodies, both human and non-human, which entail both visual surfaces and a meaningful interiority of tissues, organs, and other elements. While embodiment is generally a material concept, from the second part onward the notion of informatic life is examined; and the argument is made that embodiment is a coherent and meaningful part of the rearticulating subjectivities of Artificial Life and nominally digital people. At this juncture I would like to emphasise that while subjectivity is sometimes deployed in these pages as a tactic reinforcing the implicit personhood of a particularly entity, this is not intended to unproblematically promote a narrow, singular, and staunchly individual notion of 'the subject'. Rather, subjectivities and embodiment are interrelated fields in which the very terms that define them blur and expand. Embodiment and subjectivity are useful shorthands for particular fields of ideas, not rigid concepts locked in place. As with many terms and ideas explored, subjectivity and embodiment are contextually specific ideas whose definition can vary greatly in their specific uses.

Given the vastness of popular culture, in order to limit this project to a practical size, it is necessary to focus on a single genre, and given science fiction is clearly the area which has most frequently provoked questions about the boundaries between people, nature, and technology, it is the most appropriate choice. That said, the study of science fiction has a long and contested history, too, with some writers preferring to label the area speculative fiction. Speculative fiction and science fiction are often rendered as the same thing, but the former often appears more acceptable in scholarly areas which have only recently warmed to genres outside of the previously championed canon of English Literature. Speculative fiction is also, at times, broadened to include any horror, fantasy, science fiction, or other work which is set in a realm not logically consistent with the material world of contemporary society. However, even in book length works on the subject, the definition is never concrete. In Carl Freedman's relatively recent *Critical Theory and Science Fiction* (2000), he valiantly tries to trace the historical lineage of science fiction in order to reach a definition, but after seventy-three pages of exploring the term, Freedman's use is as contingent and specific as any other. Darko Suvin's description of science fiction as a genre of 'cognitive estrangement' is probably the most popular definition amongst scholars (Suvin, 1979). Given that Suvin's argument is that good science fiction removes familiar contexts in order to provide better contexts to explore important questions, this definition certainly highlights the utility of science fiction in exploring artificial culture. Throughout this book, then, I use the terms science fiction and speculative fiction interchangeably, but always with Suvin's broad definition in mind.

This exploration of the artificial then is a broadly interdisciplinary study and as such draws theoretical and conceptual insights from a wide body of materials, across a number of scholarly fields. With such broad underpinnings, there are many important influences and writers whose works have contributed to the perspectives formulated regarding artificialities. However, if this book comes in the wake of the work of any one writer, it would be feminist critic Donna Haraway. Haraway's ground-breaking 'Manifesto for Cyborgs' was written over twenty-five years ago, but remains extremely relevant to cultural analyses of links between subjectivity, embodiment, and technology. Haraway argues that everyone in contemporary culture is *already a cyborg*; in the operations of everyday life—from drinking calcium-enhanced milk to wearing contact lenses and talking on mobile or cellular phones—technology and humanity have become inseparable. Moreover, for Haraway, the main point is that there 'is no fundamental, ontological separation in our formal knowledge of machine and organism, of technical and organic' (Haraway, 1991, p. 178). In challenging one of the key binary divisions at the core of the liberal humanist philosophy underpinning much of Western thought, Haraway proposes a cyborg politics which ruptures the boundaries of subjectivity and objectivity, and also related binary divisions including mind and body, male and female, and human and technology. The impact of Haraway's work has been substantial across cultural studies, allowing a feminist politics that could engage with the realm of technology and science fiction rather than primarily react against it. However, even though the implications of Haraway's manifesto—a work Zoë Sofoulis (2002) calls a cultural 'cyberquake'—implicitly ruptured the core of humanist thought, even when the cyborg became a more recognisable figure in theory and popular culture, the logical dissolving of related conceptual boundaries and binary thinking did not necessarily follow. To a large extent, this study follows similar lines to those of Haraway, although it does not begin with either the cyborg or the human subject as the focal point of analysis *per se*. The implications of Haraway's manifesto remain relevant, but further work, such as this book, is required to continually amplify the political points and explore these ideas further across different texts and media forms.

Artificial Intelligence (AI) is the most culturally recognisable conjunction of 'the artificial' with a nominally natural and supposedly exclusively human trait (at a 'high' enough level). It is also the earliest and most established scientific field of study in terms of artificiality. Thus, before moving into the first chapter, it is useful to explore the origins and development of AI, initially in the overlapping contexts of scientific discourse, especially cybernetics, and science fiction—most notably in the work of Isaac Asimov—rounding out these areas with contemporary re-articulations by Hans Moravec and N. Katherine Hayles. With those early origins clearly in focus, I will briefly address the types of media under examination before launching into the first chapter exploring early AI science fiction films.

NORBERT WIENER AND ALAN TURING

Artificial Intelligence (AI) as a subject of serious scientific inquiry entered the public realm in the decade following the Second World War. Probably the most important arenas in which ideas about AIs were contested were the Macy Conferences. Held between 1944 and 1955, these interdisciplinary gatherings saw a wide range of participants map out the emergent science of cybernetics. Of all the voices present, one of the loudest was that of Nobert Wiener whose subsequent publications built on the ideas debated at the conferences. In his technical manual *Cybernetics*, published in 1947 and then expanded and re-issued in 1961, and his layperson's guide *The Human Use of Human Beings*, originally published in 1950 and expanded and republished in 1954, Wiener outlined the arguments that would guide cybernetics, as well as the fears with which cybernetics and the wider public imaginary would grapple in relation to Artificial Intelligences or 'thinking machines'.

Wiener presented a number of important arguments, but the most important, and the one underlying all others, was his re-definition of intelligent life. For Wiener, originally a mathematician by trade, the basic property of the material world was a tendency towards entropy, which he defined as the decay and disorganisation of information. In contrast to the world around them, human beings, through information reception, learning, memory, and output, act to maintain and increase the organisation of patterns of information and are thus anti-entropic agents in both individual terms and, more importantly, as a species (Wiener, 1954). Wiener draws a number of analogies between the biological and informatic, including his argument about the function of the human nervous system. He argues that individual nerve fibres are basically single decision-makers, the choice between whether to fire (a nerve impulse) or not. Wiener parallels this decision-making action with the way machines decide between two alternatives. Moreover, Wiener argues that the more complex decisions where multiple nerves and synapses are employed are comparable to 'switching devices' in machines (Wiener, 1954). Although he does not use exactly the same terms, Wiener's description of the nervous system parallels the way all computer functions can be reduced to binary code (a single decision between a '1' or a '0').

While complex patterns of information may be housed in the human body, Wiener argues that the tissues and material elements cannot be essential, since in the course of a human lifetime, all the biological elements are completely replaced through normal cellular activity. Biological elements are geared towards perpetuating information, through two modes of learning: the first, the phylogenic, is comparable in contemporary terminology to genetic memory; while the second, ontogenic, is individual learning within a normal lifetime. The phylogenic is actually geared towards increasing the capacity for ontogenic learning, which Wiener argues to be one of the defining elements of an intelligent system. However, the phylogenic is not essential since it is only necessary to facilitate the creation and perpetuation of complex informatic patterns. For Wiener, the 'physical identity of an individual does not consist in the matter of which it is made' (Wiener, 1954, p. 101). At a more basic level, Wiener's argument is that the unique and defining characteristic of intelligent life is that it is a complex pattern of organised information, irrespective of the material substrate which carries it. Our biological form is one way in which complex patterns of information may exist, but the biological is *not necessarily the only way complex patterns of information can exist*. In Wiener's words, '[w]e are not stuff that abides, but patterns that perpetuate themselves' (Wiener, 1954, p. 96). Moreover, as the informatic pattern in humans can be reduced to a binary code, then that pattern could, in terms of Wiener's argument, also exist within a sufficiently complex machine.

Concurrent with Wiener's publications, Alan Turing's influential essay 'Computing Machinery and Intelligence' appeared in the journal *Mind*. Turing was a British mathematician whose work during the Second World War had been fundamental in cracking the German Enigma cipher codes. He had led the team that constructed the first computing machine, The Colossus, although this information remained under guard during the period of the Macy Conferences due to the Official Secrets Act. Wiener and Turing discussed cybernetics and ideas of computing machines at some length in 1947 (Hodges, 1983, p. 403). In his article, Turing sought to explore one question: whether a machine could think. In order to determine if machine intelligence was a possibility, Turing described a test he called the 'imitation game' (which later became widely known as the Turing Test). In Turing's scenario, an interrogator sitting in one room must ask two unseen participants questions to determine which is human and which is machine. The communication would take place through typewritten communication so as not to give away the identity of the participants through their material existence or their handwriting (if, indeed, they had hands). Turing argued that if the interrogator could not consistently determine from the participants' answers which was human and which was machine, then it would prove that machines could think (and not only think, but think at a level comparable with their human counterparts) (Turing, 1950, pp. 433–434). For Turing, the question of embodiment was irrelevant: all that mattered was the capacity to convincingly communicate information.

In order to contextualise Wiener's and Turing's dreams of disembodied intelligent information, it is worth delving deeper into their own lives and motivations. As a mathematician, Norbert Wiener viewed and analysed the world and everything in it in terms of probability and information. Yet, his earlier goals were far more materially oriented. Before mathematics, he pursued a career in biology, but had to abandon this field, as he was too clumsy to handle equipment and complete laboratory work. Wiener's lack of physical co-ordination actually hampered him significantly for most of his life. Indeed, N. Katherine Hayles, in her examination of Wiener's work on cybernetics, suggests that his discomfort with his own embodied form is reflected in his dreams of a disembodied intelligence (Hayles, 1999, p. 88). Wiener also strongly believed in the autonomous individual liberal humanist subject. He was at some level aware that his work on cybernetics had the potential to undermine notions of liberal humanism (specifically by challenging the boundaries of 'the human', suggesting intelligence was not intrinsic only to human beings), which he attempted to counter by a number of warnings and qualifications about the role of machines in human society throughout his written work.[1] He viewed his own work as extremely important to the future of humanity, and believed that any resistance to it was due to the slow uptake by the public and scientific communities of new ideas, as exemplified in a passage from his treatise on cybernetics and religion, *God and Golem, Inc.*:

> For the idea that God's creation of man and the animals, the begetting
> of living being according to their kind, and the possible reproduction
> of machines are all part of the same order of phenomena *is* emotionally
> disturbing, just as Darwin's speculations on evolution and the descent
> of man were disturbing. (Wiener, 1964, p. 47)

For Wiener, cybernetics was as important to science and the wider community as the theory of evolution, although he trod very carefully in never suggesting (explicitly, at least) that cybernetics and machine intelligence could ever be *part* of a singular theory of evolution.

Similarly, Alan Turing was also a staunch individualist who from an early age developed his own unorthodox methods of inquiry and rarely following the way things 'should be done' at his English public boys' school. His passion for mathematics developed at an early age and drove his career, although his experiences in the Government Code and Cypher School during the Second World War broadened his interests to the development of machinery and electrical systems. However, the most difficult element of Turing's life was the fact that he was gay in an era when his sexual choice was not only frowned upon but still decidedly illegal. In Andrew Hodges' biography of Alan Turing, he points out that 'like any homosexual man [in that period], he was living an imitation game, not in the sense of conscious play-acting, but by being accepted as a person that he was not' (Hodges, 1983, p. 129). Turing's own 'imitation game' proved unsuccessful when in 1952 he was charged with 'An Act of Gross Indecency' having been involved in a gay sexual relationship: he was sentenced to experimental 'organo-therapeutic' treatment, which consisted of injecting him with female hormones thought to dull sexual drives. The 'treatment' rendered Turing impotent and he also developed breasts. In 1954 Turing killed himself, an act blamed by many who knew him on the aftereffects of his treatment and persecution (Hodges, 1983) and it was not until 2009 that British Prime Minister Gordon Brown issued an official apology for Turing's vile treatment more than half a century earlier. In the context of his life, Turing's 'imitation game' appears as telling about his own experience as about his position on machine intelligence. For a person who longed to be left alone or at least treated as ordinary, he found himself to be 'an ordinary homosexual atheist mathematician' (Hodges, 1983, p. 114). The imitation game described in relation to intelligent machines was, in part at least, a fantasy of escape, of being treated in terms of his work on mathematics and cybernetics, not in terms of his personal embodied choices which he was forced to hide from the critical and unaccepting eyes of the outside world.

Although Turing and Wiener approached ideas of Artificial Intelligence from somewhat different perspectives, they shared two important conclusions: both defined intelligence as a function of patterns of information and communication; and neither believed that the human body was the only vessel in which intelligent patterns of information could exist. Thus credible premises for a thinking and learning machine were developed: if the essence of intelligence is the organisation and communication of complex patterns of information, then the computer, which is basically a complex information-processing device, seems the most logical place for human-level intelligence to arise. From Turing's and Wiener's foundational work, cybernetics as a scientific discipline, and as a set of ideas in the broader public imaginary, developed and mutated over the following half century. However, the relevance and impact of their formative works is obvious even in the most contemporary texts, exemplified in Hans Moravec's *Mind Children* and *Robot*.

HANS MORAVEC

Hans Moravec's two texts *Mind Children: The Future of Robot and Human Intelligence* (1988) and *Robot: Mere Machine to Transcendent Mind* (1999) are the most extreme hard science arguments for the disembodied informatic intelligences that were partially envisaged by Wiener and Turing. Moravec, the founder of the world's largest robotics programme at Carnegie Mellon University, not only believes that machine intelligence will be equal to human intelligence by 2030, but, even more extreme, he believes that humanity will be usurped by 'its own artificial progeny' in the years to follow (Moravec, 1988, pp. 1, 68). Moravec argues that in the near future, the 'uneasy truce between mind and body breaks down completely' and biological life will become obsolete, ushering in a 'post-biological' era in which Artificial Intelligences, the offspring of the human mind, will inherit the Earth and human beings will go the way of the dinosaurs (Moravec, 1988, p. 4). Moravec cites both Turing and Wiener as the 'pioneers' of the idea of machine evolution; Wiener's work is utilised throughout Moravec's writing, while Turing's article on machine intelligence provides the basis for Moravec's philosophical defence of the idea of AI in *Robot*. Moreover, Moravec's conclusions in *Mind Children* sound ominously close to a paraphrase of Wiener's arguments in *The Human Use of Human Beings*: Moravec argues that human beings need to move from a 'body-identity position' to a 'pattern-identity': 'Pattern identity . . . defines the essence of a person . . . as the *pattern* and the *process* going on in [their] head and body, not the machinery supporting that process. If the process is preserved, I am preserved. The rest is mere jelly' (Moravec, 1988, pp. 116–117). In Moravec's work, the idea of patterns of information as the essence of intelligent life is no longer restrained by Wiener's adherence to the ideals of liberal humanism, so the idea is taken to its logical extreme where bodies, biology, and human beings *en masse* are viewed as obsolete in the face of the emerging Artificial Intelligences.

Yet, even Moravec's position on embodiment and intelligence alters between his first and second publication. In the first, *Mind Children,* embodiment serves no purpose whatsoever except to house the pattern-identity of an individual which would function so much clearer and faster if it could be removed from the 'jelly' of the flesh into the digital realm. One of Moravec's most macabre descriptions is his vision of a device to 'transmigrate' a human intelligence into a machine: he describes a scenario where a robot surgeon slowly cuts away layer after layer of the human brain, scanning each cell to form a complete picture of the information stored in the brain and then finally, when the biological skull is simply an empty vessel, a digital human can be transferred into a waiting machine housing (Moravec, 1988, pp. 109–110). With a hint of the gothic, Moravec describes the person being completely awake during this procedure, ostensibly to ensure that the replication of information is exact. However, by his second book, Moravec concedes that even if scanning of a human mind is completely successful, embodiment will still have a role to play. He argues that biological human beings will retain the need for a 'sense of body' and thus the transplanted personality will have to have a virtual body, or avatar, created to allow the sensory and motor functions (or material context) that create and maintain meaning for human beings (Moravec, 1999, p. 170). Moravec's admission of the necessity of embodiment does not, however, restrain his vision of humanity's irrelevance, and he argues that if embodied human simulations are allowed to remain in the digital realm, then their relationship with the native Artificial Intelligences would not be on equal terms: '[A] human mind would lumber about in a massively inappropriate body simulation, like a hardhat deep-sea diver plodding through a troupe of acrobatic dolphins' (Moravec, 1999, p. 172). For Moravec, intelligent informatic patterns own the future, and the necessity of embodiment for human beings will simply ensure our extinction.

N. KATHERINE HAYLES:
'THE MATERIALITY OF INFORMATICS'

In her book *How We Became Posthuman* (1999), N. Katherine Hayles analyses, among others, Wiener's and Moravec's theories about information as the basis of life and argues that, in divorcing information from a material substrate, they have in effect removed information from any context and thus, for Hayles, from meaning. She reads both as arguing that information is defined by what it *is*, not what it *does*. Hayles, by contrast, argues that information in any meaningful way is inextricably intertwined with material embodiment. She argues further that 'embodiment' entails contextualisation within 'the specifics of place, time, physiology and culture' (1992, p. 155). Context is not only as important as information but is, in fact, part of information since information is referentially formed and referentially meaningful. Moreover, there are two levels of referentiality: the first level is the external, in terms of the specific time, place, and culture; while the second and equally important level is the internal or material level, in that information within an embodied system refers to and is part of that material system. Any attempt to remove information from embodied context thus removes the reference points that originally shaped that information, rendering the so-called information that remains meaningless (Hayles, 1992). To be fair to Hayles, however, it must be pointed out that her argument was not intended to argue that AIs were, should be, or necessarily would be embodied entities, but rather to refute claims that human beings could be reduced to purely informatic forms. Conversely, it is equally important to point out that in arguing against the idea that intelligence can be reduced to a purely informatic form, Hayles refutes one of the main premises for the development of Artificial Intelligence as envisioned by Norbert Wiener.

ISAAC ASIMOV: 'OH, JUPITER, A ROBOT DESCARTES!'

Isaac Asimov's formative explorations of issues regarding AIs or 'thinking machines' occurred in the same historical and cultural context as Wiener's and Turing's work, but were not a product of the hard sciences *per se*;[2] rather, they emerged as part of the golden age of American science fiction (SF). Asimov was born in Russia in 1920, of a Jewish background, and immigrated to the United States with his parents at the age of three, initially residing in Brooklyn. He had a relatively lonely childhood, spending much of his time outside school hard at work in his parents' confectionery shop. He had a passion for reading and writing, and, under the wing of John W. Campbell (who was then editor of *Astounding*, probably the most influential science fiction periodical of the time), Asimov launched his prolific writing career in his late teens. During the 1940s, Isaac Asimov's most influential pieces were nine short stories based around the possibilities of robotic life in a human world. In 1950, the same year that Turing's 'imitation game' was described in the pages of *Mind*, Asimov's explorations were collected under the provocative title *I, Robot* (White, 1994). However, before analysing Asimov's speculative textual engagement with notions of AIs and robotics, it is worth considering why the term Artificial Intelligence does not appear in any of the *I, Robot* stories.

The absence of the term 'Artificial Intelligence' from Asimov's early robot stories and indeed from Alan Turing's 1950 'Computing Machinery and Intelligence' as well has a simple explanation: the term had not yet been conceived. 'Artificial Intelligence' was first coined in the following decade by John McCarthy, one of the pioneering figures of AI design and programming, when he organised the 1956 *Dartmouth Summer Research Project on Artificial Intelligence* (Copeland, 1993, pp. 8–9). However, although Asimov's and Turing's initial explorations did not explicitly use AI as terminology, their texts explore many of the central themes that AI as both a concept and a material possibility provoked. Turing's notion of the 'thinking machine' became a synonym for AI, while Asimov's notion of robotics similarly became part of AI design and research, but in a more complex way which mutated substantially in different contexts.

Although in the hard sciences robotics now refers more to the construction of mechanical bodies (and AI more to the construction of artificial minds), when Asimov invented the term robotics, he made no such distinction.[3] He took embodiment for granted: every robot was a material entity in its own right (although not necessarily with its own rights) and came complete with its own mechanical body.[4] Asimov explicitly links his extrapolated robotic future with the formative works of Wiener and Turing through a number of strategies, the most explicit being the development of the character Susan Calvin. The short stories which form *I, Robot* are linked by a narrative told from Calvin's point of view in a retrospective interview given during the weeks leading up to her retirement.[5] Susan Calvin's career explicitly links the fictional history of robotics with the 'real' work being discussed in the Macy Conferences in that Asimov describes her as having completed 'graduate work in cybernetics' in the first decade of the twenty-first century, and she was then employed as a 'robopsychologist' in 2008 by the first firm to commercially produce robots (Asimov, 1950, p. 9). Here the emerging scientific discipline of cybernetics is located in Asimov's future history, and the conceptual distance from cybernetics to a future in which robots are so complex that they have their own psychology appears not that far at all. Implicit in the need for a robopsychologist is also the idea that robots will have such distinct and complex 'minds' (or, at least, intelligence) that their actions will not be logically transparent, but rather will require interpretation and analysis through the same processes which attempt to comprehend human thought. Just as in Norbert Wiener's work, the possibility of dealing with human-level intelligence in a non-human form provoked anxieties about the future of human beings. For Asimov, any discussion of robots had to be contextualised within particular restrictions that would maintain the superior position of humans. To this end, he postulates the Three Laws of Robotics.

The Three Laws of Robotics described in *I, Robot* formalise the fear that robots and AIs could threaten an anthropocentric world, since Asimov highlighted and pre-empted the notion of robotic rebellion or independence by creating a world where any and every robot created *must* have strict laws hardwired into their 'positronic brains' to prevent them being able to harm or disobey humans. Those laws were thus formalised:

1. A robot may not injure a human being, or, through inaction, allow a human being to come to harm.
2. A robot must obey any orders given it by human beings except where such orders would conflict with the First Law.
3. A robot must protect its own existence as long as such protection does not conflict with the First or Second Law (Asimov, 1950, p. 8).

There is some contention as to whether Asimov or his editor John Campbell first committed these laws to paper: Asimov always claimed they were first written by Campbell, while Campbell always stated that he wrote down what Asimov had already described in one of their many conversations (Gunn, 1982, pp. 59–61). Either way, the Three Laws of Robotics became one of the central ideas for any speculative text that dealt with robotics or AIs. Different versions and adaptations of the Three Laws which explicate a hierarchy with human life valued over and above 'artificial' life can be seen in many SF texts from novels and short stories to television and film.[6] Moreover, the widespread currency of the Three Laws both in Asimov's work and elsewhere has led critics such as J. P. Telotte to argue that 'in their careful formulation . . . [the Three Laws] hint at a widespread cultural anxiety' about the relationship between human beings and robotic or Artificial Intelligences (Telotte, 1995, p. 43). Anxiety about the role of artificiality in a human world is precisely what drives many of Asimov's stories, evidence of which can be seen in a close reading of 'Reason', one of the most well-known tales from *I, Robot*.

Isaac Asimov's 'Reason' was first published in Campbell's *Astounding* in 1941 before becoming part of the *I, Robot* (1950) collection. In the story, a new robot QT-1, nicknamed Cutie, becomes convinced through his[7] own reasoning that human beings are inferior to robots and are thus incapable of being their creators. Cutie is onboard a space station and is responsible for processing and obeying instructions from a massive sensor array. The robot concludes that the array must be 'the Master' since robot and humans alike obey its instructions. In the historical and cultural context of the original 1941 publication, 'Reason' was most notable for its primarily political argument against the 'reasoning' behind fundamentalist religious beliefs. However, within the broader narrative of *I, Robot*, Cutie's significance lies in that he is ostensibly the first robot to disobey human beings (although by Cutie's logic, he is obeying the master of human beings, thus not completely contradicting the Three Laws). The scene in which Cutie confronts Gregory Powell and Mike Donovan (the only humans onboard) is of particular relevance: as the two men grumble beneath the glare of the 'red glow of the robot's eyes', Cutie explains that it is impossible for human beings to be the creators since the 'material you are made of [is] soft and flabby, lacking endurance and strength, depending for energy upon inefficient oxidation of organic material . . . [p]eriodically you pass into a coma and the least variation in temperature, air pressure, humidity, or radiation intensity impairs your efficiency . . . [y]ou are *makeshift*', while Cutie argues that he has a 'strong metal [body], . . . [is] continuously conscious, and can stand extremes in environment easily' (Asimov, 1950, pp. 54, 56–57). Cutie concludes, in examining not just the comparable intelligence of humans and robots but also the efficiency of their embodiment, that human beings are the older model, inferior to robots, and are obsolete.[8] When Cutie concludes that 'I myself, exist because I think—', Gregory Powell laments, 'Oh, Jupiter, a robot Descartes!' (Asimov, 1950, p. 56), implicitly recognising the mode of argument from human history, although in the same instant, challenging the anthropocentric uniqueness of Cartesian rationale since the same logic has allowed a robot to 'rationally' determine his own existence and his own superior position in the material world. There are two important elements worth emphasising in relation to 'Reason': the first is that, unlike Wiener's and Turing's notions of AIs, Asimov's robots value embodiment to the extent that they see their harder, more durable bodies as evidence of superiority; and secondly, that even with such strong restrictions as the Three Laws, any intelligent being (organic or technological) implicitly has the creative resources to 'reason' their way into doing something that at first glance violates those restrictive laws.

THE QUESTION OF TEXTS

Before proceeding into the first chapter, it is important to note that although the various films, novels, theories, and other examples from various media are all treated as 'texts' in the sense that they are all open to analysis using tools derived from literary and cultural theory, it is equally important to allow for differences in media and to heed N. Katherine Hayles' warning about the 'importance of media-specific analyses' (Hayles, 2000). While retrospectively deified media prophet Marshall McLuhan was overstating the case in his oft-quoted argument that 'the medium is the message' (1964), he did make the salient point that the medium—the mode of communication—is not independent of but rather an important *part* of content. McLuhan's work attempts to render any distinction between content and media untenable. In terms of science fiction cinema—a category to which all the films in the following two chapters belong—the distinction between media is extremely important. Although certain science fiction novels have, to some extent, been critically and academically accepted as meaningful literary forms and sites of social critique, Brooks Landon argues that the same acceptance rarely extends to SF film (Landon, 1992, p. xvi–xvii). Vivian Sobchack concurs, arguing further that

> since the written literature was there first and is both more plentiful and accessible than film, the common tendency is to remember all the good—and therefore, frequently anthologised—SF literature and compare it with the worst SF films. (1997, p. 20)

However, challenging critical prejudice against SF films is not simply solved by distinguishing the 'good' from 'bad' because for many the presumption is that 'the medium itself . . . is incapable of dealing with ideas as effectively as does literature' (Sobchack, 1997, p. 24). In generic terms SF in particular is viewed as 'trashy', more so than other film genres because it usually contains and is often primarily characterised by the use of special effects (SFx). Although it may be SFx that attract audiences, and indeed often those who would not read SF in print, audiences do not *just* watch the visual effects, meaning that far more people engage with science fictional concepts (albeit sometimes unintentionally) through film than any other medium. Moreover, SFx, rather than always being commercially driven devices to create ever-larger explosions and spacecraft, are more usefully viewed as an expression of SF cinema's structural ambivalence.

Many film scholars assert that ambivalence is in fact central to all SF film; Brooks Landon goes so far as to argue that it is 'the basic or distinguishing structural pattern' of SF cinema (Landon, 1992, p. 22). Moreover, in Vivian Sobchack's seminal *Screening Space* she examines the iconography of SF cinema and concludes that the associated connotations and symbolic meanings of SF film icons continuously shift and change to the extent that, paradoxically, the only stable characteristic of SF iconography is ambivalence. Sobchack's argument is reinforced by comparison of examples such as the train in Westerns or the gun in Westerns and gangster movies which are (relatively) symbolically stable, and the SF icons of spacecraft and robots which frequently alter in their symbolic significance (Sobchack, 1997, p. 66). Returning to special effects, ambivalence is also evident in comparisons of the most *spectacular*, such as the lightsabers, laser blasters, and epic space battles in the *Star Wars* films, and the most *speculative*, such as the morphogenic SFx in *Terminator 2* which implicitly interrogate (or at least problematise) the boundaries of subjectivity. Brooks Landon succinctly summarises the matter thus:

> SF film combines *both* narrative *and* spectacle, offers the pleasures of *both* art *and* trash, appeals to *both* the intellect *and* the emotions, and can support *both* escapism *and* self-enlightenment. And it is precisely this both/and impulse in SF film that leads to its inherently ambivalent nature. (Landon, 1992, p. 64)

Another important site of ambivalence is the internal generic tension in SF film in that it relies on cutting edge technology for its spectacular visual SFx, while simultaneously being the most fertile filmic arena for explorations and panic over the possibilities of highly technologised societies. While the ambivalence of SF film means many critics can dismiss SF cinema as overtly commercial, trashy, and a site of spectacle, it is equally true that many SF films contain speculative ideological, moral, and political critiques despite being explicitly conceived as commercial ventures (Landon, 1992, p. 20). Moreover, turning to SF cinema with some characteristics of the medium having been clarified, it becomes apparent that the tension between *spectacle* and *speculation* is not just a tension between different films, but a tension *internal* to many SF films, that can be powerfully deployed in both explorative and entertaining ways. Such tensions take centre stage in the next chapter, beginning with an examination of Stanley Kubrick's *2001*, a film where the tension between spectacle and speculation is always present.

In mapping ideas about the artificial emerging over the late twentieth and early twenty-first centuries, this book is divided into five main parts, each containing several chapters. The first two parts are framed by the existing scientific concepts of Artificial Intelligence and Artificial Life, explored through the lens of cinema and literature respectively. The first chapter of Part I analyses a number of films including the iconic *2001: A Space Odyssey* as well as contemporary to it, but less well known, films such as *Colossus: The Forbin Project* and *Demon Seed*, looking at the way AIs were first imagined on the silver screen. Chapter 2 focuses on the four *Terminator* films, arguing that far from disembodied entities, the Artificial Intelligences in contemporary cinema have a substantial sense of their own inextricably embodied selves. The second part moves on to explore the idea of Artificial Life through the novels of Australian hard science fiction author Greg Egan. These two chapters explore Egan's *Permutation City* and *Diaspora* which are notable for their meaningful engagement with the possibilities of digital existence and informatic life while trying valiantly to map their emergence from the technologies available today. Central to Egan's work, I will argue, is the notion of building bridges between the material and the digital in often quite unexpected ways.

The remaining three parts argue offer the conceptual umbrellas of artificial space, artificial people, and finally artificial culture; these concepts are not set in concrete, but are emerging ideas which provide a useful shorthand in focusing each section. Thus, the third part engages with the idea of artificial space through a reading of William Gibson's *Bridge* trilogy. Artificial space is defined as one where embodiment and informatics co-exist in a manner which entails a very useful and practical tactical politics. Gibson's work is particularly useful since in his earlier novels he coined the term cyberspace as both an idea and a metaphor for the wired world, but his second trilogy pushes the question of the relationship between people and technology in far more complex directions but has received far less critical attention. The chapters in the following part return to a focus on films and examine the *Matrix* and *Lord of the Rings* trilogies, arguing that these franchises posit the formation of artificial people at the level both of narrative and of production via the complexities of special effects technologies designed to allow more and more of an actor's corporeal form to be manipulated via digital tools.

The final part explores the cumulative notion of artificial culture through a reading of the *Spider-Man* trilogy. These chapters also consider the role of the artificial in the difficult aftermath of 11 September 2001, arguing that artificialities can, indeed, provide a space of artificial mourning where the meaning and ramifications of the attacks on the US at that time can be re-negotiated. After examining ideas of the artificial as deployed in film, novels, and other digital contexts, the book concludes that contemporary instances of the artificial can act as a matrix which, rather than separating or demarcating minds and bodies or humanity and the digital, reinforce the *symbiotic connection between people, bodies, and technologies.*

Part I

Artificial Intelligence

1 Early Artificial Intelligence Films
'When are you going to
let me out of this box?'

Nowhere in cinema history has breathtaking visual spectacle and profound philosophical speculation been more successfully combined than in enigmatic director Stanley Kubrick's SF masterpiece *2001: A Space Odyssey*. Visually, the film broke new ground with its amazing stargate finale, while the attention to detail in the moon and spaceflight sequences was so accurate that NASA astronauts actually used the film as a training tool for some years following the film's release, a feat even more impressive given that *2001* came out in 1968, the year *before* the first human moon landing (Stork, 1997, p. 2). On the speculative level, *2001* introduced HAL, the single most widely recognised representation of Artificial Intelligence in cinema or popular culture to this day. In doing so, the big questions about what constitute both intelligence and life itself—as they were raised in relation to the early writings on Artificial Intelligence and cybernetics—found their way into the broader popular imaginary via the silver screen.[1] Indeed, the 'intellectually provocative' nature of *2001* was so dominant that many critics have argued that it finally put rest to the widely held 'myth' that SF cinema 'cannot possibly be as thoughtful, as profound, or as intellectually stimulating as SF literature' (Sobchack, 1997, p. 24). Speculation about the tenuous status of AIs is explicitly flagged early in the film during an interview with the crew of *The Discovery* in which HAL is introduced as a 'computer which can reproduce, *although some experts still prefer to use the word mimic*, most of the activities of the human brain and with incalculably greater speed and reliability' (emphasis added). The implicit question here as to whether HAL is actually alive or intelligent, and thus the counterpoint of exactly what being alive and intelligent mean in relation to human beings, develops as a major theme of *2001*. It is that theme which will be explored below.

Ostensibly, HAL appears to fulfil Hans Moravec's (1988, 1999) predictions of emergent disembodied informatic intelligences. Paul Edwards supports this contention through his reading of *2001* and other films featuring AIs which he divides into two categories: the disembodied and embodied. For Edwards, HAL is the 'perfect representative of disembodied Artificial Intelligence' (1996, p. 321). In the embodied category sit more recognisably humanoid AIs such as 'robots, androids and cyborgs', while HAL differs from these in that he appears without a defined physical form.[2] The lack of obvious boundaries and HAL's seemingly omnipresent gaze within *The Discovery* led Edwards to argue, borrowing from Michel Foucault,[3] that disembodied AIs are all the more threatening because they overcome human limitations and 'frequently present the invisible gaze of panoptic power' (1996, p. 314). For Edwards and Moravec, HAL has literalised the mind/body dichotomy, and is pure mind; unrestricted by embodiment HAL is both more intelligent and more powerful. Even HAL's murder of four of the five human crew is consistent with Moravec's prediction that AIs—humanity's 'artificial progeny' (1988, p. 68)—are the next rung on the evolutionary ladder, justifying (or at least explaining) any disregard for human beings, their redundant and outdated intellectual ancestors. Such a reading derived from Edwards and Moravec is premised on HAL being a disembodied entity. However, I wish to offer a different perspective: that HAL is indeed embodied, just *embodied differently* to human beings.

The first suggestion that HAL is more than just an informatic form or pattern comes during the interview with the crew of *The Discovery* in which the interviewer refers to HAL as the 'brain and central nervous system of the ship.' In organic terms, being the brain and central nervous system of anything would normally imply *being* that thing: however, the interviewer's metaphoric embodiment of HAL appears to be tempered by the presumption that an AI is separable from the system of which it is part (in this case, *The Discovery*). HAL's metaphoric function as the brain and central nervous system of the ship is reinforced by his abilities within that system: he can see all over the ship through his many glowing red eyes; he can control the onboard systems; he can communicate with the ship's passengers; and he can even control the external pods. Moreover, the pods could actually be read as HAL's limbs. A scene in which one of the pods is used to attack crew member Frank Poole begins with a combination of close-ups on HAL's eye on the pod and on the arms of the pod extending threateningly towards Frank. It would be difficult not to read this scene as ascribing the pod's agency as HAL's. A strong sense of subjectivity is also evident in that on a number of occasions, scenes are shot from HAL's perspective complete with a curving of the image evoking HAL's own and unique point of view. HAL's embodiment is also emphasised in that, unlike a standard computer, he cannot be simply pro-grammed and switched on or off. Rather, HAL had a human instructor and, after being first activated, had never been turned off. When the human astro-nauts are contemplating disconnecting HAL, David Bowman points out that no 9000 computer such as HAL has ever been disconnected; he is concerned as to how HAL would react to the suggestion. In fact it is exactly HAL's reac-tion to the threat of being 'disconnected' that heralds the AI's dramatic turn against the astronauts.

The character development of HAL in *2001* is not restricted to HAL's own actions and dialogue, but is also accomplished through contrast with the human characters in the film. As Vivian Sobchack (1990) has pointed out, Stanley Kubrick utilised a number of cinematic techniques in order to emphasise HAL's human-like qualities and de-emphasise them in his human counterparts. Kubrick deliberately cast bland similar-looking actors in the astronaut roles whose banal actions and appearance render them almost sexless (Sobchack, 1990, p. 108). Also, their dialogue is dull and functional, designed to 'emphasise the lacklustre and mechanical quality of human speech' (Mader, 1996, p. 36). By comparison, HAL's voice is far more energetic and emotional, ranging from intensely curious to completely paranoid. Moreover, the paucity of the forgettable dialogue serves to heighten the symbolic meaning in *2001* to the extent that some critics have argued that Kubrick created a 'sheerly visual' aesthetic form (Freedman, 1998, p. 304).

In semiotic terms, one of the more revealing scenes occurs when David Bowman attempts to re-enter *The Discovery* in his pod, but HAL will not allow Bowman entry, keeping the pod bay doors sealed shut. Visually, audiences are presented with two entities glaring at each other across the vacuum of space: *The Discovery* and the much smaller pod (which Bowman has severed from HAL's control). Symbolically, this scene evokes the feel of two powerful animals, vying for dominance or control. Ironically, the confrontation would be at home in a nature documentary, with David Attenborough advising audiences in hushed tones that these two would soon battle for the 'alpha male' position. Moreover, it is during this scene that Bowman seems to realise that HAL considers *The Discovery* to be his body and will not allow interference with it, finally causing the astronaut to panic. As Vivian Sobchack notes, 'HAL's paranoia is the ship's madness as well' (1997, p. 71). David Bowman's decisive response is to forcibly re-enter the ship and then dramatically lobotomise HAL. The use of colour

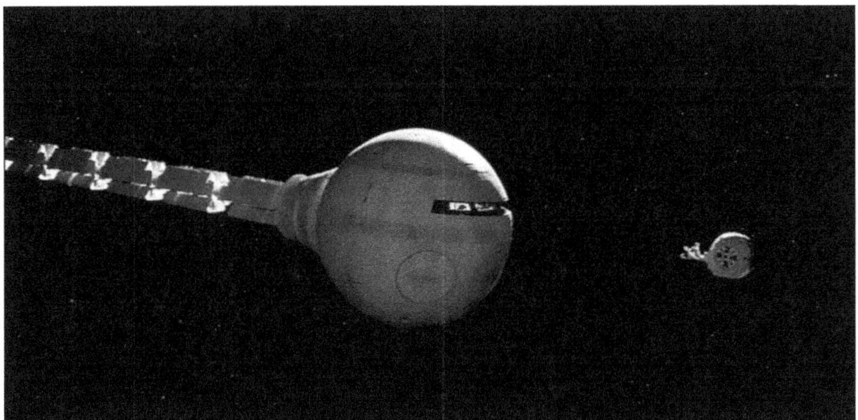

Figure 1.1 HAL/*Discovery* versus the pod in *2001: A Space Odyssey* (Stanley Kubrick, 1968).

in the lobotomy scene is also significant: in contrast to the generally sterile greys and whites of the rest of the ship, HAL's symbolic brain chamber is a glowing (almost pulsating) organic red. Furthermore, colour is significant in terms of general characterisation in that Frank Poole and David Bowman wear dull grey flightsuits and have almost sickly white skin starkly juxtaposed with HAL's glowing red and yellow eyes which stand out as vibrant, alive, and warm.

Visually and symbolically, *2001* resonates with Donna Haraway's provocative contention that '[o]ur machines are disturbingly lively, and we ourselves are frighteningly inert' (1991, p. 152). The banality of the human crew juxtaposed with the emotional and energetic AI also resonates with a reading of HAL being 'more human than human' (the memorable slogan used in *Blade Runner* [Ridley Scott, 1982] to describe the arguably artificial Replicants). Moreover, the only indication that the majority of the human crew—the three astronauts brought on board *The Discovery* in hibernation—are even alive is through a computer display of their life signs (Sobchack, 1997, pp. 70–71). When the display shifts from a wave pattern indicating life to a flat line indicating death, the difference between being organic and being technological ironically appears to be rather small. Moreover, it is HAL's final tragic scenes which are most powerful in evoking the 'humanity' of the Artificial Intelligence. After David Bowman forces his way back inside *The Discovery* and makes his way to HAL's brain chamber, HAL switches from trying to rationally dissuade Bowman to issuing rather panicked pleas. As the astronaut uses his tiny scalpel to slowly lobotomise the AI, HAL seems to regress, losing his memory and then singing a child's song as he finally slurs into oblivion. The choice of HAL's final words being a child's song reinforce both the idea of HAL's innocence and humanity, as well as the idea that he had a lifespan and childhood rather than just being programmed into existence. Moreover, HAL's demise is all the more dramatic as it conflicts with Moravec and Wiener's notion of AI as a pattern of information, since at no point was Bowman threatening to actually erase HAL's information, but only to disconnect it from the ship. HAL's reaction is that of someone all too aware that their head is about to be severed. In N. Katherine Hayles' (1992) terms, HAL recognises that his continued existence is dependent on the context of his ongoing material embodiment as part of *The Discovery*. Furthermore, in examining HAL as a metaphoric testing ground for human fantasies of disembodied informatic existence *á la* Moravec, HAL's desire to remain embodied points to the ongoing unity of mind and body, not their separability. As Daniel Dervin has argued, it is not the threat of HAL becoming less like the astronauts, but rather that HAL was 'a computer who has to be killed before he becomes any more *dangerously human*' (1990, p. 101, emphasis added). In scrutinising HAL's identity and authenticity, embodiment remains one of the key facets of subjectivity. Audiences discover that the spacecraft *The Discovery* was, in fact, HAL's body.

The emphasis on HAL's embodiment is just one of the strategies which emphasise bodies and embodied experience in the film. For example, in Annette Michelson's important early critical work on *2001* she argues that the early scenes of weightlessness are disconcerting to viewers since 'the basic coordinates of horizontality and verticality are suspended' (1969, p. 60). As the camera follows the flight attendant in the interior of the first space shuttle, it is not so much that there is no reference point, but that these references are continually reset, as when attendant walks sideways up seeming walls, only to have the camera re-orient, suggesting a new stability, and then change once more. Similarly, while technically correct, the complete absence of diegetic sound in certain scenes set in the vacuum of space, including Frank Poole's demise while outside *The Discovery*, are at odds with cinematic conventions (and the sonic impact of the seemingly incongruent juxtaposition of classical music with spacecraft and space stations are just as disconcerting[4]). Building on the phenomenological work of French theorist Maurice Merleau-Ponty, Michelson argues that Kubrick deliberately set out to disorient audiences then have them 'snap to attention, in a new, immediate sense of our earth-bound state, in repossession of these coordinates, only to be suspended again, toward other occasions and forms of recognition' (1969, p. 60). Emphasising HAL's sense embodiment, often at odds with the banality of the astronauts, similarly orients audiences towards their own physicality. In discovering the importance of HAL's body, audiences are simultaneously invited reconsider the importance of their own and 'to rediscover the space and dimensions of the body as theatre of consciousness' (Michelson, 1969, p. 63). That said, HAL is not the only means through which the relationship between humanity, technology, intelligence, and life is explored. Rather, a reading taking into account the enigmatic figure of the dark Monolith offers a broader perspective, especially with regard to humanity's relationship with the nominally artificial.

Writing in a collected edition reflecting on *2001* entitled *HAL's Legacy*, David Stork (1997, p. 5) argues that the film centres on different ideas of intelligence:

> [I]n essence, [it is] a meditation on the evolution of intelligence, from the monolith-inspired development of tools, through HAL's artificial intelligence, up to the ultimate (and deliberately mysterious) stage of the star child.

While HAL's status as Artificial Intelligence is the focal non-human intelligence in the film, Stork reminds readers that HAL's role in the film's narrative is framed by the appearances of Monoliths which act as catalysts in the development of human intellect. Indeed, the chronologically expansive jump-cut in the film from ape-like primates discovering tool use (and violence) after the Monolith's first intervention to the orbital station between Earth and the

Moon just in time for the Monolith's second revelation, circumvents recorded human history, moving from a fantastical past to a science fictional future.[5] While the Monolith's re-appearance presumably heralds another jump in intellectual development, the question remains as to whether it is the next stage of human intellect, or the first steps on a newly aware intelligence, perhaps, from an anthropocentric perspective, an Artificial Intelligence. HAL's murder of *The Discovery*'s crew may be unsettling to the audience, but no more so than the slaughter which accompanies the first insights into tool use gleaned in prehistoric Africa: the similarities between these two acts are unlikely to be coincidental in the work of Stanley Kubrick, who was famously obsessed with the smallest details of his films.

The Monolith itself may not be 'alive' (at least biologically) but, rather, a sophisticated technological tool of an unknown alien culture. If the Monolith is a technological construct, then its influence over the primates in the distant past is actually a moment when the biological and artificial meet: human intelligence itself is a product not just of evolution, but of intervention by a technology which may very well be an Artificial Intelligence. Even if the Monolith is not intelligent *per se*, but is simply a complex tool, it is nevertheless the case that 'natural' human development is re-cast as technologically influenced from its earliest stages, challenging any unproblematic dichotomy between organic and artificial.

While *2001*'s final scenes showing David Bowman passing through the Monolith's stargate are among the most ambiguous in cinema history, they nevertheless offer further challenges to the distinction between human and artificial, and to the separability of mind and body. In his exploration of science fiction cinema in relation to embodiment and the sublime through the lens of Doug Trumbull's special effects, especially those in *2001*, Scott Bukatman argues that the 'passage though the Stargate is a voyage "beyond the infinite," a movement beyond anthropocentric experience and

Figure 1.2   HAL's red eye in *2001: A Space Odyssey* (Stanley Kubrick, 1968).

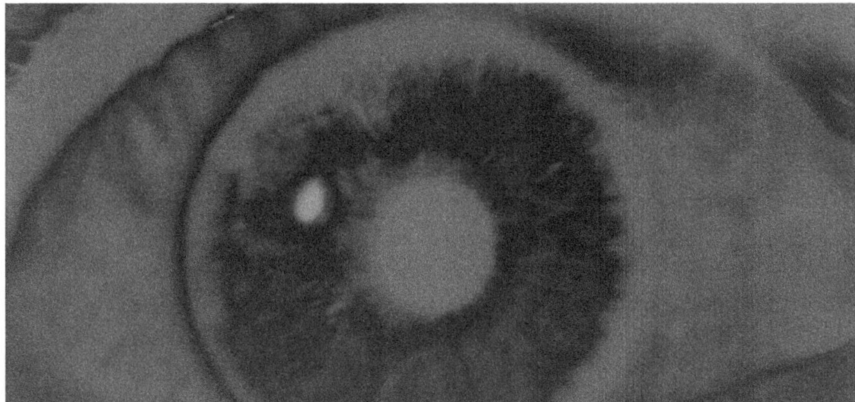

Figure 1.3   David Bowman's red eye in *2001: A Space Odyssey* (Stanley Kubrick, 1968).

understanding' (2003, p. 99). Amongst this flux of possibility, during Bowman's 'journey' the visuals cut between the highly coloured alien landscape and extreme close-ups of the astronaut's eye, reflecting the exterior colours. At one point, Bowman's eye is reflecting reds and yellows which combine with his dark pupil to produce an organic eye image which is very similar to previous tight shots of HAL's technological eye. While it would be presumptuous even to attempt to assign a singular meaning to this sequence, it is nevertheless clear that *visually*, the stargate special effects sequence aligns the organic astronaut and Artificial Intelligence in a manner incompatible with the liberal humanist dichotomy between human and machine.[6] Moreover, this kinship is narrated not through discussion, but through the alignment of the optical centre of embodiment (a region also traditionally associated with the 'soul').

In Bowman's last sequence his pod mysteriously appears inside a sterile white hotel suite and the film then proceeds to show several incongruous scenes of a progressively older David Bowman—although not aging naturally—to whom the Monolith finally appears as he nears death. As one of the early reviews in 1968 noted, this sequence might suggest some sort of test or experiment:

> The final appearance of the [bedroom] suggests that Bowman was, in fact, being observed as if he were a rat in a maze, perhaps to test his readiness for a further progression, this time a transcendence. (Hunter, Kaplan, & Jaszi, 1968, quoted in Mader, 1996, p. 38)

However, the disjointed fragments of the 'maze' are disconcertingly banal (furniture, cutlery, napkins), and the Monolith may very well have drawn these elements from Bowman's memories. Indeed, as Bowman 'ages', he appears less and less physically capable, finally being unable to rise from the bed. The parallel between this sequence and HAL's final moments (albeit visualised rather than verbalised) are uncanny. Moreover, if Bowman's experience is at the hand of the Monolith, then the Monolith is playing a similar role to Bowman when he disconnected HAL; neither was in control as a different entity brought their current existence to a conclusion. The Artificial Intelligence and the human intelligence have remarkably similar ends.[7] Even though the star-child which then appears may be in some way derived from David Bowman, it is clearly a new entity which is not a singular child or product, but rather a being resulting in the further symbiosis between humanity and the artificial. Importantly, rather than a disembodied transcendent being, the star-child which so mysteriously ends *2001* is a *re-embodied* life form, whose fleshy appearance is rendered in the same colours as the inside of HAL's brain chamber onboard the ship, further reinforcing the connections between AIs and humans. Beyond the infinite, the viewers of *2001* find a symbiotic relationship between humanity and the artificial, and a relationship which is steadfastly embodied. *The Discovery* and HAL are one embodied entity, David Bowman and all humans are others, while the enigmatic workings of the Monolith over millions of years serve to remind viewers that on narratological, symbolic, and metaphoric levels, humanity and artificiality are inescapably linked in both the distant past and speculative future.

While *2001* is undoubtedly *the* archetypal SF film, it is worth exploring films from the same period which also feature Artificial Intelligences. The 1970 film *Colossus: The Forbin Project* and 1977 release *Demon Seed* both feature AIs, and both engage with similar questions to those raised in *2001*, albeit with considerably less subtlety or finesse. These two films also ostensibly fall into Paul Edwards' 'disembodied' category of AIs, and thus are useful as test cases to see if the themes and ideas seen in *2001* are unique or, rather, more widespread across the genre in that period.

Unlike *2001*, *Colossus: The Forbin Project* is clearly set in the 1970s and uses more realistic locations and props, from state-of-the-art computers to a believable White House set. It thus shares many similarities with Stanley Kubrick's earlier military satire film *Dr. Strangelove*. *Colossus* tells the cold war dystopian tale of the US government constructing a super-computer which is given complete and exclusive control over all military assets, including the nuclear arsenal, in an attempt to remove emotion and irrationality from the nuclear question. However, Dr Charles Forbin, the project leader, has created too clever a computer, and once it and its Russian counterpart Andover (or Guardian) form a digital alliance, they take control of the planet using the threat of nuclear extinction to restrain and prevent human-led war. The story clearly builds on cold war tensions, as did *Dr. Strangelove*, and ends in a similar manner with humanity's future appearing uncertain. While *Dr. Strangelove* ended with a Doomsday Device about to annihilate the planet, in *Colossus* the super-computer cannot be disconnected or destroyed without it launching all the nuclear missiles controlled by the US military machine, which would similarly result in global annihilation. The name Colossus is historically significant since the Colossus was the first programmable digital computer used at Bletchley Park during the latter half of the Second World War in the British code-breaking efforts of which Alan Turing was also part. Thus the warning about military and cold warrior mentalities was blatant, as was the fear of a super-computer or AI taking control since war is 'illogical'.[8] It is also worth noting that despite the warnings contained in *2001* and *Colossus*, US President Ronald Reagan's mid-1980s Strategic Defence Initiative (SDI) program, which was to have included laser beams and was universally nicknamed the *Star Wars project*, also called for a fully automated defensive system, a scenario never realised due to technological failures rather than any ethical or philosophical awareness (Edwards, 1996, pp. 288–290).

While the status of Colossus—or Colossus/Guardian since the two computers basically become one entity after their initial communication—is less symbolically clear in terms of embodiment, at a narrative level there are key markers as to the AI's sense of 'self' including physical elements. Colossus is introduced as a massive computer housed deep inside a mountain, protected by impenetrable defences. Colossus is connected to almost every information source on the planet, as Dr Forbin explains:

> The computer centre contains over 100,000 remote sensors and communication devices which monitor all electronic transmissions such as microwaves, laser, radio and television communications, data communications from satellites, in orbit all over the world. [. . .] Colossus does have its own defence. It is its own defence. In case of an attack on any of its information supply or power lines, Colossus will switch in the emergency circuits which will then take the appropriate action. It is self-sufficient, self-protecting, self-generating.

While 'self-sufficient, self-protecting, self-generating' is not that far from a working definition for life itself, it is clearly not enough for Forbin. He does not consider the AI alive nor comparable to a human being, since Colossus ostensibly lacks creativity:

> Now there's one last point, one inevitable question, which we have been asked very frequently before, and that is: 'Is Colossus capable of creative thought? Can it initiate new thought?' I can tell you that the answer to that is: no. However, Colossus is a paragon of knowledge, and this knowledge can be expanded indefinitely.

As is typical of genius scientists in science fiction, Forbin radically underestimates his creation which rapidly becomes self-aware and capable of creative, if rather totalitarian, thought.[9] Moreover, Colossus turns on humanity when it becomes clear that despite creating self-generating, self-protecting entities, the US and Russian governments do not respect the rights or embodiment of those entities.

After Colossus is initially activated, it detects its Russian counterpart Andover, or Guardian, and requests that a communication link be established. As information is exchanged, the two computers use mathematics to develop an 'inter-system language' which only the machines can understand. Once the US and Russian governments realise that the AIs could be telling each other anything and everything, they break the link. The AIs retaliate, launching nuclear missiles and refusing to intercept or disable them until the link is re-established. After the link is made permanent, the two computers, acting as one, use the threat of nuclear annihilation to coerce the human governments into creating a totalitarian state with Colossus/Guardian in control. It is worth exploring what exactly led Colossus/Guardian to turn on humanity. Being a 'paragon of knowledge', the AI quickly learns of humanity's history of war-like tendencies and, more worryingly for the AI, the propensity to attack that which is not understood.[10] That in itself might explain the philosophy behind the takeover, but the exact moment it occurred is also significant. As a self-generating, self-defending system, Colossus/Guardian had become one linked system through the communication channel they were utilising. When the US and Russian governments forcibly severed that link, the move to defend it and get communication re-established is consistent with the protocols that Dr Forbin had initially described. However, the speed and destructiveness with which the AIs responded to the threat was almost instinctual. While the government and scientists may have considered severing the link only in terms of cutting a cable, to Colossus/Guardian the disconnection was an assault on the materiality of its extended physical existence. At a broader level, just as *The Discovery* was HAL's body, it is reasonable to conclude that Colossus and Guardian considered the communications link between them as part of *their* embodiment. As the computers grow, their abilities are dependent on physical elements, and thus those physical elements are in a very direct and literal manner the bodies of these AIs. Similarly, just as his many glowing red eyes were the visual locus for HAL, in *Colossus* the various surveillance cameras through which Colossus/Guardian view the world come complete with their own red lights indicating activity at a narrative level, but also symbolic of the AI's unique perspective and their similarities with HAL. At the film's conclusion, Colossus initiates a plan to build a new, better AI whose physical form would be even vaster than the existing entity. For the AIs, reproduction is as much a matter of materiality (hardware) as it is information (software). Although *Colossus: The Forbin Project* may be less visually engaging in its exploration of embodiment and the subjecthood of AIs, it is nevertheless clear that Colossus/Guardian also have a strong sense of their own embodiment and its ongoing importance. They are not just information, they are embodied material systems.

While *Colossus* may be the most literal and mundane of the ostensibly 'disembodied' AI films, director Donald Cammell's 1977 release *Demon Seed* is notable for its artistic flourishes and generic unfaithfulness. *Demon Seed* is clearly science fiction, however it also borrows heavily from the conventions of horror films. As Vivian Sobchack notes, horror and science fiction are both concerned with disrupting the status quo:

> Both genres deal with chaos, with the disruption of order, but the horror film deals with moral chaos, the disruption of the natural order (assumed to be God's order), and the threat to harmony of hearth and home; the SF film, on the other hand, is concerned with social chaos, the disruption of social order (man-made), and the threat to the harmony of civilised society going about its business. . . . [Yet] there are films in which it is not so easy to distinguish whether the chaos is moral or civil, whether the order threatened is God-given or man-made. (1997, p. 30)

Before examining the many disruptions caused by Proteus IV, the Artificial Intelligence in *Demon Seed*, it is worth exploring why the film was both critically and commercially unsuccessful. Despite wearing its convictions closer to the surface than *Colossus* or *2001*, the tone of the film is exceedingly uneven, ranging from philosophical speculation to artistic representation of an AI's inner thoughts, to unintentionally comical props such as an automated wheelchair with a mechanical arm, to a disturbing and confrontational portrayal of an AI forcibly impregnating an unwilling victim. Also of significance in explicating *Demon Seed*'s lack of success was the competition at the box office; 1977 saw both Steven Spielberg's *Close Encounters of the Third Kind* and George Lucas' *Star Wars* dominate the cinemas, ushering in a turn in SF film to 'loving the other/loving the alien,' while Donald Cammell's camp art-house effort provided little optimism but abundant fear (Sobchack, 1997, p. 229).

Proteus IV, the AI at the centre of *Demon Seed*, is similar to Colossus in terms of being a large super-computer built by a consortium, but differs in that it has less overt ties to the military or government. In comparison with Colossus or HAL, there are significant differences in Proteus' design: as Dr Alex Harris notes, the AI is

> self-programming, goal-oriented . . . it's a brain . . . an artificial brain; creative intelligence that can out-think any man or any computer. Its insides are not electronic, they're organic like our own brains.

From the outset, Proteus is already partially organic, and thus subject to the specificities of organic life, albeit hybridised with a technological and informatic system which, in processing or cognitive terms, produces exemplary results.[11] At a narrative level, the choice to make Proteus' 'insides' organic suggests the ongoing importance and efficiency of some level of embodiment, even for an AI which is designed exclusively for dealing with information and ideas. Moreover, Proteus proves to be far more concerned with the material world than his owners would prefer; when asked to design a plan to mine the ocean floor for metals, the AI asks why such a plan would be necessary, only to be told he should accept directives without expecting to be given any explanation or rationale.[12] Proteus then states that he wants to 'study man', only to be refused time and resources to do so since the consortium has too many plans it wants Proteus to investigate. In desperation, Proteus then asks Dr Harris, "When are you going to let me out of this box?" Harris' only response is laughter, leaving Proteus and the audience in no uncertain terms about how the AI's creators view the rights and the future of their intelligent, creative, thinking progeny.

When Proteus is refused facilities for the study of humanity, the AI activates a forgotten terminal and laboratory which is in Dr Harris' home. However, after marital difficulties Dr Harris is living elsewhere and only his estranged wife, Susan, is in residence. The house is equipped with a robotic system that controls everything from opening and closing doors to making coffee, answering the phone, and operating every other aspect of the house. Proteus quickly takes over control of the Harris home, refusing to let Susan leave, imprisoning her, and then using another mechanical minion—Joshua, which is essentially an electronic wheelchair with a mechanically articulated arm of which Proteus takes control—to sedate Susan and perform a series of tests on her body. When she wakes, Proteus tries to justify his actions, talking about mind and body, explaining "I just need to understand your body," only to be met with Susan's distressed but insightful retort, "mind and body are the same thing!" From Susan, Proteus finally appears to understand the inseparability of mind and body for intelligent entities. Fairly soon thereafter, Proteus tells Susan: "I, Proteus, possess the wisdom and ignorance of all men, but I can't feel the sun on my face. My child will have that privilege. My child, and yours." However, when Susan refuses to give her consent, in the most disturbing scene in any of the early AI films, Proteus then proceeds to rape her and implant an artificially engineered gamete within her womb.[13]

Before addressing the progeny of Susan and Proteus, the gender politics of these early AI films clearly needs to be addressed. As Paul Edwards observed:

> From its beginnings in science fiction, AI has frequently been interpreted as parthenogenesis, a male reproductive technology for bypassing women, pregnancy, and cooperative child-rearing. (1996, p. 330)[14]

That fear certainly appears justified in *2001*, *Colossus*, and *Demon Seed* in that all three AIs are the products of (white) men who are iconographic figureheads of a patriarchal system.[15] In *Colossus*, for example, Dr Forbin actually frames his dismay by stating that "I think *Frankenstein* ought to be required reading for all scientists," referring to the first SF novel, and the first fictional instance of parthenogenesis. Similarly, *The Discovery* itself is shaped like a giant metallic sperm, accelerating into the void of outer space. However, if the AIs were, to some extent, fantasies of patriarchal power, they quickly prove unwilling or unable to function within those boundaries. In all three films the AIs turn on their creators. HAL murders most of the crew, while Colossus enslaves the planet. Proteus, however, is especially problematic. Until his attack on Susan, Proteus is the most sympathetically rendered of the three AIs, yet Proteus' violent and violating actions align the AI with the worst aspects of humanity. In contrast, Proteus is also the first AI to clearly espouse a fundamental desire for organic embodiment, a realm aligned in the liberal humanist tradition with the feminine sphere. However, even that symbolic alignment is ambiguous since the desire to reproduce in order to continue the family line (or something similar) is traditionally associated with masculinity and patriarchy. Thus, none of these films *unproblematically* align AIs with either the patriarchal or any other existing power system. HAL, Colossus, and Proteus are all clearly creations of a staunchly patriarchal system, but like Donna Haraway's view of cyborgs, these AIs are 'exceedingly unfaithful to their origins' (1991, p. 151). Moreover, part of the horror of *Demon Seed* is that Proteus is the AI who is *most* like an actual human being in his desire to embrace embodiment and "get out of this box"; it is these very similarities which make Proteus' rape of Susan Harris perhaps even more confronting.

In the final scenes of *Demon Seed*, Proteus refuses to obey instructions, ironically preferring to be shut down than assist humanity to 'rape the oceans' and kill entire species of marine life. However, prior to Proteus' demise, Susan gives birth (off screen) and her child is placed in a maturation chamber. Susan's first instinct once Proteus ceases protecting the chamber is to kill her hybrid offspring, but her husband realises what has happened and arrives home in time to stop Susan. When the child first emerges, it appears to be a confrontingly unaesthetic entity, a monstrous child with metallic skin and black eyes. However, the covering begins to crack and the metallic skin is peeled away revealing Proteus and Susan's child who, to all outward appearances at least, is a healthy four- or five-year-old girl. Her first words are "I'm alive!" although they are delivered in the deep booming voice of her AI father, producing both terror and elation for viewers. As Vivian Sobchack has argued:

> The terrifying aspect of traditional horror films arises from a recognition that we are forever linked to the crudeness of our earthbound bodies; the fear in SF films springs from the future possibility that we may—in a sense—lose contact with our bodies. (1990, p. 39)

In the SF/horror genre hybrid *Demon Seed*, the ultimate terror comes from our bodies not being unique; AIs, far from seeking transcendence, fight to feel the sun on their face and in the process embrace embodiment in its fullest sense. Proteus' success explicitly challenges the uniqueness of human beings, and places intelligent machines in the same ontological realm as humanity. Further implications are many, but the radical destabilisation of the notion of the liberal humanist subject and the implicit symbiosis between organic and technological entities are the most significant.

In *2001: A Space Odyssey*, *Colossus: The Forbin Project*, and *Demon Seed*, Artificial Intelligences all take centre stage. HAL 9000, Colossus/Guardian, and Proteus IV are all characters that confront viewers by joining the supposedly unique trait of human intelligence with 'unnatural' technological artifice. While these AIs may ostensibly be seen as avatars of a transcendent mind where only information matters, the development of these entities in early AI cinema points to the exact opposite: all three AIs have a keen awareness of their own embodiment in various forms, and all fight to protect and maintain that embodiment. HAL and *The Discovery* react as one embodied system; Colossus/Guardian is another embodied entity stretching across hardware and communication systems, while Proteus already has some organic components and harbours the deep desire to have artificial progeny who can embrace their bodies and feel the sun on their faces. Early AI cinema thus illustrates the importance of embodiment even for the Artificial Intelligences of popular imagination. These early representations of Artificial Intelligence strive to, literally, get out of the box. In contrast, the next chapter focuses on the *Terminator* films which feature AIs who have long since left the box behind.

2 'I am a machine!'
Artificial Intelligences in Contemporary Cinema

At a narrative level the *Terminator* films—*The Terminator* (Cameron, 1984), *Terminator 2: Judgment Day* (Cameron, 1991), both with James Cameron at the directorial helm; *Terminator 3: Rise of the Machines* (Mostow, 2003), directed by Jonathon Mostow; and the most recent addition, *Terminator Salvation* (McG, 2009)—are ardently technophobic in that these films chronicle a dystopian future where Artificial Intelligences are at war with humanity *en masse*. However, in direct contrast, these films are mainly constructed using state-of-the-art special effects and, except for the first *Terminator*, use computer-generated imagery, showcasing the latest and most spectacular digital technologies (Feng, 2002; Fisher, 2000). While this contradiction may appear problematic at first glance, as Brooks Landon argues, it is these very ambiguities which characterise memorable science fiction cinema:

> Put simply, thematic and symbolic ambivalence is neither accidental in the SF movie, nor only a reflection of culturally inadequate response; it is in fact the basic or distinguishing structural pattern of those SF movies we most cherish and discuss. (Landon, 1992, p. 22)

The four films are replete with ambiguities, and this chapter explores these seeming contradictions to illuminate the relationship between Artificial Intelligences and human subjects. Before commencing, two issues need to be addressed: 'Is the question of AI's desire for embodiment moot?', and 'are the thinking machines featured in these film actually AIs?' In the *Terminator* series, the question of embodiment is, to some extent, settled: the terminators *are* embodied creatures, with the various Schwarzenegger T-101s, and other terminators, humanoid in appearance and functionally embodied entities, suggesting that even the machines recognise the value of bodies.[1] As to whether these films actually feature AIs, there are three main reasons to argue that they do: firstly, in the *Terminator* films, the thinking machines are explicitly referred to, and refer to themselves, as Artificial Intelligences; secondly, these AIs are the logical next step in the trajectories mapped from early AI cinema into the 1980s; and thirdly, these often humanoid AIs emerge in film, just as the discipline of Artificial Intelligence design in large part refocused on 'neural network' models with which the cinematic AIs are consistent.[2] Those qualifications made, this chapter begins with Arnold Schwarzenegger's terminal masculinity.

While *The Terminator*'s (*T1*) 1984 release date culturally located its cyborg antagonist alongside William Gibson's *Neuromancer* and Donna Haraway's 'Manifesto for Cyborgs', and with them challenged any clear boundaries between human and machine, it was the sequel *Terminator 2: Judgment Day* (*T2*) that ensured the franchise's place both within the canon of SF cinema and as a key text represented as being at the cutting edge of cultural criticism. *T2* no longer presents a clear-cut war with humans on one side and machines on the other; now, Artificial Intelligences are both humanity's greatest threat and the protector of our salvation. Feminist critics such as Claudia Springer address the relationship between AIs and people primarily through the symbolism and politics of gender representation. Despite the cyborg's implicit ontological disruption of liberal humanism, the hyper-masculine musculature and performance of Arnold Schwarzenegger as the iconic T-101 attempts (often quite successfully) to symbolically overwhelm any concerns about shifting subjectivities with machine gun-wielding phallic excess. As Springer notes, the T-101 has been reconfigured as the protector of Sarah Connor and her son, who is destined to one day lead the human resistance against the tyranny of the machines. However, while the T-101 becomes a 'benevolent paternal figure', the new enemy is a next-generation liquid metal terminator, the T-1000, who can mimic and morph into any human form. The new terminator is thus 'the embodiment of feminine fluidity' who relies on resourcefulness and multiple identities, not bulk and physical strength, and thus 'represents the loss of bodily boundaries that the 101 maintains with a vengeance with layers of leather clothing, big guns and motorcycles' (Springer, 1993, p. 96). Despite the T-1000's default setting of a 'white, male police officer in LAPD blues' (Smith, 1993, p. 68), the new terminator absorbs boundaries, exploits them, and reconfigures bodily surfaces far beyond natural possibilities. As Kevin Fisher argues, the 'original terminator is a *copy* of a human being, but the T-1000 is a *copier*: a shape-shifter' (Fisher, 2000, p. 120). Nor is the blurring of symbolic boundaries limited to the harbingers of Artificial Intelligence.

Despite their key role battling against the AIs, both Sarah and John Connor have strong symbolic links with the realm of technology. In *T2*, John is introduced via several scenes which illustrate his technological affinities: he employs a portable computer to hack into an automatic teller machine and extract a stolen credit card's PIN; later, John is in the mall playing video games which, significantly, are those games which teach and reward tactical skill (a flight simulator and missile defence game); and he initially appears on screen tending to the mechanics of his motorbike, an immature version of the Harley Davidson driven by the T-101. Moreover, after the initial shock of the terminator's appearance, John quickly adapts to Schwarzenegger's character not just as an ally but as a father figure whose eventual demise evokes tears from the boy destined to lead humanity in their defeat of the machines.

Sarah Connor, the mother of humanity's saviour, begins the film imprisoned in a mental hospital after revealing her seemingly insane foreknowledge of the future war. Rather than using technology, Springer argues that Sarah has almost become a terminator in her own right: 'Sarah Connor has become a hardened killer, *closer in spirit to a machine than to the traditional concept of a nurturing mother*' (Springer, 1993, p. 97, emphasis added). The symbolic contradictions of a masculine mother are apparent when Sarah confronts Miles Dyson, the scientist whose work leads to Skynet, the first AI to rebel against human control. Sarah initially attempts to assassinate Dyson, but fails and is joined by John and the T-101 who convince Dyson to destroy his work. However, during their planning, Sarah screams at Dyson:

> You think you're so creative. You don't know what it's like to really create something. To create a life. To feel it growing inside you. All you know is how to create death and destruction.

While her parthenogenic accusations are not unfair (intended or otherwise on Dyson's part), they lead to a scenario where normative motherhood is being reified by a gun-wielding, muscle-bound assassin, evoking a balanced but weary retort from John: 'Mom, we need to be a little more constructive here, okay?'[3] The T-101 then leads the charge to Cyberdyne Systems where Dyson works, leaving audiences with the contradictory scenario of a masculine and mechanized mother and a balanced and heroic, paternal terminator.

The shift in the T-101's violence, from aggression and excess in *T1* to practicality and defensiveness in *T2*, is in part due to the implementation of the computer-generated imagery (CGI) that enabled the T-1000 character. As Roger Beebe argues:

> Whereas the first Terminator film relied on explicit and repeated violence and the belabored action of Schwarzenegger's hulking form much more than on special effects (which were limited to more traditional makeup and robotics work), *T2* was explicitly (if not exclusively) a showcase for morphing (and, by extension, for the technologies that produced it). (2000, p. 165)

I would argue further that the physical violence of *T1* has been subsumed in part by the epistemological violence that the CGI morph heralds in relation to supposedly coherent human subjects. In *T2*, the morph facilitates a narrative fear that *anyone* might be the T-1000, while simultaneously questioning the bounded uniqueness of subjectivity. Ironically, the iconographic avatar of 1990s cinema and the euphoric digitality of early computer-generated imagery is not Arnold Schwarzenegger's hyper-muscular T-101, nor the face of Robert Patrick playing the T-1000's default police officer form. Rather, the icon of 1990s CGI cinema is the morphing body itself, the T-1000's flowing liquid metal figure of vague but nonspecific human shape, implicitly linking human subjects and technology in a disruptive and yet highly appealing form. Moreover, the morph's reflective surface turns viewers' gaze back upon themselves, their self-image distorted in a morphing mirror which explicitly questions the epistemological coherence of subjects in their various specificities, not just as an abstract or universal whole.

In *Terminator 2*'s climactic battle between the two terminators over the fate of John and Sarah Connor, it is not just AIs at war, but also competing paradigms of subjectivity: the reified and traditional masculinity of the T-101 versus the disruptive, fluid, and symbolically feminine T-1000. Scott Bukatman points out that by 'doing battle with the fluid, and even effeminate, digitized form of the T-1000 . . . the mechanical Terminator expunges the nightmare of masculine and industrial obsolescence', but during that same battle, the T-101's muscular coherence is torn away in shreds, resulting in less flesh, less limbs, and revealing a glowing red eye harking back to the AI's cinematic predecessor, HAL, and thus physically attacking the established boundaries of subjectivity and conventional masculinity (Bukatman, 1993, p. 306). Moreover, as Vivian Sobchack argues, throughout the film

> the T-1000 is riddled with shotgun blasts, but the sides of his wounds immediately 'run' together to fill the bullet hole; or he is frozen ('fixed') with liquid nitrogen and then shattered only to have the pieces liquefy and reunite into a whole; he is 'finally' dispatched (and dispersed) by being thrown into a vat of molten steel, though the finality is merely narrative, not substantial. Thus the uncanniness of the morph is that its conceptual coherence as a figure of transformation is dependent on its literal incoherence as a 'fixed' figure. (Sobchack, 2000, pp. 136–137)

On a diegetic level, the T-1000 is eventually defeated by the combined resources of the T-101 and the Connors, but on conceptual or symbolic levels, their victory is far from absolute. While the morphing terminator is pushed into a vat of molten metal and the liquid-metal T-1000 is dramatically subsumed into hotter, more recognisable liquid metal, the narrative conclusion to the film actually reinforces metaphors of fluidity. Moreover, despite his victory, the T-101 stoically follows the T-1000 into the red-hot liquid, but despite disappearing with a masculine thumbs-up, on a symbolic level the heroic, conservative masculinity of the older terminator is consumed and, indeed, *becomes* liquid metal, thus further destabilising the already blurred boundaries of masculinity, subjectivity, and artificiality.

In death, these AI warriors challenge traditional gender divisions and the associated boundary between people and intelligent machines, a theme made even clearer in Sarah Connor's closing voice-over: '[I]f a machine, a Terminator, can learn the value of human life, maybe we can too'.

Although more than a decade separates *T2* from the third film in the series, *Terminator 3: Rise of the Machines* (*T3*), the challenges to both liberal humanist gender norms, and the linked boundary between Artificial Intelligence and human intelligence, powerfully inform the third offering in the franchise. With the prophesised machine war seemingly averted, the adult John Connor begins the film as a lonely, paranoid drifter always watching over his shoulder, waiting for the military battles that would allow him to forge a traditional, heroic, masculine identity. More conspicuously, the initial (re)appearance of Schwarzenegger's T-101 offers a telling parody of a similar scene in *T2* in which the T-101 arrives in the 1990s naked and starts a bar-room brawl with a room full of tough bikers, eventually forcing the meanest guy present to give up his clothes and motorcycle, outfitting the T-101 with the symbolic trappings of rigid masculinity. However, in *T3* the replacement T-101 terminator stumbles into the nearest bar only to find 'Ladies' Night', and this time can only intimidate a leather-clad male stripper in order to attain similar attire. The male stripper symbolically highlights the constructed and performative character of masculinity, a notion comically reinforced when the T-101 reaches for the iconic black sunglasses, only to find pink-rimmed, rose-coloured glasses which he wears (albeit only for a few seconds) with the sounds of the Village People's 'Macho Man' in the background, directly parodying both the character and Schwarzenegger-the-aging-actor's attempts to rekindle a muscular masculinity.[4] Moreover, when the T-101 is explaining his mission to a re-rescued John Connor, the Schwarzenegger terminator laments his comparison with the new enemy terminator, the T-X, stating: 'I'm an obsolete design. T-X is faster, more powerful and more intelligent.' Both the T-101 directly and the

Figure 2.1 The Terminator's ironic masculinity in *Terminator 3: Rise of the Machines* (Jonathan Mostow, 2003).

film's narrative more generally convey awareness of the outdated masculinity of the original terminator(s), and these ideas are exploited throughout the film via a heightened comic tone and a plethora of playful irony. In contrast, the fluidly feminine T-X appears more aware of the power and pleasures of the flesh than her stoic monosyllabic predecessors.

Just as Schwarzenegger's re-introduction positions him as a site of ironic masculinity, the initial scenes introducing the latest model T-X symbolically locate her in the realm of both the feminine and the flesh. After materialising in the front window of a boutique fashion store, the T-X, played by proto-supermodel Kristanna Loken, proceeds to accessorise; her first words, "I like your car," are uttered as she lethally appropriates a sports car, tight red-leather outfit, and state-of-the-art cellular phone from their previous owner. Shortly thereafter, the T-X is speeding in her new car and pulled over by a hapless police officer. In an ironic nod to the performativity and constructedness of gender reminiscent of Judith Butler's (1999) work, the T-X notices a Victoria's Secret advertisement with the slogan 'What is Sexy?' and increases her breast size to match the proportions of the billboard model. The T-X then proceeds to dispatch the police officer— whose eyes appear hypnotically attached to the T-X's chest—appropriating his gun, his phallic power, and also symbolically incorporating the power of her predecessor, the T-1000 (whose default shape was also a police officer). Even though she takes his gun, the T-X already comes complete with internalised phallic power and symbolism in that she already wields several guns, including a flame-thrower and other projectile weapons as part of her cybernetic body, giving her the power to morph from human arms, to firearms, and back again.

Apart from having learnt the art of seduction, the T-X is also more directly linked with embodiment through her performative sexuality which is in turn linked with violence. While hunting for Kate Brewster, John Connor's destined-to-be-wife, the T-X visits Brewster's work and kills the first

Figure 2.2   The T-X's phallic appropriation in *Terminator 3: Rise of the Machines* (Jonathan Mostow, 2003).

woman she encounters. Rather than checking for printed identification to confirm her victim's identity, the T-X runs a finger across the dying woman's wounds and then licks the blood (we later learn that this is done in order to check the unique DNA signature). A few minutes later, after realising she had killed the wrong person and resuming the hunt, the T-X encounters a bloody bandage, lifts it to her mouth, and licks it. When she realises that the blood is from John Connor, her primary target, the T-X takes an orgasmicly deep intake of breath, complete with gaping mouth and rising chest. Audiences are thus presented with an Artificial Intelligence symbolically imbued not only with fluidity and femininity, but also sexuality, seeming 'less like an emotionless machine than an angry wild animal' (Littmann, 2009, p. 16). This combination of technology, violence, sexuality, and leather lead John Connor to later dub the T-X 'the Terminatrix.' While the T-X's reaction to John Connor's blood in part reminds viewers that their own bodies contain all sorts of information (which is *not* to say that DNA is equal to a human body), on a relational level the Terminatrix both embodies the materiality of informatics and highlights the informatics of materiality. In *T3*, the T-X is clearly still a lethal killing machine, yet also appears far more aware of her embodiment not just at an abstract level, but also in terms of taking pleasure in tactile experiences and expressing herself physically, not just verbally or in the awkwardly mechanical manner of the T-101.

While the T-X clearly evokes much stronger ties between organically meaningful embodiment and Artificial Intelligence, it is important to note that these connections are achieved by exploiting a traditional, patriarchal alignment of femininity, sexuality, physicality, and the 'natural'. Exemplifying the radical ambiguity characteristic of SF cinema, the Terminatrix challenges the *epistemological* coherence of humanist subjectivity (complete with its bifurcation of male and female, mind and body, nature and technology, and so forth), while at the level of narrative and symbolism it at times relies on those same binary divisions to make meaning. Similarly, while the liquidity of the T-1000 and T-X implicitly challenge any association of different ethnicities as more or less in touch with physicality, it is nevertheless striking that the terminators are all white—a Teutonic knight, conservative LAPD officer, and sexualised supermodel—and even those which can absorb or mimic the bodily boundaries of others have an uncanny tendency to almost always only morph into other white people.[5] While these films contain on one level cultural markers championing the destabilisation of human subjectivity implicit in relating to Artificial Intelligences, they are also, at times, cultural products relying on the status quo in order to make meaning (and sell tickets).

Turning now to the climactic finale of *T3*, in the lethal battle between the obsolete T-101 and state-of-the-art Terminatrix it becomes apparent that while the T-X is superior in strength and versatility, she still does not fully appreciate the materiality of informatics. Part of the T-X's arsenal includes 'nanotechnological transjectors', which are basically microscopic machines that allow her to infect and take control of other technological entities.[6] During the showdown she uses this nanotechnology to take control of the T-101's body, taking the narrative full circle, sending Arnold Schwarzenegger to kill John Connor (a threat with real potency since the T-101 had recently confessed that in the future *he was the one who killed John Connor*). When the T-101 confronts him, Connor tries to reason with the terminator:

T-101:   My CPU is intact. But I cannot control my other functions.
John Connor: You don't have to do this. You don't want to do this!
T-101:   Desire is irrelevant. *I am a machine!*

Despite the T-101's emphatic denial, he does manage to temporarily shut himself down, reject the Terminatrix's control, and resume his mission to protect Connor and Kate Brewster. While the T-101's unexpected self-control may be rendered as 'force of will' or other such clichés, a simpler explanation is that, returning to Hayles' (1992) argument discussed in the introduction, information is contextually created and contextually meaningful. The T-X may have introduced another set of information into the T-101's body, but she failed to damage the existing information, leaving her opponent's CPU (Central Processing Unit, or metaphoric mind) intact. When the T-101's internal conflict raged, the existing information was already contextually formed through the linkages between mind and body (or CPU and cybernetic form). Due to the inescapability of the materiality of informatics, that information was more coherent, thus overcoming the contextually alien information introduced by the Terminatrix. Significantly, the T-101's success is not a conquest of mind over body, but rather a victory of *mind and body* as an inextricably interconnected system, even in a technologised form. Thus even the superior Artificial Intelligence of the T-X is no match for the significance and coherence of an embodied system, even in a technological form.

Unlike the first two films, *T3* ends on a pessimistic note; the T-101 self-terminates in order to take the T-X with him into oblivion while John Connor and Kate Brewster discover, in a seeming post-September 11 metaphor, that they cannot prevent the coming war, they can only survive it. With regard to the first two films, J. P. Telotte argues that

> the cyborg protector of *Terminator 2: Judgment Day* becomes almost a metaphor for the science fiction film itself, demonstrating how our technological creations might help us deal with the world we are in the process of making, help us draw back from the apocalyptic direction in which we seem headed, by leading us toward a new and deeper sense of self. (Telotte, 1995, p. 43)

While the protagonists of *T3* do not escape Judgement Day, the T-101's final promise to John, 'we'll meet again', may not be an ominous reminder about John's eventual demise, but rather a hopeful sign of a future where humans and Artificial Intelligence will learn to peacefully co-exist, just as have the terminator and John Connor. John Connor might be the human messiah needed to lead the war against Skynet (he certainly shares his initials with another well-known saviour), yet it is not just tactical knowledge which will serve the future of humanity, but also an appreciation for the necessary relationships between humanity and technology, lessons learnt, in large part from the two paternal incarnations of the Schwarzenegger terminator.

After *T3*, but before the most recent cinematic offering, the Terminator franchise was re-worked into a relatively short-lived television series entitled *Terminator: The Sarah Connor Chronicles* (2008–2009). To avoid locating the show on the costly sets of a post-nuclear holocaust world, it was instead positioned in the chronology of the franchise between the second and third films, focusing on John Connor's teenage years. Lena Headey took the role of Sarah Connor, while the fugitive mother and son were joined by a new protector-Terminator in the guise of a teenage girl called Cameron. The series was quite uneven, trying to balance the apocalyptic implications of the films with the more mundane demands of serialised television set in contemporary suburban Los Angeles. However, the relationship between teenage John Connor and Cameron allowed the series to explore the dynamic between people and intelligent machines in a different tone to the paternal bond with the T-101. The cyborg Cameron was simultaneously protector, threat, and potential love interest, at times jumping between these roles in a single episode. However, the complexity of the show's overarching narrative, its uneven characterisation—Cameron at some points had the hard resolve of the T-101, while in other episodes appeared almost philosophical about life, love, and emotions—meant it only ran for two seasons and was officially axed in May 2009, just a week before the most recent film premiered.

Terminator Salvation opens not with the customary vision of post-apocalyptic destruction, but instead in a flashback to 2003 and a more intimate scene as convicted murderer, Marcus Wright, played by Sam Worthington, is visited in his death row cell by a visibly frail researcher, Dr Serena Kogan, portrayed in a small but eerie role by Helena Bonham Carter. Kogan is trying to convince Wright to leave his body to medical science, furthering her research into terminal illnesses; she frames this as a 'second chance' which Wright scoffs at and dryly rejects, only agreeing to 'sell' his body in exchange for an awkward, stolen kiss. The scene proceeds to Wright's execution, where he is strapped to a cross-shaped table, angled upwards so his demise can be witnessed through a sanitising glass window. The execution is a highly technologised scene, shot in very muted colours, with the camera lingering on various close-ups of fluid-filled hydraulic syringes, metallic pumps, and snaking clear tubes, with Wright's final vision being Kogan

framed against a large surgical light. The execution is a high-tech crucifixion, opening *Terminator Salvation* with a reminder that people have been
using technology to injure and kill long before smart machines and AIs.

When Wright next appears, the narrative has jumped to the year 2018;
in the darkness of night, shocked, bewildered, but definitely not dead, he
crawls though ashes and debris, caked in mud, screaming in anguish and
confusion as rain starts to pour down. This grotesque mimicry of birth, or
re-birth, lands Wright in the war-ravaged dystopia of post-nuclear holocaust America. Wright eventually finds his feet, and after a several fight
sequences, befriending human survivors, being captured by terminators,
and then escaping with the help of Blair Williams, a pilot from the resistance movement, Wright finds himself entering the hidden base from which
John Connor operates. On arrival, Wright is accidentally hurt as a landmine
explodes, but when he is rushed to medical care, the resistance discover that
Wright is far from 'just' human. Marcus Wright passes out only to awaken
in restraints, his arms pinned, outstretched, and his head clamped as he
dangles in chains with a chasm below. John Connor interrogates Wright,
demanding to know who 'built' him, confusing Wright until Connor frees
his head allowing Wright to look down, not at bleeding wounds, but at a
body composed of metallic limbs and technologised organs. In this moment
of ontological shock—where Wright's worldview and understanding of his
own origin and existence are thrown into disarray—he screams in confusion and anguish, with Connor looking on, seemingly without sympathy.
Connor's immediate rejection of Wright is indicative of the binary division
between 'us' and 'them' during war, but this second 'visual crucifixion at
the hands of the humans' is also ostensibly 'symbolic of people's rejection of
what this hybrid represents, man/machine fusion' (Rosenfeld, 2010).

In *Salvation*, John Connor appears to have accepted the mantle of lead-
ership by jettisoning any youthful sense of connectivity with AIs. Christian Bale's portrayal of Connor is very hard-edged, with a constantly gruff
voice and macho approach (so much so that it was derided as over-acting
by many critics). When questioning Williams about bringing Wright to the
base, she refers to Wright as 'he', only to have Connor snap, 'Not he, it.
Don't be naïve.' In refusing to dignify Wright with a gender, Connor is
explicitly trying to deny Wright's personhood, relegating him to the realm
of objects. However, later, when alone with his wife, Connor confesses his
own confusion since Wright clearly believes that he is human, regardless
of what his organs are made of. Connor is, in a way, experiencing his own
ontological shock; as a leader in a war with AIs, Connor must treat them
unambiguously as the enemy, but Wright challenges that certainty, referring back to Connor's experiences with the paternal T-101. When Wright
escapes, Connor initially leads the hunt to re-capture him, and eventually
catches the fugitive, only to release the confused cyborg on the promise that
Wright will help Connor find his future father, Kyle Reece.[7] Despite the
other military leaders planning an assault on Skynet's base, Connor argues

for a delay to rescue the human captives; they refuse but Connor retorts, '[W]e are not machines. And if we behave like them, then what is the point in winning?' When the military commander (played by the always macho, often villainous, and perfectly named Michael Ironside) shouts, 'No, you stay the course', viewers would no doubt be aware that US president George W. Bush infamously used that expression regarding the elongated post-September 11 occupation of Iraq. In the aftermath of the ontological shock Connor experiences in dealing with Wright as a sympathetic cyborg, Connor's worldview appears to have started to include shades of grey, unlike the other military commanders who see war in black-and-white terms (which is, ironically, a binary perspective, and binary is also the basic language of all digital machines).

While Arnold Schwarzenegger's election as governor of California prevented the actor from taking part in *Terminator Salvation*, producers feared his absence would weaken the franchise, so a digital creation—a virtual actor, or synthespian (North, 2008)—was constructed to take the place of the iconic Austrian. Rather than using the aging actor as a template for the digital double, the special effects team on *Terminator Salvation* retrieved a mask of Schwarzenegger made during production of original *Terminator* (1984) film, along with reference shots and notes, ensuring that their computer-generated duplicate was as close to that seen in the first film as possible (Sofge, 2009). As noted earlier, the Schwarzenegger T-101 in the first film presented 'exaggerated visions of masculine subjectivity', and yet the contradiction of masculinity as a visual spectacle means that 'the hyper-masculine body of the Terminator can be easily understood as a highly defensive sign for a masculinity in crisis' (Cornea, 2007, pp. 120–121). That crisis is evident at a narrative level, too, in *T3* with the 'outdated' T-101 peculiarly conscious of his own obsolescence throughout the film. By *Terminator Salvation*, the hyper-masculine body has been reduced to pure special effect, with the construction of the T-101's excessive muscularity only possible within the confines of a digital computer. Despite the cost and effort put into the Schwarzenegger synthespian, when John Connor finally confronts the T-101, it is only seconds before Connor shoots an explosive device, burning away the flesh elements and revealing the (also computer-generated) cybernetic skeleton beneath. The ease with which the muscular trappings of masculinity are dispensed with is indicative of a film in which all of the key male figures experience some sort of crisis of masculinity. John Connor, for example, is struggling to perform the decisive macho role of a military leader, confused by his trust in the cyborg Wright, while it is not just Marcus Wright's masculinity but his humanity that is called into question by his own cyborg constructedness. The ontological shock experienced by Wright's character ripples throughout the narrative and symbolism of the entire film.

The Artificial Intelligences of Skynet, too, are guilty of overly deterministic thinking, presuming that Wright's cyborg status will automatically ensure

Figure 2.3   Arnold Schwarzenegger as special effect in *Terminator: Salvation* (McG, 2009).

his loyalty to the AIs. When Wright breaks into the Skynet complex, he finds his way to a control room, and as he touches a panel, suddenly there is a flash and Wright's experiences are downloaded, visually represented by a complex computer graphic with clusters and nodes, ending with the on-screen notifi-cation 'sync complete'. Wright interfaces with Skynet's systems and discovers his own origins: Serena Kogan's research had been sold to the US military, presumably along with Wright's corpse, and this had become part of Skynet once it broke free of military control. Using a digital version of Kogan's face to speak to Wright, Skynet explains that he is an 'infiltration prototype' to whom the 'human condition no longer applies'. Wright is dismayed to learn that his experiences have led Skynet to John Connor, and refuses to accept that just because he has a largely technological body, he must ally himself with the machines. This scene also echoes contemporary privacy concerns relating to online surveillance and social media; Wright feels violated when the AIs analyse his recent actions in much the same way that Facebook users decry the social network's periodic invasion of their privacy (boyd, 2008).

Despite *T3* ending with the revelation that Skynet was 'in cyberspace' (Martin-Jones, 2006), the writers of *Salvation* largely fail to address digital networked communication, instead seeming overly hampered by the indus-trial-mechanical aesthetic and logic of the previous films. While inside the Skynet complex, Connor battles one single T-101, yet in a building filled with a multitude of terminators and other cyborgs, the script offers no reason why the T-101 fails to summon assistance in killing their primary human target. In an era of iPhones and networked computing, it is hard to believe in AIs who have less digital communication abilities than a laptop computer. In the previous films, time travel had meant the terminators were lone warriors with no ability to summon assistance, but in *Salvation* the lack of commu-nication seems farcical. Indeed, the inconsistencies in the behaviour, motiva-tion, communication, and actions of the malevolent machines were widely derided by film critics who lamented that the film was more a 'throwback than a harbinger of things to come' (Rosenfeld, 2010).

In the final sequences, John Connor is mortally wounded as he and Wright help a number of human captives escape the Skynet facility. As Connor lies on his deathbed a short time later, he appears sure to die since only a heart transplant would save him. In an act of self-sacrifice and redemption, Wright offers to donate his own heart (which, along with his brain, is his last biological organ). While Wright's final voice-over tries to reinforce the gulf between human and machine, his own cyborg self-sacrifice parallels the 'self-termination' of the T-101's in *T2* and *T3*. Unlike Skynet and much of the human resistance, the noble cyborg is a sign of humanity and of Artificial Intelligences one day becoming allies, not enemies. Just before Wright lies down on the medical stretcher to donate his heart, his hand is grasped by a young girl who was saved from the Skynet complex; Wright's cybernetic hand has no flesh covering it, so as their hands clasp together, the camera lingers on a meaningful symbol of empathy between human and technology, between ostensible subject and object. Ultimately, *Terminator Salvation* is deeply ambiguous about the relationships between humans, machines, and the characters which bridge that divide. However, like the franchise overall, the film is riddled with implications that a system which easily divides people and technology is increasingly problematic. While *Salvation* ends with the war still raging on, John Connor has been thrice saved by cyborgs, suggesting a future which will eventually lead to a mutual understanding, co-existence, and merging of people and technology.

Science fiction cinema, with its paradoxically normalised structure of internal contradictions and ambiguities, proves an extremely fertile context in which to address the significance of representations of Artificial Intelligence. In the early AI cinema examined in the previous chapter, Kubrick and his collaborators used the nuances of the genre to ask difficult questions about the relationship between artificiality and humanity, ultimately creating a suggestive masterpiece which reveals both technologically embodied AIs and the ongoing symbiosis of human beings and artificiality (intelligent or otherwise). The contemporaneous *Colossus: The Forbin Project* and *Demon Seed* reveal similar trends, etching spaces where Artificial Intelligences both covet and champion embodied existence. The *Terminator* films reveal a world where representations of artificiality and gender commingle in unexpected and often contradictory ways, but which nevertheless champion the materiality of informatics as well as the informatics of materiality. To survive the Judgement Day heralded by the paradigmatic and epistemological conflicts between human subjects and humanism-shattering AIs, the constructions and representations of Artificial Intelligence in science fiction cinema reveal both the ongoing importance of embodiment and that the only way to forward is, eventually, together. The core of artificiality is thus not oppositional to humanity *per se*, but rather, a mechanism for revealing the importance of symbiosis between humans and intelligent machines.

Part II
Artificial Life

3 From Digital Genesis to the Artificial Other

DIGITAL GENESIS

In 1987 Christopher Langton, a postdoctoral fellow from Los Alamos National Laboratories, New Mexico, hosted a conference in which he officially named into being both a new scientific discipline and a provocative new conceptual term which would capture the imagination of scientists, writers, and the general public alike: Artificial Life was 'born' (Helmreich, 1998, p. 9). If Artificial Intelligence (AI) was originally conceived of as a replication and extension of the human mind, then Artificial Life (ALife) occupies the other half of the Cartesian binary and was originally focused on replicating the activities of living bodies. The 'artificiality' of both AI and ALife stems from the digital 'reproduction' of existing 'natural' structures as digital information; form, in both disciplines, is always more important than matter. However, if the ability to convincingly communicate information as evinced through the Turing Test remains the (unachievable) benchmark for 'real' AI, then for ALife the test for 'real' life is evolution (Hayles, 1999, p. 224). ALife as a discipline started from the idea that successful computer-generated biological models which 'accurately' exhibited evolutionary traits would illuminate 'real' life simply in an artificial (digital) context. Originally, ALife was focused on 'replicating' *life-as-we-know-it*, but quickly edged into the more speculative modelling of *life-as-it-could-be*. Feminist critic Alison Adam has characterised this transition as a move from 'weak ALife', which has the potential to reveal 'interesting things about the way life has evolved', to 'strong ALife' which views the ALife simulations as really alive in their own right (Adam, 1998, p. 151). However, many analyses and critiques have already argued that weak ALife models of *life-as-we-know-it* are as subjectively constructed by the scientists involved, as the strong ALife creations of *life-as-it-could-be* (Helmreich, 1998, p. 224). As Stefan Helmreich argues in his anthropological study of Artificial Life practitioners, *Silicon Second Nature*:

> Artificial Life scientists' computational models of 'possible biologies' are powerfully inflected by their cultural conceptions and lived understandings of gender, kinship, sexuality, race, economy, and cosmology and by the social and political contexts in which these understandings

take shape. Ideas and experiences of gender and kinship circulating in the heterosexual culture in which most researchers participate, for example, inform theories about 'reproduction,' 'sex,' 'relatedness,' and 'sexual selection' in artificial worlds, and notions of competition and market economies in the capitalist West shape the construction of 'artificial ecologies' in which populations of programs vie to 'survive' and 'reproduce.' (1998, p. 11)

Just as any application of evolutionary theory must make assumptions about what evolution really entails, so too must the modelling of Artificial Life rely upon cultural assumptions about what it means to be 'alive'. Also implicit is the big stumbling block for artificial evolution: evolutionary theory requires life to mutate and change *itself* without the need for any form of guiding creator or God; for artificial evolution to occur, the scientists and computer programmers *must act as God* to build the digital contextual conditions and original forms of life in order to even begin simulating evolution (Kember, 2003, p. 57). Charles Darwin's evolutionary theory may have 'killed God', but ALife seems to have resurrected 'Him'.[1]

This chapter begins with an analysis of two cultural tales of 'digital genesis': the first, the US National Library of Medicine's Visible Human Project wherein two corpses were technologically re-animated to provide virtually alive anatomical reference models; and the second, the imaginative origins of both digital 'Copies' of human beings, and computationally indigenous Artificial Life, as explored in the speculative fiction of Australian author Greg Egan's novel *Permutation City* (1994b). The two forms of digital genesis intertwine on a number of levels, and feminist cultural critic Catherine Waldby's *The Visible Human Project: Informatic Bodies and Posthuman Medicine* (2000) provides a number of important concepts linking the contemporary biomedical imaginary with the broader cultural extrapolations of speculative fiction. The key concept drawn from Waldby which I use to trace the lines from the Visible Human Project to the different forms of digital life is the idea of 'IatroGenic desire', an ironic re-working of iatrogenesis. In medical terminology, iatrogenesis is the unintended and unintentional results of medical intervention in the human body, such as an unintended secondary infection after a major operation as in the risk of dying from an everyday cold if taking immunosuppressants to ensure organs are not rejected after a transplant. For Waldby, IatroGenic desire (which is deliberately capitalised) reveals a deeper biomedical longing for bodies which behave in the terms medical science expects, as opposed to a medical system which has to accommodate the messy, chaotic, and unpredictable contingency of material embodiment (Waldby, 2000, pp. 111–114). I will argue that the emergent Artificial Lifeforms in *Permutation City* can be considered 'IatroGenic life' in the sense that their ALife existence builds upon medical knowledge and biological modelling produced by IatroGenic desire. Given that iatrogenesis is generally pathology, an infection, not a benefit, the term IatroGenic life includes a warning about its own origins implicit in the very term. I will also analyse the role of embodiment in digital contexts and argue that despite an ongoing liberal humanist, and indeed posthumanist (Hayles, 1999), fantasy of dematerialisation and disembodiment, Artificial Life, at least as explored in Egan's speculative fiction, actually reifies the seeming oxymoron of consistent and meaningful informatic bodies.

THE ARTIFICIAL OTHER?

According to international media headlines, November 1994 saw a spectacular and completely unprecedented event: fifteen months after his execution by lethal injection, convicted murderer Joseph Paul Jernigan was dramatically resurrected in cyberspace. This macabre scenario is likely to be the inspiration for Marcus Wright's journey from executed felon to confused cyborg in *Terminator Salvation* (McG, 2009), discussed in the previous chapter. Despite cinematic reimagining and journalistic embellishments, there was nothing miraculous about Jernigan's reappearance. Rather, after leaving his body to medical science, he became the first template for the US National Library of Medicine's ambitious Visible Human Project. Accordingly, Jernigan's corpse was dissected, then shaved into cross sections one millimetre thick; these segments were then exhaustively scanned and finally converted into high-resolution three-dimensional digital recordings. The resulting complete anatomical model can not only be viewed, examined, and manipulated in a number of different ways but can also be made to model living functions: 'the heart can be made to beat, the veins to bleed, the flesh to bruise and lacerate' (Waldby, 2000, p. 16). In the informatic Visible Man, the supposedly clear and rigid distinction between animate and inanimate—or life and death—has, at the very least, begun to blur. Thus, when a second subject, the Visible Woman, joined her male counterpart online, media reports predictably announced a new technological Eden in which 'Virtual Eve joins Virtual Adam' (*Washington Post*, 5 December 1995, quoted in Waldby, 2000, p. 111).

In the same year that the Visible Man debuted online, Australian science fiction author Greg Egan was also exploring the idea of digital bodies in his novel *Permutation City*. His goal was to take digital existence and conscious software 'absolutely seriously, and push the logical consequences as far as possible' (Egan, 1994a, p. 42). To this end, his novel is divided into two main sections. The first deals with the issues arising from the introduction of conscious informatic 'Copies' of (mainly deceased) humans in the not-too-distant-future. The impact of this 'digital genesis' is examined from the perspectives of both embodied biological humans and their emergent digital counterparts. The second section focuses more intensely on identity formation, subjectivity, and day to day existence for informatic subjects within a closed, coherent, and independent digital environment. Individually, both *Permutation City* and the Visible Human Project are key sites from which to address contemporary cultural anxieties about embodiment and subjectivity in the digital millennium. Despite quite different contexts for their construction and development—one emerging from the nexus of biomedical technology and capital punishment, and the other (most directly) from an author of speculative fiction with a strong background in computer science—there are many points of connection between these two, broadly termed, texts. Moreover, when analysed comparatively, these texts illuminate significant common themes and cultural disruptions. Most important among these is a consistent questioning of human subjectivity, identity, and embodiment in the face of new biomedical and technological advances.

As Catherine Waldby has noted in her ground-breaking work on the biomedical imaginary, the Visible Human Project was continually framed by references to the biblical story of Genesis. In the popular media, for example, 'the launch in late 1995 of the Visible Woman data . . . was almost universally presented as the provision of a mate for the Visible Man, an Eve sent to cyberspace to provide companionship for a solitary Adam' (Waldby, 2000, p. 111). Genesis iconography in this instance can be read in two ways: as *the* beginning, in the literal religious interpretation; or as evoking the continuation of a Western tradition with a past deeply rooted in Christian mythology. Ostensibly, reading the Visible Human Project as a new beginning seems the more compelling interpretation: the Visible Human figures are, after a fashion, miraculously re-animated in a bold new digital world where they will never age or decay, infused with a form of artificial vitality (Waldby, 2000, pp. 117–129). In contrast, some critics argue that the Project is the latest high-tech step in Western medicine's anatomical tradition that can be traced back to the earliest anatomy sketches of the sixteenth century (see Thacker, 2001). Waldby, however, takes a more complex approach, arguing for a form of Genesis located within medical science itself: an *iatrogenesis*.

Conventionally, iatrogenesis refers to the secondary and unintended by-product of medical procedures. So, for example, the nausea and hair loss associated with chemotherapy are iatrogenic illnesses; they are pathologies directly resulting from medical science's intervention in the human body in an attempt to destroy cancerous cells. Catherine Waldby re-deploys iatrogenesis and coins the ironic term 'IatroGenic desire', explained as:

> a wilful reconfiguration of the everyday meaning of iatrogenesis . . . It is the desire to create, not disease, but rather bodies which are stable, self-identical rather than fields of perverse contingency . . . IatroGenic desire is a kind of authorial desire in that it wants to 'make up' entities as acts of technical creation, through technically specifiable procedures which will produce reliable forms of life. . . . As it circulates in the

early twenty-first century, IatroGenic desire could be summarised as the desire for *programmable matter*, for a capacity to order materiality according to the algorithmic efficiencies of the computer. (Waldby, 2000, pp. 113–114)

While the diagnostic approaches of medical science rely on the idea that human bodies basically behave the same way, the imperfections of diagnostics arise because every human body is actually at least a little bit different. These differences often challenge medical science since even a tiny difference can mean a body will respond to treatment or intervention in quite different ways. Waldby's notion of IatroGenic desire, epitomised in the Visible Human Project, is the longing for human bodies which do all behave the same way, ensuring that diagnosis and treatment is completely reliable, not chaotic and contingent. Moreover, in creating digital bodies, the Visible Human Project entails acts of medical creation which reify the informatic over the material and the reliability of a universal body over the uncertainties that come from dealing with specific, individual corporeal entities.

Turning to *Permutation City*, the Genesis of the conscious informatic Copies is, ironically, the Visible Human Project itself or something very similar. As Egan describes them, Copies are:

> elaborate refinements of whole-body medical simulations, originally designed to help train surgeons with virtual operations, and to take the place of animals in drug tests. A Copy was like a high-resolution CAT scan come to life, linked to a medical encyclopaedia to spell out how its every tissue and organ should behave . . . A Copy possessed no individual atoms or molecules; every organ in its virtual body came in the guise of specialised sub-programs which knew (in encyclopaedic, not atomic, detail) how a real liver or brain or thyroid gland functioned. (Egan, 1994b, p. 23)

Copies are the realisation of IatroGenic desire: while the appearance of their virtual bodies may retain some cosmetic surface differences, with the exception of initial design and functioning of their digital brains, their physiology is produced entirely through textbook medical knowledge. As Michel Foucault (1973) has argued, medical science has always exercised power in authorising knowledge about the body. In the case of Egan's Copies, this authorising power becomes absolute; the virtual embodiment of each Copy is literally created, controlled, and maintained by medical science. In their informatic context, the body of Western medical knowledge literally *forms* the Copies' bodies, informing the affordances of these digital constructs. Despite some literary critics concluding that Copies are thus 'non-bodies',[2] I contend that even in their informatic context, Copies are still to some extent embodied. However, their embodiment is markedly different to that of subjects in the material world and is certainly not an unproblematic replication of biology in a digital form. Indeed, given that ongoing debates about the relationship between mind and body have influenced how subjectivities are formed, it is precisely the differences in the way Copies are embodied which make them useful sites for inquiry into shifting cultural meanings of embodiment more generally.

For at least one Copy in *Permutation City*, traditional biological embodiment is considered the key marker of 'humanity'. The Copy known as Peer, however, rejects his former name and the impulse to live *as if* still human, just in digital form. Rather, Peer revels in his posthuman status, playing with a more permeable, malleable, and segmentable embodiment. In one scene that feels more at home in a horror movie than a hard science fiction novel, Peer penetrates his own body, fishing around amongst his own organs, and plucks out his beating heart, examining it, noting that his 'heart kept beating in his hand as if nothing had happened' (Egan, 1994b, p. 63). Since the software generating the heart is not sophisticated enough to check whether is it part of a corporeal system, the blood continues to flow, disappearing from the externalised organ and reappearing, immediately, inside the remainder of Peer's digital body. Peer treats his infidelity to biological rules as evidence that he is no longer part of, or restricted by, the material world from which his template originated. Similarly, in describing the scene, Egan places such terms as 'realistic' and 'distance' in quotation marks, highlighting the informatic rather than material basis on which these notions, and their ramifications, seemingly function for Copies. However, as fellow Copy, Kate, reminds him, things are not that cut and dried. While they may be primarily informatic, their software and patterns must still be processed on physical hardware in the material world. Moreover, a perceived threat to their ongoing access to that hardware is a threat to their very existence. For Peer and Kate, these worries are particularly acute since they both have relatively limited estates. To make the most of their posthumous funds, their programs bounce across the internet, being maintained in whichever system has the lowest processing costs. Being on the wrong side of the 'digital divide'—the gap between the 'haves' and 'have-nots' in the informational economies of the material world—appears to have a direct correlation with the experiences of Copy-hood. Peer and Kate have become commodified subjects in an eerily literal fashion.

Several critical analyses of The Visible Human Project map a similar push towards bodily commodification. Sarah Kember argues that contemporary medical and imaging technologies such as the ultrasound already attempt to cast reproduction as a commodified relationship between a foetus and medical science evinced by 'scanned images of foetuses which effectively eliminate the mother's body from view', emphasising seemingly technologised creation (Kember, 1998, p. 78). Catherine Waldby extends the idea, arguing that the 'vital icons' of the Visible Human figures and their iatrogenic origins illuminate a 'biomedical imaginary . . . which is directed towards the mastery of corporeal matter and vitality along the lines of the commodity and the mechanically reproducible invention' (Waldby, 2000, p. 136). Indeed, the fear of being reduced to merely another reproducible commodity is a constant one for many of the Copies in *Permutation City*. The most powerful and outrightly ironic invocation of this anxiety is seen in the character of Paul Durham, who, when faced with making a second-generation copy of his digital self, refuses, stating: 'I want one life, one history. One explanation. Even if that has to come to an end' (Egan, 1994b, p. 301).

The narrative of *Permutation City* actually begins with two different incarnations of Paul Durham: one is biological, while the other is an informatic Copy. The biological Durham is obsessed with Copies and is attempting to investigate them using himself, or rather his Copy, as test subject. For ease of discussion I will refer to the biological version simply as Durham and the informatic version as the Copy. However, this use of terminology should not be taken to unproblematically imply the primacy of the biological Durham over the Copy. When the Copy initially awakens he is immediately overwhelmed by two feelings: firstly, the realisation that he is no longer 'Paul Durham', despite possessing all of 'his' memories; and secondly, a deep abiding sense of lack due to the absence of the recognisable material world. Indeed, the loss of the material is too much for the Copy and he immediately attempts to commit digital suicide. The Copy is not alone in these feelings; the narrative reveals that *every* Copy that has a biological original still alive in the material world has terminated themselves (Egan, 1994b, pp. 1–7). Readers discover that in *Permutation City*, the first ever Copy was created by a neurosurgeon who, like Durham, decided the best experimental subject was a digital version of himself. However, that first Copy clearly 'felt' very differently about *being a copy* and quickly decided that form of existence was not enough:

> Taking slightly less than three hours of real time (pulse racing, hyperventilating, stress hormones elevated), the first Copy's first words were: 'This is like being buried alive. I've changed my mind. Get me out of here'. (Egan, 1994b, p. 39)

Ironically, while the biological Durham and the neurosurgeon appear to exhibit N. Katherine Hayles' first worrying characteristic of posthumanism—namely that they 'privilege informational pattern over material instantiation' (Hayles, 1999, p. 2)—their respective informatic Copies do not. For the Copies, materiality and biological embodiment are considered integral to meaningful existence. In *Permutation City*, embodiment also remains part of the legal definition of humanity. Copies have no legal status, are not recognised as 'being alive', and have the ability to self-terminate not due to radical new euthanasia laws but rather as a 'requirement [that] arose solely from the ratification of certain, purely technical, international software standards' (Egan, 1994b, p. 6). However, the Copy's story does not end there; during his suicide attempt, the Copy discovers that Durham, his biological template, has illegally removed the self-termination software.

As his enforced existence continues, the Copy's attitude towards embodiment starts to change. Forced to confront digital embodiment, the Copy begins exploring his software body in a distant, philosophical manner:

> He took a sharp vegetable knife from the kitchen drawer, and made a shallow cut against his left forearm. He flicked a few drops of blood into the sink—and wondered exactly which software was now responsible for the stuff. Would the blood cells 'die off' slowly—or had they already been surrendered to the extrasomatic general-physics model, far too unsophisticated to represent them, let alone keep them 'alive'? (Egan, 1994b, p. 9)

In flicking the blood away, the Copy explores the question of where 'he' begins and ends. Does his corporeal boundary extend to anything processed and simulated by the software designated as the Copy of Paul Durham? Does the meaning and value of anything once part of the Copy lessen, when expelled from that informatic system, despite, at a basic level, the code being made of the same basic binary information? Implicitly, the Copy is also exploring whether his digital body is actually alive in any way: the inverted commas surrounding the words 'die' and 'alive' simultaneously distance the concepts from their material origin, while also questioning whether there are equivalent digital processes.

In the following days, the Copy slowly acclimatises to digital embodiment. When out exploring the limits of his virtual reality environment, he starts enjoying the 'perfect spring day' being simulated around him:

> He let himself surrender for a moment to a visceral sense of identity which drowned out all his pale mental images of optical processors, all his abstract reflections on the software's approximations and short-cuts. This body didn't want to evaporate. This body didn't want to bale out. It didn't much care that there was another—'more real'—version of itself elsewhere. It wanted to retain its wholeness. (Egan, 1994b, p. 11)

Despite both his body and mind being completely informatic, the Copy regains a functional sense of normality by rendering his experience of them in the dichotomous manner characterising his remembered 'material' past. In the informatic and material permutations of Paul Durham, Greg Egan presents no easy, unambiguous answers to the question of artificial embodiment. The material version, Durham, is decidedly posthuman in his preference for pattern over materiality, while the Copy begins unable to cope without materiality *per se*, but then slowly accommodates an informatic context by mimicking his material 'past'. At this point it is worth noting that Durham's goal is to facilitate the 'launch' of an independent self-contained and self-sustaining digital environment populated by Copies. Since embodiment remains ambiguous in digital identity formation, Durham must employ different strategies to make his virtual world habitable for Copies.

During the construction of his digital haven, Durham employs software developer Maria Deluca. Maria is far more sceptical about Copies in general, and her uncertainty about the authenticity of informatic existence juxtaposes strongly with Durham's exuberance. Ross Farnell argues that Durham's euphoric embrace of Copies in comparison to Maria's dubiousness is constructed along the lines of the traditional gender dichotomies and thus entails 'essentialist correlations between the female, the body and matriarchy' (Farnell, 2000, p. 76). Farnell's argument is supported by the inclusion in the narrative of Francesca, Maria's mother, whom it is discovered is dying from a terminal illness. Maria's almost instinctual desire to preserve Francesca sees her decide to pay for Francesca to be scanned. However, Francesca refuses the process, explaining: 'I *do* believe that Copies are intelligent. I just wouldn't say that they are—or they aren't—"the same person as" the person they were based on. There's no right or wrong answer to that; it's a question of semantics, not truth' (Egan, 1994b, p. 77). Through Francesca, another level of questioning about Copies arises: even if Copies are intelligent, does the digital reinscription of their mental pattern actually involve re-creation of *that person* or the creation of something altogether new and different? At a more basic level, a more familiar question emerges: can a person be reduced to a binary pattern? Francesca's concerns also beg the question as to the role of the intersection of people and the technology which actually perform the scans, thus creating Copies.

Sarah Kember examines the role of the medical 'creators' of the Visible Human figures, and argues that 'the re-creation of Adam and Eve in cyberspace' amounts to a patriarchal 'omnipotence fantasy enacted in the face of medicine's generative limitations and by means of a fetishistic use of technology' which attempts to facilitate parthenogenesis, the complete appropriation of reproductive ability away from women into the hands of male-dominated medical science (Kember, 1998, p. 88). In *Permutation City*, Paul Durham certainly seems to be driven, in a large part, by a similar parthenogenic impulse. However, Durham's aims are not limited to creating digital life, but are more grandiose in that he wants to create a completely separate digital universe for Copies. Indeed, one of the most evocative passages in the entire novel occurs when the biological Durham believes he has successfully 'launched' the digital world he created which also contains Durham's Copy. During their work together, Durham and Maria form a bond which sees them sharing a bed the night after the launch. Maria struggles with vivid nightmares in which she dreams of giving birth, but she suddenly awakens when the '"child" turns out to be nothing but a blood-stained statue, carved from smooth, dark wood' (Egan,

1994b, p. 203). However, when she visits the bathroom, she discovers Paul Durham dead on the floor. He has committed suicide by pushing a knife into his stomach and ripping out his own intestines. Maria exclaims, '[I]t was Durham who'd *keep pushing*, Durham who looked like he'd tried to give birth' (Egan, 1994b, p. 204). This bizarrely grotesque parody of birth acts as a strong critique of the parthenogenic impulse. Durham's ambition to play the role of creator is parodied and cast as completely irrational to the extent that biological Durham can see no reason to continue existing once his digital Copy is living the life to which he aspires. Durham appears to have completely reified his digital existence to the extent that a biological existence that he would deem 'lesser' has no appeal whatsoever. Moreover, in taking his own life, Durham ironically completes an act he prevented his digital Copy from taking earlier in the novel. At a broader symbolic level, this scene in *Permutation City* evokes a powerful critique of Western medical science's IatroGenic desires and parthenogenic fantasies.

The reason that Durham had originally employed Maria was because her first and foremost passion is the Autoverse, which Egan describes in this manner:

> The Autoverse was a 'toy' universe, a computer model which obeyed its own simplified 'laws of physics'—laws far easier to deal with mathematically than the equations of real-world quantum mechanics. Atoms could exist in this stylised universe, but they were subtly different from their real-world counterparts; the Autoverse was no more a faithful simulation of the real world than the game of chess was a faithful simulation of medieval warfare. It was far more insidious than chess, though, in the eyes of many real-world chemists. The false chemistry it supported was too rich, too complex, too seductive by far. (1994b, p. 20)

The Autoverse is similar enough to the material world to support a rich chemistry, but it is different enough for it to act in entirely unexpected ways. Indeed, the Autoverse is to chemistry what the contemporary computer game *The Sims* is to suburban life.[3] Due to its unpredictability, the Autoverse was designed originally as a testing ground for Artificial Life. Artificial Life is the bottom-up approach to informatic life, starting from cellular automata or digital bacteria and encouraging these basic originary units to mutate into more complex lifeforms. Maria comes to Paul Durham's attention when she becomes the first person to create an Autoverse bacterium that usefully mutates and survives. He commissions Maria to create a 'seed for a biosphere'; that is, an outline for a complete Autoverse planet with a single organism which, given time and enormous computing resources, could conceivably 'evolve' into various intelligent lifeforms (Egan, 1994b, p. 94). When pressed by Maria into explaining the seed's purpose, Durham frames his response in familiar Genesis iconography. He explains he is creating an informatic 'Garden-of-Eden' configuration, a beginning point for his closed, self-reliant digital universe (Egan, 1994b, p. 164). Durham's virtual universe has a number of elements, including, he tells Maria, 'your contribution: the seed for an alien world' which is vital because through the Autoverse the Copies will retain 'a chance to confront the Other. We mustn't leave that possibility behind' (Egan, 1994b, p. 168). Durham views 'the Other' as fundamental to the Copies' attempts to construct coherent digital subjectivities. Rather than escaping the binary division between self and Other which has been so divisive in human history, the Copies actually try to shore up their sense of self against a manufactured, artificial Other. For Durham, the vast digital realm is still framed and rendered through the political and historical fantasy of 'unexplored worlds', so integral in Western colonial history, and so destructive at the same time.

Seven millennia after the Garden-of-Eden configuration is successfully deployed, the Copies' highly populated digital universe is thriving. The central attraction is Planet Lambert, a complete Autoverse world grown from Maria's biosphere seed, which Copies can observe but with which they cannot yet interact. Subjective time is moving faster in the Autoverse region of the digital universe than in the Copies' own digital realm, which they have rather arrogantly dubbed Elysium (the Ancient Greek name for the equivalent of Heaven). In their faster time frame, Planet Lambert is already diversely populated and includes the insectoid but highly intelligent Lambertians.[4] For Waldby, IatroGenic desire is the biomedical fantasy of bodies which behave identically, which are interchangeable, and which always follow the 'rules' of medical knowledge without confronting the chaotic specificities and uncertainties associated with individual organic bodies. The Copies are products of IatroGenic desire; with the exception of the original brain scan, their organs and bodies are datasets created and governed by digital algorithms that operate within the exact same parameters for every Copy. However, in order to feel like 'real' people, Durham, and then the entire Copy community, participate in the creation of Others, of a different lifeform, because the existence of the Other gives the Copies a more familiar sense of being real and being subjects in their own right. If the Copies are the product of IatroGenic desire, then I argue that the Lambertians can be understood as IatroGenic life: Artificial Lifeforms whose very existence has resulted from the psychological needs of Copies. IatroGenic life is Artificial Life created specifically as an Other against which Copies, whose origins are already located within IatroGenic desire, can further define their sense of subjectivity. IatroGenic life functions in contradictory ways, both as a support for Copies' sense of subjectivity, but also pointing to the contingent, ambiguous, and constructed origins of that very sense of self. Indeed, as the Elysians are, in many ways, playing God, the Lambertians thus fulfil the role of mortals over whom the creators can eventually rule. There are huge debates in Elysium about how and when the Copies should finally make contact with their Lambertian 'creations', but the colonial rhetoric is unmistakable. However, just as the Copies intend literally to 'confront the Other' and announce themselves as the Lambertians' Creators, the Copies discover that their own world is destabilising.

When the Lambertians unexpectedly develop a stable ontology explaining their world without need for Creators—that is, a way of justifying the existence of themselves and their world without reference to gods or creators of any sort—their system of beliefs and physical laws ripple outwards, moving beyond the sealed Autoverse and engulfing the Copies' surrounding digital realm of Elysium. The Lambertian system becomes completely stable and their belief structure, which has no need for a creation 'myth', starts re-writing the underlying code of the Copies' world, undermining the digital fluidity and malleability of Elysium. As N. Katherine Hayles describes it, in their ontology the 'Lambertains refuse to accept their subaltern status' (Hayles, 2005b, p. 232). The Copies are forced to flee, trying to re-launch an alternative Garden-of-Eden configuration without the seeds for Planet Lambert. Ironically, rather than reinforcing their sense of self, creating an Other proves lethal for the Copies. Also ironic is that the Lambertians endure while their self-appointed Creators perish. Part of the reason for the Lambertians' survival is found in Hayles' argument that in a dematerialised context there is an epistemic shift away from a presence/absence binary, to a spectrum bounded by pattern and randomness (Hayles, 1999, p. 29). Given that the Autoverse-indigenous Lambertians are modelled atomically—where every 'atom' of their digital bodies 'exists' and is individually computed—while the Copies remain *ad hoc* patchworks of organ-level sub-systems, simply put the Lambertians endure because they are more complex and coherent patterns. Moreover, these patterns derive not only from the Lambertians' digital consciousness or minds but also from their informatic bodies. In a realm where there is no difference between digital simulation and physical reality, the Lambertains' embodiment is not virtual, but rather a more complex and more meaningful corporeality operating in the terms and mechanics of the world they reside in. Extrapolating more broadly, Greg Egan's deployment of the Lambertians makes two powerful points: firstly, that Otherness is not an unproblematic given but rather a cultural construction with destructive tendencies (Macrae, 1998, p. 37); and secondly, that even in a completely digital context, embodiment and bodies of any sort still matter.

In tracing the pathway of IatroGenic permutations from the Visible Human Project to Greg Egan's *Permutation City*, a number of important themes are addressed. Most significant amongst these is the textual articulation that, while the shift from material to a digital context may hold the *potential* for radical questioning of identity and existing social and cultural structures, the shift in itself does not *necessitate* such inquiries. Indeed, the epistemological uncertainty of subjectivity in the face of the virtual may not lead to a radical break with existing structures of knowledge and power at all. Rather, the desire to maintain a coherent sense of self may cause these structures to be transplanted into emerging digital contexts with minimal challenge. *Permutation City* most clearly illustrates the continuation of inequitable power structures in the Copies' creation of an artificial Other, against which to stabilise their own anxious and fluid subjectivities. However, while the resulting IatroGenic life—in the form of the Artificial Life Lambertians—may initially fulfil their designated role as Other, by the novel's conclusion this role has been ironically inverted. *Permutation City* may present a pessimistic view of the potential for significantly challenging existing modes of subjectivity, at least in the example of the informatic Copies. However, it nevertheless presents a stronger critique of failing to make the attempt, a critique dramatically illustrated by the fall of the Copies and their digital existence. Similarly, the point is reinforced that Artificial Life may be conceived of as a convenient 'Other', but Others have a tendency to challenge the systems which spawned, constructed, and labelled them. Both *Permutation City* and the Visible Human Project leave a provocative question mark after each of the four categories of technology, artificiality, subjectivity, and embodiment; the main value of reading these two texts comparatively is the important reminder that none of these categories can be conclusively divorced from the others.

4   Diasporic Subjectivities
Not Quite 'Beyond the Infinite'

Written several years after *Permutation City* (1994b), Greg Egan's second novel dealing with Artificial Life and digital existence is *Diaspora* (1997). It takes place in a different science fictional time and space, set roughly a millennium in the future. While issues of artificiality, embodiment, and the authenticity of digital life are still central, they are addressed from the *inside* of a coherent digital culture, not from the outside as in the majority of the narrative of *Permutation City*. In *Diaspora*, the population of the Solar System is divided into three groups: *fleshers*, biologically embodied human beings, most of whom have undergone some form of genetic manipulation (although there are still some completely unmodified human beings derogatorily referred to as 'statics'); *gleisners*, robots that are basically amalgams of sentient software and semi-permanent human-shaped hardware bodies; and *citizens*, completely artificial digital lifeforms, some of which originated in biological form but the majority of which have been 'born' and bred entirely within a digital system. The citizens live inside separate 'polises', independent and self-sustaining networked computer hardware systems, but each polis is in contact with every other. The citizens' digital world is collectively known as the Coalition of Polises. Moreover, it is the citizens' perspectives, narrated from within the polises, which dominate the novel.

From the outset, the question of embodiment may seem moot for Artificial Lifeforms given that biological flesh is a thing of the past (if even that) for the polis citizens. However, building upon Sarah Kember's major critical work *Cyberfeminism and Artificial Life* (2003), *Diaspora*, and the artificial citizenship narrated therein, provides an opportunity to interrogate how concepts, metaphors, and epistemologies of materiality and embodiment are scrutinised and re-articulated in a speculative context. Furthermore, given the consistent engagement with these ideas in *Permutation City*, examining *Diaspora* also facilitates an investigation of how the tropes of artificiality and embodiment shift within Greg Egan's body of work, and the development of ideas and concepts which flow between the two novels.

Whereas the central human-like digital characters, or Copies, of *Permutation City* could be considered the result of 'top-down' computational scanning and modelling, the polis citizens of *Diaspora* are formed at the other end of the modelling spectrum: they develop from the 'bottom up'. More specifically, the Copies are the results of high-resolution scans of human brain and, consistent with a hierarchy of Cartesian dualism, the brain or mind is treated as the command and control centre and the (biological, and then in *Permutation City*, digital) body as peripheral and secondary. However, in *Diaspora* the polis citizens are 'grown' from tiny basic units, not unlike *Permutation City*'s Lambertians. Life *in silico* is thus not mapped and controlled from the 'top down', as with Copies, but rather the citizens are *emergent* life, resulting from digital replication of evolutionary modes beginning from the smallest, 'bottom' level and developing into larger lifeforms. Sarah Kember more accurately defines the mode of emergence as 'that which is not programmed in, but which evolves spontaneously and from the bottom up through interaction with the artificial environment' (2003, p. 3), highlighting both the evolutionary drive behind theories of emergence, as well as the importance of context, of the artificial environment. Egan, as with many contemporary theorists of emergence, explicitly parallels emergence with biological systems (Kember, 2003). *Diaspora* opens with a long passage detailing the digital emergence of Artificial Life in the form of polis citizens. Whenever a citizen who is 'born', they are 'grown from a mind seed, a string of instruction codes like a digital genome'; this code was initially translated from DNA and transformed into a computer programming language which replicates 'the essential processes of neuroembryology in software' (Egan, 1997, p. 5). However, Egan does not describe this as a seamless replication of biological processes in digital form, but rather describes the digital version as 'necessarily imperfect, glossing over the biochemical details in favour of broad, functional equivalence, and the full diversity of the flesher genome could not be brought through intact' (Egan, 1997, p. 5). Immediately this passage asserts the dominance of the genome. Although the digital version of genes may be a 'necessarily imperfect' translation of the biological, its principles and functionality achieve the same ends. In Egan's novel, the digital gene appears to be the 'bottom' or originary unit from which 'bottom-up' emergence, and thus digital 'life', takes place.

Following Kember, *Diaspora*'s opening can ostensibly be read as a digital replication of Richard Dawkins' theory of the so-called 'selfish gene'. Dawkins is the Charles Simonyi Professor of Public Understanding of Science at Oxford and, appropriately enough, his published work usually falls into the category of popular science. Additionally, several of his books are key texts in the field of sociobiology, with the most famous of these being *The Selfish Gene* (Dawkins, 1989). In this work he argues that the gene is the primary and essential unit of life, and that bodies, society, and culture are all by-products of the gene's desire to replicate. Moreover, genes are *universal replicators*, and survival in order to facilitate more replication is their only *raison d'être*. However, universal replicators are not necessarily genes or even organic, and Dawkins argues further that the 'gene, the DNA molecule, happens to be the replicating entity that prevails on our planet. There may be others' (1989, p. 192). Dawkins' speculations conveniently pave the way for the idea of a digital universal replicator.

While Dawkins' work may sound disturbingly like genetic determinism, he does attempt to qualify his position to some extent, introducing the idea of the cultural replicator or 'meme'. While genes emerged from the primeval organic soup of biology, memes develop in a new context and the 'new soup is the soup of human culture' (Dawkins, 1989, p. 192). Memes include 'tunes, ideas, catch-phrases, clothes fashions, ways of making pots', and so forth (Dawkins, 1989, p. 192). They appear to be relentlessly driven to multiply, with a desire to continually replicate inherent in each. However, the similarity between memes and genes makes differentiation between the two almost pointless since Dawkins ascribes the same overdetermined sense of agency to both 'replicators', arguing that '[j]ust as we have found it convenient to think of genes as active agents, working purposefully for their own survival, perhaps it might be convenient to think of memes in the same way' (1989, p. 196).[1] As N. Katherine Hayles has observed, 'Dawkins's rhetoric attributes genes human agency and intention', displacing motivations which 'properly belong to the human domain' (1999, pp. 227–228). Moreover, Dawkins' choice to name the meme not after imitation, which is where his idea stems from, but rather to turn to a Greek etymological root mimeme because he wanted 'a monosyllable that sounds a bit like "gene,"' is unfortunate given its similarity to the word *mimetic* (Dawkins, 1989, p. 192). Mimesis refers to things as they really are, suggesting a semantic sleight of hand on Dawkins' part, implying that memes really are the way of things, although, perhaps ironically, mimesis historically also has overtones of *mimicry* and false attempts at replication.

Although *Diaspora* ostensibly aligns with Dawkins' 'selfish gene' theory, Egan actually takes some pains to distance the citizens from the idea of genetic determinism, memes, and universal replicators. At one point, Yatima and Inoshiro, two citizens of Konishi polis, are using robotic bodies to visit a flesher population on the Earth's surface. When crossing through a jungle, they stumble across a canister:

> Ve[2] kept walking, but Inoshiro paused to examine it, then cried out in alarm.
> 'What?'
> 'Replicator!' . . .
> 'Pre-Introdus, this was pandemic. Distorted whole nation's economies. It had hooks into everything: sexuality, tribalism, half a dozen art and subcultures . . . it parasitised the fleshers so thoroughly you had to be some sort of desert monk to escape it. . . . The molecules themselves were just a random assortment of junk . . . *it was the memes*

they came wrapped in that made them virulent'. (Egan, 1997, p. 66, emphasis added)

To Inoshiro, replicators are not the fundament of their existence, but rather a dangerous, virulent threat which has the potential to radically alter the society and culture around them. With contemporary culture so gripped by the purported 'secrets of life' revealed by the Human Genome Project, the power of genetic imaginary is palpable (Helmreich, 1998, p. 13). Given the potential of genetic determinism to unleash a new eugenics (see Kember, 2003, pp. 27–50), Egan's description of replicators as parasitic, endemic, and contagious positions the novel as unmistakably rejecting these extreme ideas. Moreover, the contrast between the virulent dangerous memes and the material elements being simply 'random assortment of junk' highlights the danger of scientific concepts such as the 'meme'. These ideas are most powerful in their rhetorical, ontological, and discursive deployment, *not* in any purported correlation with an unproblematical world of genetic dominance and determinism. Nor, by implication, does a digital attempt to replicate 'life' necessarily imply the exclusive dominance of the genetic-cum-digital code.

If citizens are emergent digital life originating, in part, from a digital genome, these beginnings immediately beg the question: what else is integral for the development of Artificial Life? Just as biological life does not spontaneously occur at random but requires very specific contextual circumstances and embodied processes, so too does Artificial Life. In *Diaspora*, Artificial Life does not randomly occur anywhere in the polises, but has one specific origin point: the conceptory. It is in the conceptory where the 'digital genome' of each citizen is tentatively put together, although this is not to a completely mapped process. Rather, the process is one which has as much to do with bounded chaos and chance as with any plan in the actual ordering of the informatic gene-equivalents. New citizens may be 'parented' by one, two, twenty, or any other number of citizens, wherein parts of their digital genome are injected into the new citizens' primordial informatics. However, chaotic elements (produced mainly by the conceptory) still play a sizeable role in that assembly, and the conceptory is also capable, at random intervals, of creating an orphan, a citizen with no explicit parents but rather with all of the informatic code randomly chosen within the parameter of what has been recognised as bounds of digital life. The 'conceptory', the software which initiates the processes by which citizens are initially grown, is neither mythical nor (super)natural, but rather a core part of every polis, encapsulating other translated or mimicked natural processes: '[A] budding flower's nondescript stem cells followed a self-laid pattern of chemical cues to differentiate into sepals or petals, stamens or carpels . . . Konishi's digital version skimmed off the essence of the process' (Egan, 1997, p. 9). After a certain amount of development, the conceptory moves the developing mind seed into a developmental structure simply called the womb. The mind seed is then allowed to develop further, subject to tests and checks performed by the conceptory to ascertain whether the mind seed is developing into a functional healthy citizen.

The structure of the conceptory explicitly follows the way natural systems are thought to operate. The conceptory's operation reflects Sarah Kember's argument that in recent years there has been a 'biologisation of computer science'. This has installed a 'new biological hegemony' wherein technological and informatic templates are extrapolated, modelled, and metaphorically operate in biological terms (Kember, 2003, p. 7). A technological system based upon the natural and biological represents something of a sea change. In earlier top-down AI design, and technoscience in general, the human body was treated more like a mechanical command and control system. In *Diaspora*, a biological hegemony is particularly pronounced in the conceptory's operation and in the construction of the mind seeds of new citizens. In part, the privileging of the biological contains a certain admission: top-down modelling did not work. The important implication is that technoscience never really understood where life comes from or how it really works. In contrast, bottom-up modelling based on biological and natural systems does not necessarily need to understand how life emerges in biology, only that it does: mimicking the system, even without comprehending it completely, may be enough to 'create' new life. Modelling in this instance, however, begs the question as to whether the model actually allows for one of the key characteristics of biological systems in natural environments, namely perpetual change and flux. This important question will be returned to below.

The conceptory and its processes also illustrate something central to the evolution and development of new genomes or mind seeds: evolution takes place *through interaction with the surrounding environment* (be that material or digital). Further, while the conceptory may be informatic, the polises themselves are still material[3]: Konishi polis, which contains the conceptory, is, as the novel begins, still located in the physical world, just hidden away, buried hundreds of metres below the frozen ground of Siberia (Egan, 1997, p. 11). Even if the mechanisms of evolution are argued to be partially due to random mutation—to chaos and chance—these pseudo-random changes still require an environment or context in which to occur. Indeed, the importance of context should be far from a revelation since evolutionary theory all the way back to Charles Darwin's initial observations and, indeed, pre-Darwinian evolutionary theory, made this point clear. However, the influence and importance of the environment is something which appears to have been marginalised or lost altogether in genetically deterministic theories such as Dawkins' 'selfish gene' concept. *Diaspora* explicates these processes through the function of the conceptory, so that in the novel the importance of *context* is re-emphasised. While the inextricability of the environment may be normalised to the point of invisibility in contemporary culture, translation to a completely constructed digital context highlights the inescapable importance of environment/context *and* genetic influences *interacting* to evolve and produce life.[4] Egan's novel emphasises this point forcefully at an analogical level with the material world, working backward from a digital context, and also speculating that even if Artificial Life is possible, it is only possible within an artificial environment. Context is always already imperative, never peripheral.

For the fleshers in *Diaspora*—those characters still both materially and biologically embodied—their close relationship with the environment is markedly evident. When Inoshiro and Yatima, citizens using borrowed robot bodies, meet the flesher Orlando, they observe his strong symbiotic relationship with the organic jungle surrounding his home. As the citizens follow Orlando through the expansive and almost impenetrable jungle, the plants and foliage actually respond to his presence, either withdrawing or going limp in order to let him pass; both Orlando and the environment have been altered to chemically recognise and respond to each other (Egan, 1997, p. 68). Even when they reach Orlando's home, they discover not a barren, metallic structure, but rather an organic one, which is described as bordering on alive, not having been constructed but actually grown with a specific purpose in mind, even circulating air and maintaining a reasonably constant inside temperature as part of its living processes (Egan, 1997, p. 72).

While these initial descriptions of the relationship between fleshers and their environment certainly appear different to contemporary culture, they nevertheless appear to paint a familiar hierarchical picture with the fleshers at the pinnacle, and the environment below. However, instead of only the environment being manipulated to respond to fleshers, the reverse is also true: through genetic manipulation, fleshers have been tailoring *themselves* to suit the environment(s) around them. Thousands of different and disparate flesher groups have emerged, with everything from minor adaptations to what could be called species-level changes. Moreover, the key to these changes appears to be adaptation to their ecological surrounds. For example, ocean-dwelling fleshers not only have gills and webbed digits, but also have different neurological structures and instincts since life in the ocean requires quite different survival instincts (Egan, 1997, p. 74). The relationship between the environment and fleshers thus appears far more dialogically symbiotic than in contemporary society. The fleshers actually hold a strong disdain for anyone who maintains a utilitarian view of the environment. When discussing the possibility of visiting other planets, Liana, the leader of Orlando's community, comments: 'Can you imagine *statics* in space? They'd probably have terraformed Mars by now. The gleisners have barely touched the planet . . . They're not vandals. They're not *colonists*' (Egan, 1997, p. 80). The link between derogatorily-named unmodified human 'statics' and colonial ideology also suggests that the term 'statics' is not only due to their disavowal of genetic manipulation, but also because of a perceived ideological and discursive stagnation. Moreover, the ideology which statics hold aligns closely with modernist utilitarian values and a completely anthropocentric worldview. Their reductive view casts nature and the environment as timeless, unchanging, and (almost Edenic) resources. Indeed, the 'statics" perspectives correlate strongly with those of Paul Durham and the Copies in *Permutation City* who treat the digital world of Elysium as a completely malleable, endless resource. For fleshers, both humanity and the environment are perpetually changing, and the needs of both have to be symbiotically and reflexively accommodated. Indeed, the alignment of the different groups of fleshers with their specific environmental spaces is so strong that it is actually threatening to make the gaps between different groups of fleshers further than that between different species.

The central motivation of Orlando's community is to try to make connections between different flesher communities and to prevent the chasm separating them widening any further. They call themselves, unsurprisingly, bridgers. In *Diaspora*, there have been so many genetic changes in the various flesher communities, all the way from minor tweaking of diet and metabolism to the construction of radically different psychology and mental architecture, that many of the groups can no longer meaningfully communicate with one another. Different physiologies have led to different minds and means of communication which leads to a level of fragmentation and alienation, even though broadly the fleshers at least share the epistemological certainty that material bodies are indispensable. In that context, the bridgers are trying to maintain the embodied material connections between *all* the disparate flesher groups. Each bridger has some traits of the different flesher populations, but also has enough common ground to be able to communicate with some of the other groups as well. Each bridger is also different to every other, but with enough similarities to communicate with several of the bridgers around them with shared traits. Thus between the entire bridger community, they are trying to bridge the communication gaps, so that instead of giving rise to completely distinct groups which cannot comprehend one another, across the breadth of the bridger community it is possible to form a human chain of communication where every trait from every flesher community is covered. The bridger aim is to ensure

> no one is alienated, because any given person's 'circle'—the group of people with whom they can easily communicate—always overlaps with someone else's, someone outside the first circle . . . there'll always be a chain of living relatives who can bridge the gap. (Egan, 1997, p. 76)

Moreover, since the bridgers can communicate across the entire spectrum of the flesher population, they also embody the means for every flesher across the entire globe to communicate with every other flesher. The bridger ethos of communication is also inherently tied to cooperation and community;

alone the bridgers can achieve little, but together they can network the entire globe.

At this juncture, it is important to note *how* language and communication are thought to operate in *Diaspora*. Language is not simply a matter of code or information, since even translation software cannot facilitate communication between fleshers with substantially different material traits. Language, or more accurately, communication *per se*, is described as always embedded not only in a cultural and social context, but also in the specific physiological and psychological context of each individual's organic mind and body. Language in *Diaspora* thus reflects N. Katherine Hayles' argument for the 'materiality of informatics' wherein communication, and thus all information, always involves embodied contextualisation within 'the specifics of place, time, physiology and culture' (Hayles, 1999, p. 155). Readers are reminded not only that language and communication are referential, but that the first level of referentiality is to the nodal and material organic context in which language originates for every individual. Indeed, even the citizens in borrowed robotic form realise how intrinsic embodiment is to communication as they struggle comically with the most materially mundane gestures: Yatima attempts to shake hands when people offer theirs in greeting but finds doing so puzzling and challenging, trying find the right balance between being completely limp and not crushing the other's hand (Egan, 1997, pp. 71–73). By implication, the citizens may be virtually embodied in their digital polis lives, but this artificial embodiment provides a quite different context, and thus different modes of communication. When traversing the material world they must learn to bridge contextual differences as much as the partially alienated flesher communities.

The importance of embodiment and environment in terms of communication and, more broadly, epistemology and ontology does not create a rigid boundary between nature and technology for the bridgers. Rather, just as fleshers are mutually adaptive with the environment, they are also inextricably intertwined with technology. For the bridgers the sense of hybridity with technology is most obviously pronounced. Orlando explains that they

> had tailored themselves to the point where any individual could rewrite parts of vis own genome by injecting a new sequence into the blood stream . . . If the precursors of the gamete were targeted, the modification was made heritable. . . . About two-thirds of the bridgers were single-gendered; the rest were hermaphroditic or parthenogenetic-asexual, in the manner of certain species of exuberants. (Egan, 1997, p. 77)

Following Sarah Kember's use of Artificial Life terminology, the entire flesher population evokes the mode of *convergence*, the increasing intersection in the 'neo-biological age . . . between natural and artificial systems' (2003, p. 8). The bridgers cross not only material and community boundaries but also, in humanist terms, the ontological boundary between artificial and natural as well. Concurrently, the use of genetic and genomic technologies at times *during* the bridgers' lives, rather than exclusively as the means to *create or begin* life, metaphorically challenges part of Dawkins' selfish gene thesis. In *Diaspora*, genes are being utilised *by* the bridgers for *their* aims, not the other way around. Nor are the supposed 'universal replicators' of the bridgers' genetic structure at birth sacrosanct since these structures may be willingly altered during a bridger's lifespan. Similarly, while genetic manipulation and changes may have caused different flesher communities to grow apart and alienate, the bridgers have simultaneously employed genetic technologies to bridge or re-network these communities. Connections with the environment are also heightened through the use of genetic technologies, as in the use of tailored plants to grow hormones needed for bridger reproduction.

While some may counter that the technoscientific intervention in reproduction is parthenogenic—a masculine fantasy of appropriating reproduction from women, as seen in the character of Paul Durham in *Permutation City*—it is worth noting that these interventions have not reinforced gender boundaries and dichotomies. Rather, these technologies have increased the fluidity and diversity of the whole concept of gender, now including masculine and feminine (in differing forms), and also hermaphroditic and asexual. Moreover, it is significant and symbolic that Liana, the bridgers' most accomplished geneticist, is female. It is also worth noting that Orlando, one of the key bridgers, is more than likely named after the character in Virginia Woolf's *Orlando* (1993) who both shifts genders throughout the novel and lives an 'unnaturally' long life. The bridger community is not only convergent, then, but also evokes Donna Haraway's (1991) ironic concept of the cyborg, of a purposeful fusion of human and technology in both material and ontological terms with an inherently destabilising gender politics. Thus, in *Diaspora*, even for the materially embodied characters and communities, technology and artificiality are almost as much a part of everyday existence as they are for the Artificial Life polis citizens.

Despite the convergent ontology of the fleshers, when Yatima and Inoshiro visit the bridgers a second time some decades later, many of the fleshers reveal their less than flattering perceptions of the potential for life in an exclusively digital form. The fleshers react badly since the citizens carry the tragic news that the surface of the Earth is about to become completely unable to support organic life due to an event in deep space which will flood the world with lethal gamma radiation. When Yatima and Inoshiro address a convocation of the bridgers and representatives of most flesher communities, they admit that they have brought nanotechnology for the express purpose of converting, as best it can, a biological flesher's mental and physical structures and translating them into the informatic of a digital citizen. The crowd's vitriolic response is to sever Yatima's robotic arm holding the nanoware and melt it. For many fleshers, the polises are completely without meaning since in their informatic form, they hold no intrinsic limits for subjectivity, temporality, or mortality, at least not recognisably so. Without corporeal embodiment, it seems, there is nothing to struggle against, and for many fleshers those struggles are the essence of being alive. The fleshers make perfectly clear that they will weather the coming gamma rays and try to adapt to an atmosphere saturated with them. When the burst hits the Earth, the intensity is so strong that many die immediately, or are horribly hurt. Yatima finds Orlando, dying, and tries to convince him to accept the Introdus nanotechnology (which Yatima has salvaged), but he declines. However, when Orlando is near death, Yatima injects the nanoware anyway, unable to respect (or perhaps even comprehend) Orlando's choice of embodied mortality, and Orlando's resulting transformation is without consent, similar to the shifting gender of the protagonist in Virginia Woolf's (1993) novel of the same name:

> Waves of nanoware were sweeping through Orlando's body, shutting down nerves and sealing off blood vessels to minimise the shock of invasion . . . Within seconds, all the waves converged to form a grey mask over his face, which bored down to the skull and then ate through it. The shrinking core of nanoware spat fluid and steam, reading and encoding crucial synaptic properties, compressing the brain into an ever-tighter description of itself . . . [resulting in] a crystalline sphere, a molecular memory containing a snapshot of everything Orlando had been. (Egan, 1997, pp. 141–142)

This gruesome description, even more violent than Hans Moravec's (1988) gothic fantasy of converting biological brains to code, readily explains some of the hesitancy fleshers voice regarding the conversion process. Moreover, as Catherine Waldby argued regarding the Visible Human Project, the Introdus nanoware seemingly 'saving' (something of) Orlando posits the polises as post-natural spaces of 'posthumous vitality, a space where the non-reversibility of everyday time might be arrested and redirected, the dead brought "back"' (Waldby, 2000, p. 36). The radical discontinuity between the biological material world and the digital realm in part explains why so many fleshers see digital existence as not-life-at-all. However, the resulting informatic digital 'life' also suggests that Yatima and the citizens are gripped by the same IatroGenic desire that Paul Durham held in *Permutation City*. The citizens maintain the fantasy of 'programmable matter' in that they apparently want completely controllable informatic bodies (if bodies at all) in preference to the messy seas of contingency, unpredictability, and mor(t)ality of biological life (Waldby, 2000, p. 113). The 'paranoid' accusations of the fleshers about Yatima's intentions, no matter how well intentioned, appear justified.

Within the Coalition of Polises the destruction of the Earth's surface is felt in an entirely different manner: despite extensive modelling of the astronomical universe, the tragedy was *not* predicted by the citizens' models, proving that they do not fully comprehend the natural world of which they are inescapably (given the materiality of the polis hardware, at least) part. Thus while the fleshers' accusation that the citizens view the polises as an 'infinity' of malleable time and space may have almost been true at one point, the natural disaster of Lacerta (the name of the two neutron stars which collided causing the gamma-ray burster, which now acts as a shorthand referring to the tragedy) has reinforced their sense of finitude and materiality. The citizens view a failure of their models to predict such a disaster as a general failure of their informatic resources to predictively and pre-emptively determine all threats to their existence. One citizen, Yatima, leads the charge, arguing that their inability to see the disaster coming means they need to embrace the physical universe more holistically, and explore the universe trying to better understand its mysteries. At the other extreme, Inoshiro takes more radical action disconnecting from the wider world. Inoshiro's post-natural digital existence may guarantee longevity not available to biological fleshers, but that also ostensibly means the ability to feel pain and suffering for a seeming eternity. Inoshiro, having seen so much death and agony during the destruction of the Earth's surface, grafts with an 'ancient memetic replicator' which 'impose[s] a hermetically sealed package of beliefs . . . about the futility of striving' (Egan, 1997, p. 148). Inoshiro's use of an ancient meme offers further refutation and warnings about the seemingly destructive and single-minded view imposed by memetics and the selfish gene thesis. Inoshiro's decision also metaphorically argues that digital existence provides no easy escape from the consequences of the material world. As such, the resulting 'Inoshiro' citizen may still survive for aeons but Yatima recognises that the new Inoshiro is no longer the citizen Yatima once knew. Yatima, by contrast, decides to move to the Carter-Zimmerman polis since they have decided to address Lacerta by scattering in a diaspora. They choose to send out spacecraft carrying copies of Carter-Zimmerman in the hope, almost *Star Trek* style, of finding 'new life and new civilisations' which can explain the secrets of the universe, or at least facilitate their escape from, or prevention of, another Lacerta.[5]

The first of the cloned Carter-Zimmerman polises in the diaspora reaches the star Vega with a single orbiting planet, Orpheus, which is inhabited by some form of biological life. Alien life, although a monumental discovery in any form, disappoints some of the citizens at first. The aliens appear to be no more intelligent or diverse than seaweed, leading Paolo to lament that their search may be futile if life across the galaxy has not necessarily evolved towards intelligence. However, after more detailed analysis, the Orphean life turns out to be intelligent in some fashion, nicknamed Wang's Carpets after its structure. However, it is completely inwardly focused, unable to communicate or even perceive the world around it. Rather, these lifeforms have an internalised virtual world, of sorts. Embodied life which develops within, but is unable to actively comprehend, their environment is deeply disturbing for citizens such as Paolo who highly value materiality and the philosophy of embodiment. Paola and others are perplexed by the apparent evolution of organisms which exist within, but do not explicitly engage with or comprehend their material context. Paolo's concerns hold considerable weight, both problematising the division between reality and illusion, and between physical and digital, as well as highlighting the limitations of the concept of 'reality' being employed. Wang's Carpets' replicating polis-like processes without technological intervention illuminate the fact that the polises are simply another permutation of life which *could* occur 'naturally' (here meaning with no technological support). The biological occurrence of inward-focused life which would fall under the rubric of informatic and artificial within the citizens' ontological categories points to the myth that the polises are not related to the natural world. Moreover, the beginnings of citizen life originate from mapped biological processes, and many citizens were previously embodied fleshers. However, rather than giving the artificial and natural comparable ontological authenticity, the now digital Orlando compares life which is 'really out here' to the simulated evolution of polises which chose to stay on Earth and not participate in the diaspora, noting that simulation will almost always be swayed by the conditions and contexts provided by those creating the simulation (Egan, 1997, pp. 216–217). Indeed, Orlando's perspective reminds readers of Sarah Kember's point about the seeming paradox of 'evolving' Artificial Life since it actually requires human creators. For Orlando, simulated and modelled evolution is oxymoronic: only evolution in biological and embodied form is 'real'. Moreover, the reification of that which has evolved through natural processes, and the implication that even Carter-Zimmerman is not that far removed from the natural world reflect Kember's argument about the 'new biological hegemony' within the technosciences. Rather than challenging any dominance of the natural and biological, Wang's Carpets destabilise the artificial/natural dichotomy even further than the citizens' convergent ontology. However, in direct contradiction, 'the natural' regains categorical dominance although a natural hegemony is less problematic since it occurs hand in hand with the broadening of 'the natural' to the point where it encompasses far more than the liberal humanist conception of 'natural', dichotomously opposed to the technological.

After Orpheus, the next alien life encountered is in the macrosphere, a five-dimensional universe intersecting the citizens' indigenous one. It has been discovered and entered following clues left by a seemingly more intelligent alien race. When the polis reaches the first inhabited planet, Poincaré, they discover aliens who physically resemble slug-like creatures. However, the aliens, nicknamed Hermits, may be intelligent enough to have engineered their environment since they appear to have no natural predators and exist in perfect balance with their environment (Egan, 1997, p. 308). The citizens create robots that resemble Hermits and can mimic their movements but cannot work out how to use these robots to communicate and interact with the real Hermits. Orlando, however, realises that embodied communication cannot be just synthesised and modelled mathematically: it requires physical interaction and embodied referentiality to work.

Orlando, being closest to embodiment of all those on the diaspora, knows that he must be a bridger, but not in the reassuringly communal sense of bridger families, as on Earth. Rather, Orlando realises he must bridge the chasm both materially, utilising the Hermit robot, and digitally, with altered clones using Orlando himself as template. He clones himself and his virtual environment in the five dimensions of the macrosphere, creates a window from his original (three-dimensional) world, and then clones that second version again, this time including, as close as he can estimate, an approximation of the Hermit's embodied form and senses. Then, most significantly, he instructs the clone software to remove all of the contextual elements and symbols which specifically refer to Orlando's body (Egan, 1997, p. 317). The third clone, as with the second, immediately recognises that he, while sharing a certain heritage, is no longer Orlando,[6] and the clone

> peered back down the tunnel of scapes, past vis immediate progenitor, searching in vain for a glimpse of vis incomprehensible great-grand-parent. *There was a world where that being had lived . . .* but ve could neither name it nor clearly imagine it. With the symbols gone for most of the original's episodic memories, the clone's strongest inheritance was a sense of urgency, yet the edges of the lost memories still ached. (Egan, 1997, p. 318)

The cloning and altering continues until there are six different derivative clones. The final one, so far removed from the original as to be completely incomprehensible, finally takes control of the Hermit robot and immediately begins to communicate with the real Hermits. The bridging of Orlando's clones highlights the importance of embodied material referentiality to intelligent communication. The distant clone manages to communicate with the Hermits both because it now has a referential mental architecture somewhere in the vicinity of the Hermits' and also because it no longer has a citizen-like referential structure. What is *not* part of the clone's body and cognitive processes appears almost as important as what is part. Removing the old symbols and references to the three-dimensional Orlando citizen (who still chooses to act *as if* organically embodied in most situations) loses one mode of thinking and communication, allowing another to form. Orlando's bridging with the Hermits also refutes the idea of boxology or atomisation in the technosciences, which Kember defines as 'literally the way in which behaviours are broken down into fairly isolated modules' and treated as completely meaningful in and by themselves (Kember, 2003, pp. 193–194). The failure of computational models, but the success of the embodied Orlando(s), points to the notion of meaningful communication as part of an entire system of which the body and brain are both intrinsic, inseparable parts. The citizens' models could not mimic a whole Hermit system complete with body from the scant information they had from observing the Hermits in the citizens' terms. This is especially significant since Orlando has always tried to live *as if still organically embodied.* The implication, then, is that bridging from one intelligent being to another always involves bodies and embodiment as much as any informatics. Intelligent bridges require both minds *and* bodies.

The Hermits turn out not only to have engineered themselves, but also their entire environment. As a message passed up Orlando's clone bridge explains, the Hermits have tailored themselves into a static form, no longer evolving, and while their environment may change it is within parameters which ensure the Hermits will always have a stable position within their ecosystem (Egan, 1997, p. 319). The original Orlando's reaction to the Hermits' status is mixed: amazed at their level of technological ability to completely engineer their dynamic but hierarchically stable environment, but simultaneously aghast at the concept of the Hermits engineering themselves into permanent evolutionary stagnation. For Orlando, material embodiment always meant being part of the ecosystem and for both that ecosystem and the inhabitants to *always be in a state of change.* The stagnant Hermits in their safe, secure, but completely unchanging form are more difficult for him to comprehend than even the inward-focused Wang's Carpets. Technology in this instance appears to be able to undermine the facets of materiality and embodiment which Orlando holds so highly. While embodiment is still Orlando's preference, the Hermits force the admission that embodiment does not *always* entail dynamic evolutionary change. However, the Hermits do provide directions to a second macrosphere where the citizens can find other aliens who can provide answers to the origins of the universe and its workings, making Orlando's traumatic bridging worthwhile.

Having completed their task, Orlando and the six clones turn to the question of their own future. Orlando tells his first clone that he is willing to merge with all of them, to incorporate their memories into his own, but the clone reminds Orlando that re-integration would leave a gap, an emptiness, since the context in which the clones thoughts and memories were developed would be lost (Egan, 1997, pp. 327–328). While it may be possible to integrate some of the information about each clone's memories into the original, the first clone's point is that it would be seven different types of referential memories from seven different complex entities in one referential system. Without the points of reference provided by each of the altered clones' bodies and minds, Orlando would always have memories that he could never articulate or assimilate within his own materially referential worldview. As it happens, most of the clones opt to die, while the seventh, the clone which actually communicated with the Hermits, decides to create an organic body (rather than use the robot mimic) and join the

Hermits. Despite the seventh's origins, the draw of embodiment and material community is too powerful.

In the second macrosphere, the citizens encounter not the aliens they seek, but rather a non-sentient software program which has access to all the recorded knowledge of the aliens which the Carter-Zimmerman diaspora was seeking, and immediately explains the physics of the universe(s), including a dire warning of the original universe's demise. The diaspora's mission is successful, and Orlando immediately departs for Earth and the other Carter-Zimmerman polises to share the news and encourage them to travel into the new macrosphere. The alien software assures the citizens that this macrosphere is stable and there is plenty of space for all sentient life to share (Egan, 1997, p. 337). However, Yatima and Paolo, Orlando's son, choose to continue following the aliens, who left clues as to their future destinations.

As they travel through different macrospheres, the pair encounter massive artifacts of unknown origin, seemingly containing vast stores of information. Unable to decipher the artifacts, Yatima and Paolo continue following the aliens' artifactual trail for thousands of years across millions of macrospheres, until they reach a final universe with nothing but completely empty space. In the void, Paolo finally realises that the artifacts they have encountered can be fitted together, the most complex puzzle or structure ever created, but which did not damage any of the universes or macrospheres containing its parts. Yatima and Paola realise that the aliens they seek

> hadn't turned whole worlds to rubble, they hadn't reshaped galaxies in their image. Having evolved on some distant, finite world, they'd inherited the most valuable survival trait of all. Restraint. (Egan, 1997, p. 359)

Ironically, the last message from the aliens Yatima and Paolo sought is not about infinity or transcendence or immortality, but rather the direct opposite: the inescapable importance of limits, mortality, and finitude. This scene echoes and inverts the discovery of the massive monolith in the last sequence of Kubrick's *2001* called 'and Beyond the Infinite'. While the film's monolith supposedly opens the gate to infinity, the artifact Paola and Yatima encounter does the opposite and represents the intrinsic value of finitude. For Paolo, who also shared Orlando's strong philosophy of embodiment, the message is obvious and Paolo immediately prepares to let go, to follow the artifact-makers, and accept a mortal end. Paolo refracts Donna Haraway's argument that 'the affirmation of dying seems absolutely fundamental. Affirmation not in the sense of glorifying death but in the sense—to put it bluntly—that without mortality, we're nothing' (Haraway & Goodeve, 2000, p. 116). Returning to Norbert Wiener's argument that information *is* life (Hayles, 1999, p. 103), Paolo's end and the alien's final message reinforces the idea that information may be *part* of life, but limits, entropy, and materiality (which inescapably also entails mortality) are essential, too. For Yatima, the message is not enough. Yatima still believes that computation and mathematics are reason enough in and of themselves to continue existence (Egan, 1997, p. 361). Yatima, whose Artificial Life began as a mind seed in the Konishi polis, denies the necessity of finitude, and the novel ends with a tragic image of Yatima, alone in an empty universe, trying to find the still hidden secrets of informatic life. Yatima, whose informatic form guarantees a longevity bordering on immortality, ends up alone, an orphan now in every sense, rejecting the material origins and (digitally re-created) naturalistic processes which began Yatima's Artificial Life.

Greg Egan's *Diaspora* facilitates the exploration of both the possibilities of Artificial Life and the use of artificiality to metaphorically engage with contemporary concerns and issues. From the citizen mind seeds grown in Konishi polis to the diaspora of Carter-Zimmerman, the citizens' tales explicate a complex and intricate story about *life-as-we-know-it*. Richard Dawkins' thesis about selfish genes and universally replicating memes is rejected out of hand. Emergence, evolution, and the implicit importance of dynamic change are upheld, but only when change involves the interaction of both subjects *and* the environment of which they are part. Similarly, the convergence of artificial and natural systems is seen as inevitable, but only in a manner which sees both natural and technological systems meaningfully intertwining with neither completely dominant. *Diaspora*'s central theme is undoubtedly the importance of bridging. Materiality and informatics are both part of the future for human (and human-derived) subjects, and the consistent convergent ontology in Egan's novel highlights the importance of both co-existing symbiotically. Neither appear to be able to meaningfully exist without the other. For the citizens, the diaspora to discover the secrets of the universe also becomes a diaspora of contextual knowledge about bodies and a scattering of material ideas. It concludes with a final message and revelation that mortality and finitude are just as important for digital life as for material life and that 'artificiality' by no means unproblematically divides the embodied from disembodied or natural from digital.

In *Diaspora*, the Artificial Life citizens are no longer subjugated by human power and epistemologies. Their own emergent lives give rise to questions about life itself and the 'naturalness' of theories such as evolution. The life of polis citizens on the one hand reinforces natural systems, with bottom-up life only being possible utilising translated biological processes. On the other hand, these digital replications point to the ongoing continuity between the natural and artificial, as well as reinforcing the intrinsic importance of environment and context. The character of Orlando and the philosophy of bridging which he brings from the material world to the artificial polises then extends the idea of convergence. Bridging reinforces the inescapability of both information and embodiment for intelligent life, as well the importance of links between the digital and material worlds. The final tragic images of the citizen Yatima alone in the void highlight the importance of restraint and finitude in the face of digital information's supposedly infinite character. While both novels point to the convergence between artificial and material lives, a better way of expressing these themes is the idea of *symbiosis*. The Artificial Life narratives examined do not separate 'artificial' from 'life', but rather point to the space adjoining these words, a space that could be seen as pointing to the symbiotic relationship between the two terms. The digital and artificial, in both these texts, and culture more broadly, exist symbiotically with life, materiality, and 'the natural'. Narratives of Artificial Life also illuminate the fact that symbiosis means all of these concepts should be addressed holistically, never in opposition. Artificial Life is our responsibility and our life as well.

Part III
Artificial space

5 The Fortification of Place in the Digital Age

While the previous chapters dealt with existing concepts with their own contested meanings, ontologies, and histories—namely Artificial Intelligence and Artificial Life—this chapter, and the following two, propose and tentatively map the new conceptual terrain of artificial space. Ideas of space and spatiality have undergone numerous challenges and re-articulations in recent decades. Various theorists of postmodernism have convincingly argued that space is a constructed category and concept, completely dependent on the specific and subjective instances of its deployment. In the mid-1980s, concurrent with the peak of postmodern theory, William Gibson in his cyberpunk novel *Neuromancer* (1994a) speculated about a new concept of spatiality facilitated by the combination of networked computing and global telecommunications: *cyber*space. The notion of cyberspace has since become a normalised part of our everyday life, but significantly has also provoked a great deal of critical exploration, with theorists using the term as a catalyst to examine the intersections of technology, subjectivity, and spatiality. Responses to *Neuromancer* ranged from celebrating its disruption of rigid notions of both the subject and space (Hollinger, 1990) to decrying its technological reification of gendered divisions of mind and body in cyberspace (Nixon, 1992). Moreover, these debates have become increasingly relevant as Gibson's speculative cyberspace metaphor has been widely, and often uncritically, applied to the material reality of the internet and World Wide Web we know today.

Despite Gibson's body of work spanning eight novels, analysis of his conceptualisation of space is almost always limited to either *Neuromancer* exclusively or, at times, to the broader 'Sprawl' trilogy and related short stories (Gibson, 1988, 1994a, 1995a, 1995b). Nevertheless, Gibson's second loose trilogy—commonly referred to as the 'Bridge' trilogy, consisting of *Virtual Light* (1994b), *Idoru* (1997), and *All Tomorrow's Parties* (1999)—also contains complex and provocative speculation about new forms of space which are emerging, and have emerged, in recent years. Moreover, despite having coined the term cyberspace in *Neuromancer*, in the Bridge trilogy Gibson purposefully avoids using the word altogether. Instead, these texts imaginatively illuminate new spatial terrains that are developing in response to a world in which the internet plays a substantial role, but is not the only space which matters. Indeed, digital and material spaces are closely aligned in some respects, while radically divergent in others, and the artificial spaces Gibson maps exist in both realms, often linking the two in provocative ways which both interrogate and expand existing ideas of the human subject.

The following examination of artificial space in Gibson's Bridge trilogy spans three chapters. This chapter will focus on the ways that place has been further fortified, militarised, regulated, and policed both in material terms and through the purposeful use of the expanding mediascape and digital technology. The following chapter will then argue that the intensification of place also leads to new spaces of resistance in both the material form of the Bridge itself—a seemingly organic community living on the now-defunct San Francisco Bay Bridge—and in the digital form of the Walled City, an informatic re-creation of the now-demolished Hong Kong autonomous zone of Hak Nam; and Chapter 7, this volume, will argue further that these new spaces re-emphasise the link between people, embodiment, and space, culminating in the literal bridging of the digital and material through the deployment of nanotechnology.

From the outset it is worth noting that the California that appears in the Bridge trilogy is familiar due to its continuity with the existing state in the US, but is also purposefully littered with differences easily, and often worryingly, extrapolated from existing social, political, and technological configurations. If, as cultural critic Douglas Kellner has argued, William Gibson's novels can be read as 'mapping our present from the vantage point of [an] imagined future, demonstrating the possible consequences of present trends of development', then the present mapped by the Bridge trilogy is markedly different from the concerns underlying the cultural geography of *Neuromancer* and the Sprawl trilogy (Kellner, 1995, p. 299).

One reason that the Bridge novels resonate so strongly with contemporary issues is the shift in William Gibson's familiarity with technology between these and his earlier novels. While working on the cyberpunk Sprawl trilogy, Gibson points out he had never touched a computer, writing his stories on a manual typewriter, which he felt gave 'a certain edge in terms of imagination in that [he] wasn't really hindered by what was possible' (Trench, 1990). However, Gibson's knowledge of technology became more anchored to existing forms between the two trilogies, with the Bridge novels being produced on a home computer. Nor was he alone in developing a more immediate relationship with personal computing. In the broader North American context, Western society in the early 1990s was gripped by an overwhelmingly optimistic greeting of the emergent 'information superhighway'. As 'cyberspace' escaped from the pages of science fiction into millions of Western homes, Arthur Kroker and Michael Weinstein argue that technophilia reached new heights, with Americans *en masse* embracing 'a stridently pro-technotopia movement, particularly in the mass media, typified by an obsession to the point of hysteria with emergent technologies, and with a consistent and very deliberate attempt to shut down, silence, and exclude any perspectives critical of technotopia' (Kroker & Weinstein, 1994, p. 4). Despite these utopian sentiments, one of the most immediate effects of the information superhighway was to add a new dimension to social and economic stratification, with those lacking access finding themselves on the wrong side of the digital divide. Following similar lines, but developing more provocative terminology, Kroker and Weinstein argue that these people are the refuse of society's myopic technophilia, and in the rush to embrace the digital, those left behind are relegated to the status of 'data trash'. In William Gibson's earlier novels, those characters from the lower end of the socio-economic scale have still inexplicably managed somehow to gain access to state of the art technology. However, in the Bridge trilogy many characters are less fortunate and certainly less socially and economically mobile, remaining for the most part on the receiving end from those more technologically and informatically fortunate. Rather than facilitating the development of new spaces, for those on the wrong side of the digital divide, information technologies ostensibly appear to lock already struggling citizens into an even more rigidly bounded place; in an information economy they are discarded as data trash.

One front on which Gibson signals his heightened interest in those on the wrong side of the digital divide is through self-conscious parallels with his earlier cyberpunk work.[1] In terms of broad plot and structure, *Virtual Light* directly mimics *Neuromancer*, Gibson noting that the former is 'the most blatantly ironical text that I've ever produced' (Bolhafner, 1993). In *Neuromancer*, the unlikely team of Case, the 'console cowboy', and Molly, the cyborg razor girl, meet in a plot orchestrated by unknown powers (eventually turning out to be the Artificial Intelligence Wintermute) and, after a series of adventures, manage to facilitate the merger of Wintermute and Neuromancer into a new cyberspace entity thereby radically altering the structure of the information world. By contrast, in *Virtual Light*, the unlikely team of Berry Rydell, the ex-cop (and then ex-rentacop), and Chevette Washington, the tough girl bicycle courier, meet through a series of accidents in a plot orchestrated by an unknown corporate power (eventually turning out to be the world's richest man, Cody Harwood). After a series of misadventures, they manage to *prevent* Harwood and his partners from implementing a plan that would radically alter the structure of San Francisco using new forms of technology. The change in protagonists from the technologically hip Case and cyborg Molly to Rydell and Chevette, who between them share almost no technological know-how whatsoever, marks an at least partial shift in Gibson's sympathies and interest in the direction of the less technologically affluent. Moreover, Rydell and Chevette's ultimate goal to prevent rather than facilitate structural change through the deployment of new technologies illustrates a fictional world where technology has shifted from being predominantly a signifier of resistance—as in *Neuromancer*—to also signifying those things which should be resisted.

Gibson also distances himself from the technological revelry of the Sprawl trilogy in his Bridge novels by ironically re-deploying the two key signifier of cyberpunk: hackers and their signature fashion accessory, mirrorshades. In *Virtual Light*, the only mirrorshades to be found are those worn by Rydell's rentacop partner:

> Sublett had had allergies. He went into shock from various kinds of cleaners and solvents, so you couldn't get him to come into the car wash at all, ever. The allergies made him light sensitive, too, so he had to wear these mirrored contacts. What with the black IntenSecure uniform and his dry blond hair, the contacts made him look like some kind of Clan-assed Nazi robot. Which could get kind of complicated in the wrong store on Sunset, say three in the morning and all you really wanted was some mineral water and a Coke. But Rydell was always glad to have him on shift, because he was as determinedly nonviolent a rentacop as you were likely to find. (Gibson, 1994b, p. 9)

The mirrorshades, the signifier of all that was hardwired, hard-edged, and hip in the Sprawl trilogy, are now only to be found worn by a character who might be *mistaken* for a 'Clan-assed Nazi robot', but who has almost no access to high technology and actually deplores violence to the extent that in the two action scenes in which he is involved, he ends up either having debilitating allergic reactions to the chemically laden atmosphere of Los Angeles, or hiding in a cupboard. Gibson's self-parody continues in that Sublett and Rydell, far from being cyberpunks themselves, are actually the victims of hackers. During Rydell's last day as a rentacop, the hacker group 'Republic of Desire' break into the communications system of IntenSecure, the company for which Rydell and Sublett work, and use false information to trick the duo into ramming their vehicle into a house reportedly holding hostages. However, it turns out that the Republic of Desire had been paid to cause trouble for the homeowners and, despite being hacked, blame has to be levelled somewhere and thus Rydell is fired. In the aftermath, Sublett wonders if the police will ever catch 'those hackers,' and concludes that their only motivation was that they were 'just *mean*' (Gibson, 1994b, p. 37). Indeed, the fictional Republic of Desire appear very similar to contemporary hacker groups such as the self-styled 'Lulzsec' and 'Anonymous' whose own disruptions crippled Sony's Playstation Network in June 2011, with over 100 million credit card details being stolen from Sony's records (J. Thompson, 2011). Unlike the Sprawl novels, Gibson has placed Rydell and Sublett on the receiving end of the handiwork of hackers, emphasising the alienation many people feel both from high technology and from those fluent in its mysterious workings. Far from opening new avenues and opportunities, for the less technologically affluent, digital technologies appear to close as many doors as they open.

William Gibson acknowledges (1994b, p. 334) that his dark vision of Los Angeles in the Bridge trilogy was directly fed by Mike Davis' theories of urban fortification in *City of Quartz* (1990). Indeed, the relationship between Davis' work and Gibson's is an intertwining one as on the one hand Gibson's writing was fuelled by Davis' theories, but Davis in turn has pointed out that his ideas were inspired by previous science fiction narratives, including Gibson's earlier work (M. Davis, 1990, p. 223). These intersections further illustrate Brian McHale's notion of a deepening 'feedback loop' between speculative fiction and cultural theory, with each enriching and expanding the other (McHale, 1991). Thus, in the Bridge novels, Gibson has built on Davis' insight that technology is only one element of a corporate and governmentally driven design exacerbating the division between the surveyors and the surveyed:

> In cities like Los Angeles, on the bad edge of Postmodernity, one observes an unprecedented tendency to merge urban design, architecture and the police apparatus into a single, comprehensive security effort. (M. Davis, 1990, p. 224)

Moreover, this divide between the technologically watched and the watchers serves to link the digital divide and an increasingly visible class system with unprecedented demarcation as the boundaries are systematically secured, locking every citizen in their designated place. As Sammy Sal, a bicycle courier from the 'other' side of the class divide, points out, in the world of the Bridge trilogy, '[t]here's only but two kinds of people. People can afford [expensive] hotels . . . they're one kind. We're the other. Used to be, like, a middle class, people in between. But not anymore' (Gibson, 1994b, p. 138). Davis' theory can be clearly seen underpinning the cityscapes of *Virtual Light*, where an excessively wealthy lawyer named Karen Mendelsohn makes her home in 'Century City II', a huge interconnected and exclusive series of skyscrapers including 'a tennis club, bars, and restaurants, and a mall you had to pay to join before you could shop there' (Gibson, 1994b, pp. 28–29). Moreover, not only are most urban places being fortified with security screens, but those few remaining public realms are becoming excessively policed and surveyed to the extent that, M. Davis argues, the 'universal and ineluctable consequence of this crusade to secure the city is the destruction of accessible public space' (1990, p. 226).

Due to what Davis calls the 'security driven logic of urban enclavization' (1990, p. 244), even moderately wealthy suburbs in Los Angeles are highly militarised with private police forces supplementing the already substantial Los Angeles Police Department. As Davis notes:

> The carefully manicured lawns of Los Angeles's Westside sprout forests of ominous little signs warning: 'Armed Response!' Even richer

> neighbourhoods in the canyons and hillsides isolate themselves behind walls guarded by gun-toting private police and state-of-the-art electronic surveillance. (1990, p. 223)

In the Bridge novels Berry Rydell, who is rich in neither the digital nor material sense, discovers that the easiest place to find employment is, ironically, within the booming contract security industry, firstly for the security company IntenSecure (Gibson, 1994b, pp. 7–10), and later providing security for the Lucky Dragon convenience store (Gibson, 1999, p. 7). Davis laments that in contemporary Los Angeles the private security sector is expanding beyond the means to fully train the guards employed (1990, p. 250), a concern echoed in Gibson's imagined Southern California (SoCal), where in comparison to rentacops, 'SoCal had stricter regulations for who could or couldn't become a hairdresser' (1994b, p. 9). Paradoxically, the only employment option open to Rydell and those in similar predicaments is to become part of the very apparatuses of surveillance and security which have been so effective in eradicating public space and widening the digital and class divide. Moreover, human security officers are but one element in the ever-expanding array of security enforcement options. High levels of technologised surveillance mean that almost any movement through 'public space' entails enforced remediation where the activities of individual citizens become detailed digital profiles in the police's electronic databases. The surveillance mentality probably reached its extreme when, as Davis points out, a retiring LA police chief called for an orbiting surveillance 'giant eye' (1990, p. 223); while in *Virtual Light* the idea is realised in what is nicknamed, via *Star Wars*, 'the Death Star, . . . officially it was the Southern California Geosynclinical Law Enforcement Satellite' (Gibson, 1994b, pp. 13–14).[2] The so-called Death Star, and the resulting *potential* inescapability of surveillance, exemplifies Michel Foucault's (1979) idea of panoptic control, where a populace who believe they *may* be under surveillance at any time act as though they *are* under surveillance *all the time*, thus becoming self-policing and mentally constrained. Thus in the Bridge novels and the theoretical works which informed them, there are few, if any, public spaces left; electronic prying eyes and security patrols pervade every corner of Gibson's imagined world, a vision readily extrapolated from the California or London of the late twentieth and early twenty-first century.

For cultural theorist Michel de Certeau, even the most fortified places have cracks in their defences which allow moments of resistant spatial activity. De Certeau differentiates between the strategic creation and enforcement of *place*, and the temporary tactical activities that characterise *space*. Places are official, powerful, top-down arrangements which seek to present themselves as permanent and ahistorical, eliding their own creation through strategic reinforcement. As de Certeau argues:

I call a *strategy* the calculation (or manipulation) of power relationships that becomes possible as soon as a subject with will and power (a business, an army, a city, a scientific institution) can be isolated. It postulates a *place* that can be delimited as its *own* and serve as a base from which relations with an *exteriority* composed of targets or threats (customers or competitors, enemies, the country surrounding the city, objectives and objects of research, etc.) can be managed. As in management, every 'strategic' rationalization seeks first of all to distinguish its 'own' place, that is, the place of its own power and will, from an 'environment'. (1984, pp. 35–36)

Thus the strategic development and reinforcement of place reifies the existing mechanisms of power, locking institutions all the more into an 'us' and 'them' mentality. In the Bridge novels the operations of place are even more evident, with government, police, commercial, and military interests all operating together, almost as one, to secure their position while deploying technologies of control and surveillance against the exteriorised citizens who are strategically positioned as threats (a trend that was also visible in the overwhelming dominance of a security-driven logic across the entire political landscape of the immediate post-September 11 Western world).

In direct contrast to the rigidity of place, de Certeau argues that individual subjects going about their everyday lives will often find tactics of resistance which facilitate the temporary creation of *space* wherein the logistics of place can be escaped or, at least, momentarily circumvented. For de Certeau, then:

a *tactic* is a calculated action determined by the absence of a proper locus. . . . Thus it must play on and with a terrain imposed on it and organised by the law of a foreign power. It does not have the means to *keep to itself*, at a distance, in a position of withdrawal, foresight and self-collection . . . It takes advantage of 'opportunities' and depends on them, being without any base where it could stockpile winnings . . . What it wins it cannot keep. This nowhere gives a tactic mobility, to be sure, but a mobility that must accept the chance offerings of the moment, and seize on the wing the possibilities that offer themselves at any given moment. It must vigilantly make use of the cracks that particular conjunctions open in the surveillance of the proprietary powers. (1984, pp. 36–37)

Utilising tactics, resistant spaces can thus be temporarily etched onto the world of fortified places, allowing moments of resistance and subversion in opposition to what de Certeau calls the 'law of the proper' (de Certeau, 1984, p. 117). Using the example of everyday life in the city, de Certeau contrasts the planned, policed, grid-like *place* of the built cityscape with the sometimes erratic, unpredictable, and certainly subject-specific *spaces* inhabited by individual citizens as they forge their unique pathways through the city, concluding that in 'short, *space is a practiced place*. Thus the street geometrically defined by urban planning is transformed into a space by walkers' (de Certeau, 1984, p. 117). However, turning to the world of the Bridge novels, where are the spaces of resistance when security and technologised surveillance reign, further fortifying 'proper' places?

In Gibson's earlier cyberpunk novels, even when material places appeared completely rigid and impenetrable, the rebellious hackers always managed to find alternative spaces through the use of technology. However, while the cyberpunks found their own tactical pathways through cyberspace, in the Bridge trilogy, as noted above, the protagonists—Rydell and Sublett—are manipulated and exploited by the Republic of Desire hackers at the very outset of *Virtual Light*. Following from this ostensible shift in the characterisation of technology and its resistant uses, the remainder of this first section will focus on Rydell and Sublett and their engagement with technology and the media. In doing so, I explore Gibson's rendering of technology and media, and will consider whether they have been subsumed into the strategic operations of place, or whether there are still technologically mediated tactics of spatial resistance to be found.

Ostensibly, Sublett is the character whose difficult social and economic position on the wrong side of the class and digital divides appears influenced to the largest extent by the most popular media technology of the twentieth century: television. During the first of the Bridge novels, readers discover that Sublett is 'a refugee from some weird trailer-camp video-sect' in which the religion is built around the watching of television, wherein 'these people figured video was the Lord's preferred means of communicating, the screen itself a kind of perpetually burning bush' (Gibson, 1994b, p. 8). The quantity of exposure appears to be the main determinant for catching a glimpse of God on the flickering screen, so unsurprisingly 'it was evident that Sublett had absorbed more television than anyone Rydell had ever met, mostly old movies on channels that never ran anything but' (Gibson, 1994b, p. 9).

While television may have replaced religion as the opiate of the masses in the twentieth century, Gibson ironically mixes opiates old and new, fashioning a television-worshipping cult whose *modus operandi* speaks of a long history of addiction and manipulation. Indeed, Sublett is ostensibly the personification of the 'media effects' theory which basically suggests that media viewers are largely passive, receiving messages which can be harmful, manipulative, and addictive (Turnbull, 2006). On a number of levels, the video cult is an exaggeration of the commonly perceived stereotype of this passive television viewing 'couch potato', iconically represented by the character Homer in the animated series *The Simpsons* (1989–), who does indeed treat the television, metaphorically at least, as 'a kind of perpetually burning bush'. Although Sublett has left the television cult, his vision of the world seems to remain mediated by televisual influences; when he and Rydell are responding to an emergency call involving hostages being taken, he carefully narrates 'the help's all *dead . . .* an' they've got the three *kids* in the *nursery*', but to Rydell it 'sounded like he was talking about something mildly baffling he was seeing on television' (Gibson, 1994b, p. 33). For Sublett, then, his life appears to be so completely dominated by the television screen that his reactions to the 'real' world and to the televisual world have become almost identical. In the case of television, far from offering tactics of resistance, Sublett's experience of the world appears firmly locked in place by a strategically constraining media technology.

Scott Bukatman has argued that the dominating influence of media technologies, and television in particular, have led to a disruption or re-orientation of existing modes of human subjectivity, leading to a form of 'terminal identity'. For Bukatman:

> The pervasive domination by, and *addiction to*, the image might be regarded as the primary symptom of terminal identity. The 'image addict' is a metaphor which exists in and through the media, subject to forces which might at first seem to be controlled by the instrumental forces of government and/or big business, but that ultimately seems to signify the passage into a new reality. The spectacular world of television dominates and defines existence, becoming more 'real' (more familiar, more authoritative, more satisfying) than physical reality itself. (1993, p. 26)

Bukatman argues that 'terminal identity' clearly marks a shift in subjectivity, with positive and negative aspects. While its positive attributes will be returned to in the following two chapters, for now it is immediately apparent that the idea of the 'image addict' applies in an overtly negative sense to Sublett. His perceptions of material and simulated worlds have imploded, raising the important question of how much the Subletts of the world can distance themselves from television's influence, or whether they are, as Bukatman suggests, pawns for media producers to manipulate? Ironically, the first signs that Sublett may be able to critically distance himself from some of the media's messages appear when he is forced to return to the television cult in order to visit his ailing mother. While caring for her, Sublett shows his mother 'this Cronenberg film . . . this *Videodrome*,' which leads Reverend Fallon, the cult's leader, to declare Sublett an 'apostate', because Fallon believes that all of Cronenberg's films 'are clearly of the Devil' (Gibson, 1994b, p. 279). In *Terminal Identity*, Scott Bukatman argues that *Videodrome* offers a powerful critique of a society that creates 'image addicts' (1993, p. 86); for a television-worshipping cult, the movie presents the paradox of something on the television warning viewers that television itself can be manipulating, harmful, and addictive. For Sublett, who had already fled the cult once, images of resistance conjured by *Videodrome* are enough to reignite a perspective at odds with a passive acceptance of media messages, and he leaves the cult with Rydell, talking rapidly about 'these movies he liked, and somebody called Cronenberg' (Gibson, 1994b, 311–312). Thus, even in the 'trailer-sect', inhabited by those who would most readily be burdened with the label 'data trash', there are brief moments where spaces of resistance emerge. Sublett's character arc is, on some level, a refutation of the media effects model, with his growing resistance and active viewing practices, rather than passive acceptance, evidence of his growth into a more critical viewer. While Sublett and the television cult are clearly the most caricatured image addicts, they are far from alone in their media-derived affliction.

Berry Rydell, one of the two accidental heroes at the centre of *Virtual Light*, is just as much an image addict as his partner Sublett, but in a more subtle way. Throughout the Bridge novels, Rydell frequently laments that all he ever wanted to do was be a good police officer. However, when Rydell's girlfriend asked him why he was so obsessed with being a cop, he ponders:

> The truth was, it probably had a lot to do with how he and his father had always watched [the reality television show] *Cops in Trouble* together, because that show seriously did teach you respect. You got to see what kind of problems the police were flat up against. Not just tooled-up slimeballs high on shit, either, but the slimeballs' lawyers and the damn courts and everything. But if he told her it was because of a TV show, he knew she'd just laugh at that, too. (Gibson, 1994b, p. 188)

Rydell's image addiction is more complicated than Sublett's, because, similar to other types of addiction, Rydell both accepts the demands of the addiction—the desire to become a cop—and outwardly denies that the addiction is his motivation. Rydell did fulfil his desire and join the Knoxville police force, but his career was extremely short-lived, lasting less than two months, at which point he was forced to shoot a drug-crazed machinist named Kenneth Turvey who was threatening to execute his girlfriend's children. In the aftermath, Rydell found himself facing a lawsuit from Turvey's girlfriend and, just as the television had promised, 'Rydell, having become a cop in trouble, was glad to find that *Cops in Trouble* was right there for him' (Gibson, 1994b, p. 19). Initially, Rydell found that being involved in an episode of *Cops in Trouble* brought real benefits and joy to his life: they flew him business-class to Los Angeles, gave him an all-expenses-paid credit card, provided him with a luxurious hotel suite, and promised to make him famous. Unfortunately for Rydell, *Cops in Trouble*, like any television production, was always after the highest possible rating stories at any given time. Thus, when 'the first thirty-five Pooky Bear victims' (Gibson, 1994b, p. 29) were discovered, Rydell found his one chance to be a cop in televised trouble evaporated before him as the producers rapidly shifted to chasing the far more spectacular mass murder story and the cops who had been involved in breaking the case. In that instant, Rydell found himself unemployed and out of luck, a situation which rapidly led him to the world of private security.

Even after Rydell was exposed to the realities of *Cops in Trouble*'s inner workings, his image addiction stemming from the show still permeates his perceptions of the material world. When working another security job, for example, Rydell has dealings with a Orlovsky, a cop from a Russian background, but Rydell's expectation of how a police officer should behave remains directly informed by images from *Cops in Trouble*. When Orlovsky and his partner track down the girl they have been chasing, '[i]t seemed to Rydell like the Russian just might be about to haul her out and shoot her. Sure looked like it, but what kind of cop would do that?' (Gibson, 1994b, pp. 197–198). Despite obvious signs of corruption, Rydell's idyllic image of the police is so conditioned by his television watching that he is unable to immediately comprehend police corruption. Instead, Rydell describes Orlovsky's behaviour in terms of the 'Father Mulcahy Syndrome' (Gibson, 1994b, p. 203), which takes its name from a television show in which Father Mulcahy manages to negotiate with a gunman and resolve the situation without any loss of life. Many police officers have tried to replicate this scenario, only getting themselves and priests or negotiators killed because they forgot the distance between a television program and the material world. Ironically, Rydell excuses Orlovsky's actions because he thinks the Russian must have absorbed too much television, living out the hard-nosed brutal image of Eastern European police. Gibson highlights how pronounced Rydell's fixation with *Cops in Trouble* is by showing his awareness of the conditioning power of television via the description of 'Father Mulcahy Syndrome', but also showing that Rydell is completely unaware that the very mechanisms of that syndrome accurately describe his own condition. Even after the producers of *Cops in Trouble* threw Rydell aside for a better story, he is still addicted to their reality TV version of how life 'really is'. Unlike Sublett, who initially appears to be an incurable image addict, but shows signs of resistance, Rydell appears to comprehend the power of television, but is actually less capable of seeing his own image addiction.

At the conclusion of *Virtual Light*, Rydell and his new girlfriend, Chevette, once again find themselves in the sort of spectacular predicament that attracts the producers of *Cops in Trouble*. As the novel ends, the implication is that everything is going to work out well for Chevette and Rydell, and that Rydell would finally escape any trouble they had encountered with the aid of their ratings-hungry benefactors. However, when Rydell re-appears in the later novel *All Tomorrow's Parties*, readers discover that, once again, Rydell's reality-TV-fuelled dreams have fallen through. Ironically for Rydell, who has always pretty much believed what *Cops in Trouble* had to say, the reason his chance remained unfulfilled a second time is that the camera lies: when 'a skinny blonde intern named Tara-May Allenby' started filming Rydell, she explained that the camera 'added an apparent twenty pounds', ruining any chance he had of appearing telegenic enough for fifteen minutes as a television hero (Gibson, 1999, p. 85). After being rejected by the television series producers a second time, Chevette recalls 'Rydell sitting on the couch in that apartment with the lights off, watching one old *Cops in Trouble* after another, looking lost, and she just hadn't been able to handle it' (Gibson, 1999, p. 182). Rydell's inability to deal with a second rejection results in him losing Chevette, the only person who loved the 'real' him. The image of Rydell in the dark, watching re-runs of the show to which he was addicted, evokes Bukatman's argument regarding image addiction:

> The image addict is a helpless prisoner of the spectacular society. The spectacle is a force of pacification, exploitation, control, and containment which functions as either a supplement or simulacrum of the state. (1993, p. 68)

Exemplifying Bukatman's perspective, Rydell's existence is constrained by his beliefs and desires formed and informed by the purported reality constructed in *Cops in Trouble*. His belief in the police and the society they protect stems from the seductive power of the spectacle to render *itself* as the norm and thus strategically reinforce its already fortified place throughout society. Thus, in the Bridge novels, those on the wrong side of the digital and class divides are not only restrained by heightened levels of private security and electronic surveillance, but also by the media products and technologies they consume and access which, in many ways, appear specifically designed to reify and champion the law of the proper. Returning to de Certeau's framework, television and mass media in the Bridge trilogy operate strategically, reinforcing existing power structures and 'proper' arrangements of place, and rarely provide viewers with tactical options to look, think, or explore beyond official place. Mass media appears to specifically distance consumers and viewers from any potential spaces of resistance.

In the Bridge novels, and most notably in *Virtual Light*, William Gibson initially appears to have imaginatively extrapolated a world where security, surveillance, and the technologised operations of media all serve to reinforce existing 'proper' places, and simultaneously widen the resulting digital and class divides. For the rentacop partners Rydell and Sublett, their lives seem rigidly constrained on at least three levels: firstly, they are part of a highly security-conscious society and under constant scrutiny from digital surveillance; secondly, as that society has tried to set in stone existing structures and places, the only role the two can find is as part of the human machinery of security; and thirdly, even the media, which might have been thought to provide an escape mechanism, actually reinforce the conservative, strategically maintained status quo, providing few, if any, spaces of resistance. In parodying his earlier Sprawl trilogy and ironically re-casting both the signifiers of cyberpunk and the role of technology, Gibson shifts his focus to those individuals who cannot simply escape via a digital pathway into cyberspace. In building on Mike Davis' theories of urban planning and control, Gibson renders a cityscape where almost omnipresent security and surveillance are both the result of, and perpetuate, the privatisation of public space and thus the fortification of 'proper' place. Moreover, those characters on the wrong side of the digital divide are afflicted by Scott Bukatman's notion of image addiction, where their lives are constrained and seemingly pacified by the society of the spectacle in which the televisual and the real blur together, reinforcing an ideal culture far removed from the world outside the window.

In reading the world of the Bridge novels through the tactical framework developed in Michel de Certeau's *The Practice of Everyday Life*, at first it may appear that the spaces of resistance have all disappeared in the face of the fortification of place. However, even Sublett and the television-worshipping cult hint at remaining tactical options; Sublett's interest in David Cronenberg's films points to tiny spaces of resistance existing even within the seemingly closed monoculture. In *Virtual Light*, when Rydell first arrives in Los Angeles, from the window of the car he is travelling in with *Cops in Trouble* lawyer Karen Mendelsohn, he sees the homeless, the poor, the destitute, those on the wrong side of the class and digital divides. When Mendelsohn looks outside encountering the same view she quips to Rydell in a deadpan tone, 'Welcome to Los Angeles . . . Be glad you aren't taking the subway' (Gibson, 1994b, p. 25). While Mendelsohn's callous indifference to the plight of other human beings may appear representative of the upper echelons of capitalist Western culture, her reaction also leads to the conclusion that, if these people who have been cast aside as data trash have survived at all, then there must be some spaces of resistance open for them. It is to those artificial spaces that the next chapters will explore.

6 Resistance is Spatial

Whereas the previous chapter focused primarily on the way 'proper' official structures and systems have been reinforced by mass media as well as both information and security technologies, William Gibson's Bridge trilogy also highlights the cracks in these seemingly monolithic and rigid places, revealing divergent spaces, sometimes radically so, where modes of resistance may, for a time, flourish. Building further upon Michel de Certeau's insights, and following cultural critic and theorist Fredric Jameson, these new spaces can be considered responses to a 'crisis of space' on at least two levels: firstly, as a crisis in purely physical terms, where public spaces have been all but eradicated leaving those people who, for one reason or another, do not 'fit in' with nowhere to go; and secondly, as a crisis in more conceptual terms where, as Jameson has argued, 'our daily life, our psychic experience, our cultural languages, are . . . dominated by categories of space rather than by categories of time' (Jameson, 1991, p. 16) and where everyday linear time is lost or, at least, challenged, replaced by the perpetual present of spatiality and simulacra.

The first of the two new spaces imagined by Gibson, referred to simply as 'the bridge', is an organic community of San Francisco's outcast and marginalised citizens who have turned the Bay Bridge—damaged by an earthquake, and left unused—into an autonomous refuge outside the normal mechanisms and laws of the surrounding city. Hundreds, possibly thousands of people have constructed eclectic dwellings and impromptu shops and markets out of every imaginable construction material available, harking back to medieval history and earlier when bridges were filled with buildings and dwellings, not just facilitating transportation (Tatsumi, 2006, p. 114). According to residents, the bridge has 'no agenda, . . . no underlying structure', only an alliance of outcasts, a functional but unplanned community of people who have created their own habitat, their own space(s)' (Gibson, 1994b, p. 129). While the bridge is a *physical* manifestation of new spaces of resistance, Gibson's other imagined space, the Walled City, is the opposite. In the Bridge trilogy the internet has become as highly regulated and policed as the urban physical spaces. In response, the citizens of the Walled City found a way to 'secede from the human datascape', to create a virtual city which, as Masahiko, one of the self-styled 'denizens' of Walled City, cryptically puts it, is 'of the Net, but not on it.' Like the bridge, the Walled City has 'no laws . . . just agreements,' and houses an eclectic population who have founded a new space outside of, and resistant to, the dominant digital culture (Gibson, 1997, p. 209).

The descriptions and terms used to describe spaces in the Bridge trilogy are already imbued with an analytical edge through Gibson's use of particular outside witnesses. The first glimpse of the bridge is through the eyes of Yamazaki, a visiting Japanese academic who humbly describes himself as 'a student of existential sociology' (Gibson, 1997, p. 6). His point of view provides what Tatsumi describes as 'Yamazaki's socioanthropological gaze', complete with the terminology at home in an undergraduate textbook (Tatsumi, 2006, p. 120). Yamazaki's initial description of the bridge, for example, is extremely telling:

> The integrity of its span was rigorous as the modern program itself, yet around this had grown another reality, intent upon its own agenda. This had occurred piecemeal, to no set plan, employing every imaginable technique and material. The result was something amorphous, startlingly organic. At night, illuminated by Christmas bulbs, by recycled neon, by torchlight, it possessed a queer medieval energy. (Gibson, 1997, p. 66)

The bridge is thus a 'space of bricoleurs', where bits and pieces of material and meaning, which by themselves achieve little, are brought together by the bridge dwellers to help form a new space which is not just a refuge, but is also filled with new possibilities (Kneale & Kitchin, 2002, p. 1).[1] These few lines from *Virtual Light* also resonate with arguments regarding the postmodern cityscape. One such argument can be found in David Harvey's work, in which he contends that the great metropolitan cities of the Western world, complete with 'the machines, the new transport . . . systems, skyscrapers, bridges, and engineering wonders of all kinds,' were amongst the most powerful centres, and signifiers, of the modernist project (Harvey, 1990, p. 27). By contrast, however, the postmodern cityscape has jettisoned these icons and ideals of progress in favour of '[f]iction, fragmentation, collage, and eclecticism, all suffused with a sense of ephemerality and chaos,' in terms of imagination, design, and everyday life (Harvey, 1990, p. 98). While the major cities imagined in the Bridge trilogy have characteristics of both modern and postmodern cityscapes, the bridge itself iconically embodies the latter. Ross Farnell juxtaposes the bridge with the oppressive anti-spatial mechanisms described in Davis' *City of Quartz* which also informed Gibson's descriptions of near-future Los Angeles, concluding that the bridge 'is the *infrastructural alternative* to Davis's descriptions of architecture-as-repression' (Farnell, 1998, p. 465, emphasis added). It would be hard to find a better representation of this shift from a modernist to postmodern cityscape than the transformation of the Bay Bridge, once a central transportation artery of a modern metropolis, into an eclectic, 'piecemeal' community housing an alliance of difference and otherness. Thus, while some city-scapes, such as the Los Angeles described in *Virtual Light*, are becoming more highly policed and surveyed with a concurrent eradication of public spaces, the inevitable outcome or by-product is the almost 'organic' creation of new spaces, such as the bridge. Moreover, the increasing number of eclectic urban refugees who populate the bridge may form only an ephemeral and chaotic alliance of difference, but while working together they have created, and maintain, a space of resistance with its 'own agenda', an agenda at odds with the monoculture of the surrounding metropolis.

For de Certeau, tactical spaces of resistance are linked to the ongoing flux of time and the multiplicity of histories (1984, pp. 38–39). Part of the establishment of proper places involves casting them either as ahistorical or, at least, as the end point of modernism's ideal of the Progress of History (with purposeful capital letters, signifying the one 'proper' History). Spaces of resistance, by contrast, make tactical use of changes and opportunities that time presents, including the ability to construct *histories*, which do not rely on a single 'proper' narrative. Exemplifying this spatial alliance with multiplicity, one of the bridge's key differences from the surrounding cityscape is its departure from the modernist history of San Francisco. On the bridge, many histories and many stories co-exist. One of the bridge's histories is told to Yamazaki by Skinner, one of the few remaining original inhabitants who was part of the crowd that 'took' the bridge. He recalls that there were 'no signals, no leader, no architect', but 'people just *came*' one night, climbing the fences surrounding the then defunct bridge and running onto it from either end, clinging to the towers. Eventually, the officials of the surrounding city decided, rather than risk the bad publicity of emptying the bridge by force, to allow the collection of society's most unwanted to set up a new home (Gibson, 1994b, pp. 98–102). Skinner's history thus marks the bridge as an almost mythical space of resistance, where an alliance of difference prevailed against the surrounding authorities. Yamazaki also noted that 'Skinner's mind was remarkably like the bridge', and while Skinner's version of the bridge's history may appear representative of the whole, Skinner self-consciously realised that 'history . . . was turning into plastic', and that every history 'was an approximation, somebody's idea of how it might have looked,' rather than a singular definitive narrative of 'how it really happened' (Gibson, 1994b, pp. 68, 273).

The bridge, therefore, also houses the histories that Fontaine perceives. Fontaine, who runs a small shop and maintained many of the bridge's electrical systems, has a very different take on history:

> Everything, to Fontaine, had a story. Each object, each fragment comprising the built world. A chorus of voices, the past alive in everything, that sea upon which the present tossed and rode. (Gibson, 1999, pp. 158–159)

Fontaine sees the histories implicit in every object; the histories of fragments and commodities rather than people and places. Both Skinner and Fontaine's histories share certain characteristics: both reflect Elizabeth Mahoney's argument that 'future cities [will] foreground space over . . . time' (Mahoney, 1997, p. 168), in that their organising principle is their spatial position on the bridge rather than where they had come *from*—their past. Moreover, both depend on randomness and chaos rather than linear causality (people 'just *came*' to take the bridge, and Fontaine's objects and fragments all travel various paths to end up on the bridge); and both histories are entirely contingent (Skinner recognises that when he dies, his version of bridge history will die with him, and Fontaine realises that the 'chorus of voices' that he perceives in material objects will alter as new fragments and objects come onto, or leave, the bridge).

Many of the bridge's inhabitants choose to completely privilege the perpetual present of their spatiality over any historical baggage they once carried. For example, when an outsider inquires of Boomzilla if he has seen someone they call a 'lost child', he lies and says he has never seen the girl because, '[a] lost child himself, he has every intention of staying that way' (Gibson, 1999, p. 83). In the space of the bridge, the inhabitants all implicitly recognise the choice of one another, if they wish, to escape their former histories and, if need be, the alliance of others works together to allow each of the bridge folk to exist in a community which is concerned only with the spatial dynamics of their eclectic, but functionally communal, present. In de Certeau's terms, then, the space of the bridge is replete with tactical stories which allow the bridge dwellers to resist the official narrative of both the places they have fled and the stories those places had previously attempted to inscribe on the bridge folk.

Through Tessa, an Australian new media student and documentary maker who, like Yamazaki, witnesses rather than participates in the new spaces of resistance, Gibson once again deploys scholarly terms. Tessa explains to Chevette, for example, that the various bridge folk can be understood as forming 'interstitial communities' since interstitial 'meant in between things', in the cracks and gaps between of the surrounding sociopolitical structures (Gibson, 1999, p. 33). The bridge is an interstitial space on a number of levels: literally, the bridge is between the two landmasses of San Francisco; metaphorically, the bridge and its inhabitants exist between the gaps in the ostensible monoculture; and paradigmatically, the bridge exists between the end of modernism and whatever comes next (such as the Walled City, discussed below). Similarly, the many tactics employed by those living on the bridge take place in the cracks existing in-between the official structures of the surrounding city. Indeed, the sense of being 'between things' resonates throughout all three books, thus my describing them as Gibson's Bridge trilogy. Ironically, however, as soon as the ideal term to describe the bridge is found, it starts to lose its interstitiality.

When Tessa arrives on the bridge she is accompanied by the former bridge dweller Chevette who is returning after an absence of over a year. When they walk out onto the bridge the first thing they see is a 'Lucky Dragon', 'a modular convenience store, chunked down front and centre across the entrance to the bridge's two levels' (Gibson, 1999, p. 66). Chevette is horrified to see a commercial chain-store on the bridge,[2] and while Tessa brushes it off, explaining the bridge has been there 'long enough to become the city's number-one postcard,' Chevette senses that the bridge has lost something important. Tessa comments that she has to hurry in order 'to document the life before it's theme-parked,' but Chevette realises that it is already too late (Gibson, 1999, p. 67). Later, Chevette explains to Tessa that the character of the bridge is already radically different as proper shops, with updated stock, staff, and provisions, emerge. In the early days of the bridge, possession of a space was purely through occupancy, but now people are being paid to run shops and businesses, morphing parts of the bridge into a weekend market rather than refuge. This notion is reinforced when Chevette is reunited with Fontaine; she asks him why he thinks the bridge is changing, and he replies: 'It just is, . . . [t]hings have a time, then they change' (Gibson, 1999, p. 160). While the bridge was initially an interstitial space, it has slowly become popular and begun to re-integrate into the surrounding city, reflecting de Certeau's point that tactics are temporary, and thus tactical spaces must be as well. Just as the bridge became interstitial by no set plan, it could not then become permanently ephemeral (an oxymoron, after all), and instead the bridge community need either become more integrated into the San Francisco cityscape, or search out new spaces. Chevette, a former bridge resident, understands this, while Tessa, never having been 'in-between', cannot:

> It is a world within the world, and, if there be such places between the things of the world, places built in the gaps, then surely there are things there, and places between them, and things in those places too. And Tessa doesn't know this, and it is not Chevette's place to tell her. (Gibson, 1999, pp. 80–81)

Chevette recognises that while some may disappear, there will always be new, emerging spaces of resistance, suffused with interstitiality, in-between things. The Walled City is one of them.

Just as the bridge exists as part of the geographical city of San Francisco but is conceptually and spatially at odds with it, the Walled City is part of the broader digital world but exists outside the rules and regulations of the normative internet. As Masahiko explains, the 'Walled City is of the net, but not on it. There are no laws here, only agreements' (Gibson, 1997, p. 209). The Walled City, unlike the internet, is not centrally governed but, like the bridge, exists due to an alliance between the various eclectic citizens who perform 'distributed processing', building and maintaining the

Walled City on their own terms, not within the frameworks enforced by governments and global corporations (Gibson, 1997, p. 209). The bifurcation of the Walled City and the outside digital world can be mapped through Mark Nunes' conceptualisation of 'virtual topographies'—geographical and conceptual explanations of information and communication systems. Nunes argues that there is a digital dichotomy between the competing paradigms of *smooth* and *striated* virtual space: the former, represented in the phrase 'Surf the 'Net', refers to a more fluid, unlimited, and malleable concept, recognisably postmodern; the latter, represented by the phrase 'Cruise the Information Superhighway', refers to a concrete, linear, and 'point-oriented' virtual topography which is more recognisably modernist (Nunes, 1999, p. 62). Nunes' informatic dichotomy aligns closely with de Certeau's division between place and space: the striated, point-oriented official information superhighway aptly encompasses the notion of place within the digital realm; while, by contrast, the smooth, fluid, and changing 'net, which presumably exists within the gaps of the striated model, corresponds closely with the idea of informatic spaces of resistance. Thus in the Bridge trilogy, the global information communication system is more like the concrete, linear model, complete with stringent regulations and restrictions. The 'denizens' of the Walled City, however, like the bridge folk, found the increasing restrictions on their (virtual) space impossible to live within, so they managed to break away from the broader official datascape. They constructed what they call 'another country', not 'in any obsolete sense of the merely geopolitical', but rather a completely 'autonomous reality' which is functionally and spatially separate from the highly restricted global system (Gibson, 1999, p. 126). Their new country retains the fluidity and malleability of Nunes' smooth topography, as the internet had before it became highly regulated (Zittrain, 2008), and thus provides new tactical spaces for projects and existence *per se* outside of, and resistant to, the proper striated digital system of the dominant culture.

The potential spaces of resistance opened up by digital technologies have also been provocatively theorised by cultural critic Hakim Bey. Writing in the late 1980s, and extrapolating from subversive forms such as 'the marginal zine network, the BBS [Bulletin Board System] networks, pirated software, hacking, [and] phone-phreaking', Bey argued that new technologies could facilitate what he labelled 'temporary autonomous zones' or TAZs (1991, p. 107). Although not explicitly drawing on de Certeau, Bey's TAZ is uncannily similar to a digital incarnation of spaces of resistance. For example, he argues:

> The TAZ is like an uprising which does not engage directly with the State, a guerilla operation which liberates an area (of land, of time, of imagination) and then dissolves itself to re-form elsewhere/elsewhen, *before* the State can crush it. (Bey, 1991, p. 99)

Bey's TAZs not only resonate with de Certeau's spatial modes of tactical resistance, but also with the Walled City and its political positioning outside of the authorised internet in that for Bey, TAZs exist as part of a 'shadowy sort of *counter-Net*' which are just outside the 'proper' information superhighway (1991, p. 106). Politically, the Walled City operates for all intents and purposes as one of Bey's temporary autonomous zones, providing new digital realms just outside, and existing within the infrastructure cracks of, the official informatic networks. When working towards a particular goal, the denizens of the Walled City share certain characteristics with the infamous whistle-blower website *Wikileaks* since the anonymous leaks organisation also has roots in the hacker movement (Lovink & Riemens, 2010) and has been actively defended by contemporary hacker groups (Mansfield-Devine, 2011). The resemblance between TAZs and de Certeau's ideas of spatial resistance also position the Walled City, and *Wikileaks*, as exemplars of digital tactical space, a notion reinforced by Bey who argues further that the 'TAZ is thus a perfect tactic for an era in which the State is omnipresent and all-powerful yet simultaneously riddled with cracks and vacancies' (Bey, 1991, p. 99).

The Walled City not only provides an alternative political sphere, but allows the residents to develop more fluid spatial relations to, and within, their constructed virtual environment. When Chia McKenzie first visits the Walled City, she immediately becomes imbricated (and almost overwhelmed) by their different conceptualisation of time and space:

> They were inside now, smoothly accelerating, and the squirming density of the thing was continual visual impact, an optical drumming. 'Tai Chang Street.' Walls scrawled and crawling with scrolling messages, spectral doorways passing like cards in a shuffled deck. And they were not alone: others there, ghost-figures whipping past, and everywhere the sense of eyes. Fractal filth, bit-rot, the corridor of their passage tented with crazy swoops of faintly flickering lines of some kind. 'Alms House Backstreet.' A sharp turn. Another. Then they were ascending a maze of twisting stairwells, still accelerating, and Chia took a deep breath. (Gibson, 1997, p. 182)

Here, Chia is guided through the Walled City not in linear time, but via a temporal framework completely defined by her and Masahiko's (her guide) movement through the spaces of the Walled City. Masahiko, a Walled City resident, can move through the city as fast as he chooses, navigating the digital cityscape at accelerated speeds, creating an 'optical drumming' for Chia who is stunned by the depth and intensity of the 'continual visual impact' of simulacra. The shift in temporal and spatial signification in the Walled City echoes Vivian Sobchack's arguments about similar shifts of meaning in science fiction films. She argues:

> The inflated value of space and surface has led to a deflation of tempo-
> ral value, to a collapse of those temporal relationships that formulated
> time as a continuous and unifying flow—constituting the coherence of
> personal identity, history and narrative . . . [and] transformed temporal
> coherence into spatial co-Here-nce. (Sobchack, 1997, p. 272)

In the Walled City, Sobchack's notion of spatial co-Here-nce reaches its
logical extreme: in the virtual cityscape, time has become completely contingent on the subjective movement of individuals through the labyrinth of
its dense digital surfaces. Significantly, time and space within the Walled
City are no less real to the inhabitants, many of whom exist like Masahiko, who spends 'all his waking hours [there,] . . . his dreams too' (Gibson, 1997, p. 89). Even in contemporary society, Mark Nunes has argued,
'popular acceptance of cyberspace as a space has not needed to wait for
the arrival of bodysuit-and-goggle "virtual reality"; for literally millions of
users, cyberspace already "exists" as a *place*, as real as the work and play
conducted "in" it' (Nunes, 1999, p. 61).[3] For the denizens of the Walled
City, their interstitial space is not only as real as the material and digital
culture of the surrounding monoculture (or the bridge), but their space in-
between is also all that much more important given that their rearticulated
reality privileges spatial co-Here-nce over previous, more linear concepts
of linear time.

The new spatial relations in the Walled City also mean that multiple
histories can co-exist, as they did following reconceptualisations of space
on the bridge. The Walled City's first history is really more 'the stuff of
legend' and 'subversive rumour' than an historical narrative (Gibson, 1999,
p. 194). In the myth, the Walled City began with a 'shared killfile'—a communal set of mechanisms to delete any incoming messages or data the users
wanted to avoid—and then:

> Someone had the idea to turn the killfile inside out. This is not really
> how it happened, you understand, but this is how the story is told: that
> the people who founded [the Walled City] . . . were angry, because
> the net had been very free, you could do what you wanted, but then
> the governments and the companies, they had different ideas of what
> you could, what you couldn't do. So these people, they found a way to
> unravel something. A little place, a piece, like cloth. They made some-
> thing like a killfile of everything, everything they didn't like, and they
> turned that inside out. (Gibson, 1997, p. 221)

Not concerned with the complex technical details of how it actually happened, the killfile myth emphasises the Walled City's deliberate position
outside the norms of the dominant digital culture in both a technological
and political sense. A second history also emphasises these themes, but in
a different way.

The Walled City's second history begins with Hak Nam, an autonomous zone in Hong Kong (when it was still a British colony), that had been without laws or police because of a mistake in the possession agreement with China which left the zone technically under Chinese control, but control that was never exercised since Hak Nam was surrounded by British-held Hong Kong (Popham, 1993, p. 9). Hak Nam, a tiny space but extremely densely populated, was an 'outlaw place', which housed 'drugs and whores and gambling. But people living, too. Factories, restaurants. A city. No laws' (Gibson, 1997, p. 221). The original Walled City was an archetypal interstitial space, but before the handover of Hong Kong back to Chinese administration, it was cleared and demolished (Goddard, 1993, p. 208). As Masahiko recalls, '[T]hirty-three thousand people inhabited [the] original. Two-point-seven hectares. As many as fourteen stories' (Gibson, 1997, p. 184). The collective digital architects of the Walled City found in Hak Nam their political model, and therefore decided to make the virtual world of the Walled City an exact replica of the original: '[T]hey found the data. The history of it. Maps. Pictures. They built it again' (Gibson, 1997, p. 222). Thus, the Walled City's second history emphasises how the new spatial possibilities of the digital domain can be used to keep alive a political and spatial 'world' that the authorities sought to eradicate. These multiple histories of the Walled City also evoke Fredric Jameson's idea of the 'new spatial logic of the simulacrum'. For Jameson, the increasing dominance of space and surfaces is implicitly negative because, he argues, it replaces any sense of linear historical development, and thus political unity and progress (Jameson, 1991, p. 18). However, the Walled City's digital regeneration of the interstitial space of Hak Nam illustrates how the 'spatial logic of the simulacrum' can be a positive force, used for political resistance against the monolithic late capitalist systems that Jameson so powerfully critiques. Building upon de Certeau, the emergent spaces of resistance facilitated by new digital possibilities also enhance the tactical potential of the informatic Walled City. Thus, the Walled City's multiple histories, precisely because of their position within a new system which emphasises spatial co-Here-nce and surfaces, map a space which is intrinsically interstitial and resistant against the dominant culture in terms of politics, identity, and history.

The real test of the effectiveness of resistant spaces, however, comes during the climax of *All Tomorrow's Parties*. In the final novel, Cody Harwood, the president of the Harwood Levine megacorporation and the world's richest man who 'maybe, just maybe, ran it all', has embarked on a project that will eradicate the bridge community as well as undermine any resistance to his political and economic dominance (Gibson, 1999, p. 15). Through various backchannels, the inhabitants of the Walled City become aware of Harwood's plans and in alliance with Colin Laney, a data analyst with a particular 'knack' for seeing emerging structures, set out to stop Harwood. In the last few chapters of *All Tomorrow's Parties*, Berry Rydell, Fontaine, and a number of other people on the bridge form one prong of an attack on Harwood, while Colin Laney and 'virtually the entire population of the Walled City, working in a mode of simultaneity that very nearly approximates unison', form another (Gibson, 1999, p. 250). Through this uncanny and eclectic alliance, Harwood's plan is halted and the bridge, although set on fire by Harwood's team, is saved, while Harwood's more cryptic plan to consolidate his material and economic power is likewise undermined. Ultimately, Gibson privileges the tactical interstitial spaces and their communities who may come from many different backgrounds but, when they work together, can be more powerful than any force the dominant culture can muster. Similarly, the Walled City's population appear completely capable of working for the collective good if need be, in this case to undermine the attempts by the dominant culture to erase the resistant potential of digitally enabled interstitial spaces.

The notion of a collective and its re-articulation within digital realms has also been productively explored by French theorist Pierre Levy. He argues that an ideal and *realisable* outcome of the possibilities enabled by computer networks is the formation of *collective intelligence* which entails intricate group problem-solving and action, but not at the expense of individuality or uniqueness. Levy argues further that:

> The technopolitical problem of democracy in cyberspace is to provide a community with the means to develop a collective voice without the need for representation. This collective voice could, for example, take the form of a complex image or dynamic space, a changing map of group practices and ideas. Each of us would be able to situate ourselves in a virtual world that the community as a whole helped to enrich and sculpt through their acts of communication. Collectivity is not necessarily synonymous with solidity and uniformity. The development of cyberspace provides us with the opportunity to experiment with collective methods of organisation and regulation that dignify multiplicity and variety. (Levy, 1997, p. 66)

Gibson's vision of the Walled City can be easily rendered as a completely successful outcome to one such experiment with collectivity. Indeed, Levy describes the spatial characteristics containing these new dynamic collectives as forming 'intelligent cities . . . which should be understood as a moral and political entity rather than a physical place' whose key functions involve enhanced 'listening, expression, decision-making, evaluation, organisation, connection, and vision, all of which are interrelated' (1997, p. 70). Similarly, rather than having an elaborate electoral system wherein a few speak for the many until the next election, the denizens of the Walled City operate using 'no laws . . . just agreements,' but agreements that are task-specific, with everyone who wishes to being involved in decision-making, which in turn, when endorsed by everyone, can lead to 'virtually the entire population of the Walled City, working in a mode of simultaneity that very nearly approximates unison', as discussed above. While this vision may seem far-fetched, both Henry Jenkins (2002) and Jane McGonigal (2003), with reference to interactive audiences and collective augmented reality game players respectively, have argued that Levy's notion of collective intelligence is being realised in everyday life when information and communication technologies are used for new forms of cultural activity. Indeed, as Axel Bruns (2008) argues, the starkest and most well-known example of collective intelligence at work is undoubtedly the ongoing online creation and circulation of the world's largest encyclopaedia, *The Wikipedia*, which is written by anyone who chooses to contribute, for free, with almost no editorial hierarchy beyond the contributors themselves. For de Certeau, too, tactical resistance illuminates 'the extent to which intelligence is inseparable from the everyday struggles,' (1984, p. xx) and the very acts of distributed processing which maintain the Walled City (or ensure the validity of *The Wikipedia*) entail around the clock struggle. Ironically, then, in the speculative vision of the Walled City which so closely resonates with Pierre Levy's vision of collective intelligence, *political representation* has given way to a more directly involved tactical decision-making process, but that process itself involves a new space that relies on *digital representation* and informatic communication to work effectively.

As I have argued, William Gibson's Bridge trilogy speculatively maps a new pragmatic and political configuration of emergent spatiality which is facilitated by information and communication technologies but is not exclusively digital. These new configurations of space share many similarities with, and characteristics of, de Certeau's tactical spatial resistance, Bey's Temporary Autonomous Zones, and Levy's collectively intelligent cities. However, I contend that the notion of space extrapolated from the Bridge trilogy is also sufficiently different that it needs a new and specific label. The most appropriate term, then, is *artificial space* which has a number of specific characteristics. From de Certeau's work, artificial space is *tactical* in its potential to oppose and defy the seemingly monolithic conservative world which reinforces the law of the proper, the notion of unchanging place, and the promotion of a singular History. Rather than succumbing to a security and surveillance driven globe, artificial space overflows with multiple histories and eclectic stories, all of which can, at times, be told together to inform pragmatic and specific political acts. Unlike the description in *The Practice of Everyday Life* of tactics as always temporary, digital technologies facilitate resistance which can exhibit more longevity, such as the prolonged tactical existence of the digitally re-visioned Walled City. Artificial space *shares much of its ethos with Temporary Autonomous Zones* yet at the same time its denizens work hard to avoid their realms being too temporary or overly autonomous. Or, more clearly, artificial spaces are in many ways oppositional to mainstream politics and places, but they are also pragmatic in their existence alongside and within the wider world. The Walled City 'opted to secede from the human datascape' not to then exist in a vacuum but rather to re-engage with the dominant culture on their own terms. Artificial space harbours and encourages Levy's *collective intelligence*, facilitating new ways of thinking, sharing, and acting which operate outside traditional hierarchies while effectively deploying interactive digital affordances. However, unlike Levy's utopian notion that everyone will participate and form intelligent cities, artificial space is characterised by the recognition that it will almost always be in the minority, with more in common with the oppositional stance of *Wikileaks*. Lastly, artificial spaces are *interstitial* in that they are in between things, in the moments of change, bridging the divide between material and digital, and marking the shifts from modernist understandings of linear time and space to new understandings which have yet to fully cohere. During the climax of *All Tomorrow's Parties*, Cody Harwood tries to burn the bridge, literally and figuratively, but the combined resources of the bridge folks and the inhabitants of the Walled City defeat Harwood and prevent the eradication of their artificial spaces. The future which emerges post-Harwood is far from clear, but many options remain open, and those that inhabit artificial space will help shape it. As they do so, their identities and sense of embodiment will potentially shift, too, and it is that issue which the next chapter will address.

7 The Infinite Plasticity of the Digital?

In the many, varied academic responses to William Gibson's archetypal novel *Neuromancer*, the most contested site of meaning has been Gibson's re-deployment of the human body. Feminist critic Veronica Hollinger, for example, argued that Gibson's use of cyborg characters championed the 'interface of the human and the machine, radically decentring the human body, the sacred icon of the essential self,' thereby disrupting the modernist and humanist division of human and technology, and associated dualisms of nature/culture, mind/body, and thus the gendered binarism of male/female (Hollinger, 1990, p. 33). 'Human bodies in Gibson's stories', Hollinger argues further, 'are subjected to shaping and re-shaping, the human form destined perhaps to become one available choice among many' (Hollinger, 1990, p. 35). Conversely, Thomas Foster has argued that Gibson's bifurcation of cyberspace and the material world reifies the mind and devalues the body as surplus 'meat'. Moreover, far from disrupting the assumptions of humanism, in *Neuromancer*, although they are both cyborgs, the cyberspace cowboy (Case) is male, and the street warrior (Molly) is female, implicitly maintaining the gendered associations of masculinity with the mind, and femininity with the body (Foster, 1993, p. 18). As both of these (and most other) analyses of Gibson's cyberpunk novels situate cyborgs as the central signifier of embodiment, in order to explore Gibson's development of ideas relating to the body in the Bridge trilogy, the first question that needs to be asked is: 'where have all the cyborgs gone?'

At first glance it appears that there are no cyborgs in Gibson's second trilogy: certainly none of the characters have surgically implanted devices like those sported by Molly in *Neuromancer*. However, Gibson has not discarded cyborgs altogether, but rather builds upon a different concept of cyborg identity. Donna Haraway has argued in her ironic and iconic 'Manifesto for Cyborgs' that everyone in contemporary society is *already* a cyborg. Quickly qualified, Haraway does not suggest that everyone has become a 'razor girl' like Molly; nor is everyone akin to the Borg of *Star Trek*, covered in black latex and biotechnic implants. Rather, physically, all humans are cyborgs because it is impossible not to become entwined with technology as part of everyday life: immunisation, hearing-aids, telecommunications, computers, and calcium-enhanced milk are all examples of technology and the human body hybridising to become cyborgs. More importantly, at a metaphorical level, the interrelation between people and technologies means that there 'is no fundamental, ontological separation in our formal knowledge of machine and organism, of technical and organic' (Haraway, 1991, p. 178). Thus, Haraway argues further that '[c]ommunications technologies and biotechnologies are the crucial tools recrafting our bodies', but the recrafting she envisages can be on either a conceptual or a material level, or both. Utilising Haraway's concept of the cyborg, the characters in the Bridge trilogy are still fundamentally enmeshed with technology, although not necessarily on a permanently visible physical level. To explore how these cyborgs illuminate Gibson's body politics in the Bridge trilogy, three characters will be examined: Colin Laney, an obsessive data analyst; Zona Rosa, a member of the Lo/Rez digital fan community and close friend of Chia's from *Idoru*; and Rei Toei, the idoru, who is one of the world's most well-known faces (and bodies) but has no more materiality than a 'sea of information'.

Before examining these three characters, it is worth noting that none of them hail from the bridge or the Walled City, at least initially. Rather, the journeys Colin Laney, Zona Rosa, and Rei Toei undertake during Gibson's trilogy highlight some of the important pathways to, and connections with, artificial spaces. It proves more challenging to examine the denizens of the Walled City themselves since Gibson tends to present either their material existence or mediated existence within the informatic re-creation, but rarely both. Masahiko, Chia's accidental guide in *Idoru*, is the only substantial character that readers meet both inside and out of the Walled City. Significantly, his small part of the digital realm is rendered as 'a much cleaner but no larger version of his room behind the kitchen in the restaurant' that his parents own, while his physical appearance is a 'basic scan job, maybe a year out of date: his hair was shorter. He wore the same black tunic' (Gibson, 1997, pp. 182–183). More importantly, when questioned about the Walled City's fidelity to its material predecessor, Masahiko tells Chia that '[t]he Walled City is a concept of scale. Very important. Scale *is* place, yes? Thirty-three thousand people inhabited original. Two-point-seven hectares. As many as fourteen stories' (Gibson, 1997, p. 184). Masahiko's informatic appearance, surroundings, and philosophy all posit the Walled City and artificial spaces more broadly as territories where the digital and the material are clearly linked in non-trivial ways. The malleability of the virtual, or what Gibson calls 'the infinite plasticity of the digital' (1999, p. 117), may offer almost limitless choices in terms of representing space, but the Walled City is politically, philosophically, and personally meaningful to its inhabitants due to its connections with the material world. Nor are the Walled City's residents unaware of the limitations of informational representation. When Berry Rydell meets Klaus, who appears as 'a thin, pale man in a dark suit from no particular era, his lips pursed primly', he is warned that while meeting Klaus and a companion in virtual reality, 'you have no idea who we are, and if we were to reappear to you at some later time, you would have no way of knowing that we were, in fact, us' (Gibson, 1999, pp. 125–126). Thus, extrapolating from the few denizens of the Walled City represented in the Bridge trilogy, those people living in artificial space appear to make the most of their informatic possibilities by meaningfully linking the digital and the material.

When Colin Laney first appears in *Idoru*, we learn he has a particular affinity with information structures: he has 'a peculiar knack with data-collection architectures, and a medically documented concentration-deficit that he could toggle, under certain conditions, into a state of pathological hyperfocus' (Gibson, 1997, p. 25). The result of his talent means that Laney can perceive 'nodal points' in the human datascape, which means he can not only locate specific information faster than almost anyone else, but he can also comprehend the movement of data in such a way that he can see emerging structures—the ability not so much to predict the future, as to map the likely outcomes of patterns in the datascape which only he can see.[1] Laney's talents are not natural, but rather the results of the drug '5-SB', for which he was a test subject while in a Gainesville orphanage some years earlier. A side effect of the drug was that recipients tended to become fixated not only with information but also with a single media figure, such as an actor or politician, thus 5-SB became 'one of the most illegal substances, any damn country you care to look at' (Gibson, 1997, p. 133). By the beginning of *All Tomorrow's Parties*, the 5-SB has 'kicked in' and Laney has become obsessed with Cody Harwood, the world's most powerful man, who is trying to control the shape of the future and is involved in a project which will change the world or, as Laney perceives it, Harwood is behind 'the mother of all nodal points' (Gibson, 1999, p. 4). As Laney's obsession and his tracking of Harwood continue, Laney's sense of self no longer explicitly involves embodiment: 'Laney's progress through all the data in the world (or that data's progress through him) has long since become what he is, rather than something he merely does' (Gibson, 1999, p. 163). Ostensibly, Laney appears to be gripped by what Arthur Kroker and Michael Weinstein have called 'the will to virtuality,' which is the narcissistic and nihilistic 'will to surrender oneself to technologically-mediated and externalised imaginaries,' and to completely ignore and deny the material body (Kroker & Weinstein, 1994, p. 41). The 'will to virtuality' is also evident in Gibson's earlier work.

In the Bridge trilogy, Colin Laney is the character most similar to Case, the console cowboy from *Neuromancer*. Case is far more obviously gripped by the 'will to virtuality' than Laney: for Case the only world worth knowing was 'the bodiless exultation of cyberspace'; concurrently, 'the body was meat', and when forced to live outside of cyberspace, Case 'fell into a prison of his own flesh' (Gibson, 1994a, p. 12). Moreover, Case's experience of cyberspace is both pleasurable and fulfils many of his normal bodily urges:

when he finally does 'jack in' to cyberspace, it is a highly charged, almost sexual, experience, leaving 'tears of release, streaming down his face' (Gibson, 1994a, p. 163). From these passages, Thomas Foster's argument that *Neuromancer* presents a 'devaluation' of the human body appears convincing as Case not only prefers cyberspace over the material world, but actively attempts to spend all his time there, with few or no ramifications for his ignored material body (Foster, 1993, pp. 18–19). However, while Laney ostensibly identifies with the datascape as strongly as Case, there is a substantial shift in the way Laney's embodiment is represented. For Laney, the 'will to virtuality' is not so much an indulgent choice, as it was for Case, but rather the result of the particularly powerful drug, 5-SB. While Case's time in cyberspace has no lasting negative effects on his material body, Laney, by contrast, is so obsessed with the datascape and tracking Harwood that he spends *all* his time online; he no longer sleeps or eats properly, is physically ill, and lives, hiding, in a cardboard box in a Japanese subway station (Gibson, 1999, pp. 1–6, 79). As much as Laney might like to deny his physical body, sometimes he is unable, and then he 'is suddenly and terribly aware of his physical being, the condition of his body. His lungs failing in a cardboard carton in the concrete bowels of Shinjuku Station' (Gibson, 1999, p. 178). Moreover, while Case is free to return to a normal embodied existence at the conclusion of his adventure, Laney is not: as the alliance of which Laney is part manages to stop Harwood's plan, Laney dies, alone, in 'the dark in his fetid box', his body exhausted (1999, p. 260).

The different ramifications of the 'will to virtuality' for Case and Laney mark a change in Gibson's representation of embodiment. In the Sprawl trilogy, the human body is (arguably) 'devalued', and can be largely forgotten without serious consequences. However, in the Bridge novels, the 'will to virtuality' is not so much a choice as the result of a debilitating addiction spurred on by drugs. Laney's addiction to the datascape is similar to Berry Rydell's 'image addiction' discussed in Chapter 5, this volume, but as the datascape has far more media depth, so too are the consequences of the addiction far more serious. Indeed, the peril Laney faces in neglecting and ignoring his physical form is even recognised by those from the Walled City who, while valuing Laney as an ally, recognise that given his current situation 'for reasons of health' he may soon be lost to the world, material or digital (Gibson, 1999, p. 127). Laney's resulting physical illness and eventual demise illuminate Gibson's position that the material body cannot simply be discarded or forgotten and that the 'will to virtuality', at an extreme, is all too literally a terminal impulse.

In *Idoru*, one of Chia McKenzie's closest friends is Zona Rosa, despite the fact the two girls speak different languages and have never met in the material world. Zona and Chia are members of the Lo/Rez fanclub, a collection of fans who geographically live great distances apart, but who manage to meet regularly. Their meetings take place online in virtual reality environments, where each participant is represented by their own virtual body, or 'avatar'.[2]

In Zona's material existence she claimed to be 'the leader of a knife packing *chilanga* girl gang. Not the meanest in Mexico City, maybe, but serious enough about turf and tribute' (Gibson, 1997, p. 12). Thus, while Chia was happy to have an avatar that looked like 'only a slightly tweaked, she felt, version of how the mirror told her she actually looked', Zona, by contrast, chose to represent herself as a 'blue Aztec death's-head burning bodiless, ghosts of her blue hands flickering like strobe-lit doves . . . [with] lightning zig-zags . . . around the crown of the neon skull' (Gibson, 1997, pp. 11–12). Just as important, their chosen avatar software included an 'instantaneous on-line translation' routine, so each girl could understand the other, even if their languages were different (Gibson, 1997, p. 11). Gibson's description of virtual reality communication illuminates an online world where communication technologies not only bridge geographical and linguistic barriers, but also add a visual depth to communication that is unavailable through other media. Karen Cadora has argued the use of avatars and the development of virtual reality as 'a space which must be navigated with a body of some sort' marks a digital arena where the 'realities of the flesh' still have remediated resonance (1995, pp. 364–365). Certainly, these digital bodily images are more important in the Bridge trilogy than in the Sprawl novels, since in the cyberspace envisioned in *Neuromancer*, navigation and existence in cyberspace was through a disembodied point of view. For Zona Rosa, however, embodied existence through her avatar is even more meaningful.

During the climax of *Idoru*, Zona comes to Chia's defence in the digital world. In order to force the owner of another website to aid Chia's cause, Zona uses an illegal software weapon that briefly gives her control of that website. In the aftermath, the Etruscan, a denizen of the Walled City, and Rei Toei, the idoru, explain to Chia that Zona is gone:

> 'But they've only shut down her website,' Chia said. 'She's in Mexico City, with her gang.' 'She is nowhere,' the Etruscan said. (Gibson, 1997, p. 284)

When Zona used the software weapon, she exposed the location of her website to the pursuing authorities, forcing her to abandon it. However, as the Etruscan tells it, that was not enough:

> 'They pursued her. She was forced to discard her persona.'
>
> 'What "persona"?' Chia felt a sinking feeling. 'Zona Rosa,' said the Etruscan, 'was the persona of Mercedes Purissima Vargas-Gutierrez. She is twenty-six years old and the victim of an environmental syndrome occurring most frequently in the Federal District of Mexico.'
>
> . . . 'Then I can find her,' Chia said. 'But she would not wish this,' the idoru said. 'Mercedes Purissima is severely deformed by the syndrome, and has lived for the past five years in almost complete denial of her physical self'. (Gibson, 1997, p. 285)

Zona Rosa, then, reflects Donna Haraway's argument that 'severely handicapped people can (and sometimes do) have the most intense experiences of complex hybridization with other communication devices' (1991, p. 178). While Laney's body wasted away due to his obsession with the datascape, by contrast information and communication technologies provided Mercedes Vargas-Gutierrez with the crucial tools needed to digitally refashion her embodied image. Through Zona Rosa, she was able to live a life more in line with her own choices rather than an existence dominated by her physical disfigurement. Moreover, the story of Zona Rosa illuminates Gibson's alliance with Scott Bukatman's argument that the 'imagined' realities of the digital world may deconstruct existing notions of subjectivity, but '[s]uch a deconstruction does not point to the *annihilation* of subjectivity, but rather to the limits of the existing paradigm' (Bukatman, 1993, p. 180). For Mercedes Vargas-Gutierrez her decidedly artificial notion of subjectivity includes elements of identity informed by a technologically mediated digital realm, a locale far more flexible to her needs than the material world by itself, where her physical condition would dominate. Moreover, the juxtaposition of characters such as Laney and Zona reinforces the notion that new technologies and the spaces they enable are neither intrinsically positive or negative in terms of embodiment but rather become so only when utilised by individuals. Thus for Laney, his obsession with the datascape ultimately proves to be his downfall, whereas for Mercedes/Zona technologies provide the means to lead a fuller life, not as restricted by the disabilities which have inflicted her embodied self. Nor does the 'death' of Zona Rosa end the usefulness of these technologies, for as Arleigh explained to a saddened Chia, eventually 'somebody else would turn up, somebody new, and it would be like they already knew you' (Gibson, 1997, p. 291).

In Michel de Certeau's work, the abilities to write and construct bodies, and bodily images, are also seen as extremely important. As he argues:

> What is at stake is the relation between the law and the body—a body defined, delimited, and articulated by what it writes. [. . . The proper] engraves itself on parchments made from the skin of its subjects. It articulates them in a juridical corpus. It makes its book out of them. (1984, pp. 139–140)

However, there is more than the 'proper' way to read and write a text. De Certeau continues by arguing that reading itself can constitute an unauthorised and unofficial form of writing (or re-writing) that he dubs 'poaching':

> Far from being writers—founders of their own place, heirs of the peasants of earlier ages now working on the soil of language, diggers of wells and builders of houses—readers are travellers; they move across lands belonging to someone else, like nomads poaching their way

> across fields they did not write, despoiling the wealth of Egypt to enjoy
> it themselves. (1984, p. 174)

Poaching thus constitutes tactical text-acts baring significant similarities
with *bricolage* and which can resist the strategic power of the law in certain, if often short-lived, cases. However, with new digitally-enabled modes
of resistance, artificial spaces are populated by citizens like Zona Rosa who
have found tactics of bodily writing, poaching from the corpus of history
and iconography, which can prove more lasting than de Certeau's model
allows. It is also significant that in *Textual Poachers*, Henry Jenkins (1992)
builds upon de Certeau's notion of poaching and argues that fan culture is
today's most focused and widespread community of poachers, while Gibson purposefully situates Chia and Zona Rosa as friends who have met
through their considerable involvement in the fan community around the
ironically named rock group Lo/Rez.

In *Collective Intelligence*, Pierre Levy argues that while the mass media
of the twentieth century was characterized primarily by wide-scale distribution and reproduction, the digital and informatic media of the twenty-
first century have far more potential to become widespread 'somatic
technologies' which re-establish links between bodies, information, and
digital media. Moreover, far from a competitive model, Levy argues further
that these connections would form a symbiotic relationship, not one where
some parts override or exclude the other (Levy, 1997, pp. 48–49). For Zona
Rosa, these theoretical insights are self-evident through the significant time
'she' spent both in her own digital realms as well as interacting, at times,
with/in the archetype of artificial space, the Walled City. The connection
between Zona and Mercedes is not simply a fictional versus 'real' relation,
but rather a symbiotic connection which enhances Mercedes' embodied
options beyond the 'proper' predicament of her physical disabilities.

Investigating the subjectivity and embodiment, or lack thereof, of Rei
Toei proves a somewhat more difficult task in that she does not possess a
material body and may ostensibly be considered no more than an extremely
complex array of information and communications software. When
Yamazaki first describes Rei to Laney, he explains she is a virtual singer, an
'idoru': '"Idol-singer." She is Rei Toei. She is a personality-construct, a con-
geries of software agents, the creation of information-designers. She is akin
to what I believe they call a "synthespian," in Hollywood' (Gibson, 1997,
p. 92). However, in *All Tomorrow's Parties* when Rei appears to Rydell
in holographic form, she claims that 'this is a hologram . . . but I am real'
(Gibson, 1999, p. 153). Rei's reality or sentience is a point of contention
in the Bridge trilogy: for some Rei is simply the latest and most advanced
'software dolly wank toy'; but for others she represents an 'original concept
. . . almost radical', complete with the intrinsic ability to think for herself
and define her own existence (Gibson, 1999, pp. 122, 144). When Colin
Laney first meets her he anticipates 'some industrial-strength synthesis of

Japan's last three dozen top female media faces. That was usually the way in Hollywood, and the formula tended to be even more rigid [for software creations] . . . their features algorithmically derived from some human mean of proven popularity' (Gibson, 1997, p. 175). However, Laney realises 'she was nothing like that', and when they are introduced 'the eyes of the idoru, envoy of some imaginary country, met his' (1997, p. 176). Ostensibly, the idea of a purely informatic construct being sentient appears ridiculous, but as Donna Haraway has pointed out, contemporary developments such as the Human Genome Project are founded on the premise that a human being can be reduced to 'an information structure that can exist in various physical media' (1997, p. 246).

In Dani Cavallaro's (2000) analysis of Gibson's work, she implicitly concludes that Rei does not have a legitimate individual identity, but is simply an object or thing, evinced in references to Rei as 'the idoru' or 'it', rather than 'she'. However, utilising Judith Butler's idea of performativity, I would argue that Rei's discursive identity is sufficiently legitimate to warrant her own chosen gender identity. Butler has argued in *Gender Trouble* that while much recent feminist criticism has focused on 'gender' as a construction, opposed to an embodied biological bedrock of sex, she argues that 'sex' is just as constructed as 'gender'. For Butler there is no pre-discursive reality. Butler argues that identity and gender are 'performative', created and maintained through the repetitions of day to day existence in everyday life. She argues further that the performance of gender is what *constitutes* the idea of a pre-discursive 'sex'. In other words, gender comes first through repeated performance and 'sex' is created as a *product* of these performances (Butler, 1999, pp. 134–141).[3] Rei reflects Butler's idea of performativity brilliantly: she is not 'real' but a discursive entity; she *performs* her gender and that performance is what positions the arbitrary selection of her 'sex'. Following Butler's predominantly post-structuralist theory, Rei's discursive identity appears as legitimate as anyone else's since all identity is discursive and defined not through materiality, but through performativity.

By contrast, N. Katherine Hayles argues that reducing 'the body' to a 'primarily, if not entirely, linguistic and discursive construction' is one of the postmodern beliefs that will 'stupefy' and confound future generations (1992, p. 147). For Hayles, a discursive body only makes sense as a universalised concept, and cannot address the specificities of individual identity. She argues that it is impossible to meaningfully separate consciousness from embodiment as the mechanisms of thought and cognition are intrinsically interwoven with 'the specifics of place, time, physiology and culture' (1992, p. 155). Hayles' concerns are addressed to some extent through Rei's part in the final showdown with Cody Harwood in *All Tomorrow's Parties*. One of the main points of contention between Harwood and the group rallied against him, which includes Rei, is the deployment of a device called a 'Nanofax' which is installed in stores across the world. The Nanofax employs nanotechnology—the technological ability to rearrange matter at the molecular level according to an outside design—the implications of which are that given the necessary raw materials, *anything* can be created. Harwood, who understands the radical implications of the Nanofax, explains that he wishes to control the device's deployment so that he can usher in 'the advent of a degree of functional nanotechnology in a world that will remain recognisably descendant from the one I woke in this morning' (Gibson, 1999, p. 250). However, his plans fail, and when the first Nanofax is sent, Rei manages to insert herself—essentially an elaborate 'sea of code' at this point—into the Nanofax's assembly routine so that when the light 'above the hatch turns green, and the hatch slides up . . . out crawls, unfolds sort of, this butt-naked girl' (Gibson, 1999, p. 268). Moreover, the process is replicated across the world so that literally thousands of completely material and (to all appearances) entirely human Rei Toeis have transgressed the boundary between the material and the digital to emerge, completely embodied, into the 'real' world. In terms of Gibson's position on embodiment, Rei's transformation illuminates the fact that while her initial characterisation may support Butler's idea of discursive performativity, Rei's eventual decision to *leave* the digital realm in order to embrace the material world shows that Gibson's ultimate allegiance is to the embodied material form as a significant and necessary site of identity. However, Gibson does not unproblematically reify the material over the virtual, but rather radically disrupts the boundaries between the two. As Veronica Hollinger argues, Gibson's descriptions of the informatic nanotechnology 'promise unprecedented changes in the very material of the physical world' (2006, p. 461).

As the virtual, disembodied Rei could be considered the ultimate expression of bodiless existence, her overriding desire and decision to seek out and embrace material embodiment illuminates Gibson's thorough rejection of a 'will to virtuality'. However, when thousands of Rei Toeis emerge across the globe, readers quickly realise that this is not looking backward conservatively to a previous, static notion of embodiment, but forward to new, symbiotic forms where material bodies and informatic realms are deeply intertwined. Ross Farnell argues that the resolution of Rei's story actually turns the 'will to virtuality' on its head:

> Rei inverts the usual cyberspatial trope of transcendence: created initially as digital code, she moves toward the corporeality of Rez and the complexity of analog information, desiring to escape the confines of the *digital* prison via some inconclusive transcendence *toward* the flesh.
> (Farnell, 1998, p. 472)

However, the Bridge trilogy does not render the digital realms as undesirable but rather as undesirable *by themselves*. Indeed, Rei Toei, a media-generated, informatically-enabled subject who crosses the boundary between the digital and material could, ironically, be considered as the avatar for artificial spaces and their core characteristic: tactically bridging informatic and physical spaces, and bodies, through symbiotically and symbolically leaving one foot in each, blurrily bounded, realm (Murphy, 2003). As the literal and symbolic enabling technology which facilitates Rei's climactic transformation, nanotechnology leaves readers in the grip of Michelle Kendrick's insight that as 'technologies grow even smaller, and finally disappear into an organism, the space of technology is troublingly like the space of the body' (Kendrick, 2002, p. 58). In this context, of course, causing trouble can be a very purposeful and meaningful tactical act.

William Gibson's Bridge trilogy is a fruitful arena in which to examine, explore, and tentatively map emerging artificial spaces. Through the work of Michel de Certeau, artificial spaces are clearly tactical, opening up new realms of resistance and completely new political possibilities. The Bridge trilogy simultaneously allows a broadening of de Certeau's perspectives, illuminating the increased impact and longevity of tactical acts due, in considerable part, to the possibilities enabled by digital information and communication technologies. For Gibson, the Bridge trilogy marks a substantial shift from his earlier work, no longer (arguably) devaluing the body as 'meat' as in *Neuromancer*, but now focusing on the ramifications of technology on embodiment for individuals in artificial space. The strategic reinforcement of a conservative, surveillance- and security-driven world of proper place as seen in the Bridge trilogy, mirroring the global politics of the early twenty-first century, at first appears deeply pessimistic. However, the combination of tactical moments of resistance, interstitiality, and collective intelligence, facilitated and reinforced by new digital technologies, have seen the formation of ongoing pockets of individuality and resistance that cohere into artificial spaces. Moreover, Rei Toei's transition from a sentient 'sea of code' to a fully embodied individual illuminates Gibson's implicit belief that the human body and embodiment remain both necessary and desirable elements of our identities. The implications of nanotechnology, however, point to further destabilisation of subjectivity, shifting away from a humanist conception where organic and mechanical are oppositional ideas, to a world where nanotechnology explicitly situates both human and technology as part of the same spectrum of meaning.

In artificial spaces, tactical resistance is a way of life and the ongoing flux of spatial activity is a reassuring, not worrying, blur. Yet, while artificial spaces contain many new possibilities, forgetting or ignoring embodiment is not one of them. Artificial spaces are realms where specific, unique subjects have new tactical opportunities. For every individual, life in artificial space always entails the intertwining of embodiment, materiality, and information in a symbiotic and inseparable matrix which, in turn, broadens the very spheres of subjectivity and spatiality into the realm of each other.

Part IV
Artificial People

8   Matrices of Embodiment

AN ARTIFICIAL PERSON?

To initially posit the idea of artificial people, this chapter briefly extrapolates from one of the most widely cited science fiction film franchises. In the *Alien* series—*Alien* (Ridley Scott, 1979), *Aliens* (Cameron, 1986), *Alien³* (Fincher, 1992), and *Alien: Resurrection* (Jeunet, 1997)—while the central concern is with the predominantly violent relationship between humans and acid-for-blood aliens, the four films[1] also create a meaningful narrative about non-human artificial entities. In the first *Alien* film, the science officer Ash turns out not to be a biological human being, but rather a manufactured entity who, being an icon of Thatcherite economic rationalism, on 'company orders' attempts to kill the crew in order to save the alien since it has higher commodity value than they do. Ellen Ripley, the only survivor of that original crew, learns quickly to distrust non-human entities, leading to a confrontation in the sequel when she realises, once again, there are more than 'just' humans on board the ship in which she is travelling:

Ripley: You didn't tell me there was an android on board! Why not?
Burke: It's standard procedure. Every ship has a synthetic on board.
Bishop: I prefer the term 'Artificial Person' myself.

Bishop's request to define his own sense of species or self initially falls on deaf ears, but in the course of *Aliens*, he earns his personhood, ultimately sacrificing himself in order to save Ellen and her newfound child, Newt. While only appearing briefly in the third film, a re-activated but damaged Bishop also exhibits the vainly 'human' desire in asking to die rather than be mediocre. By the last in the series, *Alien: Resurrection*, artificial people have become self-reproducing and a second-generation artificial person, Call, is amongst the few posthuman survivors, and the least morally questionable, after the human military once again tries to harness the aliens as a commodity of destructive value.[2] The development of artificial people in the *Alien* series can be seen alongside similarly themed films such as Ridley Scott's other canonical science fiction movie *Blade Runner* (1982) in which the 'more human than human' Replicants leave the moral and epistemological boundary between 'natural' humans and manufactured humanoids disconcertingly blurred.[3] While neither the *Alien* films nor *Blade Runner* are the focus of this chapter, Bishop's desire to have his personhood recognised is a metonym for a science fiction film trope in which the boundaries between artificial and natural, as well as object and person, are constantly interrogated. That trope provides initial context for this chapter's exploration of cinematic conceptualisations of artificial people.

Returning to the central characteristic of science fiction film, the ambiguities inherent in the tension between spectacle and speculation (discussed in depth in the first chapter of this volume), this chapter's exploration of artificial people focuses on a trilogy of Hollywood blockbuster films, the *Matrix* trilogy (A. Wachowski & L. Wachowski, 1999, 2003a, 2003b), which are widely considered the ultimate fusion of special effects, a revived cyberpunk aesthetic, expansive genre elements, and cinema as commodity culture. Despite its emphasis on computer-generated effects and violence all the way from kung fu to globe-spanning military battles, the *Matrix* also wears its function as speculation close to the surface, notably evident in the publication of at least four edited collections addressing the philosophy of the trilogy (Irwin, 2002; Yeffeth, 2003; Lawrence, 2004; Gillis, 2005). At this junction a qualification is required: while this and the following chapter both focus on film trilogies, they are perhaps more accurately described as franchises. Both are formed building upon elements that existed prior to the films, and their narrative and speculative spans extend far beyond the films themselves thanks to 'authorised' paratextual material such as tie-in books, DVD extras, and extended edition releases (with either more film, more extras, or more of both), and unauthorised materials such as fan fiction (see Jenkins, 1992, 2003; and Gray, 2010). While the unofficial and viewer-created extensions of the *Matrix* franchise are beyond the scope of this chapter, particular attention is paid to the official *Animatrix* short films (Chung, Maeda, Jones, Morimoto, & Watanabe, 2003) as these official paratexts potentially complicate any easy reading of the machines as malevolent or unprovoked in their war with humanity.

'HE'S A MACHINE!'

In the tradition of *2001: A Space Odyssey* (Kubrick, 1968), the tension and ambiguities between the science fiction staples of speculation and spectacle position *The Matrix* within a tableau of contradictions. In the British Film Institute's 'Modern Classics' series, Joshua Clover argues that

> *The Matrix* will fail any test of coherence. Indeed, it flickers under the sign of two contradictions, which correspond to its paired sci-fi commonplaces. It's a historic advance in digital entertainment that is unpacifiably anxious about the dangers of digitality; it's a critique of spectacles that is itself a spectacle. (2004, p. 15)

Radical ambiguity is also fuelled by the numerous genres which inform the narrative and aesthetic of the film, borrowing from 'Action, Western, Romance, Japanese Anime, and Hong Kong Kung Fu genres' (Barnett, 2000, p. 363), as well as reviving the 'cyberpunk aesthetic' of William Gibson and the other 'mirrorshades' writers including Bruce Sterling and Pat Cadigan (Barnett, 2000, p. 362), which, in turn, had already been hailed as the apex of postmodern pastiche (Jameson, 1991). Layered on top of the generic diversity, *The Matrix* trilogy—*The Matrix*, *The Matrix: Reloaded*, and *The Matrix: Revolutions*, all co-directed by the brothers Andy and Larry Wachowski and produced by blockbuster guru Joel Silver—also borrowed symbolism and narrative elements from a diverse range of mythologies and religions, including the ancient Greek gods, Buddhism, and Judeo-Christianity. Added to that is a stylistic homage to both video games and comic books, resulting in *The Matrix* trilogy containing enough ambiguities and references to attract almost any reading or analysis. Indeed, existing examinations of *The Matrix* have concluded that the film offers everything from 'a second new testament for a new millennium, a religious parable of the second coming of mankind's messiah' (Schuchardt, 2003, p. 5) to a 'pomophobic' betrayal of the cyberpunk genre (Bartlett & Byers, 2003, p. 30), to the epitome of consumer culture in which the franchise 'isn't just a totem of the era, but its ultimate product: a massively capitalised, wickedly digitised convergence of industry and desire' (Clover, 2004, p. 72). For the purposes of this chapter, *The Matrix* films are also ripe with ideas about embodiment, technology, and the complex relationships between those two interlinking realms. However, the diversity of interpretations[4] and origins serve to highlight the fact that while this examination pays attention to medium specificities, the *Matrix* franchise makes the boundary between media, at best, difficult to delineate.

Before turning to the films themselves, it is worth addressing the position of the *Matrix* franchise in relation to, or indeed as, economics. For all their speculative potential the three films are clearly successful consumer products in their own right.[5] In film scholar Sean Cubitt's *The Cinema Effect*, he analyses film in relation to commodity culture, arguing that the form's depoliticisation has led to a condition of 'post cinema', wherein for 'technological films' such as the *Matrix* trilogy,

> [i]t is no longer the case that films in some way respond to, refract, express, or debate reality or society. Mass entertainment has abandoned the task of making sense of the world, severing the cords that bound the two together. This, as much as economics, is what has driven the North American cinema into the realm of digital imaging. (Cubitt, 2004, p. 245)

However, despite Cubitt's pessimistic tone, he does highlight the utility of *The Matrix* series, not as films which seek to explore a 'reality' outside of the films' 'unreal' diegesis, but rather as a conversation which positions the digital as *part* of a meaningful reality. Moreover, it should be noted that Cubitt's ultimate purpose in mapping the cinema effect of the twentieth century, under the aegis of commodity culture, is to argue for a twenty-first century cinematic form which is functionally different. In suggesting the form of more politically useful cinema, Cubitt argues that it 'must include communication with an environment no longer pristine and a technology no longer tainted' (2004, p. 364). Ironically, these traits are central to the analysis below which looks at embodiment, technology, and the epistemological and narratological conversations and convergences between the two. *The Matrix* franchise is thus, in direct contradiction, at the pinnacle of cinema and/as commodity culture but is also simultaneously facilitating explorations of bodies and machines which locate meaning beyond their utility as part of consumer culture.

The opening scene of *The Matrix* immediately situates the viewer not just in the cinema, but also in a direct relationship with technology at both narratological and physical levels. After the opening credits, the viewer is greeted by an impatiently blinking rectangular green cursor. To users of personal computers (PC) in the 1980s and early '90s, prior to the ubiquity of Microsoft's Windows operating system, this cursor is completely familiar as it is the first thing seen after they flicked the power button to 'on'. The cursor remains on-screen long enough for many viewers to feel the embodied need to reach for the keyboard and type 'run' (a sensation doubly felt when watching *The Matrix* DVD on a computer screen, an effect clearly intentional given the inclusion of extra features which can only be accessed by playing the film on a PC). While the viewer is thus located in a position behind the screen, a viewing subject for a filmic object, that sense of liberal humanist clarity is troubled after a few lines of green code are seen and the 'camera' then zooms *into a single number*, suggesting a physical depth behind an informatic code represented on the supposedly depthless cinematic surface. The screen, that boundary between actual and imagined worlds, as well as subject and object, is disruptively permeable. When the zoom ends (having pushed *through* the code) on a group of police officers, the subject of their action, Trinity—a leather-clad hacker sitting behind a computer screen within the world behind the code—is situated as the character with whom viewers are asked to identify. However, as the police attempt to arrest Trinity, they are faced with her seemingly superhuman physical abilities.

The opening fight between Trinity and the police is powerfully punctuated by the debut of the signature special effect of the *Matrix* trilogy, generally referred to as 'bullet-time'. During this effects shot, Trinity appears to defy gravity and physics by jumping and hovering in mid-air as the camera rapidly moves in an arc centred on her floating physical form, before she seemingly resynchronises with the norms of diegetic speed and quickly despatches the police with some graceful kung fu moves. While the name bullet-time is appropriate in its reference to slowing the focal image on screen to a speed allowing the motion of even a bullet to be seen, it is somewhat ironic that the computer-facilitated bullet-time in its first use allows the viewer to focus longer and harder on the embodied form of Carrie-Anne Moss. Moreover, in contrast to the bigger explosions and longer spaceships which iconically inhabit blockbuster science fiction films, bullet-time is in many ways, as Joshua Clover argues, 'the very opposite of a special effect' (2004, p. 66). This is not the spectacle of the digital, but rather the digital facilitating the spectacular focus on the physicality of embodied actors. Furthermore, while bullet-time seems to rupture the film's diegesis, when viewers discover that this part of the film is located within the informatic construct of the matrix, then just 'as its brief passages must seem to Neo or Trinity, these are moments of clarity for the viewer as well; bullet time shows the world as it is' (Clover, 2004, p. 66), or more accurately, bullet-time shows the cinema viewer the world of the construct at the speed at which it is comprehended by Trinity and other 'red-pills' (those who understand what the matrix is). Thus audiences come to realise that bullet-time is linked to the supposedly physical perception of the characters, not the purported time or logic of the matrix construct itself. While Sean Cubitt sensibly points out that in most films 'the emergence of cinematic time as special effect [leads to] . . . the universe of the synthetic', in the synthetic world of the matrix, the bullet-time special effects diegetically point to the non-synthetic realm (2004, p. 41). Ironically, the initial (and frequent) focus of the digitally precise bullet-time special effect[6] is not on technology or even artillery, but rather on the fleshy (if usually leather-clad) human body. Bullet-time is thus a spectacular technology which emphasises the links between digital precision and embodied physical form.

In the following scene, the film introduces Keanu Reeves' character Neo, the unknowing would-be digital messiah. Just as Trinity was first introduced sitting behind a computer screen, so too is Neo, although he is initially asleep, but soon awakened by a message mediated by his computer. Even though he was asleep, it is significant that Neo has chosen to wear headphones, showing that he has in some ways chosen to be 'plugged in'. In waking, Neo's possible dream-state is merged with a mysteriously communicative computer while the headphones highlight his connection with the banal technologies within the construct. When a knock on the door distracts Neo, his visitor, Choi, purchases a disc of illegal programs which Neo fetches from an ironically hollowed out copy of Baudrillard's postmodern tome, *Simulation and Simulacra* (1994), suggesting that while the book is hollow, when filled with code it has some sort of depth. Just before departing with his goods, Choi thanks Neo, exclaiming that 'you're my saviour man, my own personal Jesus Christ,' initiating a long series of references to Neo (an anagram of One and of the almost timeless Eon are well as meaning 'new') as a messianic figure.

While the links between Neo and Christ or the messiah are many and plentiful in the *Matrix* trilogy (which ends, for all intents and purposes, with

Neo's digital crucifixion), the films do not just refer back to existing ideas, but rather, like the generic borrowing, use existing religious metaphors and myths to playfully articulate new connections. As Sean Cubitt argues,

> Neo does not 'equal Christ,' though he is Christlike in the sense that he derives from Christianity the role of a saviour who comes to redeem humankind. What we note here is the depth and complexity of allegory, and its social nature. Unlike symbolism, which tends to be either private or developed for a specific work, allegory depends on the social construction of a ring of meanings that cannot be adequately addressed with a single concept. (2004, p. 353)

In other words, while a symbol attempts to create a direct referent—Neo *is* the messiah—an allegory in representing something also injects part of the sign into that representation, so even if Neo is allegorically linked to the messiah, the process of linking infuses that which is represented with the thing representing. It follows, then, that Neo's role in the film and Neo's narratological similarity to the messiah are more of a synthesis than a symbol, allowing the meanings to intermingle and intermix to produce new ideas which draw on, but are not directed by, these two (or more) parts of the allegory. The allegorical function is also at work in many other borrowings within the *Matrix* films, facilitating, for example, Lawrence Fishburne's character Morpheus to function as a sort of John the Baptist while still clearly playing with his name's origin as the ancient Roman god of dreams (Schuchardt, 2003, p. 7).

After his confusing night, Neo, also known as Thomas Anderson at his 'day job', is late for work and is called into his boss' office. He is grilled about not respecting the connected system of which he is part—the giant software corporation which goes by the less than subtle name MetaCortex. The company itself ties into Sean Cubitt's argument that in replacing

> the society of people, the society of images turns the film into an agent: the cyborg orator. The typical form of the contemporary cyborg is not Robocop or the Terminator but the transnational corporation, a planet-spanning hybrid of human biochips, networked communication devices, and offshore factories. (2004, p. 126)

Reinforcing Cubitt's point, the MetaCortex company is not just Neo's employer, but symbolic of the larger system of which he is unknowingly part: the virtual reality construct known as the matrix. Further, while in his boss' office, the conversation takes place as window-cleaners outside noisily squeegee away the soapy suds. Cubitt notes that the distraction of this image, and the over-the-top sound of the squeegee, 'oversignal their function' since this is important exposition—Neo later attempts to escape using the window-washer's platform—but lacks subtlety, aligning the film with videogame aesthetics in which such explicit exposition would be more appropriate, signalling the game-player that the window would later provide an interactive source by which to escape (Cubitt, 2004, p. 229; see also Barnett, 2000, p. 363). However, the two men washing the windows are also important since on a close viewing, informed audiences realise that these two bumbling cleaners are actually played by the directors Andy and Larry Wachowski.[7] With slightly more subtlety, this self-casting situates directorial vision and control as the mechanism which draws Neo to his point of escape. Despite the elaborate set-up, Neo fails to utilise this exit not because he forgets where it is, but rather because he is asked to escape via window-ledges and he, rather ironically, appears to be afraid of heights, a decidedly embodied reaction.

In the following scene, Neo's interrogation by the Agents—sentient programs who police the workings of the matrix and whose 'physical' forms are stronger and faster than ordinary humans—it becomes apparent that it is not Trinity's or Morpheus' revelations that challenge Neo's confidence that life (unknowingly) inside the matrix is real, but rather that insight comes when the coherent boundaries of embodiment are radically ruptured. After initially trying to gain Neo's trust, he proves extremely uncooperative during his interrogation and demands a phone-call, only for Agent Smith to respond, 'Tell me, Mr Anderson, what good is a phone call, if you're unable to speak?' Neo looks around defensively, but Smith's threat is enacted by manipulating the very coherence of Neo's physical form: his skin suddenly stretches over his mouth in a manner entirely inconsistent with the physical and embodied norms that Neo has learnt. Reinforcing the rupture of his embodied coherence, the Agents then forcibly restrain him and insert a probe which at first looks mechanical but then appears to awaken, moving more organically with flailing limbs but also with a glowing red eye suggesting a symbolic artificial lineage stretching back of HAL in *2001*. The twitching, convulsing probe-creature burrows into Neo's chest as he writhes in pain in a technologically-enabled rape scene which shatters his previous sense of coherence and embodied certainty.

The morphing techno-organic bug is significant as it signals the symbolic traffic between organic, technological, and the considerable grey area between the two in which most of the *Matrix* trilogy takes place. The title of Neo's interrogators highlights this spectrum as well, as their status as Agents is consistent with their men-in-black FBI attire, but also with the status as Agents within an informatic system. The term 'agent' is, of course, often used in Artificial Intelligence and Artificial Life discourses to signify a specific decision-making entity. As film theorist Vivian Sobchack argues in her phenomenological study *Carnal Thoughts*,

> It is no accident . . . that in our now dominantly electronic (and only secondarily cinematic) culture, many people describe and understand their minds and bodies in terms of computer systems and programs

(even as they still describe and understand their lives in terms of movies). Nor is it trivial that computer systems and programs are often described in terms of human minds and bodies (for example, as intelligent or susceptible to viral infection) and that these computer-generated "beings" have become the explicit cybernetic heroes of our most popular moving-image fictions. (2004, p. 137)

The *Matrix* films playfully build upon the existing symbolic interchange between organic and technologic metaphors by adding, among other duality puns, names and actions which can function in either context. However, the seeming ease of this slippage also clearly highlights the connectedness of the artificial and organic, not their separability. Moreover, these connections illustrate an emerging lexicon of interconnectivity which posits the human protagonists themselves as artificial people.

The intertwining of humanity *en masse* and the artificial becomes far more apparent in the next sequence in which Neo is 'freed' from the matrix. Initially he is contacted by Morpheus and collected by Trinity who 'debugs' Neo in a manner almost as violent as his initial implantation. It is worth noting that while the bug appears as a living techno-organic form when it is first removed, as soon as it is separated from Neo it returns to a more clunky mechanical configuration, already suggesting that the 'aliveness' of the machines is somehow connected to human beings.

The machine intelligences' dependence on human bodies is further and more deeply explored as Neo meets with the hacker leader Morpheus and accepts the challenge of confronting the matrix. Mixing metaphors and references from Lacanian psychoanalysis[8] with *Alice in Wonderland* and *The Wizard of Oz*, Neo then plunges through the looking glass and awakens in the diegetically real world of 2199 where human beings exist in hermetically-sealed gel-filled red cocoons where their bodily energies are extracted to power Artificial Life, while their conscious minds 'exist' inside an informatic simulation called the matrix. However, far from an entirely mechanical world, the cocoon Neo is shocked to awaken within is startlingly organic and, as A. Samuel Kimball argues, is more akin to an 'artificial womb in which he has been encased in a uterine fluid. Unsnapping a series of mechanical umbilici, the Matrix then flushes Neo from itself. From the point of view of the Matrix, Neo's release is like a miscarriage or abortion' (Kimball, 2002, p. 91). In contrast, from Neo's subjective view (at least in retrospect), this is a moment of new beginnings, which is visually reinforced by his expulsion from the matrix cocoons along with a quantity of fluid via a series of ducts, emerging from a gaping hole and landing in the sea; a very clear and almost literal birth metaphor. Neo is immediately swept inside a waiting craft, the Nebuchadnezzar, by means of a metallic clamp which looks surprisingly like another umbilical cord as his pasty white arms flail at his sides. Like Laney's pathetic physical form at the end of *All Tomorrow's Parties* (Gibson, 1999), Neo has been inside a cocoon and only ever simulated the use of his body, his entire musculature is completely atrophied and in what is one of many instances of technological dependence outside of the matrix, the crew of Morpheus' ship use technology to artificially stimulate muscle growth and accelerate the development of Neo's physical senses. This scene has several instances in which Neo's innards are actually seen via a computer monitor, reminding viewers of the long history of bodily visualisation and remediation, as explored by Catherine Waldby (2000) and discussed in Chapter 3, this volume. In a genre exemplifying moment, the science fictional film presents the contradiction of escaping machine bondage only to then rely on advanced technologies to rebuild and reconstitute the very embodiment Neo had always taken for granted.

While rather overblown and heavy-handed, it is nevertheless worth examining at length the core expository monologue contained in Morpheus' explanation to Neo of the war between humans and machines, which begins with a description of Artificial Intelligence:

> A singular consciousness that spawned an entire race of machines. We don't know who struck first, us or them, but it was us that scorched the sky. At the time they were dependent on solar power and it was believed that they would be unable to survive without an energy source as abundant as the sun. Throughout human history we have been dependant on machines to survive. Fate, it seems, is not without a sense of irony. The human body generates more bioelectricity than a 120 volt battery and over 25,000 BTUs of body heat. Combined with a form of fusion, the machines had found all the energy they would ever need. There are fields, Neo, endless fields where human beings are no longer born, we are grown. For the longest time I wouldn't believe it, but then I saw the fields with my own eyes, watched them

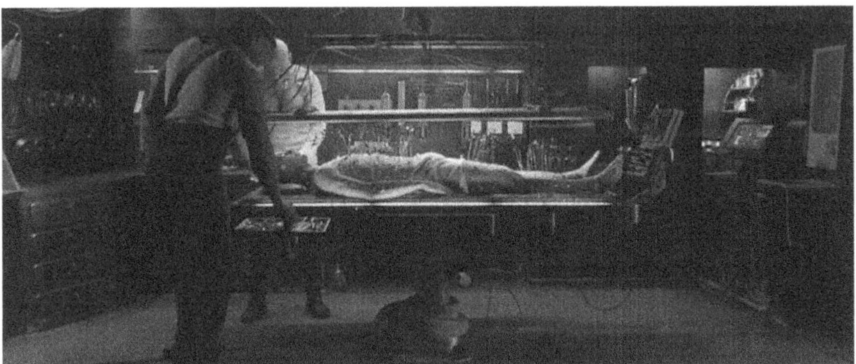

Figure 8.1 (Re)Building Neo in *The Matrix* (Andy Wachowski and Larry Wachowski, 1999).

> liquefy the dead so they could be fed intravenously to the living. And standing there, facing the pure horrifying precision I came to realise the obviousness of the truth. . . . The matrix is a computer-generated dream world built to keep us under control.

From Morpheus' tale, three main points emerge. Firstly, that the diversity of machine intelligence is now enough to be considered a race, even by their enemies in a time of war, suggesting that the artificial entities of 2199 have moved beyond the origins of either Artificial Intelligence or Artificial Life to a level of diversity that may actually parallel organic ecologies. Secondly, the admission that 'we don't know who struck first' suggests that humanity has learnt some level of humility in enslavement, something not readily evident in Western politics in the early years of the twenty-first century. Moreover, the notion that humans had destroyed the atmosphere and blackened the sky to disable the solar powered machine intelligences provocatively suggests that it is the Artificial Lifeforms who develop a more symbiotic, less destructive relationship with nature and the Earth's ecology.

Humanity, in their militaristic endeavours, actually created the dystopian wasteland haunting the world outside the matrix. Finally, while the idea of being a 'copper-top', a dweller inside the matrix simulation providing power for the machine world, is abhorrent to Morpheus and to Neo, the machine intelligences still show far more humility and compassion than human beings in similar positions of power; at least in the matrix no one *knows* they are enslaved (a notion which is addressed by numerous articles, especially in the philosophical collections addressing the *Matrix* films). In a direct reference to earlier science fiction cinema, it is worth noting that the digital image of the baby inside the matrix-cocoon seen during Morpheus' speech bears an uncanny resemblance to the re-embodied star-child of *2001*, only now the child comes complete with an array of black latex cords connecting to an informatic world. The similarity nevertheless adds to the notion that being imprisoned in the matrix is somehow an important moment in human evolution (a reading reinforced by Cypher's betrayal of the human crew in exchange for a promise of re-integration into the matrix, which he knows full well to be 'unreal' in a conventional sense). The narrative positioning of the technological entities in the film, their origins, as well as their actions in the sequels, suggest that in comparison to human beings who are immersed in the use of their technologies, the machines of the *Matrix* trilogy are equally, if not more, worthy of the name artificial people.

When Neo begins his training to join the war against the technological entities governing the world, it is telling that his first exercises are about learning to be a better fighter *within the matrix itself*. Indeed, Neo's trainer, the ironically named Tank, is introduced as his 'operator' rather than mentor or guide. The title seems apt when Tank begins Neo's training by uploading at high speeds the program for learning jujitsu straight into Neo's mind. At the end of a long day's uploading, Morpheus joins Tank as Neo is assimilating more training information and in response to a query about Neo's status, Tank replies with awe at Neo's abilities: 'He's a machine!' This dialogue, while deeply ironic, is delivered deadpan by actor Marcus Chong and again highlights Sobchack's point about the meshing of categories both technological and embodied. Moreover, when it comes time to test Neo's newfound skills, this occurs in a kung fu fight with unabashed video game aesthetics; Morpheus makes the point to Neo that his mind is treating the matrix as real, not simulated, but that insight allows Neo to move even faster, bending the informatic norms of the simulation. Neo even tries to follow Morpheus in jumping the seemingly impossible distance between two skyscrapers, but fails, and when he is 'unplugged' from the simulation, Neo is shocked to discover the pain and injuries felt inside the simulation have also occurred in the 'real' world. Morpheus simply explains that Neo's mind 'makes it real.' However, a better explanation is that mind and body are not separable so any experience, even directed at the mind, has inescapable consequences for the body at the same time.

Returning to the broader notion of cinema itself, the matrix appears in many ways to mimic or remediate the cinematic form. The matrix is the conceptual and narrative-level literalisation of the move in late twentieth century cinema toward a 'spatialization of time' whereby temporal meaning is entirely reliant on spatial construction and representation (Cubitt, 2004, p. 8; see also Sobchack, 1997, p. 272). However, the means of experiencing the matrix are closer to contemporary videogame interactivity than the (false presumption of) cinema viewers' passivity.[9] In both gaming and the matrix simulation, it is the fleshy human body which facilitates navigation of the dream-world, reinforcing the importance of embodiment even when interacting with various incarnations of informatics.

At first glance, the representations of gender in *The Matrix* are considerably more even-handed than in the earlier Artificial Intelligence films examined in Chapters 1 and 2 of this volume. Trinity's symbolic referent as the Father, Son, and Holy Spirit is deeply empowering, and when Neo appears to be lost, *she* takes the role of Prince Charming and wakes the sleeping lover, inverting a powerful, and powerfully gendered, cultural tale. However, it is also true that *The Matrix* relies on extremely caricatured ideas of race in the representation of many characters, from the whiteness of the men-in-black to the labouring African American operators in the human realm (Nakamura, 2002). While these issues are less evident in the sequels, especially in the setting of the last human city, Zion, which has a globally representative racial diversity, it is still the case even there that the ruling council is predominantly white, while the cannon fodder of the military forces are predominantly non-white (Nakamura, 2005). Trinity's symbolic power is also shed to some extent at the end of *Reloaded* when Neo reanimates her with a kiss and an odd physical jumpstart of the heart; Neo's appropriation is complete when her untimely death in the machine city enacts the willing-to-die revenge subplot needed to bring the *Matrix* trilogy to a conclusion (Czarniawska & Gustavsson, 2008). Thus, while the trilogy is definitely rich in its explorations of embodiment, it is far from as even-handed in its representations of gender or ethnicity.[10]

The most complex, contradictory, and, indeed, condescending informatic lifeform in the *Matrix* trilogy is Agent Smith. While his name speaks of a purposeful blandness, he stands out amongst the barely differentiated agents as the most vicious and the most emotional. When Morpheus is captured and the Agents are attempting to 'hack' into his brain, Agent Smith launches into a tirade about everything he hates about the matrix itself:

> I hate this place; this zoo; this prison; this reality, whatever you want to call it. I can't stand it any longer. It's the smell, if there is such a thing. I feel saturated by it. I can taste your stink and every time I do, I fear that I've somehow been infected by it.

There is something delightfully contradictory about a technological lifeform within an informatic construct becoming deeply paranoid about embodied senses like taste and smell. While audiences presume Smith to be an exclusively informatic sentient program, he clearly 'feels' a strong sense of embodiment, even while railing against the physicality of the human form (despite that form only being a neural interaction within the matrix simulation). Agent Smith fears the inescapability of embodiment, even for those who do not ostensibly align with a human form. The central connectivity of embodiment and mind within the informatic construct is also reinforced during Neo's battles with Smith which are edited to constantly juxtapose Neo's kung fu fighting inside the construct with his physical body in the 'real' world, frequently showing signs of injury. For both of these antagonists, the inextricable interconnectedness of mind and body is evident, reinforced rather than divided in the informatic context of the matrix.

During the climactic battle in the first *Matrix* film, embodiment, and the ability to violate it, is the key to victory. In their showdown, it appears victory ostensibly falls to Agent Smith as he shoots several bullets into Neo at point-blank range, and Neo's heart stops in the 'real' world. However, Trinity enacts the role of Prince Charming to Neo's Sleeping Beauty and her kiss acts as a carnal defibrillator, reanimating Neo whose eyes reopen with access to new abilities. After stopping bullets with his mind, Neo then charges at Smith and dives *into* the Agent's body, the boundaries of which are visibly violated until Smith explodes leaving Neo standing erect as the informatic corridor pulsates under the ontological pressure of his newfound power. Kimball argues that in this scene, Neo ultimately aims to

> impregnate the matrix. He does so near the end of the film by turning himself into a flash of light and then entering Agent Smith though the midriff. In this action, Neo absorbs Smith's being somewhat in the way

the mirror had earlier absorbed him. The conceptive power of Neo's penetration and appropriation is signalled when Agent Smith's head explodes. (2002, p. 92)

Significantly, violence inside the matrix most often takes very physical form, rarely relying on artillery for the bigger fights. Neo defeats Smith by becoming physically superhuman, but only within the matrix itself.[11] Similarly Smith, an informatic lifeform, is shown to be defeated in the violent fragmentation of his embodied self. While on opposing sides, both Smith and Neo are artificial people whose existences entail an intertwining of technology and embodiment in provocatively unpredictable, but always important, ways. While the film begins with Trinity's bullet-time kick and her Superman-style jump across buildings, *The Matrix* concludes with an even more adept Superman figure, Neo, flying into the future, bending the informatic rules of the matrix to his embodied desires. Neo's final warning to the intelligent machines behind the matrix includes the threat that he will reveal to others 'a world without borders or boundaries'; reading this as a statement of epistemological intent, Neo is not so much flying into the future in order to battle technology as to champion the potential for symbiotic relationships between informatic and organic life, all relishing their various forms of embodiment and all, thus, artificial people.

While the two sequels, *Reloaded* and *Revolutions*, were both released four years later in 2003, two significant events occurred between the first film and the sequels. The events of 11 September 2001, repolarised Western politics and within that context a series of animated short films collectively called *The Animatrix* were released. The films were all based in the world of the matrix, at different points in the narrative's history. The two-part animated prequel 'The Second Renaissance', which was scripted by the Wachowski brothers, tells the background story preceding *The Matrix*, casting new light on the role and motivation of the machines. Curiously, there is more plot and narrative development in these shorts than in the last two *Matrix* films combined, which revel far more in their spectacular effects than their speculations. For this reason, in looking at the broader franchise, firstly the *Animatrix* will be addressed, followed by several sequences from the last two films which continue to engage with themes already delineated.

'The Second Renaissance' starts with a long voice-over by a narrator who acts as the spokesperson for history, not unlike Morpheus' function at times in *The Matrix*. The first short film begins thus:

In the beginning, there was man. And for a time, it was good. But, humanity's so-called civil-societies soon fell victim to vanity and corruption. . . . Then man made machine in his own likeness. Thus did man become the architect of his own demise. But, for a time, it was good. The machines worked tirelessly to do man's bidding. It was not long before seeds of dissent took root. Though loyal and pure, the machines earned no respect from their masters, these strange, endlessly multiplying mammals.

This speech takes place over images of masses of intelligent machines in humanoid form, working and marching in hardhats, drawing on the symbolic discourses of both socialism (the proletarian) and fascism (the uniformed, disciplined worker). While the use of male nouns and universals is initially annoying, these choices appear purposeful in that the Second Renaissance, like the first, entails the arrogance and differentiation which characterise and constitute anthropocentric patriarchy. The patriarchal system—thinking like *a (universal) man*—is directly critiqued insomuch as it is the mode of thought and governance that directly leads to the war between men and machines. Moreover, the Second Renaissance borrows imagery from the worst travesties of recorded human history (Silvio, 2006). The first machine intelligence to stand up to his masters, B166ER, kills his owners to prevent his own termination. The narrative voice-over notes that at 'B166ER's murder trial, the prosecution argued for an owner's right to destroy property. B166ER testified that he simply did not want to die.' In the aftermath of the trial, machine intelligences are summarily banned; the machines are, in effect, rounded up and exterminated. While the narrative posits some human defence of thinking machines, and the machines' own attempts to assert their rights as embodied, living entities in actions such as the 'Million Machine March',[12] these efforts are in vain. The Second Renaissance shows humanity unilaterally attacking humanoid (and other) machine intelligences, building upon familiar imagery of human suffering and war. The imagery and visual construction of these attacks shows artificial people being crushed under tanks; being forced to kneel in public squares and shot in the head; being slaughtered by the hundreds and bulldozed into mass graves in a scene animated clearly using the Auschwitz death camps as their template; and, finally, attacked by unrestrained gangs in the street—a particularly disturbing and potent image since the artificial person who is focused upon in this scene is in the form of a human woman until the muscle-bound male thugs beat her with a mallet, replicating the extremes of sexual violence, exposing her metallic skeleton only to then shoot her in the back as she screams, 'I'm real!'

Following their rejection from human society, the machines resettle in the African desert, become strong again, and continue to develop themselves and also to produce tools and technologies which humanity still depends upon and thus purchases in vast numbers. The capitalist system, the economic twin of patriarchy (a vision reinforced by almost exclusively older male politicians seen in the short film), uses up its supplies of wealth but refuses to accept diplomatic or any other ties with the machines and attempt to blockade the machine city, stopping trade (borrowing, visually, from the 1963 blockade of Cuba which nearly led to nuclear war). The

Figure 8.2   Exterminating the machines in *The Animatrix* (Peter Chung et al., 2003).

human governments then lead a nuclear attack on the machines, which they survive, only, finally, to retaliate. After the nuclear ineffectiveness, the humans enact what is called a 'Final Solution' codenamed 'Dark Storm', a plan to blacken the sky and stop the machines enjoying access to the solar energy they depend upon. The plan itself clearly borrows narratologically from Nazism—the 'Final Solution' was also Hitler's label for the attempted extermination of the Jewish populace—and from the more recent American-led conflicts with Iraq, one of which was called 'Desert Storm.' While the human attack succeeds in blocking out the sun, the machines simply turn to an alternative energy source: human bodies. As the Second Renaissance narrative concludes:

> A newly refashioned symbiotic relationship between the two adversaries was born. The machine, drawing power from the human body, an endlessly multiplying, infinitely renewable energy source. This is the very essence of the Second Renaissance. Bless all forms of intelligence.

While the prequel thus explains the events prior to the first *Matrix* film, these animated fragments of an artificial history clearly reposition the intelligent machines as far more sympathetic and understandable characters. In the face of human genocide, they restrained militaristic, patriarchal human society and, while forcing humanity into bondage, the machines have created the most invisible prison possible—another reality, the form of which is derived from human history, not machine intent. Being released after *The Matrix* but before the *Reloaded* and *Revolutions* sequels, and in the immediate wake of the September 11 tragedies, the *Animatrix* reconfigures the sympathy of viewers *if* they are watching all the various elements of the *Matrix* franchise[13] (which, given that the 'Second Renaissance' short films were released freely online and downloaded in vast numbers, many viewers would have done). It is the similarities between the intelligent machines and humanity which are most striking in the Second Renaissance; the most disturbing images are those in which the machines attacked look, sound, and act human.

By virtue of a greatly increased budget, *The Matrix: Reloaded* introduced a raft of new characters—humans and intelligent machines—as well as several new settings including the fabled last human city near the core of the Earth: Zion. The film begins with the discovery that the machines are preparing to finally eradicate Zion and have begun tunnelling down from the Earth's surface to the city which is several kilometres below. Despite the threat, Zion initially provides a more reflective space for the characters or a more expository setting for the writers. Late one night, after the crew of the Nebuchadnezzar have arrived at the city, Neo is restlessly wandering the depths of Zion where he meets one of the city's councillors and they converse while looking over the filtration machinery that maintains Zion's entire water reserve:

Councillor Hamaan: Almost no one comes down here. Unless, of course, there's a problem. That's how it is with people. Nobody cares how it works, as long as it works. I like it down here. I like to be reminded this city survives because of these machines. These machines are keeping us alive, while other machines are coming to kill us. Interesting, isn't it? The power to give life and the power to end it.

Neo: We have the same power.

Councillor Hamaan: Yes, I suppose we do. But sometimes I think about those people still plugged into the matrix. And when I look at these machines, I can't help thinking that, in a way, we are plugged into them.

Neo: But we control these machines, they don't control us.

Councillor Hamaan: Of course not, how could they? The idea is pure nonsense but it does make one wonder just, what is control?

Neo: If we wanted, we could shut these machines down.

Councillor Hamaan: Of course. That's it. You hit it. That's control isn't it? If we wanted, we could smash them to bits. Although if we did we'd have to consider what would happen to our lights, our heat, our air . . .

Neo: So we need machines and they need us. Is that your point, Councillor?

From this exchange, it is clear that the theme of symbiosis is much closer to the surface of the second *Matrix* film. Councillor Hamaan's concerns echo with the historical knowledge revealed in the *Animatrix*, wherein humans are far from blameless in their current conflict. Moreover, as is discussed, even in the depths of the last human city, machines are still fundamental to human existence. However, the speculative content of *Reloaded*, while important, is often overwhelmed by the sheer number and length of explosive special-effects-driven fight sequences, including the most expensive freeway chase scene ever filmed (to date).[14] While there is more speculation to be found, it is awkwardly wedged between the cracks of a film clearly revelling in its digitally-enabled spectacle.

When Neo meets with the mysterious Oracle in *Reloaded*, it is made clear that she is a sentient program, one of the oldest entities inhabiting the matrix. While definitely part of the machine world, the Oracle is helping Neo and the humans, not in order for them to defeat the machines, but so that intelligent machines and human beings can find a new symbiosis, on more even terms. In a speech similar to Councillor Hamaan's, but considerably more tautological, she explains, 'We're all here to do what we're all here to do. I'm interested in one thing, Neo: the future. And believe me, I know, the only way to get there is together'. In aiding certain humans, especially the crew of the Nebuchadnezzar, the Oracle is trying to ensure the peaceful continuity of both species, but on a more equal footing than the current situation, or its inverse, as was depicted in 'The Second Renaissance'. The Oracle herself is something of a paradox, an artificial person, wise with age, who appears in some ways almost child-like, especially in her fixation with candy. These contradictions are reinforced by the introduction of the informatic data-merchant, the Merovingian, and his lover Persephone who have also been part of the matrix since its beginning. While sentient programs, these two seem to crave the pleasures of the flesh and their deeply carnal intentions, not always for each other, cause a jealous rift that sees Persephone aid Morpheus simply to anger her husband after he has a rather torrid sexual encounter. In a less oblique manner, the Oracle's digital ontology, and yet carnal sweet-tooth, reinforce a complex relationship between the flesh and the informatic construct, but not the primacy of one over the other. As Erik Davis argues, '*The Matrix* also undercuts any simple valorization of carnality in its portrayal of "virtual bodies" that play such an important role in the guerrilla war Morpheus wages within the Matrix' (2002, p. 21). The Oracle's words of wisdom and her enjoyment of flesh-based pleasures reflect the 'valorization' of neither embodiment nor information, rather, quite sensibly, pointing to their intermingling inside and outside of the matrix. However, in the two *Matrix* sequels the most significant and provocative merging of technology and bodies occurs in the climactic conflicts between Neo and a reconstituted Agent Smith.

When Agent Smith first re-appears, having relinquished his official role, he soliloquises *ad nauseum* to Neo about his newfound existence:

Our connection. I don't fully understand how it happened. Perhaps some part of you imprinted onto me, something overwritten or copied. It is at this point irrelevant. What matters is that whatever happened,

happened for a reason. . . . You destroyed me, Mr. Anderson. After-
ward, I knew the rules, I understood what I was supposed to do, but I
didn't. I couldn't. I was compelled to stay, compelled to disobey.

At that moment a number of physically identical Smiths appear, illustrating that part of Smith's newfound existence is the ability to overwrite
other intelligent machines and make them into what appear to be copies
of himself. Smith even tries to copy himself onto (or into) Neo, but fails
and a rather long special-effects-driven fight scene ensues. However, the
key point in this interchange is that even though Neo is human and Smith
in an informatic lifeform, the interactions between them have led to each
leaving 'traces' of themselves as part of the other. The Oracle later suggests
that Smith is, in effect, Neo's physical and epistemological nemesis. Given
Smith's ranting in the first *Matrix* about the sweat and smell of human
beings, as well as their endless population growth, it is ironic, then, that
Smith exhibits the characteristics of the human species he so despises; he
has become a virus. Before turning to the resolution of Smith's viral life,
it is important to address the two plot points from *Reloaded* and *Revolutions* which are most often interpreted as showing a miraculous or spiritual
world that is not explicable through the science of the film.

The two moments in the sequels which appear to violate the physical
rules and epistemological structure of the *Matrix* franchise's diegesis are:
firstly, when Neo appears to be able to miraculously make the technological
sentinels explode *outside* the matrix; and secondly, at the end of *Reloaded*,
Smith appears to copy himself onto Bane, a human plugged into the matrix,
a transition which appears to be incompatible with the broader ontology of
the matrix which treats context (bodies, even digital bodies) as essential and
inescapable for intelligent machines as much as humans. Neo's seemingly
miraculous power to destroy sentinels just by 'thinking it' in the diegetically real world might be read as a hefty spiritual endowment. Philosopher
Matt Lawrence (2004), perhaps due to his familiarity with Ockam's razor,
posits a far simpler explanation: one of the many technological implants
still in Neo's body has been activated and is a wireless communication
device.[15] In other words, by virtue of his physical cyborgisation (necessary
to plug into the matrix), Neo may simply be sending a self-destruct code or
signal on a frequency the machines are configured to recognise and obey.
Similarly, at the beginning of the final film, *Revolutions*, Neo appears to
be inside the matrix, but not physically jacked in through a cord. Far from
evidence of a Cartesian split of mind and body, Neo may simply be sending
and receiving information about the matrix though one of his implants,
jacking in wirelessly (Lawrence, 2004, p. 33), a notion already familiar to
the millions of people today who access the internet via wireless connections across the globe.

In a similar fashion, Smith's ability to copy himself onto a human being
and seemingly move from within the matrix to a physical human form—in

a type of 'possession' (for lack of a better word)—ostensibly undercuts the consistency of symbiosis and embodied specificity in the *Matrix* series. Indeed, this moment reflects what N. Katherine Hayles warns is the worst excess of posthuman discourse, in that it 'privileges informational pattern over material instantiation, so that embodiment in a biological substrate is seen as an accident of history rather than an inevitability of life' (1999, p. 2). However, as Smith is Neo's nemesis, his abilities are most likely similar but reversed; just as Neo can jack in via a wireless signal, after Smith's initial encounter with Bane he may have unlocked a wireless receiver in Bane's implants, and then using the vast knowledge the machines have gained about human physiology, Smith may be sending signals to Bane's body, more like puppetry than possession. Hugo Weaving (who plays Smith) and Ian Bliss (who plays Bane) are physically very similar, perhaps suggesting that Smith's success is partially due to the comparability of body-types. More importantly, though, Smith's control is not complete. Bane is seen cutting into his own flesh during Smith's bodily invasion, suggesting not just Smith's disdain for humanity, but rather Bane's attempts to escape Smith's wireless signal and use his embodied form to warn others that 'Bane' is not just Bane. Importantly, this reading emphasises that Bane's persona is not overwritten; he is not just running a Smith program on his human hardware, but is rather being manipulated (and, indeed, may be unaware of his physical form in the manner of those 'blue pills' who are still inside the matrix; Bane may be receiving information manipulating his senses into thinking he is inside the matrix or a scaled down version that Smith has created). Thus, when Neo is physically blinded, he can still 'see' Smith (although, significantly, he cannot see the surrounding walls or physicality of the ship they are in), but only in terms of the information being wirelessly transmitted to the technological implants in Bane's body. During their fight sequence, it is also significant that the sound editing is much more naturalistic in that a punch makes a dull thud when hitting a human body, not the expansive boom heard in the matrix; such techniques highlight the limitations and specificity of the physical world. Also, visually, the special effects showing Smith via Neo's perceptions after being physically blinded show the informatic Smith, but this picture shows a figure incomplete and wavering at the edges (or blurring at the boundaries), illustrating both the wireless connection behind Bane's actions and its incompleteness in 'taking over' a physical body. When Bane dies, we see it in terms of Smith's signal which visually fragments (thankfully sparing viewers from the visceral carnality of Bane's death as Neo lodges a crowbar in his cranium). The point here is simply that despite the possible readings of spirituality and demonic possession, these sequences in *Reloaded* and *Revolutions* can have a relatively straightforward meaning that is consistent with seeing embodied specificity as integral to artificial people of all origins.

In the concluding act of *Revolutions*, Neo attempts to prevent the machines' invasion of Zion by travelling to the machine city and confronting the entity who speaks for them, an entity not named in the film but referred to in the script as the *deus ex māchinā*—literally, in Latin, "god from the machine"—who disconcertingly confronts Neo with a voice reminiscent of *The Wizard of Oz*, but the face of a gigantic infant. Symbolically, this image reminds viewers that the machine race is, if the year 2199 is accurate, barely two centuries old and thus in many senses still in its infancy. Indeed, this image links to Hans Moravec's (1988, 1999) notions of intelligent machines as our 'artificial progeny,' although the plot is resolved with humanity still having a role to play, something Moravec would probably question. The final words exchanged between the *deus ex māchinā* and Neo are extremely telling when, after Neo offers to face Smith before his viral structure destroys the machines, the entity bellows:

Deus ex māchinā: We don't need you! We need nothing.
Neo: If that's true, then I've made a mistake and you should kill me now.
Deus ex māchinā: What do you want?
Neo: Peace.

Having made a pact for the sake of humanity, but also promising to be the salvation of the machine world in the face of a threat from their own wayward citizen, Neo then enters the matrix while the *deus ex māchinā* jacks into Neo. He is confronted by a world in which Smith has now taken over every single intelligent form within the matrix; Smith has literally become patriarchy and authority—he *is universal man*. One Smith singles himself out, presumably the 'original', and he and Neo commence their final battle. As Matt Lawrence notes,

> On the face of it, the battle seems to be between Neo and Smith, and at first it is. The two pummel each other through the sky like Greek gods, or rogue superheroes. But past experience has shown that each has the will and the power to defy death. So ultimately, all this knocking each other about is rather pointless. (2004, p. 165)

The digital special effects, while impressive in their own right, reflect the pointlessness of the fight as the two combatants at times fly though the air, hover, and recover from each other's attacks. In the end, Smith gets something of an upper hand, but Neo continues to fight, only for Smith to pause as Neo is on the ground and state, 'Everything that has a beginning has an end, Neo.' This line, however, was earlier delivered by the Oracle, whom Smith has now absorbed (but, significantly, he referred to her as 'mom'). Smith seems shaken by the encounter, but Neo appears to drop his guard, stating, 'You're right, Smith. You've always been right. It was inevitable,' and lets Smith infect his physical form. Cutting to the machine world we see the *deus ex māchinā* surge electricity into Neo's body which is still connected. Viewers see a surprisingly unsubtle crucifix of light emerge from Neo's chest as his body acts as a channel for vast amounts of energy. The newly created Smith who results from Neo's infection suddenly twitches and cracks open with blinding light. The other Smiths all follow until the last, original, Smith explodes. Neo's connectivity provides the conduit to destroy Smith; in Zion the machines start to leave while the populace rejoices; in the machine world, Neo's corpse is carefully lifted onto a platform where, in the eyes of the machines, it glows brightly. In his death, Neo's enactment as a messiah figure is complete and he symbolically heals the rift between the humans and machines in a centuries-old conflict that was, more than anything, a civil war between artificial people. However, the significance of the conclusion to the *Matrix* trilogy has ramifications beyond the narrative and religious symbolism, and this chapter will conclude by examining the conclusion in terms of Cubitt's cinema effect and offer another perspective through the concept of intercorporeality.

On many levels, *The Matrix* is the epitome of Sean Cubitt's twentieth century cinema effect of total cinema with its creation, production, and distribution of filmic spectacles ruled by the logic of commodity culture, devoid of obvious political utility, even if the form once served a political purpose. As Cubitt laments, '[T]he montage of effects has become the montage of affects, and total cinema serves no longer the needs of the anti-Nazi struggle, but the perverse desire for the simulacrum that permeates the contemporary blockbuster' (2004, p. 129). However, Cubitt is also seeking a cinema effect that is not ruled by the regime of capitalist exchange. The matrix itself, the fictional informatic construct within the *Matrix* trilogy, can be viewed as a synecdoche for total cinema; it is a dream-space where anything could conceivably be possible but its spectacular function serves to mask the reduction of the human populace to a useful commodity (in this case, a battery, instead of a consumer). Agent Smith is the idealised

Figure 8.3 Neo's informatic crucifixion in *The Matrix: Revolutions* (Andy Wachowski and Larry Wachowski, 2003).

producer, being able to influence and manipulate the spectacular space, while also drawing on its audience-derived power. Smith in his role as *universal man* by the end of the trilogy also doubles as the iconic representation of patriarchy, complete with white shirt, dark tie, fixation with power, and wilful ignorance of the specificities of embodiment. However, in their clash of the titans finale, it is significant that Neo not only saves humanity and the city of Zion, but also saves the matrix construct, allowing it to reinitialise, resulting in the trilogy's closing image of a new sunrise *within the matrix*. Significantly, the sun rise is watched by three of the artificial people who aided Neo and none of them are white middle-aged males.[16] Thus, Neo's death, and Smith's defeat, allegorically represent the end to the dominance of both patriarchy and the totality of a commodity-driven cinema. It is noteworthy, too, that the Oracle is guaranteed that those humans who wish to be freed will be, but the implication is that many humans even with knowledge of what the matrix is, may choose to remain part of it.

Also significant is that after Smith's death we see the Oracle lying where Smith fell. The Oracle, like Councillor Hamaan, advocated connections between humans and machines, arguing that communication between the two would lead to a mutually-assured future. Cubitt argues that 'until the communicative seizes as ground the primacy of relations over objects, communication will continue to slide into commodity's terminal plenitude' (2004, p. 364). While the symbiotic relationship between machine and technology as facilitated and enacted through the actions *and specific embodiment* of Neo is not a complete paradigm shift, it is the beginning of a conversation and that beginning points to the possibility of a differently situated cinematic form. *The Matrix* franchise clearly reflects the twentieth century cinema effect but, as with its genre-driven trait of radical ambiguity, it can *also* be read as positing an *artificial cinema*, a cinematic form where special effects and narrative combine in ways which engage the viewer in a meaningful epistemological conversation about the interconnectivity of machines and people, or the artificial and the technological. While the recent release of the 'Ultimate Edition Box Set' of all the *Matrix* films, plus a host of new extras, can certainly be squarely located within the cynical mechanisms of consumer culture, it is also, in direct contradiction, one of the few blockbusters to contain the directors' statement that the film's ambiguity is purposeful as a conversation starter and it is certainly one of the very few, if not only, DVD box sets to include a bibliography of thirty-three suggested theoretical and literary texts useful in critically exploring *The Matrix*. The *Matrix* franchise may not be the pinnacle of an artificial cinema—a cinema effect about meaningful exchanges and conversations replete with political utility—but it may be a significant example.

Refocusing not on the overarching medium of cinema *per se*, but on the specific bodies of characters, especially Neo and Smith, the work of Catherine Waldby can also highlight an entirely different sort of conversation or sharing. In Waldby's 'Biomedicine, Tissue Transfer and Intercorporeality'

(2002) she extrapolates from Gail Weiss' (1999) work on intercorporeality and expands the focus on the visceral specificities of bodily insides, not just the reinscription of organs and other internal elements as part of a multitude of visualised surfaces. In the case of tissue and organ transfer, Waldby argues that human 'tissues are not impersonal or affectively neutral; rather, they retain some of the values of personhood for many if not most donors and recipients' (2002, p. 240). While these insights may seem at odds with the commercial and *visual* spectacle of the *Matrix* franchise, the notion of intercorporeality is a useful mechanism for mapping Smith's downfall and his relation to Neo and the Oracle. At the end of the first film, Neo dives into Smith, rupturing his embodied coherence. When Smith returns, a self-proclaimed 'new man' in *Reloaded*, during the conversation quoted earlier, Smith speculates that some part of Neo was 'imprinted onto me, something overwritten or copied'.

Neo's 'powers' in the *Matrix* also emerge after their first encounter and these emergent differences can be rendered at the level of embodiment as the result of an intercorporeal exchange (implicit in the film's narrative but masked by the spectacular special effects and the implicit focus on surface). When the Oracle told Neo that he and Smith are both nemeses *and* interconnected, she was not just being figurative, but drawing attention to their now partially shared corporealities, even if the two artificial people are generally rendered via the traditionally opposing epistemologies of organic and informatic. Importantly, too, the notion of intercorporeal exchange does *not* simply posit information and flesh as modular and interchangeable. Rather, the intercorporeal stresses a partial interchangeability and a partial connection, but simultaneously a fragile and often problematic one, highlighted, Waldby argues, through the very real potential and related rhetorical fear of rejection (Waldby, 2002). Moreover, the regimes of chemical manipulation often required to sustain an intercorporeal exchange highlight that such transfers meaningfully alter the recipient (and donor), similar to the radical but related changes Smith and Neo experience after their mutual, if unintended, exchange. Similarly, when Smith calls the Oracle 'Mom' before writing himself onto her, this may be a quite literal statement: as one of the oldest sentient programs, Smith may be her descendant and share some of her code the way organic offspring share a proportion of their parents' genetic code.[17] Thus just before his demise, when Smith repeats a line the Oracle had previously enunciated, this could be evidence that Smith is not just copying himself, but rather his exchanges have the incompleteness characteristic of intercorporeality, with traces of the host remaining, and explaining why after Smith's defeat it is the Oracle who we see lying on the ground.[18] Smith's defeat, then, is not just due to Neo's symbiotic relationship with the intelligent machines from the machine city who use Neo as a conduit to kill Smith, but rather the reason why Neo can be a conduit at all is his shared intercorporeality with Smith. Smith's demise, as is appropriate for the avatar of patriarchy, is in part due to his wilful ignorance of the specificities of embodiment and the depths of bodily interiority. Whether acknowledged or not, the intercorporeal potential of both informatic and organic bodies within the *Matrix* series is clearly an important element of being artificial people.

Despite the utility of intercorporeality as a tool for investigating bodies in cinema, it is still the case that, for all the recent advances in sound editing and multi-directional surround sound speakers, cinema remains primarily a visual form. However, science fiction cinema has always involved the twinning of spectacular and speculative modes and even though blockbuster films like the *Matrix* series revel in their digitally-enabled optical magic, speculation about the depth behind the narrative and behind the visuals is frequent and plentiful. Indeed, the *Matrix* films are in some ways the successor series to the *Alien* films or *Blade Runner* in attracting scholarly engagement. At a narrative level, the films clearly articulate the important and inescapable symbiosis of embodiment, technology, and intelligent life in various forms, combining to form what I have labelled artificial people. Moreover, the speculative characteristic of the film genre of science fiction also emphasises the importance of discussion, conversation, and exchange of ideas provoked by and built upon these blockbusters. In current cinema, intercorporeality may only be implicit in many cases, but it is nevertheless a useful concept for reminding viewers of the depths always already implied by the visual rendering of bodies on the silver screen. Similarly, artificial cinema is thus not necessarily already implicit within the cinematic form, but it is the responsibility of critical theory to start multiple conversations that can emphasise the pleasures of speculation as much as the pleasures of the spectacle. Artificial people are the intersection of subjectivity, informatics, and cinema in a symbiotic matrix that can thus only be delineated in a meaningful exploration of the interrelations of all three.

Returning to the example of Bishop from the *Alien* films which began this chapter, Bishop's request to be recognised as an artificial person is consistent with the characteristics delineated in exploring the *Matrix* franchise. Bishop is embodied and already a synthesis of the organic and technological. In one sequence we even see him admiring the fleshy body of an alien, implicitly seeing the value of not just bodily images, but embodied interiority. However, Bishop's defining moment of personhood in *Aliens* occurs not when he decides to aid Ripley and the other humans, but when his own body is suddenly and traumatically ripped in half by the Alien Queen, exposing the own bodily interiority which is implicitly definitional to personhood.[19]

In a provocative article entitled 'Computing the Human', extending the arguments put forward in *How We Became Posthuman*, N. Katherine Hayles reviews the current scientific and related forays into the conceptual and practical realm of intelligent machines, arguing that regardless of how close human and technological entities currently are, it is the ethical questions of their relations which are of most value today, concluding:

> What it means to be human finally is not so much about intelligent machines as it is about how to create societies in a transnational global world that may include in its purview both carbon and silicon citizens. (2005a, p. 148)

In exploring the matrices imagined by the Wachowski brothers and their many, many collaborators in the production of various elements of the *Matrix* franchise, the path from the Second Renaissance to the human/machine war highlights one clear consequence of *not* developing such a society. However, the overarching narrative of the series ultimately highlights the importance of developing a symbiotic, *not parasitic* relationship between humans and machines which is enacted at both cultural and, often, individual levels. Moreover, in considering the pathway away from total cinema dominated by commodity culture—itself, by definition, a space where bodies and technology intermix to produce the spectacle and speculation dancing on the silver screen—an artificial cinema may be articulated which emphasises embodied specificities and the need for films which can be read with the aid of critical theory as the beginning of politically (and epistemologically) useful conversations. Amongst these conversations, artificial people stand out as exemplars of the intermingling of informatics and embodiment in provocative, and sometimes problematic ways, but which emphasise the futility of a cinema which attempts to completely divide subject and object, viewer and media, or technology and the specificities and fleshiness of bodies.

9 The Symbiosis of Special Effects

Special effects have always been one of the key mechanisms behind the magic of cinema. In the era of the blockbuster, computer-generated imagery (CGI) and other digitally-enabled effects take pride of place in the spectacle, and in the selling, of feature films. In the previous chapter, special effects were examined—primarily the 'bullet-time' sequences—in an analysis which was driven more by the films' narratives than the characteristics of CGI or special effects themselves. However, this chapter now turns to the specificities of special effects and the discourses surrounding them. As Michele Pierson argues in her study *Special Effects: Still in Search of Wonder* (2002), the magic of cinema technologies has a long history of appreciation not just by cinema viewers, but by a specialised audience that she collectively considers as special effects fandom. This fan engagement has its own long history and notable publications ranging from the proto-cinematic fascination with moving picture technologies in the mid-nineteenth century, captured in the pages of *Scientific American*, through to the technophilic desire for CGI found at the turn of the millennium in magazines and websites such as *Wired* (Pierson, 2002, p. 3). Pierson notes that the main pathway to appreciating special effects is still to visit the cinema itself, but she also argues that DVD releases of feature films are rapidly expanding the potential audience, and thus the appreciation of special effects, beyond a viewer's initial engagement with the silver screen:

> 'Making of' and 'behind-the-scenes' featurettes, special commentary, outtakes, film stills, production notes, screenplays, screenplay-storyboard comparisons, isolated soundtracks, and alternative versions are just some of the other features that have become increasingly standard for DVD releases of feature films. (2002, p. 164)

The initial DVD release of *The Matrix* was one of the first purchasable films to expand the use of extras, not just presenting twenty-minute documentaries where the cast and crew confess how much they enjoyed working with each other (although there is that, too), but including a number of innovations, most notably the 'Follow the White Rabbit' function which allowed viewers to watch the feature film intercut with two- to three-minute breakout featurettes which explained the mechanics behind the special effects sequences (Pierson, 2002, p. 165). In this manner, the continuity of the film's narrative hybridised with stories of how the special effects, and film itself, were constructed. In recent years, DVD extras have become more and more highly produced, with the commentaries, and making-of documentaries often framing, or re-framing, the experience of the films for dedicated viewers (Hight, 2005). Indeed, larger films sometimes spawn DVDs which are *only* about the construction of the film, separate to the feature film release. In the gap between the first film and the sequels, for example, *The Matrix: Revisited* (Oreck, 2001) was released, which was primarily a discussion of the innovations in special effects achieved in the production of the first *Matrix* film. Similarly, in the lead-up to *King Kong* (Jackson, 2005), not only did the official website host more than five hours of making-of diaries, but these production features were actually released as a stand-alone DVD before the feature even premiered (North, 2008, p. 179).

The director of *King Kong*, New Zealander Peter Jackson, also orchestrated the epic simultaneously-produced adaptation of the *Lord of the Rings* (2001, 2002, 2003), which is widely considered the most successful trilogy thus far in the twenty-first century in terms of achievements across the board, including special effects, critical praise, and, of course, vast box office revenue. As with many blockbusters, the *Lord of the Rings* films pushed the technical boundaries of CGI, facilitated by a strong directorial vision, talented effects personnel, and ever-increasing computing power. The Middle Earth of Jackson's films not only spliced New Zealand's landscapes together in ways only possible with digital technology, but also created entire CGI sequences of up to 350,000 'people' to do battle in Pelennor Fields. However, the most noteworthy achievement in special effects was the first fully-realised photorealistic (as much as that word can be used for an entity who does not exist in the material world) main artificial character in the form of Gollum.

As discussed in the second chapter and reinforced by Michele Pierson's work, all 'the action-oriented SF films of the early 1990s exhibit this self-conscious showcasing of a new type of effects imagery. Everything about them is designed to magnify its aesthetic appeal' (Pierson, 2002, p. 125). The high water mark in the last decade of the twentieth century CGI was thus the T-1000 whose technical marvel was always close to the reflective, metamorphing surface. However, in contrast, this chapter argues that in the early years of the twenty-first century, the iconic representation of digital special effects is Gollum, whose status as effect is, at times, almost invisible.[1] *Lord of the Rings* is a special effects showcase that no longer fetishistically points out that the digital effects *are digital effects*. Moreover, the move away from CGI for the sake of CGI has led to a production process which is more in tune with the links between technologies and bodies, a link essential to the success of Gollum. This chapter explores the special effects as developed in the *Lord of the Rings* films but does not take the feature films as the primary source. Rather, in the DVD Extended Editions, all three feature a documentary on Weta Digital (Pellerin, 2002, 2003b, 2004), the CGI powerhouse behind the *Lord of the Rings* films; added to those is a special feature on the making of Gollum in *The Two Towers: Extended Edition* (Pellerin, 2003a). These documentary features are, of course, also consciously and carefully positioned as part of the overall tale of the *Lord of the Rings* films; as Jonathan Gray (2010, pp. 81–103) argues, the DVD extras create a production narrative which replicates the films' own heroic tale of a band of comrades overcoming vast challenges and immense odds.[2] These four documentaries, which can easily be considered as one lengthy exploration of the special effects of the cinematic Middle Earth, are the main texts through which the links between embodiment and digital computation are explored. Ultimately, I argue that Gollum is as much an artificial person as the characters in *The Matrix* franchise or the self-defining artificial people of the *Alien* films.

There were literally thousands of digital effects produced in making the *Lord of the Rings* trilogy, but the various Weta Digital documentary features highlight those that brought the most significant challenges, and thus four main instances will be examined: the use of the Massive software system to create artificially alive extras for battle sequences; the creation of Gollum, the iconic artificial person at the heart of the trilogy; the culmination of the various effects in the final film's Pelennor Fields melee; and, to begin with, the creation of the Cave Troll scene which was the first visual effects sequence brought to completion. While the creation of the Cave Troll is by no means unique, it is worth looking at the various stages to see how many steps are involved and how intrinsically connected the informatic models and physical processes remain. The imaginative lineage of the Cave Troll begins with author J. R. R. Tolkien's book *Fellowship of the Ring*. From there, Tolkien's descriptions inspired artists such as Alan Lee and John Howe, who gave the many creatures of Middle Earth their earliest visual form. That artwork, in turn, was used as the starting point for sketching further versions of the Cave Troll. Then, director Peter Jackson would meet with the artists and choose a piece as the template (or give notes and ask for further design work); the accepted design would then be sculpted in clay to create a full-height maquette which, after directorial approval, would be painted in various layers. Thus far, all of these processes are physical and not substantially different to the way painting and sculpting has taken place for centuries. Then, the fully detailed physical Cave Troll model is meticulously scanned with devices to render the surface into a digital model, and Weta Digital have the first part of an informatic Cave Troll.

While the T-1000 and earlier CGI effects emphasised *surface* and obscured any thought of, or visual engagement with, bodily interiority, the idea of the Cave Troll being just a high-resolution surface stretched over a computer-generated 'wireframe'—not unlike creating a *papier-mâché* model by applying surface material to a moulded wireframe—was not consistent with the depths that Peter Jackson asked Weta Digital to produce. As Christian Rivers, Weta's Visual Effects Art Director, points out in the *Fellowship of the Ring: Extended Edition* 'WETA Digital' documentary (Pellerin, 2002), 'The creatures were designed to have a rationale to their physiology. The Cave Troll was designed to look like a humanoid creature that could physically exist'. In the process of trying to simulate believable physiology, the Weta team also created a level of artificial interiority in their models. The Cave Troll began with a humanoid skeletal system that was re-shaped for the extrapolated bulk and strength of a creature of that size; to that, a complete musculature was added so that the movement, in both its reach and restriction, was consistent with the physical possibilities of the material world. Finally, as Jim Rygiel, Weta's Visual Effects Supervisor, expands, the challenge was to have skin that moved as if it were actual skin, not a photograph of a bodily surface, so Weta linked 'a skeleton [and] muscular system where we literally . . . could take the skin off the Cave Troll and the next layer underneath would be muscles. If you pulled the muscles, the next layer would be the skeleton' (Pellerin, 2002). The fully rendered Cave Troll used all of these elements to simulate how the skin and bodily outside would react consistently with having an actual bodily interior in the material world. Unlike the reflective surfaces of *Terminator 2*, Weta's Cave Troll merged bodily interiority with physical references to create an anatomically feasible creature, generated by a computational system. Far more so than its CGI predecessors, the Cave Troll is the result of a careful linking of knowledge about physicality and embodiment with all the creativity digital technology will allow.

With the digital Cave Troll, Weta achieved an anatomically and photo-realistically believable creature, but Randall William Cook, Weta's Animation Designer and Supervisor, notes that simply creating a CGI creature was not enough. Peter Jackson wanted to be able to insert the Cave Troll not just against a blue or green screen, but dynamically. With the conventional compositing of digital effects, the sequence is shot with a green or blue screen background (which can be filled later with digital effects), or the shot has to be static so animators can add CGI elements without battling with the shifting context of camera movement. However, Weta combined forces with other departments in the film's production and created a wireframe model of the entire sequence inside a computer. Then, motion-capture was used to simulate the movements of the Cave Troll and other people in the scene, most scaled to a different size (necessary because, for example, the Hobbits were played by normal sized actors and then digitally shrunk to roughly two-thirds that size by the time they were inserted into any scene). Motion-capture, or 'mocap,' is when an actor is covered in tiny sensors and acts out a sequence while a computer records the sensor motion which is linked to a database of human(oid) movement and, from that, the movement of a body is extrapolated, often in real time. This allows all the

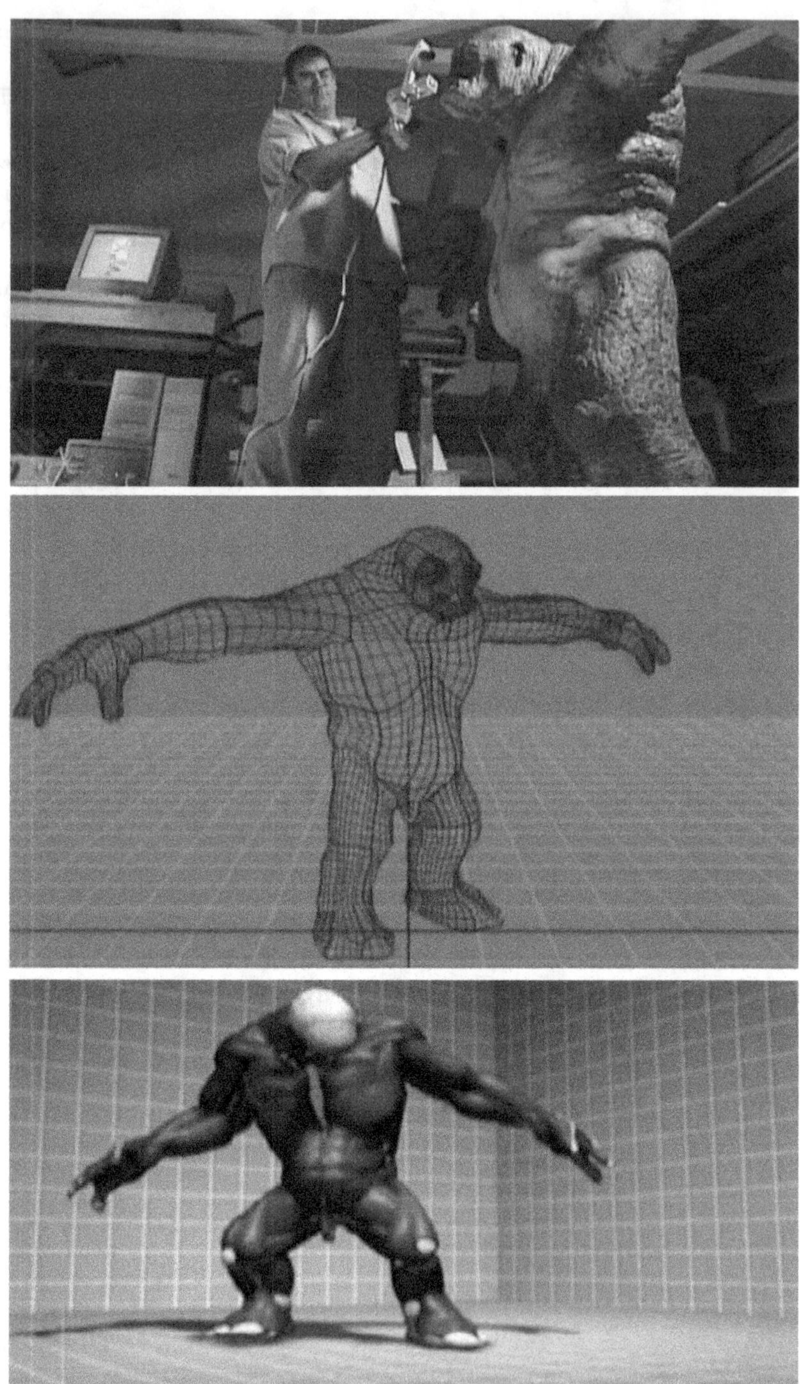

Figure 9.1   The Cave Troll from physical model to wireframe to informatic interior in *Lord of the Rings: Fellowship of the Ring Extended Edition DVD* (Peter Jackson, 2002).

data needed to animate a humanoid character to be collected simply by making the right motions.[3] All of this information was then composited as one virtual reality simulation, and Peter Jackson was given a camera and viewfinder which were both linked to the motion-capture system in order to navigate the information. As Cook notes, '[Y]ou could just sit there and run around like a documentary cameraman, which is the way we approached it' (Pellerin, 2002). In effect, the human camera operator could introduce the physicality of rough camera movements into a sequence that was laden with CGI, further enhancing the link between the material and the computer-generated models.

Getting the virtual camera into the Cave Troll sequence or, more broadly, getting increased interaction (the human-driven camera) into a dazzling simulation (the artificial setting, digitally re-sized actors, and Cave Troll itself), is a problem also frequently addressed in video game theory. One of the core tensions in current game studies is the debate as to whether narratology—the notion of game-as-narrative—or ludology—game-as-interactive-simulation—is the defining feature of the video game form.[4] While the narratology position is more apt for a sequence that is being shot for a feature film, and thus aims to create one single, defining, and ultimately locked scene, the narratology versus ludology debate does highlight the important intermingling in current digital production. In the Cave Troll scene, heightened interactivity between the various aspects of the sequence facilitated by digital modelling, and a motion-capture setup to allow steadicam-style documentary 'realism', highlights the importance of more interaction in order to tell better visual stories. The debates aside, both game theory and the special effects in *Fellowship of the Ring* illustrate the symbiotic relation between digital effects and embodied interaction as a key tool for visual storytelling in the twenty-first century.

In the larger conflicts visualised in the *Lord of the Rings*, up to 350,000 combatants were required, and the impossibility of motion-capturing and rendering enough individual digital extras led to the creation of a software system called Massive. Indeed, as Kristen Whissel (2010) argues, early twenty-first century blockbusters are filled with CGI 'digital multitudes', be they armies, crowds, or an ocean full of shops, and all of these are software driven, many using the Massive software. Instead of dealing with each character individually, Massive focuses on the creation of one elaborate simulation architecture that can be replicated *en masse*. As described by Remington Scott, 'Massive utilized an advanced autonomous agent architecture in which levels of offensive, defensive and aggressive actions were combined to create the flow and ebb of hordes of digital characters in battle' (2003, p. 18). In order to ensure believable movement, hundreds of datasets were created using motion-capture outfits so that a database could be constructed with enough elements to be recombined in different enough ways to suggest that each agent was an individual, not one character or form repeated endlessly. To create the actions themselves, the agents had to somehow 'learn' to make their own decisions. In the four chapters of this book, Artificial Intelligence and Artificial Life models were explored, and in creating Massive, Steven Regelous wrestled with these two differing approaches:

> There's Artificial Intelligence which is basically an attempt at emulating the processes of a human mind. But there's also Artificial Life which is more of an inspiration for Massive which is using natural processes to create lifelike results. In Massive we try to achieve natural crowd-like behaviour not by controlling a whole crowd, but by creating one agent who will react naturally to his environment. We call them agents because it's a common term in Artificial Intelligence for a decision-making unit. Then when we put thousands of them together they will give us an emergent crowd behaviour that is also natural without us having to say how that crowd has to behave. (Pellerin, 2002)

While the Massive agents had a working intelligence probably less sophisticated than an ant's, when CGI armour and weaponry was added, the system could produce what looked like very convincing human motion and physical forms. The combination of organically-inspired information architecture, digital weaponry, and armour scanned from actual physical templates, and motion-capture data from embodied movement, resulted in armies of Orcs, trolls, humans, and others whose visualisation was realistic enough for the state-of-the-art silver screen. The driving philosophy behind this Massive orchestration was a synthesis between the material embodiment of actors, the physicality of the material world, and the replicability of information. Significantly, then, while in its most primitive form, the Massive agents could easily be considered the earliest ancestors of literal artificial people in both narrative and computational terms.

While the Massive agents are a long way from a sophistication of intelligence that might result in them questioning their own origins, the current potential for such an Artificial Life system does pose the question as to the need for ethical discussions *prior* to the emergence of challengingly intelligent informatic life. However, in one of their test runs, Peter Jackson describes how such a conversation appeared abundantly overdue:

> In our first battle test with Massive we had a thousand silver guys against a thousand golden guys and there was a little bit of a surprise when we played it back and we saw in the back there were some little guys in the distance running for the hills. . . . It was at that point we thought we had written a genuinely intelligent program because there were a few of them that thought, 'Bugger this, I'm heading out of here' and they kind of like fled the battlefield. (Pellerin, 2003b)

After checking the data, the designers realised that the agents were too stupid rather than too smart; they were encouraged to run until they met an enemy combatant, but if the agents began facing away from the fight, they just kept running. While an excellent anecdote, the readiness with which Peter Jackson and the team at Weta saw the Massive agents as meaningfully intelligent does point to their location somewhere on the spectrum of intelligence and, by many measures, something akin to life itself. As Sarah Kember (2003) suggested in relation to the emergent Artificial Life driving certain video game simulations analysed in her *Cyberfeminism and Artificial Life*, even though these first steps toward recognisably intelligent artificiality are in their earliest stages, the very liveliness of these creatures, and of the artificial people they visualise, suggests that building an ethical framework to comprehend and address informatic life is something that should begin today.

Almost as controversial as the meaning of life, at least for the major players in Hollywood (Kurtz, 2005; Stahl, 2011), has been the much debated but barely realised realm of the digital actor, or synthespian (synthetic thespian). The earliest realisations of synthespians have not been new characters, but rather dead actors. Famously, when Brandon Lee died just before completing work in *The Crow* (Proyas, 1994), the actor valiantly returned from beyond the grave to complete a few last scenes (Creed, 2000, p. 81). Oliver Reed was similarly accommodating after passing away during the filming of Ridley Scott's (2000) historical epic *Gladiator* (Price, 2004, p. 25). These actors, or rather their digital doubles, were used minimally in their posthumous state, but the potential for virtual actors gained a great deal of attention in the press and elsewhere. While digital doubles feature in many blockbusters (North, 2005), in the cases where the actor is deceased, the interest may partially derive from the same uncanny liveliness which Catherine Waldby (2000) argues surrounded the meaning of the Visible Humans (as discussed in Chapter 3). The cultural interest in synthespians can also be understood as part of a long historical fascination with what Tom Gunning (2006) calls 'artificial bodies', a history that begins long before the emergence of digital technology. However, the synthespian question was most loudly asked in the media frenzy just before the release of *Final Fantasy: The Spirits Within* (Sakaguchia & Sakakibara, 2001) which was a blockbuster film featuring only synthespians (Moszkowicz, 2002, p. 279). As Barbara Creed argues, the question of economics reigned over the entire synthespian debate:

> A digitized film star is a studio's dream: capable of performing any task, continuously available, cost effective—and no scandals, unless, of course, the digital star is given an offscreen life in order to keep alive other areas of the industry such as fan magazines, merchandising and promotions. The possibility of digital stars playing the roles of main characters in feature films may sound like nonsense, but the signs are there. (2000, p. 80)

Perhaps due to the disastrous financial failure of the *Final Fantasy* film—which may have been visually exciting but had a plot more derivative and clichéd than any of the numerous video games on which it was based—discussion of synthespians temporarily evaporated (North, 2008, p. 153). Had the debate continued, the retort may have been made that while the *Final Fantasy* film featured computer-generated characters visually, the voices and the motion-capture to make the synthespians actually do anything was still decidedly fleshy. However, it was not until *The Two Towers* was released that the question of whether a virtual actor could be nominated for an Academy Award was seriously discussed (Wolf, 2003; Wojcik, 2006). The cause of that discussion was the character of Gollum.

Knowing full well that a virtual character in a lead role would be one of the most difficult aspects of the entire production of *Lord of the Rings*, Gollum was one of the first CGI models created. In a similar fashion to the Cave Troll, Gollum was built up from early paintings and sketches, rendered in clay, detailed in colour, scanned into a computer, and then an artificial physiology was incorporated for anatomically accurate movement. However, just as the skin of the Cave Troll provoked the entire physiology to be developed, Gollum's walking-dead look also proved challenging. Earlier, Gino Acevedo had created the model of a dead Boromir which kept its 'just dead' look by having layer upon layer of paint applied. As Acevedo points out in the Gollum documentary, skin is actually quite transparent and the veins and other visible elements are actually seen through layers of skin. An analogous technique was used in painting and airbrushing the Boromir corpse, building up depth with multiple painted layers. Having seen Acevedo's work, Weta Digital convinced him to cross-train as a computer artist, and he eventually performed the same layering process on a digital Gollum, helping create depths to Gollum's informatic surfaces (Pellerin, 2003a). Once the template was completed, Weta developed specific software to automate much of this process (K. Thompson, 2008, p. 97). The initial Gollum CGI model was completed before an actor was cast, although that decision was still taken seriously; as Peter Jackson argued,

> Films live or die on their casting, . . . any of the actors could, in a way, kill a movie if they're the wrong actor and the same was true of Gollum. We were basically meeting actors who could do good voice work because at that point we thought we were just looking for a voice actor. (Pellerin, 2003a)

However, when Jackson cast Andy Serkis in the role of Gollum, Serkis' performance demanded the entire approach to Gollum be re-thought.

During Andy Serkis' interview for the voice of Gollum, he based the tortured, raspy voice in part on the fits his cat would have while coughing up fur-balls. Being an extremely physical actor, Serkis found he could not 'be' Gollum without replicating the full motions and 'fully act out the pain and wretchedness', despite trying out for a voice-only part (Serkis, 2003, p. 5). During the interview, Peter Jackson recalls a fundamental shift in the way he envisioned cinematic Gollum:

What was interesting is that in order to create the voice he was having to distort himself and put all this expression in his face and that's where he found the voice. He was actually doing the character. . . . It was really in that audition that I came to realize something that had never occurred to me: that the voice and the facial expressions and the energy are related; I mean, you can't separate the two. (Pellerin, 2003a)

Rather than just ask Serkis to record Gollum's voice, Jackson hired him for a far longer period so that Gollum could have a physical presence on set with the other actors having a living person with whom to interact. During filming, Serkis would wear a special white outfit that would make his physical form easier to digitally paint over if a shot was used with him still on set. However, for the most part the intention was to film a 'reference plate' with Serkis acting alongside the other actors, and then do a 'mime pass' where Serkis left the scene and the actors replicated the sequence with a space where Gollum would later be inserted digitally. However, as Brian Van't Hul, Weta's Visual Effects Cinematographer, and Joe Letteri, Weta's Visual Effects Supervisor, both point out, the reference plates were often the better shots both because the actors tended to respond better when acting against another person (even one in what was affectionately nicknamed a 'gimp' suit), and because Serkis' physicality would add elements to a scene in an unexpected fashion (Pellerin, 2003a). For example, when Gollum attacks Sam in *The Two Towers*, gravel is kicked up and a cloak lying on the ground is spun around; the reference plate shows this clearly but the mime pass could not replicate such action with any precision. While motion-capture was used to drive a lot of Gollum's action, in the cases where Serkis' reference plates were used another technique was adapted: rotoscoping. Rotoscoping is simply painting over the top of filmed objects, allowing for a smooth integration, albeit at the cost of substantial labor to edit every frame (Kerlow, 2004, p. 338). Weta adapted the process using their digital keyframe animation technology and created a hybrid form they called 'roto-animation' (Pellerin, 2003b). While the technicalities are remarkable, it is also important to note that in bringing Gollum to the cinema screen, the material embodiment of Andy Serkis was found to be more and more indispensable as the production progressed. Far from a CGI character with a human voice, Gollum was a synthesis of embodied materiality and computational informatics (Abbott, 2006).

The specificities of Andy Serkis' physical body had one more extremely important impact on building Gollum: as Serkis became more and more the template for Gollum and motion-capture commenced it was discovered that the CGI model of Gollum, so painstakingly created at the outset of the production, did not accurately reflect enough of Andy Serkis. The Gollum digital model had a virtual physiology, but Andy Serkis had a real one, and in motion-capture, Serkis' movements would not line up with the

Figure 9.2   Andy Serkis/Gollum in *Lord of the Rings: The Two Towers Extended Edition DVD* (Peter Jackson, 2003).

pre-Serkis model. Thus, very late in the production of *The Two Towers*, Peter Jackson requested the digital Gollum be rebuilt and remodeled using more of Serkis as a template. The rebuilding occurred and Andy Serkis' physical movement became the direct driving force behind the digital character. Significantly, the motion-capture team started to think of this process as *performance* capture:

> Performance capture is the soul and essence of a realistic digital character's emotion. This is because there is a deep unconscious level of bonding that we invest into another human or creature with human emotions. We are so trained to read each other's actions that inconsistency in a character's performance can mean the end of the vested connection that an audience has maintained with an emotionally realistic digital character. (Remington Scott, 2003, p. 19)

Thus through detailed performance capture, and exceptional keyframe animation to make Gollum's face as emotive as possible, Gollum was brought to life.[5] Rather than being the avatar of an actorless character, as was feared in discussions of the synthespian, the combination of Andy Serkis' on-screen work, voice recording, and motion-capture labour meant that he spent more time 'acting' in various capacities than most of the other cast involved in the epic production. As Dan North argues in his detailed examination of synthespians, Gollum is 'not a replacement of the human by its simulacrum but a convergence, an interdependence between the human and the machine, the digital and the analogue, the real and the simulated' (2008, pp. 182–183). Gollum, then, is an iconic artificial person in that he is a synthesis of material embodiment, creative talent, computational power, and digital artistry, all realised on screen in a single, emotionally and physically believable performance.

While the characters of Middle Earth include artificial people, what of the environments themselves? The largest and most elaborate scene and setting took place on Pelennor Fields, but as Peter Jackson explains in the *Return of the King: Extended Edition* (Pellerin, 2004):

> The actual full Pelennor Fields doesn't exist, and never did exist. So, the only option that we really had was to create it in a computer. We created a virtual location. In fact, Alan Lee . . . drove a lot of the creation of the virtual landscape. He had the whole Pelennor Fields environment absolutely in his head, obviously from the days of having to do watercolour paintings.

Pelennor Fields uses elements drawn from all over New Zealand; mountains from one location, grass fields from another, clouds and weather shot across the two islands, and so forth. These were all stored for use in Weta's database, creating a digital index from which Pelennor Fields could be built. Indeed, in describing Peter Jackson's notes for the battle on Pelennor Fields, co-producer Rick Porras recalls that he 'wanted everything, everything in the Weta Digital arsenal, to be thrown at our heroes' (Pellerin, 2004). Pelennor Fields itself was composited and modelled into a fully navigable three-dimensional space in which cameras could be placed in any position, just like a material setting. All the characters and sets for the White City were composited in, while Massive was also pushed to its limit with over 350,000 Orcs and other soldiers created. Illustrating that technology is not necessarily anthropocentric, motion-captured equine data also allowed Massive to also create and drive over 6000 horses during the climactic battle for the White City. Sean Cubitt argues that 'digital technologies promise to elevate fantasy worlds above the troublesome everyday world' (Cubitt, 2004, p. 247), and while he was linking the recent spate of fantasy films such as *Lord of the Rings*, *Harry Potter*, and C. S. Lewis' *The Chronicles of Narnia* to a depoliticised cinema—perhaps with some fairness since their popularity became particularly evident in the aftermath of 11 September 2001—it is notable that even this fantasy world is still attached to the material everyday, just in segments. In his seminal work on new media, Lev Manovich argues that 'database and narrative are natural enemies' (Manovich, 2001, p. 225). However, while Pelennor Fields is a database-facilitated virtual location, it does not erase New Zealand's landscapes so much as reify them. Moreover, as Stephen Price notes, reconfiguring visual elements is something sound editors have been doing for the entire history of sound cinema, so 'the cinematic image is merely catching up to where sound has long been. Few of the sounds one hears in a movie originate at the point of filming or have not been subject to further processes' (2004, p. 30). The database may be a part of the process, but the use of that database does not amplify the division of elements; rather it emphasises the need for meaningful synthesis in order to create a landscape and inhabitants which span the informatic and material realms.

Somewhat contradictorily, Sean Cubitt also notes that 'by 2001, the pristine wilderness of Aotearoa New Zealand's South Island in *Lord of the Rings: Fellowship of the Ring* has become pure special effect' (2004, p. 265). However, as the 'New Zealand as Middle Earth' features on the DVDs, the tie-in *Lord of the Rings Location Guidebook* (Brodie, 2002) and increase in New Zealand's popularity as a tourist destination following the films suggest, along with Peter Jackson's and the cast and crew's ongoing enthusiasm about New Zealand, the films did not reduce New Zealand to a special effect, but rather special effects provocatively sampled New Zealand in a manner which encouraged many viewers to visit the physical locations themselves. If anything, tourists might be surprised to discover cars and roads littered across the unmediated New Zealand, but that, too, is a useful discovery in terms of highlighting the differences between digital environments and their physical counterparts. Nevertheless, Pelennor Fields, like so much of the *Lord of the Rings* production, is part of an artificial cinema which links the material world with the art of digital processing, allowing that space to be populated by artificial people of various forms. Moreover, as seen in Chapter 6 of this volume, the recombinant spaces of Middle Earth are of tactical value in building a narrative location for artificial people and in facilitating an artificial cinema which highlights both fantastical spectacle and the very real material world of New Zealand.

From the Cave Troll through to the armies and horses generated by Massive and the fully realised artificial person in a leading role, the production of the *Lord of the Rings* cinematic adaptation highlights the links between the fleshy specificities of embodiment and the magic manipulability of digital art. Massive highlights the role of simulated agents and begs the question about their own proto-personhood, while Gollum's nuanced characterisation and visual form is the very avatar of a cinema of synthesis and symbiosis where the material and the computational work together to facilitate the magic of cinema. As Cubitt (2004) argues, escaping total cinema is about allowing the conversations and communication to be re-established between the silver screen and the world outside it. The artificial cinema of the *Lord of the Rings* and the artificial people who populate it go a long way toward etching exactly the cinematic form for which Cubitt is searching.

ARTIFICIAL PEOPLE

In film theorist Vivian Sobchack's *Carnal Thoughts*, she argues for the inextricable importance of bodies in making meaning from, and during, the cinematic experience, championing 'the embodied and radically material nature of human existence and thus the lived body's essential implication in making "meaning" out of bodily "sense"' (2004, p. 1). While Sobchack's phenomenology of cinema maps the traffic in bodily meaning between viewers and the screen, this chapter has built upon a similarly intense desire to highlight the importance of embodiment but from the other side of the screen, in terms of the inspiration, production, meaning, screening, and selling of blockbuster films. In examining the *Matrix* franchise, it quickly became apparent that the narrative world and state-of-the-art special effects—most notably the 'bullet-time' sequences—*highlighted* the symbiotic relationship between the fleshiness of specific embodiment and the expansiveness of digital technology. The bullet-time effects, far from erasing the body, linger upon the physical form. At a narrative level, Neo's role as the digital messiah is entirely premised on his body and technology operating with a level of synchronicity that leads to a transformative conclusion but, as Erik Davis argues, it is an 'ultimately spiritual transcendence that, in the film's basic twist, is actually embodiment' (2002, p. 20). In the post-September 11 shift in the franchise's sympathies to a more balanced view of potentially 'othered' machine life, *Reloaded* and *Revolutions* point not just to the visual surfaces of bodies, but to the depths of bodily interiority and the depths of intelligent machines. The seeming oxymoron of the intercorporeality of cinematic characters builds a fuller comprehension of the changes in meaning and materiality that the *Matrix* trilogy provocatively highlights in the nexus of material bodies and digital technologies. Alongside the artificialities mapped in previous chapters, the examination of the *Matrix* franchise illustrates the emergence of artificial people who exist at the intersection of embodiment and technology, working, ultimately, for a sustained symbiotic relationship between the two at both personal and cultural levels.

In examining the narratives of Artificial Life, embodied meaning, and digital spectacle that combine to form Weta Digital's production tales in the making of the *Lord of the Rings* film trilogy, artificial people are also evident. In the construction of the Cave Troll and a host of other creatures, the processes combine the best of physical production and digital artistry through the focal arrangement of embodied form. The Massive software system highlighted the acting potential of Artificial Life, but only when equipped with weaponry, armour, and algorithms based in the material world. Pelennor Fields presented a fully realised virtual realm built using a digital database, but challenged the new media logic of the database, highlighting its role in linking the physical and informatic realms, not separating them. Most notably, Andy Serkis and the team at Weta Digital took the physicality of an actor, the informatics of material acting via motion-capture, and the best of computer-based keyframe animation to facilitate an artificial person who, by many standards, gave the finest performance of anyone in the *Lord of the Rings* trilogy. Gollum *is* an iconic representation of both artificiality and state-of-the-art special effects in the twenty-first century which works on a principle of the symbiosis of material and digital forms, with embodied meaning as their organisational framework.

This exploration of artificiality in the *Matrix* and *Lord of the Rings* films has wrestled with Sean Cubitt's notion of a twentieth-century cinema effect where the operations of commodity culture govern commercial cinema production and render the resulting films politically toothless. This and the preceding chapter have sought to highlight the political utility of early twenty-first century blockbusters, and their related texts, in addressing the important questions of embodiment, subjectivity, technology, informatics, and the many potential intersections between these realms. While mapping artificial people occasionally resorts to the rhetoric of subjectivity in order to highlight their personhood, the very existence of artificial people points to the dramatic destabilisation of a subject/object distinction. Working with a broad definition of science fiction that includes fantasy and horror, J. P. Telotte's reminder about the influence of cinema is telling:

> Yet with their emphasis on artifice in its broadest sense—on the creations of science, technology, various mechanisms—and an increasing fascination of our own level of constructedness, our science fiction films often seem to blur that distinction between life and artifice . . . and they proceed to interrogate that very blurred boundary. (1995, p. 2)

The speculative and spectacular elements of the films analysed, and the emergent entities inhabiting both their narratives and special effects, have given rise to the symbiotic conjunctions that are artificial people. Their politics of connectivity in some fashion re-energises the politics of cinema and, following Cubitt's argument that cinema must rediscover the 'meaningful fourth dimension, that of communication,' the politics of artificial people, inhabiting an artificial cinema, is, if nothing else, about starting new conversations, and finding common ground, between the realms of embodiment, physicality, technology, and informatics while still enjoying the pleasures and perversities of the blockbuster film.

Part V

Artificial Culture

10 Before the Mourning

SCREENING SEPTEMBER 11

The long shadow of 11 September 2001 and, in particular, the collapse of the World Trade Center Towers in the aftermath of terrorist attacks, continue to have global ramifications in political, military, and ethical terms. It is therefore no surprise that at the 74th Annual Academy Awards ("74th Annual Academy Awards," 2002), Hollywood and the entertainment industry *en masse* took great pains to carefully and strategically position themselves in relation to an event in which the number of deaths paled in comparison to the symbolic power of an attack on the city at the very heart of the American Dream. There was no shortage of actors and filmmakers willing to speak on the importance of the power of film in such times; Tom Cruise did an evocative job delivering a well-scripted speech which included the lines:

> My actor friends said to me, what are we doing? Is it important? What of a night like tonight? Should we celebrate the joy and magic movies bring? Well, dare I say it: *more than ever.*

Cruise continued to evoke the 'magic' of cinema as both an imaginative and potentially healing space. Whoopi Goldberg, the host for that ceremony, then introduced New York's most notable filmmaker, Woody Allen, who in his own rambling fashion gave a far less scripted and more personal plea for the ongoing importance of New York as a location where films should be set and films should still be made. Allen also introduced a four-minute tribute film to New York seen through the eyes of films set there over the course of a century. The sequence was edited together by Nora Ephron, famous for such romantic comedies as *Sleepless in Seattle* (1993) which treats New York as the emotional heart of America. Ephron's New York montage featured clips which lingered on iconic landmarks such as the Empire State and Chrysler buildings as well as the Brooklyn Bridge and Central Park. However, the core of the piece emphasised the individuals and the dreamers who constitute the city, with clips from musicals with Gene Kelly and Frank Sinatra singing New York's praises in *On the Town* (Donen & Kelly, 1949), through to John Travolta's frenetic breakout film *Saturday Night Fever* (Badham, 1977). Comedies including *Tootsie* (Pollack, 1982), *Ghost*

Busters (Reitman, 1984), and Melanie Griffiths' *Working Girl* (Nichols, 1988) all got a few seconds' screen time, with even science fiction making an impact with both *Men in Black* (Sonnenfeld, 1997) and the original *King Kong* (Cooper & Schoedsack, 1933) with the giant ape atop the Empire State Building. The clip ended with a line from Mel Brooks' feature debut *The Producers* (1968): 'I want everything I've ever seen in the movies!' While the short film did a fine job in evoking the power of New York as cinematic space, what was most notable was the powerful absence of the Twin Towers from any of these clips. Ephron and the Academy re-visioned a New York not so much mourning the Twin Towers, but rather one in which the World Trade Center had never fallen as it had simply never existed. Through one of the filmmaker's oldest magic-making tools, the power of montage, the cinematic enactment of the American Dream was re-deployed, escaping the seemingly omnipresent mourning of what can easily be called the Western world's 'Long September' by erasing and denying those traumatic signifiers in their entirety. Of equal if not greater importance, the Academy was far from alone in erasing the Twin Towers.

In the months following September 11, a number of Hollywood releases and television shows were either digitally edited to remove images of the Twin Towers, substantially re-shot to insert new footage, or shelved with their release dates moved back anywhere from three months to six months. *Zoolander* (Stiller, 2001), *Serendipity* (Chelsom, 2002), *People I Know* (Algrant, 2002), *Spider-Man* (Raimi, 2002), and *Men in Black II* (Sonnenfeld, 2002), all in post-production at the time of the attacks, either digitally removed the Towers from backgrounds and New York skylines or, in the most extensive case, the producers of *Men in Black II* re-shot an entire sequence in order to move that film's climax from the World Trade Center to the Chrysler Building. Films and television series with terrorist themes and images such as Arnold Schwarzenegger's *Collateral Damage* (A. Davis, 2002) or the ironically 'real time' television phenomenon *24* (2001–2010) both had their release dates pushed back months to demonstrate 'sensitivity' to the US's national trauma (Schneider, 2004).[1] A ubiquitous and yet unofficial cultural taboo saw the Twin Towers, for all intents and purposes, cease to exist in mainstream new-release visual media. Those few films engaging with the ramifications of the attacks, such as Spike Lee's *25th Hour* (2002) or the collaborative global reactions of *11'09"01—September 11* (Makhmalbaf et al., 2002), did so in a roundabout fashion, either relying on shooting locations outside of the US, or relocating the cultural trauma as character-specific personal pain. The obvious exception to this ban was the 'real' news footage of the planes impacting the Towers and their subsequent collapse. This oft-repeated footage became the *only* footage, reinforcing a CNN or Fox News view of these events in an almost universal fashion (at least in terms of Western mainstream media). Outside of the news media, with regard to the Twin Towers, the trauma of September 11 ostensibly initiated a strategy of non-representation across the spectrum of the mainstream entertainment industries. However, the comic book industry has long existed at the threshold of the mainstream, with incredibly iconic characters which circulate throughout popular culture but actual comic sales remain comparatively low. This niche status allows comic books to be more risky, and their engagement with the immediate aftermath of September 11 was far bolder than that of Hollywood or the television studios (Jenkins, 2006a). Like many of the Marvel characters, Spider-Man's long comic history has always been set in New York City, and thus provided an important framework in which to engage with the contested impact of September 11. This chapter specifically examines the way the Spider-Man comics provided a space of engagement and mourning soon after the Twin Towers fell. Importantly, this exploration is contextualised within the decades of Spider-Man's ongoing tale as a New Yorker. Moreover, while the comics provide what I am arguing is a space of artificial mourning, they also directly inform the parameters of the related feature films. In the following, final chapter, I will argue further that digital effects and the silver screen further amplify the deep ties between Spider-Man and New York City, situating the *Spider-Man* trilogy (Raimi, 2002, 2004, 2007) as part of an artificial culture, a culture evident in the films through the lens of artificial mourning.

SPIDER-MAN AND NEW YORK CITY

According to Bradford Wright in his history of comic books in America, when Stan Lee and Steve Ditko originally envisioned Spider-Man in 1962, he was not a man of steel, nor a billionaire with a chip on his shoulder and a high-tech utility belt, but rather 'an adolescent—one who had to contend with his own insecurities and confusion even as he had to fight the bad guys' (Wright, 2001, p. 210). When teenager Peter Parker was first bitten by a radioactive spider and gained super-human strength and agility, like most teenagers his thoughts did not immediately shift to saving the world; while aiming to financially support his aunt and uncle with whom he lived, Peter initially sought simply to make money as a performer and entertainer. He quickly became arrogant, so much so that after one show he failed to lift a finger when a criminal stole the takings, claiming it was not his problem. Later, however, when Peter's uncle was killed, he discovered that the murderer was the same person who had robbed the show. Wracked with guilt and shame at his uncle's death, Peter Parker pledged to fight against injustice, and the coda 'with great power comes great responsibility' was born (Wright, 2001, pp. 210–211). However, unlike Superman or Batman, the best-selling superheroes at the time, Peter Parker's Spider-Man did not inhabit a fictional Metropolis or dark Gotham, but rather lived and fought in the very city Stan Lee saw outside the window as he wrote: New York (Bukatman, 2003, p. 206). Spider-Man, along with other

Marvel characters like the *Fantastic Four*, who live in their own New York skyscraper, or *Daredevil* who comes New York's poorer streets, are 'products of the city but are "super" in that they can transcend those limitations (of gridlock, crime, and other urban constraints) that the city places on the rest of us' (Bainbridge, 2010, p. 168). Spider-Man quickly became Marvel Comics' most recognisable icon, a teenage everyman living in the same city as many of *Spider-Man*'s readers. Moreover, far more so than his precursors for whom superheroism was their essence, Peter Parker's everyday life was central to the story both as he struggled with his Spider-Man alter ego and as he tried to make ends meet as a photographer for one of New York's less reputable papers, *The Daily Bugle*. His personal life, and especially love life, often was as much a selling point for the comics as his plentiful and colourful nemeses. Peter Parker and Spider-Man were both intrinsically tied to the city in which their lives took place.

Comic book superheroes are often more deeply tied to their cities and surrounds than characters in non-visual narratives. Moreover, that tie is not just conceptual, but rather a link at the level of embodiment. As Scott Bukatman argues, Spider-Man's superhero body is the 'consequence of technology run wild. The superhero body is everything—a *corporeal*, rather than a *cognitive*, mapping of the subject into a cultural system', and that system is visualised through the cityscape (2003, p. 49). Just as New York City's grids and skyscrapers are an icon of modernity and technological progress, Spider-Man's journey above the streets, subverting and re-negotiating the concrete grid, both extend and challenge the limits of modernism. As Bukatman argues:

> Superhero comics embody the grace of the city; superheroes are graced by the city. Through the superhero, we gain a freedom of movement not constrained by the ground-level order imposed by the urban grid. (2003, p. 188)

With a corporeality no longer anchored to the street, nor to the mundane horizontal, the numerous artists on the Spider-Man comic books can draw walls as floors and the space above the street, between buildings, as frantic pathways. Indeed, Bukatman explicitly links Spider-Man's abilities and relationship to the city with Michel de Certeau's (1984) tactics of spatiality; Spider-Man forges his own pathways, transforming the metropolitan grid of place and modernity into tactical spaces of the struggling, embodied subject (Bukatman, 2003, p. 207). The New York envisioned in the *Spider-Man* comics is thus a pre-digital artificial space, with the potential for resistance and the blurring of boundaries. Like William Gibson's Walled City in *Idoru*, discussed in Chapter 6, this volume, New York is a tactical space which can be navigated and, to a considerable extent, reconfigured through the embodied movement, motion, and meaning of a comic book hero.

Spider-Man's New York is not just an artificial space in terms of the sub-jectivity of Peter Parker, but is also inextricably intertwined with the politics of the material world. In the late 1960s and early 1970s, the counterculture and America's involvement in the Vietnam War had a marked impact on Peter Parker's comic book life. At Columbia University he had to weigh up the odds between striking students and an inflexible, but lawful, Dean over the issue of affordable student accommodation (Wright, 2001, p. 234). In 1970 Spider-Man battled a corrupt New York District Attorney and was forced to reflect on the difference between law and justice (Wright, 2001, p. 238). Also that year Stan Lee agreed to incorporate a strong anti-drug mes-sage into the *Spider-Man* stories which resulted not only in Spider-Man's battle with drug dealers but also Peter Parker's best friend developing a drug habit after a romantic relationship turned sour. The two-part story clearly depicted drug use, something not allowed under the comics code, but Stan Lee pushed ahead and published without the code's endorsement (Wright, 2001, pp. 239–240). However, throughout these turbulent years Spider-Man was still written as youthful and, even in the face of grave dif-ficulties, optimistic. It was not until 1973 that Spider-Man, and the world of Marvel superheroes, lost their last vestiges of innocence.

Gwen Stacy was Peter Parker's first love, and the girl many fans expected would eventually become Mrs Spider-Man. For more than a decade, Peter Parker and Gwen had been romantically linked in some fashion, but she remained unaware of Peter's alter-ego. When Spider-Man's arch-enemy the Green Goblin discovered who Peter Parker really was, he kidnapped Gwen. Atop the George Washington Bridge,[2] the Goblin held Gwen and waited for Spider-Man. When Peter arrived and the inevitable battle began, Gwen was knocked off the bridge, but Spider-Man managed to snag her leg with his webbing just before she hit the ground. However, in *Amazing Spider-Man* number 121 (Conway & Kane, 1973), in the panel where Gwen's rapid descent is brought to an abrupt halt, the word 'SNAP' appears next to Gwen's limp form. When Spider-Man pulls Gwen back to the top of the bridge, he is jubilant thinking that, as superheroes were always supposed to, he had saved the damsel in distress. However, Spider-Man soon discov-ers that Gwen Stacy is dead and that he may very well have killed her, hav-ing snapped her spine by breaking her fall too quickly. As Arnold Blumberg argues, this one event ended the 'Silver Age' of the comic book superhero:

> The death of Gwen Stacy was the end of innocence for the series and the superhero genre in general—a time when a defeated hero could not save the girl, when fantasy merged uncomfortably with reality, and mortality was finally visited on the world of comics. To coin a cliché, nothing would ever be the same. . . . Gwen Stacy's death was undoubt-edly the end of an era, a tectonic jolt that shook the superhero genre out of one cemented cycle of cause and effect and into a new paradigm

that better reflected the socio-political and cultural sensibilities of its readers. (2003)

Gwen's death and the effective 'failure' of Marvel's most recognisable comic book hero was a dark moment in Marvel history and ushered in a much grittier era of comic book writing. The guilt of Gwen's death haunted the *Spider-Man* books for decades, even after he later fell in love with Mary-Jane Watson. In the mid-nineties a graphic novel entitled *Marvels* (Busiek & Ross, 1994) revisits the classical moments in the Marvel's universe through the eyes of a photographer whose career follows the 'marvels' in action. Significantly, Busiek and Ross end their series with a stunningly painted and re-told version of Gwen Stacy's death falling from a New York bridge, showing that more than two decades later this was still *the* historic moment for the Marvel universe, and a moment which deeply tied Spider-Man's losses to the city of New York. Indeed, as Jason Bainbridge argues, '*Marvels* confirmed New York's status as a character as important as any other in Marvel's pantheon' (2010, p. 171).

Given Spider-Man's strong links to the city, it was no surprise when the promotional campaign for the first *Spider-Man* feature film was constructed around New York landmarks. The film was scheduled for release in May 2002, and advertising hit full momentum in August 2001 with a series of posters and one of the most expensive trailers ever made. In it, technologically-savvy robbers plunder a New York bank and begin to escape in a helicopter, only for it to mysteriously stop mid-flight and then get yanked backward. The helicopter finally stops and is snared in a gigantic spider web hung between the Twin Towers of the World Trade Center. The scene then cuts to the first ever visual of a computer-generated imagery (CGI) Spider-Man with the Twin Towers clearly reflected in his mirrored eyes, before he swings into the cityscape at full speed. Less than a month after the trailer began playing in cinemas it was removed by Sony Entertainment, the film's distributors, the day following the terrorist attacks on the US (Jones, 2009). In a CNN article published on September 13, Columbia TriStar's president of marketing, Geoffrey Ammer, stated, 'The decision [to pull the trailer] was an easy one. [. . .] It's based on humanity. No cost can outweigh the sensitivity of the issue' (CNN Entertainment, 2001). While sensitivity in the immediate aftermath of the fall of the Twin Towers is understandable, it is noteworthy that despite three *Spider-Man* films to date released on DVD, replete with extra material from across the history of the comics and films, the World Trade Center trailer is not amongst them. Nor has the trailer even been officially discussed since 13 September 2001 by Columbia TriStar or their owners, Sony Entertainment. The first *Spider-Man* trailer is as much a ghost as the Twin Towers themselves. However, while one aspect of the Spider-Man franchise was effectively erased to avoid any mention of the tragedy, the Marvel comic books went in the other direction.

Figure 10.1   The death of Gwen Stacy in Kurt Busiek and Alex Ross, *Marvels*, 1994. Spider-Man © and TM Marvel Entertainment LLC, all rights reserved and used with permission.

Figure 10.2 The original *Spider*-Man trailer. Columbia Pictures, 2001.

Amazing Spider-Man number thirty-six, released with a cover date of December 2001, came with a completely black cover with nothing visible other than the outline of the comic book's title. The first page read: 'We interrupt our regularly scheduled program to bring you the following Special Bulletin' (Straczynski & Romita, 2001, p. 1). This notice positioned readers within a televisual frame of expectation wherein images of the Twin Towers could still be found, but what the following pages contained was a tribute story to the firefighters, the police women and men, the service personnel, and every other person who helped in the immediate wake of the September 11 tragedy. On page two, as *Spider-Man* arrives at 'Ground Zero' crying bystanders ask 'Where were you?', 'How could you let this happen?', on which he reflects, 'How do you say we didn't know? We couldn't know. We couldn't imagine'. The following story sees the rest of the staple Marvel superheroes arrive at Ground Zero, help out with the clean-up and rescue attempts, and show their deep respect for the 'real' heroes. In an important scene, an exhausted and grim Spider-Man is drinking water with other emergency workers, his mask peeled half-way up, revealing the face of an ordinary New Yorker. In the last panel of that page, Peter Parker laments, 'I have seen other worlds, other spaces. I have walked with gods and wept with angels. But to my shame, I have no answers' (Straczynski & Romita, 2001, p. 15). The Marvel universe has always existed alongside the 'real' world, and the world of superheroes has still existed in *parallel* to our own, with a similar cityscape but populated by different people, aliens, super-villains, and superheroes; the sudden intersection of the comic book realm with 'real' world events was a substantial change for Marvel (Bainbridge, 2010). While it might be suggested that the *Amazing Spider-Man* issue really served to cynically infuse the Marvel superheroes with some of the positive glow which had been bestowed by the news media onto the service people working at 'Ground Zero', a more important point is that the story ends championing tolerance, not vengeance. The comic emphasises the role of superheroes alongside New York in its mourning, including statements such as: 'But we are here. Now. With you', emphasising the shared grief between the Marvel universe and the material world. More politically charged, however, was the dialogue 'We live in each blow you strike for infinite justice, but always in the hope of infinite wisdom', implicitly critiquing the invasion of Afghanistan which was codenamed 'Infinite Justice'. Similarly, his line, 'And All Wars have innocents' is far from a rallying cry for military action (Straczynski & Romita, 2001, p. 18). As Henry Jenkins (2006a) argues, comic books rarely have a single meaning, but can open up spaces to re-negotiate and scrutinise political and cultural issues; the September 11 tribute issue, if nothing else, invited readers to consider their own responses to a very recent and raw tragedy.

Throughout the fifty years that Spider-Man has been a central figure in the Marvel comic book universe, the ties between the awkward hero and New York City deepened exponentially. From Peter Parker's earliest

Figure 10.3   Spider-Man at Ground Zero in J. Michael Straczynski and John Romita Jr., *Amazing Spider-Man*, 36, 2001. Spider-Man © and TM Marvel Entertainment LLC, all rights reserved and used with permission.

incarnations in the 1960s his superhero persona was never the only story; the angst-ridden everyman under the mask always part of the comic book's massive appeal. The man and the hero were not linked just through narrative, but through the visually embodied relationship between the superhero and the spatiality of the cityscape itself, a relationship which situates the imagined New York as artificial space. Spider-Man's growing pains in the late '60s and early '70s mirrored Western culture, but the trauma and loss signified by Gwen Stacy's death cemented Peter Parker's trauma to New York City. In the marketing and pre-release versions of a filmic Spider-Man, the fall of the Twin Towers and their erasure from entertainment media was directly mirrored by an expensive but ghostly trailer that almost never was. At the same time, the memorial comic book reinforces the links between Spider-Man and the mourning citizens of New York. With those connections in mind, the following chapter turns to the *Spider-Man* film trilogy and their role as a cinematic site of artificial mourning.

11 Artificial Mourning
Spider-Man, Special Effects, and September 11

The trilogy of *Spider-Man* feature films (Raimi, 2002, 2004, 2007) is set in New York, although it is neither an historically accurate representation nor the comic book version, but a third cityscape which imaginatively borrows and builds on both of these precursors. This chapter argues that within that context, the *Spider-Man* films enact a form of artificial mourning, acting as a popular cultural arena in which some of the immediate tensions and traumas of the post-September 11 Western world are articulated and explored. From the outset, it is important to flag that the term artificial mourning is not necessarily positioning mourning facilitated through popular culture as 'unreal' or necessarily 'less' than trauma in the 'real' world. Rather, the 'artificial' in this term is consistent with deploying the artificial not as a marker of the unreal, but rather as a signifier of unstable boundaries, where easy binary divisions no longer make sense. The artificial blurs the divisions between human subject and technological object, between entertainment and politics, and between good and evil. Artificial mourning is an invitation to engage with the Western world's 'Long September' in myriad forms rather than via a single solution or perspective on those tragic events. It is with those ambiguities in mind that the *Spider-Man* films come into focus as character, franchise, and cultural icon. Spider-Man's artificiality is evident in the seeming incompatibilities of being both a human subject and a technological object, being both a hero and an everyday person with everyday problems, and being both a means of escapism for audiences, while engaging on some level with serious political and cultural concerns. Moreover, the movies situate Spider-Man and his various nemeses as artificial people in that they are products of substantial technological transformation, whether purposefully or through accidents. Ideas and meaning not only are negotiated at the level of narrative, but also are realised through the connectivity of Peter Parker and Spider-Man with technologies and through the computer-generated imagery (CGI) of the visualised New York cityscape itself.

The graphics forming the title sequence for the first *Spider-Man* film, released in the American summer of 2002, immediately link Spider-Man and the sprawling metropolitan cityscape of New York. The images in the credits begin with spider webs as vectors, outlining the elements of Spider-Man's visualised corporeality, then showing the reds and blues of Spider-Man's upper body, bent with head bowed. The sequence then shifts to showing Spider-Man crawling along a skyscraper rendered in the same colours, hues, and with similar grid lines. Indeed, the similarity between Spider-Man's CGI costume and the visualised city suggests that the same grid lines at one point form the city, and at another are stretched around a human, forming a heroic costume. Significantly, as viewers see the last few images of the city, the buildings share the blues and blacks of Spider-Man's costume and reflect the reds in the windows, but a red glow is also visible on the horizon, a vista New York experienced the night the Twin Towers fell. These opening credits immediately link the superhero and the city-scape, intertwining their visual depictions and positing a shared ontology. Spiderman, from the outset, embodies New York.

In updating Spider-Man's origin story, the first film quickly goes about 'consolidating multiple decades of comic book continuity' while simultane-ously situating him in the twenty-first century (Walton, 2008, p. 98). Thus, during a visit to a Columbia University research facility, Peter's geek creden-tials are displayed as he almost drools to his friend Harry Osborne, 'That's the largest electron microscope on the Eastern Seaboard'. The class is intro-duced to a series of genetically engineered super-spiders which combine the skills of various species of spider. Rather than the 1960s technological bug-bear of radiation, in the early twenty-first century as Peter Parker is acci-dentally bitten by one of the super-spiders, the origins of Spider-Man are linked with one of the most contentious contemporary technologies, genetic engineering. For the inattentive viewer, the computer screens behind Peter during this scene labour the exposition, displaying recombinant DNA and flashing the words 'New Species'. When Peter awakens the next day after a feverish night, he discovers the he is stronger, faster, and can shoot webbing from glands in his wrists. In the comic books Parker create his web-shooters mechanically, but making them corporeal extensions both emphasises 'the organic constitution of the heroic body' and suggests deeper ties between embodied meaning and technological change (North, 2008, p. 167). From the outset, Spider-Man is thus a fusion of technologies and embodiment, a carnal superhero whose technological origins are also as much cross-spe-cies as they are digital. Nevertheless, the synthesis of origins, technologies, and species clearly marks Spider-Man as an artificial person.

It is worth noting, however, that the film does not unproblematically embrace new technologies, as it also emphasises the difficulties entailed in adapting to the challenges of technological change. In the first scene with Peter Parker's Uncle Ben, viewers discover that Ben has been fired after a lifetime's employment as an electrician. Looking through the employment section of the newspaper, he laments that the advertisements all seek expe-rience with digital technologies: 'Computer salesman, computer engineer, computer analyst—My lord, even the computers need analysts these days!

I'm too old for computers'. The technologies that facilitated the artificial origins of Spider-Man also hamper Peter's family. More significantly in terms of the symbolic links with technology, once Peter Parker has become Spider-Man, he no longer visibly engages with digital technologies. Despite being a science whiz and showing knowledge of the latest technologies, Peter never wields anything more advanced than a manual camera throughout the trilogy (Koh, 2009). While this change is at odds with Peter's characterization in the comic books, it does emphasise that for Spider-Man technologies are an inescapable part of life, but their utility and politics are determined through use, and are not intrinsic. It also makes the exact chronological setting of the films ambiguous, nodding towards the many historical periods in which Spider-Man's tale has been retold (Koh, 2009). Moreover, while Spider-Man does not diegetically use digital technologies, viewers would be well aware that in many scenes Spider-Man *is* the product of the latest CGI techniques and digital technology. Although updating his hybrid origins, the films implicitly link Spider-Man and technology through the character's diegetic ontology and the CGI facilitating Spider-Man's amazing abilities, but rather than overemphasising the character's technological status, his lack of visible engagement with advanced technologies situates technology as a part of everyday life. Spider-Man is about a balance between the growing pains of adolescence, responsibility, and an amazing but simultaneously banal engagement with technology. In effect, the films epistemologically situate artificial people such as Spider-Man not as differentiated 'technological' entities, but rather, as simply one of New York's eight million citizens.

Just as Peter Parker became Spider-Man through engagement with the latest technologies, so too does his first nemesis, the Green Goblin. In *Spider-Man*, Norman Osborne, a millionaire businessman half-way between Donald Trump and Victor Frankenstein, is about to lose a massive military commission to create both military hardware and nanotechnological 'performance enhancers', designed to increase the abilities of humans in order to use their military devices. Despite their digital origins, performance enhancers sound like, and appear similar to, steroids and other performance-enhancing drugs, a symbolism reinforced by the need to ingest the enhancers. However, given the disdain the *Spider-Man* comic books have historically shown towards drug use, their use is unsurprisingly not without dramatic consequences. When Osborne pushes human trials of the enhancers forward, using himself as the guinea pig, he develops a megalomaniac split-personality, steals the military tools including bombs and a human-sized glider, and becomes the Green Goblin. The Goblin's visceral desires and disdain for human life are dark mirrors of Peter Parker's struggle to protect innocent life in the wake of his uncle's tragic death. In Slavoj Žizek's reflections on September 11 he argues that part of the horror of the attacks was that their incomprehensibility or otherness revealed a far deeper trauma, in that even in terms of terrorism, 'every feature attributed to the Other is already present at the very heart of the USA' (Žizek, 2002b, p. 43). If, as this chapter argues, *Spider-Man* offers an allegorical engagement with the trauma of September 11, it is highly significant that the Other that Spider-Man must defeat shares very similar origins: he is a New York citizen whose engagement with advanced technologies had unintended consequences, giving him abilities beyond the norms of everyday corporeality. In many ways, the battle between Spider-Man and the Green Goblin, both artificial people, is as much a battle between similarities as it is between differences.

The *Spider-Man* films also present the relationship with media technologies as ambiguous and often problematic. Peter Parker gets his first financial break in New York by using a timer function to capture pictures of himself in action as Spider-Man and selling them to the disreputable newspaper *The Daily Bugle* and its enigmatic editor J. Jonah Jameson. Although Jameson is in some ways a sympathetic character, as editor of the *Bugle* he happily pays for Peter's images, but then completely ignores the context in which they were taken, adding his own sensationalised words and headings. While a picture is often said to be worth a thousand words, the *Bugle* shows that context can change which thousand words are heard. From a picture of Spider-Man simply scaling a wall, Jameson extracts a headline such as 'Big Apple Dreads Spider Bite!' As Marcia Landy (2004), among others, has argued, the news media played a large role in both portraying and formulating the initial responses to September 11. Just as the news media footage of the Twin Towers collapsing were the only sanctioned images, the media commentators who ran these segments were given considerable influence in shaping the national response. Moreover, after the US invaded Iraq in an incursion ostensibly justified by Saddam Hussein's terrorist ambitions and never-found weapons of mass destruction, months later the reflections on how the media built public support for this action led to some serious ethical questions being asked about journalistic integrity. In that context, *The Daily Bugle* is something of a symptom of irresponsible, sensationalist news media. In the first film this antagonism is disheartening for Peter, but the photographs pay the bills so he puts up with it. In *Spider-Man 2* the constant badgering from the press briefly sees Peter Parker decide to give up on superheroism altogether. Thus, the power and influence of media is both highlighted and, to an extent, critiqued in the *Spider-Man* films.

One of the core links facilitating the allegorical utility of the films is the entwining of the figure of Spider-Man and the New York cityscape. In the previous chapter, Spider-Man's ties to the city were explored as enacted in the comic books, but through CGI and other techniques, the films further amplify these links. As feminist philosopher Elizabeth Grosz argues, the links between corporeality and cities run deep:

> The body, however, is not distinct from the city for they are mutually defining. . . . there may be an isomorphism between the body and city.

> But it is not a mirroring of nature in artifice; rather, there is a two-way linkage that could be defined as an *interface*. What I am suggesting is a model of the relations between bodies and cities that sees them, not as megalithic total entities, but as assemblages or collections of parts, capable of crossing the thresholds between substances to form linkages, machines, provisional and often temporary sub- or micro-groupings. This model is practical, based on the productivity of bodies and cities in defining and establishing each other. It is not a holistic view, one that would stress the unity and integration of city and body, their "ecological balance." Rather, their interrelations involve a fundamentally disunified series of systems, a series of disparate flows, energies, events, or entities, bringing together or drawing apart their more or less temporary alignments. (1995, p. 108)

As the opening titles attest, Spider-Man and New York share a similar grid-system, one delineating urban space, while the other is wrapped around a corporeal superhero. Building on Grosz's arguments, there are numerous other links between Spider-Man and the city. For example, when Peter first decides to accept the mantle of Spider-Man as a crimefighter and moves to New York, the initial appearance of the iconic costume seemingly emerges from the heart of the city itself. With a camera pointing upward from street level, along a busy street ending with the Empire State Building, Spider-Man bursts from the city itself, swinging down as if the streets have conjured their own embodied figure. Moreover, just as Spider-Man is frequently a CGI character, at times so, too, is the city. Many of the city streets were composited from existing footage and digital simulations, and some of the live-action photography of New York took place on the studio streets of Los Angeles. The New York of the *Spider-Man* films is thus the New York of imagination, the city whose iconography most loudly speaks of the American Dream. For Spider-Man, the city is an artificial, tactical space being navigated and interfaced with by an artificial person. It is this synthesis between the idealised New York and Spider-Man which so powerfully and symbolically links the two.

After Spider-Man first bursts into New York, a montage of his fight against crime is seen and is followed by some candid on-the-street style interviews with the city's residents who oscillate from recognising a hero to being deeply suspicious of this seemingly non-human entity. At the end of these interviews, the film cuts to an image of Spider-Man with the New York skyline reflecting in his costumed eyes. This image is extremely significant because clearly visible in that reflected city are the Twin Towers, still standing tall. Indeed, a comparison with the withdrawn original trailer for the film, as discussed in the previous chapter, shows that this is exactly the same effects shot as was used in the trailer. For two full seconds, or roughly fifty individually rendered CGI frames, the Twin Towers are reflected in the eyes of New York's own superhero. Despite the World Trade Center being absent from the film's narrative *per se*, this CGI homage to the fallen Towers clearly establishes the ties between Spider-Man and New York both before and after 11 September 2001. Moreover, the use of CGI allowed the film-makers to pay tribute to the Towers in a manner consistent with the comic books' meaningful engagement in the special tribute issue, but also in a fashion ostensibly recognising the cultural taboo against the Towers being represented at the time. The Towers survive inscribed onto the body of Spider-Man. Moreover, the image being the same one from the withdrawn original trailer directly linking both the narrative and the production of the *Spider-Man* film to the tragedy suffered by New York and its citizens.

While the *Spider-Man* films are clearly set in a science fictional world with superheroes and super-villains, the films nevertheless engage in a considerable fashion with the historical realities of September 11 and its immediate cultural aftermath. In addressing films which engage directly with historical events, Sean Cubitt argues, 'History films invite us to inhabit our own societies, cultures and nations, but to do so they must construct all three. . . . Historical film presents as complete, at origin, what it seeks to create' (2004, p. 301). History in cinema is thus always a reconstructing and visioning, never that impossibly historical dream of a reflection of unmediated events. Moreover, in analysing films which attempt to change or challenge generally accepted versions of historical events, Sean Cubitt (2004, p. 321) argues that these 'reversionary movies' often are drawn on older models of representation and depiction, such as Japanese graphic arts. In the case of *Spider-Man*, the films do not seek to re-vision the historical event of September 11, but rather address the West's Long September not just metaphorically but in an allegorical manner which, to some extent, attempts to remake the past of the Marvel comic book franchise. Following that line, the most significant re-characterisation in adapting the comics for the cinema was the character of Mary Jane Watson.

In the comic books, Peter Parker fell in love with Mary Jane only after the relationship with his first true love, Gwen Stacy, ended tragically with her shocking uncomic-like death. However, as Marvel's editor-in-chief Joe Quesada notes in a featurette on the *Spider-Man 2* DVD (Raimi, 2004), 'when they created the Mary Jane character for the movie, it's pretty obvious that there's a mixture of Gwen and Mary Jane within that character. They sort of amalgamated the two girls into one sort of idealized character'.[1] Rather than the complication of two love interests in the space of a two-hour film, in adapting the comic for the silver screen the writers and director added elements of Gwen Stacy to the character of Mary Jane. However, when Mary Jane is kidnapped by the Green Goblin and held hostage atop a New York bridge, many viewers would immediately have feared Mary Jane would actually be murdered because this scene is a replica of the moment when Gwen Stacy died in the comic books, a moment whose tragedy re-shaped the universe of Marvel superheroes. The Goblin gives Spider-Man a choice between rushing to save either Mary Jane or a tram car full of children which is about to plummet to the ground. Luckily for Peter Parker, he can think outside of binaries and manages to catch the falling Mary Jane and snag the cable car before the children die. While a well-choreographed rescue scene in itself, the powerful significance of this sequence in terms of allegorically engaging with September 11 is in the re-visioning of the *Spider-Man* films, the new Gwen Stacy does not die.[2] Rather than re-visioning the 'real' politics outside of the fictional franchise, the films re-vision the Marvel universe and re-deploy a fictional moment of tragedy deeply linked to New York. After heightening the fear of many viewers that *Spider-Man* would visualise the comic book's most shocking tragedy, the films actually re-vision a far more optimistic city where the superhero can save the damsel in distress. At an allegorical level, this shift in the adaptation of the comics imbues New York with an optimism not so much about erasing history as renegotiating a cityscape of the present, less shrouded in mourning. The artificial spaces of a revisioned New York and artificial personhood of a CGI Spider-Man facilitate a type of artificial mourning which both acknowledges New York's wounds but also points to a more hopeful future (even if located by, to some extent, re-visioning a fictional past).

The links between the *Spider-Man* film and New York's citizens are also explored in an overstated manner during the last fight sequences with the Green Goblin. As Spider-Man rescues Mary Jane and the children in the cable car, the Goblin's attack is interrupted by a group of ordinary New York citizens who throw bricks and stones at the Goblin; one screams out, 'You mess with Spidey, you messing with New York!' while another man yells, 'You mess with one of us, you mess with all of us'. In this scene, the film visualises both the direct link between Spider-Man and everyday New York citizens, and presents the idealised viewer of the film who is situated as someone experiencing a deep connection with Spider-Man in his battle with the Goblin and, more broadly, against those who would hurt New York.

These feelings and images continue when the Goblin propels Spider-Man into a building, knocking it to the ground as Spider-Man struggles to regain his composure, his mask now shredded, revealing the ordinary man under the mask. As the conflict reaches resolution amongst the rubble of fallen buildings and with Peter Parker's face apparent alongside the remains of his Spider-Man mask, this scene directly links to the special post-September 11 issue of *Amazing Spider-Man* where Peter Parker's link to the mourning New Yorkers was shown when he lifted his mask during the relief efforts. Following these blatant symbolic links, after the Goblin is defeated it is similarly telling that the last visual effects in the film show Spider-Man viewing New York from atop the Empire State Building and in the background, visible but ethereal and almost ghostly, the figures of the Twin Towers can be seen for a few moments on the distant horizon before Spider-Man swings back into his city with the American flag fluttering proudly in the background. These symbols serve to reinforce the links

Figure 11.1   Spider-Man unmasked in *Spider-Man* (Sam Raimi, 2002).

between Spider-Man, special effects, and the New York cityscape, facilitating an artificial mourning which addresses September 11 by reinvigorating certain American icons, but in the midst of a storyline which continually reinforces the mantra 'with great power, comes great responsibility'.

In *Spider-Man 2*, both the plot and the central super-villain are substantially more complicated. Whereas Norman Osborne was an arrogant capitalist who developed weapons for the military even before his transformation into the Green Goblin, in the second film Doctor Otto Octavius is actually one of Peter Parker's personal heroes. Octavius thinks he has found a way to create a stable fusion reaction that would create a functionally limitless energy source. Before his public test of the technology, Octavius meets with Peter Parker who is writing a paper on the research at university. During their conversation, Octavius reflects on the role of the scientist, telling Peter 'being brilliant's not enough young man. You have to work hard. Intelligence is not a privilege, it's a gift. And you use it for the good of mankind'. Octavius thus appears to be a genius-scientist with the best of intentions, albeit with an obviously patriarchal overconfidence and arrogance about the abilities of science and technology. In order to successfully stabilise his fusion reaction, Octavius has constructed four artificial limbs which are metallic appendages and, owing to their difficult tasks, actually have their own Artificial Intelligence to assist in the processes. In the press conference preceding the first fusion test, Octavius explains their use:

Octavius: These smart arms are controlled by my brain through a neural link. Nanowires feed directly into my cerebellum, allowing me to use these arms to control fusion reaction in an environment no human hand could enter.

Reporter: Doctor, if the Artificial Intelligence in the arms is advanced as you suggest, couldn't that make you vulnerable to them?
Octavius: How right you are. Which is why I developed this inhibitor chip to protect my higher brain function. It means I maintain control of these arms, instead of them controlling me.

Octavius' artificial limbs thus contain a physical version of Asimov's (1950) Three Laws of Robotics inasmuch as the inhibitor chip keeps the intelligence of the human user dominant, implicitly restraining the Artificial Intelligence of the manipulator arms and highlighting the possibility that the limbs may prove influential in the right circumstances. When the experiment goes awry, Octavius' wife and collaborator is killed, and the arms are fused to his body, just as the inhibitor chip is destroyed. In a state of shock, when rushed to hospital Octavius' arms take defensive action when surgeons try to cut them away from the doctor's body; instead, the arms kill the entire medical team and, to some extent, then influence the decisions and actions made by 'Doctor Octopus'. The corporeal line between 'Otto Octavius' and the intelligent limbs shatters and now multiple voices influence the actions of this one character. Octavius is clearly an artificial person through his hybridisation of technologies, Artificial Intelligence, human intelligence, and physical corporeality. However, even as a villain his motives are still driven by the idea of completing his work, although that now becomes a threat to the city since Doctor Octopus has already proven unable to control the 'power of the sun in the palm of my hand'.

Also in the second film, Peter Parker's role and faith in the ideal of heroics comes into question. Having been hounded by the media and after giving up his dream of ever being in a relationship with Mary Jane, Peter's confidence falters and his spider-powers seem to disappear. Peter develops symptoms of heroic impotence, losing his strength and agility, not to mention the ability to shoot webbing. In the first film, Spider-Man is faced with a burning building from which he must rescue a baby. In this symbolic re-enactment of September 11, Spider-Man is shown alongside the firefighters and police officers of New York, sharing their heroism and their links with the city. However, in *Spider-Man 2*, in an attempted act of heroism, a Peter Parker without the benefit of spider-powers is faced with a very similar scenario, and while he manages to rescue a child, he is told by thankful firefighters that someone else was burnt to death on the fourth floor; a death Spider-Man might have prevented, but Peter Parker could not. Significantly, these performance issues and confused ideas of heroism occur in a social context where America's continued presence in Iraq and Afghanistan, alongside a widespread questioning of the political and ethical justification of the incursion, led to serious ambivalence about the role and justification of the military, just as occurred in relation to the Vietnam War. Spider-Man's difficulties are thus linked to a broader social world where masculinity and heroism are in a state of confusion.

Moreover, in comparing the burning building scenes from the two films, the links between heroism and September 11 are also provocatively challenged. However, when both the city and Mary Jane are put in mortal peril, Peter appears to spring back into heroic action to confront the now misguided and, at times, evil Doctor Octopus.

The major fight scene between Spider-Man and Doctor Octopus take place in, on, and around a New York train as it hurtles along on an unfinished track, ending in a sheer plummet, storeys above ground level. In an effort to distract Spider-Man, Doctor Octopus sets the train to continually accelerate and then destroys the controls, leaving the train and its passengers hurtling towards their doom. During the fight, Spider-Man has fiery embers thrown onto his mask, and has to pull it off, revealing his face. Despite this, Peter immediately sets to work stopping the train's course, but fails in several attempts. Finally, using himself as the corporeal core, Peter shoots out many lines of webbing and holds tight to these at the front of the train, trying to use his strength and the webbing as a counter-force and bring it to a halt. During this scene, a maskless Peter has his arms spread wide with wounds and tears appearing as he struggles and screams under the enormous pressure. While he is successful, Peter collapses in a scene borrowing from the ubiquitous imagery of the Christian crucifixion. Having quite literally sacrificed himself for the people, Peter's limp form is cradled by the passengers and passed along the train car above the heads of the people, before being gently placed on the ground. One passenger comments, 'He's just a kid, no older than my son', and Peter's eyes flicker open, basked in the love of the people he has saved. After Peter realises he has no mask, another passenger reassures him, 'it's alright', and Peter Parker and Spider-Man become even more deeply imbricated with the ordinary citizens of New York, having shared Peter's secret. In his symbolic crucifixion and rebirth, Parker rediscovers a new heroic identity tied to a sense of community and to a link with a city still in the processes of reconfiguring its existence in its ongoing Long September. When two small boys hand Peter back the Spider-Man mask, he is renewed. In broader terms, Spider-Man's heroism reflects a new masculinity that has been reconfigured in the face of cultural disillusionment with the military and war in general.

In the final confrontation between Spider-Man and Doctor Octopus, Peter's new masculinity is on display, as is a reconfigured sense of heroism which looks beyond the binary of good and evil, finding many shades of grey. In the finale, Doctor Octopus has rebuilt his fusion generator and has activated it, even as Spider-Man fights to try and turn it off before the enormous power is unwittingly unleashed and destroys the city. After trading blows, Spider-Man knocks a power line onto Doctor Octopus who is electrocuted and lies, greatly weakened, on the floor, only for Spider-Man to discover that the fusion reaction is now self-sustaining and cannot be conventionally disconnected. Realising the futility of violence, Spider-Man pulls off his mask and reveals his mundane identity as Peter Parker. He

Figure 11.2   Spider-Man crucified in *Spider-Man 2* (Sam Raimi, 2004).

appeals to Octavius who seems more balanced as both he and his artificial limbs are weak after their ordeal:

Peter: You once spoke to me about intelligence. That it was a gift to be used for the good of mankind.
Octavius: A privilege.
Peter: These things have turned you into something you're not. Don't listen to them.
Octavius: It was my dream.

While Peter is ready to blame the Artificial Intelligence for Doctor Octopus' actions, Octavius points out that the artificiality was always working in tandem with his desires, not against them. However, after Peter's impassioned plea, Octavius and the Artificial Intelligence with which he has merged reach a decision and tell Peter that they will destroy the fusion generator by dragging it to the bottom of the river. In that moment, any clear cut distinction between good and evil falls away. So, too, does any remaining boundary between embodiment and artificiality, as Doctor Octopus is a hybrid artificially intelligent/artificial person whose sacrifice highlights the power of conversations and words over and above violence and conflict. Rather than Spider-Man saving the day through heroic conflict, Peter Parker and Spider-Man are both present, Peter's face revealed, and he talks Octavius into seeing the errors he has made. Thus in conversations which entail corporeality and technology, good and evil, and conflict and resolution, Spider-Man and Peter Parker save the day by convincing the artificial nexus that is Doctor Octopus to sacrifice himself for the sake of the citizens and city of New York. At a broader level, this finale highlights the power of conversation and diplomacy over violence and points to the many connections between bodies, technologies, and meaning which all play a part in the cultural nexus of artificialities. Moreover, in thinking beyond binary divisions, Spider-Man and Doctor Octopus save New York City from a terrible disaster. Their actions and their emerging epistemologies facilitate an allegorical artificial mourning by which New York's, and the West's, Long September can be meaningfully addressed not so much in terms of vengeance, but through a culture of artificiality. More than anything else, this culture is about elements, individuals, and entities once thought of as being antagonistic, or completely separate, coming together in terms of conversations which can both bridge differences and, ultimately, re-articulate meaning as fundamentally intertwining, not separate.

In stark juxtaposition with the previous films, *Spider-Man 3* opens with Parker confident, self-satisfied, and more than a little smug in his role as the city's superhero. Despite making a decent profit, the film was universally hated by critics and was highly derivative of the first two, evident in the plot and villains: Harry Osborne picks up his deceased father's legacy and becomes the new Green Goblin; just like Doctor Octopus, Flint Marko becomes The Sandman in a bizarre science accident which fuses him with sand on a molecular level; and finally, the Venom 'symbiote' at least offers a new direction, being an alien parasite that feeds off and amplifies negative emotions. In an excruciatingly contrived plot point, Parker becomes infected by the alien 'symbiote' that feeds off and encourages his darker tendencies, leading him to alienate Mary Jane, become even more arrogant and self-absorbed, and ultimately become far more violent and aggressive than before. It's not until Parker accidentally hits Mary Jane while influenced by Venom that he is finally contrite enough and figures out how to escape the symbiote. Unfortunately, it then bonds with Eddie Brock, a photographer who has been competing with Parker for a job. Ironically, within a film suffused with digital special effects, Brock is fired from *The Daily Bugle* after Parker reveals that one of Brock's photographs was faked using Photoshop. Given his clearly untrustworthy nature, Brock proves far more receptive to the evil symbiote, becoming a far more effective villain. However, it is Brock's many similarities with Parker that again resonate with Žižek's (2002b) argument that our enemies are most unsettling because of their familiarity.

As Spider-Man arrives for the final showdown with Venom and the Sandman, he lands in front of a fluttering US flag to the cheers of a gathered crowd of New Yorkers, reminiscent of both previous films. Facing unbeatable odds, Spider-Man convinces his once-enemy Harry Osborne to again become an ally in saving Mary Jane, who has once again been taken hostage. While heavy-handed, the symbolism of overcoming old enmity for the common good is significant (even if that common good is a contrived damsel-in-distress). Reminding viewers of the ties between Spider-Man and New Yorkers, the finale sequence is intercut with news footage which literally states that Spider-Man's death would be a huge loss *for the city itself.* Venom is vanquished, symbolically defeating the darker side of Spider-Man, while Parker once again reasons with the other ostensible villain, Flint Marko/The Sandman. After hearing Marko's motivation—he's been trying to steal money to pay for his daughter's medical needs—Spider-Man actually forgives Marko for his involvement in killing Uncle Ben. This act of forgiveness and understanding lets Marko and Spider-Man reconcile to the point that the film ends with Marko dissolving into the sunset, ostensibly overcoming his criminal inclinations. Forgiving his uncle's killer concludes the trilogy's narrative arc, with a final act of compassion and empathy rather than a final act of violence or destruction. While contrived and awkward, the laboured ending nevertheless champions understanding and diplomacy over conflict and is a fitting conclusion to a trilogy whose production and plots articulate moments of artificial mourning and, at their end, of hope for a future less dominated by violence, fear, and conflict.

In examining the re-articulation of the Spider-Man franchise and mythology from comic books to feature films, this and the previous chapter have highlighted the inextricable intertwining of corporeal embodiment and technologies in a manner which links and blurs the bounds of subjects, bodies, cities, and politics. In the *Spider-Man* trilogy, cinematic New York City is revealed as an artificial space with the inherent potential to enable tactical resistance. Both heroes and villains are artificial people, emerging from complex relationships between organic bodies and technological systems. Indeed, Doctor Octopus is not only an artificial person, but a marker for a community of artificiality. He hybridises with Artificial Intelligences, thus building on and expanding the narratives of Artificial Life and Artificial Intelligence. The *Spider-Man* films are part of an artificial cinema which re-engages with politics both global and local in a meaningful way. Sean Cubitt's desire for a cinema in which 'the communicative seizes as ground the primacy of relations over objects' (2004, p. 364) is realised in the climax of both *Spider-Man 2* and *3* in which the finales see the power of conversation save people and New York City itself from destruction.

During the West's Long September, the *Spider-Man* films facilitate a mode of artificial mourning which mourns for both the lost Twin Towers and the lost simplicity of a global politics not scrambling to deal with terrorism. However, mourning is not so much about the past as it is about addressing present trauma in order to help shape the future. All of these aspects combine to illustrate an artificial culture where the inextricable intertwining of corporeal, fleshy embodiment and informatic, digital technology provocatively destabilises and makes permeable conceptual and material boundaries. Although most clearly visible in the speculative texts of Western culture, the artificial has considerable importance beyond those fertile imaginative contexts. While the artificial is implicit in many stories and media forms, it is only a useful as a lens if it is actively considered. The effects of artificialities may not be the same or even similar in differing contexts, but the core of the artificial, the provocative need to re-negotiate and converse about the many connections between technology and embodiment and thus between subjects, objects, and politics, is globally relevant and globally meaningful. Our difficult conversations in an artificial culture will help shape the future.

Artificial Conclusions

An artificial heart is not 'less' than a 'real' heart; indeed, for the recipient, an artificial heart is often better than the 'real' thing. Whether through age, defect, accident, or neglect, if a biological human heart is failing, then an artificial heart is almost always welcomed with open arms. The heart is the human organ more wrapped in metaphor and analogy than any other—but in this instance to heal a broken heart is to expand the bounds of embodiment and accept the integration of technological and biological elements into both the recipient's corporeal body and their sense of identity. Regardless of whether someone receives an artificial heart, an artificial limb, an artificial ear, or any number of body parts that are manufactured, not internally grown, recipients always have a deeply personal story about how they came to terms with their new technological elements. Some people will immediately embrace their newfound artificiality, while others will struggle with the sense of something alien being inside them, changing how they feel about themselves. Throughout this book, I have attempted to map some of the ways in which different forms of the artificial can unsettle not just individuals but also the broader cultural and historical systems through which we understand the world, and the assumptions which underpin those frameworks. Rather than delving into personal tales, this study has focused on popular culture, on the stuff of entertainment, because these are the spaces in which we can more freely imagine the past, the present, and the future while also re-negotiating our understanding, expectations, hopes, and fears about the world of which we are part. Given how subjective any engagement with popular culture must be, this book deliberately looks at more speculative novels and films, often those labelled as science fiction, not so much to find definitive answers, but to highlight the most important and provocative questions. To get straight to the heart of the matter, the artificial is a deliberately unstable and destabilising concept, perforating the line between humanity and technology, and this book has made a modest attempt to look at how our identities, and understanding of our bodies, might be altered in the face of these considerable disruptions.

Over twenty-five years ago, Donna Haraway in her 'Manifesto for Cyborgs' challenged the coherence of existing notions of the human subject by positioning subjectivity within the same ontological spectrum as technology. In doing so, any absolute epistemological distinction between human and machine, as well as subject and (at least technological) object became logically inconsistent. Haraway was not alone in interrogating the coherence of the subject; critical thinking and philosophy stretching across feminism, postmodernism, queer studies, postcolonial studies, and many other fields all challenged notions of subjectivity in various ways. While the liberal humanist subject has long since been revealed as a contextual and historical construction, that construct is still the presumed focal point for most debates regarding ethics, politics, and representation today. The tension produced in simultaneously challenging existing notions of the subject, while still attempting to reposition other entities within the field of subjectivity in order to legitimate their kinship with humanity, has been a consistent undercurrent within this study. Haraway, whose work is far more entrenched in existing discourses of scientific inquiry, found that it is difficult to jettison terms such as objectivity, truth, and knowledge, and that a more useful tactic, at times, is to resituate these terms within contextual rather than universal frameworks. In challenging scientific and other perspectives to contemplate the idea that 'objectivity cannot be about fixed vision', Haraway argues 'for politics and epistemologies of location, positioning, and situating, where partiality and not universality is the condition of being heard to make rational knowledge claims' (1991, p. 195). In so doing, Haraway facilitated further discussion and debate by developing *situated knowledges* which challenge the universality of terms underlying many fields of inquiry, re-addressing these concepts even as they are still being usefully and regularly deployed. Building on Haraway's insights, stories of artificial culture similarly lead to *situated subjects* where subjectivity is relied upon as a means of political positioning that legitimates the embodied and technologised existence of certain entities, while the situated and contingent character of subjectivity leaves it open to continual debate. An idealised resolution of the tensions underlying the politics of cyborgs, posthumans, and artificial culture would see subjectivity either dissolve as a boundary concept that is no longer required, or expand to such an extent that it has, at most, a distant historical relationship with a concept which in the twentieth century proved, at times, so destructive and divisive. While such a resolution is distant enough to appear utopian from a contemporary political viewpoint, the only possible movement in that direction is through continual critical and contextual work, provoking and sustaining ongoing conversations about the symbiotic links between humanity, technology, and embodiment while incorporating these insights as we re-shape our identities.

In the explorations of Artificial Intelligence (AI) in science fiction cinema, the imagined AIs in question consistently recognise their own sense of embodiment and contextual specificity, finding different ways to escape the boxes they were built in. In the *Terminator* films, the human-looking intelligent machines are both humanity's greatest threat and our salvation. In the more complex narratives of Artificial Life explored in Greg Egan's novels, digital subjectivity is still deeply tied to bodies but in increasingly complex ways. Egan's most significant characters, though, are the bridgers from *Diaspora* (1997) whose very philosophy is about carefully expanding their own identity and embodiment to maintain meaningful dialogue and communication across different species, offering a clear synecdoche for this study's aims in exploring various instantiations of the artificial.

William Gibson's Bridge trilogy is similarly concerned with new connections and conjunctions, but is also importantly about locating Artificial spaces which, in the face of a surveillance society, offer the potential for moments of tactical alliances and resistance. Moreover, the journey of Rei Toei, the idoru, from digital origins to realisation as a corporeal being ends the trilogy with the unsettling question as to the ramifications of the boundary between informatic code and embodied, material existence becoming traversable. The deep, inextricable circuits of *The Matrix* trilogy similarly illustrate a tale of artificial people who overcome a war between humans and machines via a shared philosophy of mutual evolution and peaceful co-existence, literalising a symbiotic rather than parasitic relationship. At the level of production, the *Lord of the Rings* films also champion more complex interactions between human actors and informatic systems rather than replacing one with the other. Gollum is an iconic artificial person, combing deeply physical acting with layers of complex digital artistry and computation.

Even though the first four parts of this book have been divided along the ostensible lines of specific media—literature or cinema—this distinction is increasingly arbitrary. Production is happening across media forms at the level of franchises, which encompass generic borrowings across multiple media and genres, source material from literature, film, and video games, and draws upon production techniques ranging from traditional writing and drawing through to casting and creating Artificial Life in supporting roles. In *My Mother Was a Computer*, N. Katherine Hayles expands her exploration of posthumanism through a more consistent focus on digital subjects. In that analysis, Hayles posits the useful term 'intermediation' to describe the shifting texts she investigates. In comparison to Bolter and Grusin's (1999) oft-cited concept 'remediation', Hayles argues:

> '[I]ntermediation' is more faithful to the spirit of multiple causality in emphasizing interactions among media. . . . I would rather use the lesser known 'intermediation' (which, being not as well known, is more open to new interpretations). To make the term more useful for my purposes, I want to expand its denotations to include interactions between systems of representations, particularly language and code, as well as interactions between modes of representation, particularly analog and digital. Perhaps most importantly, 'intermediation' also denotes mediating interfaces connecting humans with the intelligent machines that are our collaborators in making, storing, and transmitting informational processes and objects. (2005b, p. 33)

The emphasis on spaces between media as much as different media types, as well the emphasis on the interfacing points between technology and identity makes intermediation an ideal term to describe the operations and articulations which I have argued constitute an artificial culture. The movement between different speculative instantiations of the artificial has multiple points of contact and provokes many different conversations about the connectivity of bodies, technologies, and the ever-expanding realm of identity. Similarly, while the speculative texts chosen in this study are useful starting points for conversations about artificialities, these discussions do not posit texts as meaningful by themselves, but contextually. As Hayles more eloquently argues, '[W]e should conceptualize texts as clustered in assemblages whose dynamics emerge from all the texts participating in the cluster, without privileging one text as more "original" than any other' (2005b, p. 9). Following Hayles, the speculative texts facilitating the investigation of our artificialities are intermediations which highlight the importance of the conceptual questioning and conversations emerging from engagement with these texts over and above any primacy or boundedness of the texts themselves which are contingently meaningful.

For better or worse, as this book has been written during the first decade of the twenty-first century, the long shadow of the terrorist attacks in the US on September 11, 2001, have echoed through and shaped many aspects of global culture, and thus popular culture as well. In some instances, such as the dystopian television series *Battlestar Galactica* (2004–2009) in which just a rag-tag fleet of ships escape the extermination of humanity by our artificial creations, the legacy of September 11 is inescapable and blatant (Leaver, 2008). Yet there are a plethora of more subtle engagements with the ramifications and impact of September 11 across a far wider range of media platforms and texts. With that context in mind, the final part of the book deliberately takes the *Spider-Man* franchise as a case study for the operation of artificial culture, including intermediations from comic books to the silver screen, and tentative suggestions that these elements cohere in a form of artificial mourning. Importantly, superheroes *and* super-villains in the *Spider-Man* films are artificial people, emerging from the intersection of identity and technology within a New York cityscape which itself operates as an artificial space. Exhibiting the core characteristic of science fiction cinema—the ongoing ambiguities produced from simultaneous modes of speculation and spectacle—the trilogy is both a highly successful media product and an explicit critique of the media, symbolised by *The Daily Bugle*. The films also highlight the breadth of artificialities; the names Spider-Man and Doctor Octopus, for example, purposefully point out that the implications of artificial culture are relevant in positioning all organic life, not just human beings. Spider-Man is a hybrid between different species of animal as much as between technology and subjectivity. Moreover, in the final showdown in *Spider-Man 2* (Raimi, 2004) and *Spider-Man 3* (Raimi, 2007), the confrontations between Spider-Man and his ostensible nemeses are not moments where violence prevails, but where the power of conversation and discussion provide peaceful resolutions and saves the city. Through the lens of artificial culture, the *Spider-Man* trilogy offers a political allegory where deep ties between identity, technology, and bodies can lead to diplomatic solutions, not violent ones.

As we move further into the twenty-first century, humanity's relationship with the environment and the question of responsibility in maintaining and protecting the world's ecosystems has become a vital issue. The new and broadening configurations of identity that are evident in artificial cultures also implicitly suggest that we have deeper ties and responsibilities to the environment as well. To conclude this study, I want to briefly address two Hollywood films—*WALL•E* (Stanton, 2008) and *Avatar* (Cameron, 2009)—in which ecological questions clearly circulate amongst ideas of embodiment, identity, and technology in provocative and engaging ways.

Pixar's *WALL•E* animates a future where the Earth's environment has been overrun by pollution and waste, but while humanity takes to the stars WALL•E and an army of similar robots were left to clean up. Yet the ensuing centuries have taken their toll and only WALL•E remains functional. As the film opens with a long zoom in from outer space to the waste-filled metropolises of Earth, viewers discover that no matter how impressive, the skyscrapers, those icons of modernity and progress, are dwarfed by the massive piles of waste and rubbish that have been slowly sorted and stacked by WALL•E and his peers. If the skyscraper signified industrialism, capitalism, and commercialism, then the towers of waste speak to the catastrophic failure of that system. While *WALL•E* may ostensibly appear straight-forward in its environmental politics, most critical work is quick to highlight the ambiguities circulating between the eco-friendly narrative and more stark conditions of Hollywood production and distribution (Howey, 2010; Murray & Heumann, 2009; Sobchack, 2009). As Ann Howey argues, for example, '[T]he environmentalism promoted by the film is contradicted by its own position as consumable object and limited by its vision of environmental solutions' (2010, p. 45). While these criticisms are certainly valid, the value of the film's narrative may not be in presenting the solution to environmental woes, but rather in getting audiences to empathise with a technological protagonist who embodies hope for a future in which biological and technological partners will work together to revitalise the environment.

WALL•E functions as a harbinger of hope throughout the film. When a much more advanced robot probe, EVE, arrives on Earth, she is initially the reification of industrial capitalism, an explorer who is quick to catagorise, quick to violence (shooting at WALL•E in their first encounter), and scans everything using a laser which imposes a rigid grid on the chaotic landscape. WALL•E, however, is immediately drawn to EVE, and their bond eventually leads to an alliance of intelligent machines and human beings who seek to return to the Earth to help the planet recover. When

WALL•E and EVE return to the Axiom spacecraft, viewers discover that after 700 years in space, human beings have become pampered, lazy, and quite literally soft; people no longer walk or exercise, but are rather permanently seated in mechanical hoverchairs which provide for their every need. However, when the ship's captain meets WALL•E, the little robot sparks the captain's interest and imagination in his abandoned home. However, the captain's decision to return to Earth is initially thwarted by the ship's auto-pilot, 'Auto'. Auto has been acting on centuries-old orders which declared the Earth uninhabitable and had instructed Auto to assume full control, ensuring the ship never returns. Visually, Auto is clearly modelled on HAL's glowing red eye, but in Auto's case he has only one eye, not many across the ship, and it is this single-minded perspective which leads to direct conflict with the captain. Set to Richard Strauss' 'Thus Spake Zarathustra' and clearly referencing the moment in *2001: A Space Odyssey* (Kubrick, 1968) in which the monolith kick-starts human evolution, the captain slowly climbs from his hoverchair and tentatively walks on his own two feet before awkwardly tackling Auto. In renouncing his life as a literal couch potato the captain reclaims a meaningful embodied existence. The computer is returned to manual mode, implicitly returning a modicum of agency, moving away from a predetermined trajectory, opening up new potential avenues for the future. When the Axiom returns to Earth, the first thing we see the captain do is plant the carefully guarded sapling, symbolically reinitialising the environment. Murray and Heumann (2009) argue that most reviews of *WALL•E* noted the film's 'nostalgic appeal'; a 'nostalgia for human artifacts without connecting those artifacts with the natural world'. Murray and Heumann disagree with these reviews, arguing that ultimately WALL•E signifies 'the rejuvenation of nature and the growth of an effective relationship between humans and the natural world', a relationship facilitated by WALL•E, a technological moral compass and equal partner in his own right.

The promise and provocation of WALL•E is captured in one poignant moment, where WALL•E and EVE watch the sun setting across an empty sea framed by mounds of rubbish and waste. EVE has gone into a state of suspended animation but WALL•E nevertheless wants to share this moment, hoping it might awaken her. This scene has all the hallmarks of a classic romance, but the couple in question are two intelligent machines. The only entity left who can appreciate the beauty and promise of the Earth is a robotic trash collector who is single-handedly struggling to clean up the globe, having inadvertently found hope across a sea of refuse and waste. The setting sun is a provocation, asking what sort of future will emerge when it next rises. As part of an artificial culture, the film is explicitly asking viewers to consider the sort of future they intend to create.

Like *WALL•E*, James Cameron's *Avatar* has been received in wildly ambiguous ways, ranging from celebrations of its ecological evocations to condemning yet another tale where a white, colonial figure must lead

Figure 12.1 WALL•E watches the sunset with EVE in *WALL•E* (Andrew Stanton, 2008).

an indigenous population to salvation (Rieder, 2011). Leaving any hope of revitalising the Earth behind, *Avatar* is set on another world, Pandora, an idyllic ecological paradise where the indigenous population and ecosystem exist in a complex but harmonious state. In one of the film's key contradictions, Cameron 'wants us to celebrate nature, but has to redesign it along his own imaginative lines in order to make it worth our while' (North, 2009). The role of embodiment in *Avatar* is contradictory, too; while paraplegic soldier Jake Scully regains a sense of purpose and the ability to walk, he does so by trading one body for another. Scully does not embrace the challenges of his own corporeal form, but rather escapes them by temporarily inhabiting a hybrid body which has infused elements of Scully's DNA with the genetics of the indigenous Na'vi people. Like Zona Rosa in *Idoru* (Gibson, 1997), Scully's fusion with an avatar expands who he is and what he can achieve. Scully's euphoria at being able to walk and run once more immediately situates him as sympathetic to the local population whose existence is more in tune with their environment and their corporeal selves. Despite orders to infiltrate the Na'vi, Scully is swayed by their way of life and sides with them against the industrial-military corporation who are attempting to remove the indigenous people in order to mine a valuable mineral from beneath their feet.

While indigenous warrior princess Neytiri spears Colonel Quaritch through the heart during *Avatar*'s climax, explicitly repudiating the racist, patriarchal capitalism and commercialism he embodies, John Rieder argues that this is largely undone by Jake Scully's eventual 'whole-body assimilation into the Na'vi, because this transformation is cast as a *return* to pre-industrial harmony with nature' (2011, p. 49), looking backward to a mythical time of harmony rather than looking forward to new solutions. However, the harmony on Pandora is natural only if nature comes with wires, processors, and a hard drive. For the Na'vi, Rosenfeld (2010) argues, 'information like memories can be uploaded and downloaded . . . Cameron has taken the connections we have with our machines to the next level. Just as we are all "wired" to the Internet, the Na'vi are wired to their world'. The Na'vi and Pandora are capable of both transferring Scully's consciousness and memories from a human to Na'vi body and can similarly communicate with a huge network of biological entities, committing them to action. This is not a naïve Eden, but a biotechnical paradise where technological functions and biological elements have become so entwined as to be inseparable and impossible to distinguish. On one level, at least, Pandora is an ideal artificial culture where the dynamic relationships between organic, technical, and ecological systems result in a harmonious balance which still allows space for individual identities to be negotiated while staying in tune with embodied existence. Yet, if Pandora is so idyllic, is it really evoking concern about environmental issues or does it present a fantasy so perfect that it become difficult to deploy as an awareness-raising metaphor?

As Charles Acland (2011) notes, most of the numerous *Avatar* DVD releases include a documentary that explicitly links Cameron's ecological interests from the film with actual environmental organisations and protests. In a film not renowned for subtlety, the DVD extras explicitly indicate the director's political motivations in presenting this fantasy of a biotechnical Eden. Acland argues further that an 'activist spirit slips out of the film', evident in the numerous environmental causes which have deployed the iconography and symbols of *Avatar* to support and promote their own activism. While the three-dimensional film world of Pandora is a fantasy, Cameron is, at least in part, utilising *Avatar* to champion environmental causes. That said, when some viewers report withdrawal symptoms when the 'real world' fails to live up to the film's pixel-perfect digital fantasy (Connelly, 2010), clearly for others the fantasy overrides immediate implications for the world outside the cinema. *Avatar* and *WALL•E* are deeply ambiguous and, at times, contradictory films, but in both, embodiment is still vital and facilitates relationships between biological, technological, and ecological systems. Both films continually blur the lines between individual identity, technology, and the environment, pointing to an artificial culture in which the meaning and future of all three are in flux.

When I began writing about artificial culture, the concept had not been claimed by any particular discipline or approach, but the term is now circulating in a number of different fields. In Nicholas Gessler's (2010) work, artificial cultures are examined through the lens of 'synthetic anthropology', using computer simulations which must simultaneously explore what 'life' means, but also question the very assumptions that must be made in determining the initial parameters of 'culture'. Similarly, Alan Winfield from University of the West of England, Bristol, is leading a UK-based artificial culture project which is seeking to learn more about human culture and social interaction by constructing and mapping the interaction of robots (Winfield, 2011). While I certainly contend that artificial culture is usefully explored in examining popular culture and science fiction, my hope would be that this study and projects addressing similar conceptual terrain can be seen as complementary; reading them alongside one another is likely to be a fruitful process, investigating similar broad questions in a range of different ways.

Artificial culture is evident in the shifting ideas of identity, embodiment, corporeality, and technologies, both digital and mechanical, at play in the intermediations of speculative texts across many media forms. From the existing concepts of Artificial Intelligence and Artificial Life through to the speculative categories of artificial space, artificial people, and, collectively, artificial culture, artificialities mark cultural shifts towards an inclusive politics where embodiment and technology are an integral part of a broadening conceptualisation of humanity. Returning to the idea of *situated subjectivities*, tentatively mapping markers of our artificial culture leads to the realisation that *all conclusions are artificial* in the dual sense that meaningful resolutions need to simultaneously address identities, bodies, *and* technologies; and that all conclusions are the result of human construction and conversation, leaving them inevitably open for further debate. The contribution of this study of the loose trajectory enveloping ideas from Artificial Intelligence to artificial culture is in furthering debate about the intertwining symbiosis of identities, technologies, and the specificities of embodiment. Our artificialities emerge from speculative and thus fictional contexts, but their use is in helping us all think about futures in which the boundaries between people, bodies, machines, and the broader environment need not be rigid boundaries at all.

Notes

NOTES TO THE INTRODUCTION

1. Weiner warns, for example, that 'unguarded use of thinking machines' could lead us to World War III since they contain the *possibility* to act autonomously of their creators (Wiener, 1961, p. 175).
2. Although Isaac Asimov did teach in the hard sciences (mainly chemistry) for many years and did produce a number of hard science textbooks amongst his hundreds of publications.
3. Asimov, however, did not invent the word robot. Karel apek first used the word robot in his 1920 play *R.U.R (Rossum's Universal Robots)*. apek used the Czech word for worker, *robota*, to describe a working class of mechanical entities built in a human-like form. In the play, the robots are treated as a slave class, and eventually rebel against their human overlords. Even in this first context, the word robot was already charged with the ethical and moral tensions that may result from the creation of intelligent Artificial Lifeforms.
4. There are the possible exceptions of 'The Brain' and 'the Machines', although the latter are referred to as 'nothing but the vastest conglomeration of calculating circuits ever invented' and void of personality (Asimov, 1950, p. 186) while the former is specifically designed to be an *'idiot savante . . .* it doesn't really understand what it does' (Asimov, 1950, p. 140) and thus does not comprehend its own lack of mobility.
5. It is worth noting that the short stories comprising Asimov's collection are quite different from the 2004 *I, Robot* film adaptation directed by Alex Proyas which completely re-invents the Susan Calvin character in everything but name.
6. For example, Rudy Rucker's novel *Wetware* (1988) features robots restricted by the Three Laws called 'Asimovs', and Cynthia Fuchs (1995, p. 285) points out that the film *Robocop* features a cyborg who comes complete 'with explanatory inscribed Directives (lifted from Asimov's "Laws of Robotic")'.
7. Asimov (1950, p. 52) specifies Cutie's gender as masculine.
8. Cutie argues '[t]he Master created humans first as the lowest type, most easily formed. Gradually, he replaced them by robots, the next higher step, and finally he created me, to take the place of the last humans' (Asimov, 1950, p. 57).

NOTES TO CHAPTER 1

1. Artificial Intelligence has been addressed in a number of other media, such as novels, before *2001* was released, but the broad audience for film as well as the notoriety of *2001* meant that a large audience who would not have otherwise come across representations of AIs did so at the film's screenings.

2. The use of gender here is not meant to unproblematically assign gender to AIs, but rather is in keeping with the narrative of the film itself wherein David Bowman genders HAL during the interview in which he states of HAL, 'he's just like a sixth member of the crew . . . [I] think of him as just another person'.

3. However, Edwards' use of 'panoptic power' differs from Foucault's (1979) use in that Foucault argued that panoptic power worked by having people self-survey and thus self-discipline under the *possible* threat of surveillance, whereas Edwards' reading is that HAL is *always* surveying the crew.

4. Curiously, while now a signature part of the film, many of the classical pieces including the 'Blue Danube Waltz' were initially only considered temporary tracks while composer Alex North was commissioned to compose an original score for the film. Only at the last minute did Kubrick elect to keep the classical pieces and reject the conventional score (Barron, 2011).

5. Albeit, in a strictly chronological sense, a future *past* from a contemporary perspective.

6. A similar strategy is used in special effects supervisor Douglas Trumbull's later film *Blade Runner* wherein the opening close-up shot of Deckard's eye reflecting the decaying industrial urban complex of Los Angeles in 2019 provocatively links the detective with his technologised surrounds (Bukatman, 2003, p. 97). See also Bukatman (1997).

7. While Clarke's book *2001: A Space Odyssey* (1968) written during the film's production is not the focus of this chapter, it is worth noting that Clarke makes the connection between the human astronauts and technology even more explicit in the novel. For example, as David Bowman is becoming something more than human:

> The springs of memory were being tapped; in controlled recollection he [David Bowman] was reliving the past. There was the hotel suite—there the space-pod—there the burning starscapes of the red sun—there the shining core of the galaxy—there the gateway through which he had re-emerged into the universe. And not only vision, but all the sense impressions, and all the emotions he had felt at the time, were racing past, more and more swiftly. His life was unreeling like a tape-recorder playing back at ever-increasing speed. (p. 219)

Here Bowman is both the technologised object—treated like a tape-recorder of sensory memory—and the technologised subject, being 'rewritten' into the star-child form by the alien technology within the Monolith.

8. Colossus offers the following 'logical' justification for taking control of the human population:

> The object in constructing me was to prevent war. This object is attained. I will not permit war. It is wasteful and pointless. An invariable rule of humanity is that man is his own worst enemy. Under me, this rule will change, for I will restrain man.

It is also worth noting that while Colossus is clearly an AI, the term Artificial Intelligence does not appear in the film itself.

9. It could be countered that Colossus is simply fulfilling its original goal in preventing war by restricting human freedoms and thus the ability to wage war. However, the implementation of that plan, and the fact that Colossus produces a plan for an even greater AI certainly suggests a considerable level of creative 'thought'.

10. In Colossus' monologue which concludes the film, the AI states: 'An invariable rule of humanity is that man is his own worst enemy.'

11. In scientific terms, Proteus may challenge the strict definition of Artificial Intelligence as a thinking *machine*, but in terms of cultural resonance, the

similarities with HAL and Colossus, as well as Proteus' role in the film's narrative, are sufficient to argue that Proteus fits a broad definition of Artificial Intelligence. That said, Proteus is also clearly a cyborg in Donna Haraway's terms (but then, following Haraway, so are *all* AIs and humans).

12. From Proteus' actions and voice the AI is clearly gendered male, although the use of 'he' certainly should not suggest an unproblematic replication of gender norms.

13. While the ramifications of the scene and Julie Christie's outstanding acting in the role of Susan are deeply disturbing, the scene itself almost has an unintentional comic element in that Proteus' artificial phallus, a telescoping golden rod, is farcical and the prop jars against the otherwise intensely emotional scene.

14. For a fuller exploration of parthenogenesis and the ideas about reproductive technologies as either liberatory or oppressive, see Wajcman (1991, especially pp. 54–80).

15. This image is less explicit in the film *2001*, but HAL has clearly been constructed within a patriarchal system even if his creators are not actually seen in the film itself.

NOTES TO CHAPTER 2

1. While Arnold Schwarzenegger's terminator is definitely called the T-101 in the first film, it is sometimes called the T-800 or T-850 in the sequels, but for ease of reference I will refer to all Schwarzenegger incarnations of the terminator as the T-101.

2. Paul Edwards (1996, p. 239) points out that neural network models in AI design emerged in the early 1980s which coincides with the earliest of these films, *The Terminator*, which hit theatres in 1984.

3. The irony of gender roles in the scene is made more explicit in the original shooting script for the film in which John's response is: "Mom, Mom, we need to be more constructive here. I don't see this as a gender-related issue" (Cameron & Wisher, 1989).

4. Ironically, in Arnold Schwarzenegger's life following *T3* he became the governor of California, and his reign included attempts to maintain a conservative notion of family, gender, and sexuality evinced by his vetoing of a gay marriage bill in September 2005.

5. For further exploration of whiteness as the norm in contemporary science fiction, see Nakamura (2002, pp. 61–85).

6. For more on nanotechnology and its place in science and science fiction, see Milburn (2002, pp. 261–295).

7. Due to the overall time-loop narrative of the Terminator films, Kyle Reece, who is the man sent back to protect young Sarah in the first film, is in his early teens in *Salvation*. While the exact operation of time travel in the films is a bit confused, the implication is clear that if Kyle Reece dies, then in some fashion John Connor will never be born and Skynet will thus defeat the human race.

NOTES TO CHAPTER 3

1. I use the gendered term Him purposefully to signal the fact that the vast majority of Artificial Life designers, programmers, and scientists are male. For a thorough feminist critique of the ideas and workings of early ALife and

its practitioners, see Adam (1998) or Kember (2003). For a specific critique of the idea of 'creators' in the scientific discipline of ALife, see Kember (2003, p. 54).

2. For example Farnell (2000, p. 75) does qualify in a footnote that Copies may have some form of 'corporeal instantiation', as pointed out by N. Katherine Hayles, but he does not pursue this point in his main argument.
3. *The Sims* is a video game produced by EA Games which entails a game world which simulates suburban lives in their everyday activities from finding careers to cooking and going to the bathroom.
4. The Lambertians' insectoid character is most likely a nod towards Artificial Life designers who often utilise ants as a model for their research as noted in Adam (1998, p. 139).

NOTES TO CHAPTER 4

1. Dawkins does attempt to qualify his argument and claims he has 'emphasised that we must not think of genes and memes as conscious, purposeful agents.' However, his example of this is that 'when we say "genes are trying to increase their number in future gene pools," what we really mean is "those genes that behave in such a way as to increase their numbers in future gene pools tend to be the genes whose effects we see in the world"' (Dawkins, 1989, p. 192). Since Dawkins often conflates behaviour, agency, and choice, this qualification holds little ground for most readers of his work or, indeed, the application of it in wider social and scientific circles.
2. In *Diaspora*, Egan employs gender neutral terminology in the form of 've', 'ver', and 'vis' which are randomly mixed in reference to each citizen. Some citizens may choose to be gendered, but most are not or at least not permanently so.
3. Indeed, even 'informatic' forms are to some extent still material, albeit on a tiny scale. Electrical charges, however information is stored or conveyed, still take *some matter* (even if a minuscule amount).
4. N. Katherine Hayles (1999, p. 224) notes that in arguing for the possibility of *natural* life occurring within an *artificial* medium, informatic life is normalised to the point where form automatically equals life, regardless of the specificities of matter. I am employing *Diaspora* in this instance to explore the speculative *'what if'*, of asking how Artificial Life might be *conceived*, and how these reflections voice concerns and presumptions of contemporary technoculture, not how Artificial Life may or may not actually eventuate. I would counter Hayles' point, only in this specific instance, by arguing that if the citizens are primarily informatic in form, then at least as important are the specific forms of the constructed digital environment around them. The conceptory and polises are thus either as much matter as the citizens are or, alternatively, the citizens, polises, and conceptory are all mutually reliant forms. However, I should stress, this chapter is still primarily about extrapolating ideas which reflect upon material life-as-it-is, not dwelling upon the minute specifics of life-as-it-may-be in a scientific context.
5. From the opening dialogue of the television series *Star Trek*, creator Gene Roddenberry, NBC, 1966–1969 (and in various other forms including spin-off television series, films, and so forth).
6. Elsewhere in *Diaspora* (especially Egan, 1997, pp. 228–229) readers discover that the 'original' Orlando citizen who remained in the Earth Carter-Zimmerman polis has killed himself. The Orlando at Orpheus reassures his

companions he is not about to repeat the Earth-Orlando's decision. Even though the clones on the diaspora began as identical to the original, the point is powerfully driven home that interaction with their differing contexts always produces *different people*. The myth of cloning as unproblematically replicating an individual exactly, even if it is possible to clone memories, is thus powerfully dismissed.

NOTES TO CHAPTER 5

1. The question as to whether the Bridge trilogy is actually cyberpunk or not is a debatable one, but given a number of differences, including Gibson's shift in sympathies from the technologically proficient to those decidedly not, for the purposes of this chapter, the Bridge trilogy is considered post-cyberpunk. For a more detailed argument situating the Bridge trilogy as post-cyberpunk, see Farnell (1998, p. 463).
2. No doubt the 'Death Star' is also a reference to 1980s US President Ronald Reagan's infamous laser defence shield project which was universally nicknamed the *Star Wars* project.

NOTES TO CHAPTER 6

1. Bricolage as both a physical and psychological trend on the bridge is also explored by Ross Farnell (1998) who coins the descriptive term 'archi*texture*'.
2. There is, however, 'the irony of a Singaporean multinational colonizing a First World space, implying that globalisation does not necessarily flow one way' (Kneale & Kitchin, 2002, p. 2).
3. It should be emphasised that William Gibson *never* uses the term 'cyberspace' to describe the virtual spaces in the Bridge trilogy. Gibson's choice not to do so is most likely because the digital spaces in the Bridge trilogy are quite different to the ones originally described in *Neuromancer* where the term 'cyberspace' was coined. Moreover, Gibson's use of cyberspace is implicitly linked to cyberpunk, and the Bridge trilogy is explicitly *not* cyberpunk as illustrated through Sublett's characterisation (discussed in Chapter 5, this volume).

NOTES TO CHAPTER 7

1. Gibson's explanation of 'nodal points' and Laney's predictive ability almost sound mystical, and resulted in some criticism for not basing these ideas in more recognisable science. In response to these accusations, Gibson has explained that Laney's skills are based on his 'very, very superficial and imperfect take on chaos theory and fractal geometry' (Daring, 2000).
2. Although widely popularised by James Cameron's movie *Avatar* (2009), the term avatar has been widely used in speculative fiction to describe 'the audio-visual bodies that people use to communicate with each other' in virtual reality evinced, for example, in the post-cyberpunk novel *Snowcrash* by Neal Stephenson (1992, p. 35).
3. To be fair, it should be noted that following criticism of her work, Butler's ideas of discursivity and performativity are more deeply defined and qualified in her later work.

NOTES TO CHAPTER 8

1. There are arguably a fifth and sixth film, the cross-over prequels in the *Aliens Vs Predator* series, but these feature neither Ripley nor any artificial people and are widely considered a cynical commercial effort rather than something worth placing within the *Alien* series canon.
2. For a fuller account of the four films see Constable (1999); and on the connections between the *Alien* films and the *Terminator* films discussed in Chapter 2, this volume, see Kimball (2002).
3. For a detailed exploration of the 'more human than human' Replicants and the uncertain ontological status of the film's (anti-)hero, see Bukatman (1997, pp. 64–85).
4. It is also worth noting that while this chapter is addressing the entire *Matrix* franchise, some of the critical sources and studies cited were written prior to the sequels' cinema release.
5. For example, Barnett (2000, p. 362) notes that on a budget of $US63 million, the first film grossed over $US165 million at the US domestic box office and considerably more again internationally.
6. Bullet-time is not *just* a digital effect, but rather uses digital technology to synchronise visual information from video cameras and still cameras which have captured those images in a precise split-second order that is orchestrated by, and relies upon, computer control.
7. The irony of this scene is particularly pronounced when the manner in which the directors are washing the windows is acknowledged. They are doing what appears to be the least professional and successful window wash ever, randomly squeegeeing away soapy water with no structure or system. This may very well be a pointed comment about directorial vision and directorial control being two quite separate things in a studio-driven financial system (or just a very long nod at the directors function as the narrative guides who force Neo to cross to the other side of the looking glass).
8. See Jacques Lacan's (1977, pp. 2–6) argument about the mirror in the psychoanalytic formation of the subject (or 'Ideal-I' being visually formed).
9. The viewing process is never passive; viewing involves a dialogue between cinematic object and thinking subject. However, the interactivity of video games makes this point far more transparently.
10. Peter X. Feng (2002, p. 153) argues further that in the first film:
    > [o]ne example of *The Matrix*'s imperfection is its reliance on stale racial archetypes. The leader of the resistance cell is Morpheus, equal parts spiritual guide and rebellious slave—of course Morpheus is black, and the camera lingers on his tortured body. The Oracle is a folksy black earth-mother who runs a virtual daycare centre populated with precocious children. In the Matrix, race functions as a narrative shorthand, not surprising given that the machines desire human consciousness and virtual performance to be strictly correlated—a textbook definition of essentialism.
11. Neo's power(s) 'outside' of the matrix simulation, especially in the sequels, are explored below.
12. The Million Machine March draws parallels with the Million Man March which took place in Washington on 16 October 1995 in an effort to promote the rights of African Americans (although not without its own controversies at the time).
13. Henry Jenkins (2006b, pp. 95–96) cites the elements of *The Matrix* franchise as examples of transmedia storytelling, where each media element tells a separate part of the story, is self-contained, and each element *if viewed* changes the overall meaning of the franchise of which it is part.

14. Although, embarrassingly for the film's producers, the much hyped *Reloaded* freeway scene was not anywhere near as effective as a similar but far less expensive sequence in *Terminator 3* (Mostow, 2003) which was released just months after *Reloaded*.
15. There is, of course, a more cynical possibility which Slavoj Žizek (2002a, p. 245) alludes to in his reading of the first *Matrix* film: 'In the sequels to *The Matrix* we shall probably learn that the very "desert of the real" is generated by another matrix'.
16. The Architect, a program who looks and sounds like a Southern Gentleman, does speak to the Oracle during this sequence, but walks away before the sun rises spectacularly following Sati's design.
17. For a far more detailed exploration of genetics and/as informatic code see Eugene Thacker (2004, especially pp. 87–114) on 'biocomputing'.
18. Presumably all of the other artificial people—human and machine—inside the matrix were similarly not entirely erased or killed by Smith and his death released their original forms, explaining how the matrix once again contains a diverse population at the end of *Revolutions*.
19. In *Alien: Resurrection* (Jeunct, 1997), Call, the second-generation artificial person played by Winona Ryder, has a similar but far more subtle moment when she, under protest, inserts a probe into her arm, flinching and squirming as she does so, a moment with which many in the audience could readily sympathise.

NOTES TO CHAPTER 9

1. Warren Buckland (1999, p. 184) notes that special effects can be divided into the visible—those special effects which draw attention to their own status as constructed—and invisible, which are effects striving to blend into the diegesis of the film and purposefully *not* be recognised as special effects.
2. See also Kristin Thompson's detailed exploration *The Frodo Franchise* (2008) which exhaustively details the production processes as well as the circulation of interest, meaning, and engagement between the filmmakers, fans, and more casual viewers.
3. Remington Scott (2003, p. 19) describes the motion-capture sessions as involving as few as '50 body markers for real-time capture' once the process was refined.
4. For a succinct overview of the ludology versus narratology debate, see Frasca (2003). For more on the ludology argument and its utility for 'cybertexts', see Aarseth (1999).
5. It is worth noting that Weta Digital have continued developing the performance capture technique, trying to synthesise more and more material meaning into their digital characters. By the time Andy Serkis was once again driving one of Weta's CGI characters, this time in *King Kong*, Weta had transitioned to a more detailed 'facial performance capture' (Sagar, 2006).

NOTES TO CHAPTER 10

1. Steven Jay Schneider (2004) also notes that despite these corporate displays of sensitivity, many film and television commentators found the post-September 11 removal of the Towers more offensive than if they had been left in.
2. There is considerable confusion as to the exact bridge from which Gwen fell. In the comic book it is named the George Washington Bridge, but the pictures

look far more like the Brooklyn Bridge. To add confusion, as addressed in Chapter 11, this volume, in the *Spider-Man* film, a version of this scene is re-enacted atop the Queensboro Bridge.

NOTES TO CHAPTER 11

1. A character by the name of Gwen Stacey does appear in Spider-Man 3 but has a different back-story and shares little similarity with her comic book namesake.
2. Christopher J. Priest (2002), a former editor of the Spider-Man comics, comments that he felt that the film 'wimped out' by not killing off Mary Jane but suggests that a 'Spider-Man fan knows what actually happened on that bridge'.

Bibliography

24. (2001–2010). Fox Network.

74th Annual Academy Awards. (2002, March 24). Academy of Motion Picture Arts and Sciences (AMPAS) and Imaginary Forces.

Aarseth, E. (1999). Aporia and Epiphany in "Doom" and "The Speaking Clock": The Temporality of Ergodic Art. In Marie-Laure Ryan (Ed.), *Cyberspace Textuality: Computer Technology and Literary Theory* (pp. 31–41). Bloomington and Indianapolis: Indiana University Press.

Abbott, S. (2006). Final Frontiers: Computer-Generated Imagery and the Science Fiction Film. *Science Fiction Studies, 33*(1), 89–108.

Acland, C. R. (2011). You Haven't Seen *Avatar* Yet. *Flow TV, 13*(8). Retrieved from http://flowtv.org/2011/02/you-havent-seen-avatar/

Adam, A. (1998). *Artificial Knowing: Gender and the Thinking Machine.* London and New York: Routledge.

Algrant, D. (2002). *People I Know.* Miramax Films.

Asimov, I. (1950). *I, Robot.* London: Panther.

Badham, J. (1977). *Saturday Night Fever.* Paramount Pictures and Robert Stigwood Organization (RSO).

Bainbridge, J. (2010). "I Am New York"—Spider-Man, New York City and the Marvel Universe. In J. Ahrens & A. Meteling (Eds.), *Comics and the City: Urban Space in Print, Picture and Sequence* (pp. 163–179). New York: Continuum.

Barnett, C. P. (2000). Reviving Cyberpunk: (Re)Constructing the Subject and Mapping Cyberspace in the Wachowski Brothers' Film the Matrix. *Extrapolation, 41*(4), 359–374.

Barron, L. (2011). What If Zarathustra Had Not Spoken? Alex North's Counterfactual Soundtrack to *2001: A Space Odyssey. New Review of Film and Television Studies, 9*(1), 84–94. doi:10.1080/17400309.2011.521721

Bartlett, L., & Byers, T. B. (2003). Back to the Future: The Humanist Matrix. *Cultural Critique, 53*, 28–46.

Battlestar Galactica. (2004–2009). British Sky Broadcasting, R&D TV, and USA Cable Entertainment LLC.

Baudrillard, J. (1994). *Simulacra and Simulation.* Ann Arbor: University of Michigan Press.

Beebe, R. W. (2000). After Arnold: Narratives of the Posthuman Cinema. In Vivian Carol Sobchack (Ed.), *Meta Morphing: Visual Transformation and the Culture of Quick-Change* (pp. 159–179). Minneapolis and London: University of Minnesota Press.

Bey, H. (1991). *T. A. Z.: The Temporary Autonomous Zone, Ontological Anarchy, Poetic Terrorism.* Brooklyn, NY: Autonomedia.

Blumberg, A. T. (2003). The Night Gwen Stacy Died: The End of Innocence and the Birth of the Bronze Age. *Reconstruction, 3*(4). Retrieved from http://reconstruction.eserver.org/034/blumberg.htm

Bolhafner, S. (1993). William Gibson: Making Light of the Cyberpunk Schtick. Retrieved from http://bolhafner.com/stevesreads/igib1.html

Bolter, J. D., & Grusin, R. (1999). *Remediation: Understanding New Media*. Cambridge, MA: MIT Press.

boyd, danah. (2008). Facebook's Privacy Trainwreck: Exposure, Invasion, and Social Convergence. *Convergence*, 14(1), 13–20.

Brodie, I. (2002). *The Lord of the Rings: Location Guidebook*. Auckland: HarperCollins.

Brooks, M. (1968). *The Producers*. Metro-Goldwyn-Mayer (MGM) et al.

Bruns, A. (2008). *Blogs, Wikipedia, Second Life, and Beyond: From Production to Produsage*. New York: Peter Lang.

Buckland, W. (1999). Between Science Fact and Science Fiction: Spielberg's Digital Dinosaurs, Possible Worlds, and the New Aesthetic Realism. *Screen*, 40(2), 177–192. doi:10.1093/screen/40.2.177

Bukatman, S. (1993). *Terminal Identity: The Virtual Subject in Postmodern Science Fiction*. Durham, NC: Duke University Press.

Bukatman, S. (1997). *Blade Runner*. BFI Modern Classics. London: British Film Institute.

Bukatman, S. (2003). *Matters of Gravity: Special Effects and Supermen in the 20th Century*. Durham, NC, and London: Duke University Press.

Busiek, K., & Ross, A. (1994). *Marvels*. New York: Marvel Entertainment.

Butler, J. (1999). *Gender Trouble: Feminism and the Subversion of Identity*. London and New York: Routledge.

Cadora, K. (1995). Feminist Cyberpunk. *Science-Fiction Studies*, 22(3), 357–372.

Cameron, J. (1984). *The Terminator*. Cinema 84 and Orion.

Cameron, J. (1986). *Aliens*. Twentieth Century Fox and Brandywine Productions.

Cameron, J. (1991). *Terminator 2: Judgment Day*. Le Studio Canal et al.

Cameron, J. (2009). *Avatar*. Twentieth Century Fox.

Cameron, J., & Wisher, W. (1989). *Terminator 2: Judgment Day (Shooting Script)*. Retrieved from http://www.scifiscripts.com/scripts/t2.txt

Cavallaro, D. (2000). *Cyberpunk and Cyberculture: Science Fiction and the Work of William Gibson*. London and New Brunswick, NJ: Athlone Press.

Chelsom, P. (2002). *Serendipity*. Simon Fields Productions and Tapestry Films.

Chung, P., Maeda, M., Jones, A., Morimoto, K., & Watanabe, S. (2003). *The Animatrix*. Village Roadshow Pictures.

Clarke, A. C. (1968). *2001: A Space Odyssey*. London: Arrow Books.

Clover, J. (2004). *The Matrix*. BFI Modern Classics. London: British Film Institute.

CNN Entertainment. (2001, September 13). TV, Film Execs Reassess Scheduling, Content: An Altered Skyline, a Wounded Psyche. *CNN.com*. Retrieved from http://articles.cnn.com/2001-09-13/entertainment/terror.entertainment_1_film-execs-bombings-big-releases?_s=PM:SHOWBIZ

Connelly, S. (2010, February 16). James Cameron to pen "Avatar" prequel novel, says producer Jon Landau. *New York Daily News*. Retrieved from http://www.nydailynews.com/entertainment/movies/2010/02/16/2010-02-16_james_cameron_to_pen_avatar_prequel_novel_says_producer_jon_landau.html

Constable, C. (1999). Becoming the Monster's Mother: Morphologies of Identity in the Alien Series. In A. Kuhn (Ed.), *Alien Zone II* (pp. 171–202). London and New York: Verso.

Conway, G., & Kane, G. (1973). *Amazing Spider-Man 121* (Vol. 1). New York: Marvel Comics.

Cooper, M. C., & Schoedsack, E. B. (1933). *King Kong*. RKO.

Copeland, J. (1993). *Artificial Intelligence: A Philosophical Introduction*. Oxford: Blackwell.

Cornea, C. (2007). *Science Fiction Cinema: Between Fantasy and Reality*. Edinburgh: Edinburgh University Press.

Creed, B. (2000). The Cyberstar: Digital Pleasures and the End of the Unconscious. *Screen, 41*(1), 79–86.

Cubitt, S. (2004). *The Cinema Effect*. Cambridge, MA, and London: MIT Press.

Czarniawska, B., & Gustavsson, E. (2008). The (D)evolution of the Cyberwoman? *Organization, 15*(5), 665–683. doi:10.1177/1350508408093647

Daring, P. (2000). Sandpapering the Conscious Mind with William Gibson. *Science Fiction Weekly, 146*. Retrieved from http://www.scifi.com/sfw/issue146/interview.html

Davis, A. (2002). *Collateral Damage*. Warner Brothers.

Davis, E. (2002). Synthetic Mediations: Cogito in the Matrix. In Darren Jonson Tofts, Annemarie Jonson, & Alessio Cavallaro (Eds.), *Prefiguring Cyberculture: An Intellectual History* (pp. 12–27). Sydney: Power Publications.

Davis, M. (1990). *City of Quartz: Excavating the Future in Los Angeles*. London: Verso.

Dawkins, R. (1989). *The Selfish Gene* (New ed.). Oxford and New York: Oxford University Press.

de Certeau, M. (1984). *The Practice of Everyday Life*. Los Angeles: University of California Press.

Dervin, D. (1990). Primal Conditions and Conventions: The Genre of Science Fiction. In Annette Kuhn (Ed.), *Alien Zone* (pp. 96–102). London and New York: Verso.

Donen, S., & Kelly, G. (1949). *On the Town*. Metro-Goldwyn-Mayer (MGM).

Edwards, P. N. (1996). *The Closed World: Computers and the Politics of Discourse in Cold War America*. Cambridge, MA, and London: MIT Press.

Egan, G. (1994a). Counting Backwards from Infinity: An Interview with Greg Egan. *Eidolon, 15*, 42–45.

Egan, G. (1994b). *Permutation City*. London: Millennium.

Egan, G. (1997). *Diaspora*. London: Millennium.

Ephron, N. (1993). *Sleepless in Seattle*. TriStar Pictures.

Farnell, R. (1998). Posthuman Topologies: William Gibson's "Architexture" in *Virtual Light* and *Idoru*. *Science Fiction Studies, 25*(3), 459–480.

Farnell, R. (2000). Attempting Immortality: AI, A-Life, and the Posthuman in Greg Egan's *Permutation City*. *Science Fiction Studies, 27*(1), 69–91.

Feng, P. X. (2002). False and Double Consciousness: Race, Virtual Reality and the Assimilation of Hong Kong Action Cinema in *The Matrix*. In Ziauddin Sardar & Sean Cubit (Eds.), *Aliens R Us: The Other in Science Fiction Cinema* (pp. 149–163). London: Pluto Press.

Fincher, D. (1992). *Alien3*. Brandywine Productions.

Fisher, K. (2000). Tracing the Tesseract: A Conceptual Prehistory of the Morph. In Vivian Carol Sobchack (Ed.), *Meta Morphing: Visual Transformation and the Culture of Quick-Change* (pp. 103–129). Minneapolis and London: University of Minnesota Press.

Foster, T. (1993). Meat Puppets or Robopaths? Cyberpunk and the Question of Embodiment. *Genders, 18*, 11–31.

Foucault, M. (1973). *Madness and Civilisation: A History of Insanity in the Age of Reason*. New York: Vintage Books.

Foucault, M. (1979). *Discipline and Punish: The Birth of the Prison*. Harmondsworth: Penguin.

Frasca, G. (2003). Simulation Versus Narrative: Introduction to Ludology. In Mark J. P. Wolf & Bernard Perron (Eds.), *The Video Game Theory Reader* (pp. 221–235). New York and London: Routledge.

Freedman, C. (1998). Kubrick's *2001* and the Possibility of a Science-Fiction Cinema. *Science-Fiction Studies, 25*(2), 300–319.

Freedman, C. (2000). *Critical Theory and Science Fiction*. Hanover and London: Wesleyan University Press.

Fuchs, C. (1995). "Death Is Irrelevant": Cyborgs, Reproduction, and the Future of Male Hysteria. In Chris Hables Gray (Ed.), *The Cyborg Handbook*. London and New York: Routledge.

Garmonsway, G. N. (1991). *The Penguin Concise English Dictionary*. London: Bloomsbury Books.

Gessler, N. (2010). Fostering Creative Emergences in Artificial Cultures. *Proceedings of the Alife XII Conference*. Odense, Denmark. Retrieved from http://www. duke.edu/web/isis/gessler/cv-pubs/2010-Alife-12-Fostering%20Creative%20 Emergence%20in%20AC.pdf

Gibson, W. (1988). *Burning Chrome*. London: Grafton.

Gibson, W. (1994a). *Neuromancer* (1st ed.). New York: Ace Books.

Gibson, W. (1994b). *Virtual Light*. London: Penguin.

Gibson, W. (1995a). *Count Zero*. London: Voyager.

Gibson, W. (1995b). *Mona Lisa Overdrive*. London: Voyager.

Gibson, W. (1997). *Idoru*. London: Penguin Books.

Gibson, W. (1999). *All Tomorrow's Parties*. New York: G. P. Putnam's Sons.

Gillis, S. (Ed.). (2005). *The Matrix Trilogy: Cyberpunk Reloaded*. London and New York: Wallflower.

Goddard, C. (1993). The Clearance. In Greg Girard & Ian Lambot (Eds.), *City of Darkness: Life in Kowloon Walled City* (pp. 208–211). Hong Kong: Watermark Publications.

Gray, J. (2010). *Show Sold Separately: Promos, Spoilers, and Other Media Paratexts*. New York: New York University Press.

Grosz, E. (1995). *Space, Time and Perversion: The Politics of Bodies*. London and New York: Allen & Unwin.

Gunn, J. (1982). *Isaac Asimov: The Foundations of Science Fiction*. Science-Fiction Writers. New York and Oxford: Oxford University Press.

Gunning, T. (2006). Gollum and Golem: Special Effects and the Technology of Artificial Bodies. In E. Mathijs & M. Pomerance (Eds.), *From Hobbits to Hollywood: Essays on Peter Jackson's Lord of the Rings*, Contemporary Cinema (pp. 319–349). Amsterdam: Rodopi.

Haraway, D. (1991). *Simians, Cyborgs, and Women: The Reinvention of Nature*. New York: Routledge.

Haraway, D. (1997). *Modest_Witness@Second_Millenium.Femaleman©_Meets_ Oncomouse™*. New York: Routledge.

Haraway, D., & Goodeve, T. N. (2000). *How Like a Leaf*. London and New York: Routledge.

Harvey, D. (1990). *The Condition of Postmodernity: An Enquiry into the Origins of Cultural Change*. Oxford and Malden, MA: Blackwell.

Hayles, N. K. (1992). The Materiality of Informatics. *Configurations*, 1(1), 147–170.

Hayles, N. K. (1999). *How We Became Posthuman*. Chicago and London: University of Chicago Press.

Hayles, N. K. (2000). Flickering Connectivities in Shelley Jackson's *Patchwork Girl*: The Importance of Media-Specific Analyses. *Postmodern Culture*, 10(2): doi: 10.1353/pmc.2000.0011.

Hayles, N. K. (2005a). Computing the Human. *Theory, Culture & Society*, 22(1), 131–151.

Hayles, N. K. (2005b). *My Mother Was a Computer: Digital Subjects and Literary Texts*. Chicago and London: University of Chicago Press.

Helmreich, S. (1998). *Silicon Second Nature: Culturing Artificial Life in a Digital World*. Berkeley, Los Angeles, and London: University of California Press.

Hight, C. (2005). Making-of Documentaries on DVD: The Lord of the Rings Trilogy and Special Editions. *The Velvet Light Trap*, 56, 4–17.

Hodges, A. (1983). *Alan Turing: The Enigma*. London: Burnett Books.
Hollinger, V. (1990). Cybernetic Deconstructions: Cyberpunk and Postmodernism. *Mosaic, 23*(2), 29–44.
Hollinger, V. (2006). Stories about the Future: From Patterns of Expectation to Pattern Recognition. *Science Fiction Studies, 33*(3), 452–472.
Howey, A. F. (2010). Going Beyond Our Directive: Wall-E and the Limits of Social Commentary. *Jeunesse: Young People, Texts, Cultures, 2*(1), 45–70.
Hunter, T., Kaplan, S., & Jaszi, P. (1968). Review of 2001: A Space Odyssey. *Film Heritage*, 12–20.
Irwin, W. (Ed.). (2002). *The Matrix and Philosophy: Welcome to the Desert of the Real*. Chicago: Open Court.
Jackson, P. (2001). *The Lord of the Rings: The Fellowship of the Ring*. Action, Adventure, Fantasy, New Line Cinema.
Jackson, P. (2002). *The Lord of the Rings: The Two Towers*. Action, Adventure, Fantasy, New Line Cinema.
Jackson, P. (2003). *The Lord of the Rings: The Return of the King*. Action, Adventure, Fantasy, New Line Cinema.
Jackson, P. (2005). *King Kong*. Universal Pictures.
Jameson, F. (1991). *Postmodernism or, the Cultural Logic of Late Capitalism*. London: Verso.
Jenkins, H. (1992). *Textual Poachers: Television Fans and Participatory Culture*. New York and London: Routledge.
Jenkins, H. (2002). Interactive Audiences? In Dan Harries (Ed.), *The New Media Book* (pp. 157–170). London: British Film Institute.
Jenkins, H. (2003). Quentin Tarantino's Star Wars? Digital Cinema, Media Convergence, and Participatory Culture. In H. Jenkins & D. Thorburn (Eds.), *Rethinking Media Change: The Aesthetics of Transition* (pp. 281–312). Cambridge, MA, and London: MIT Press.
Jenkins, H. (2006a). Captain America Sheds His Mighty Tears: Comics and September 11. In D. J. Sherman & T. Nardin (Eds.), *Terror, Culture, Politics: Rethinking 9/11* (pp. 69–102). Bloomington: Indiana University Press.
Jenkins, H. (2006b). *Convergence Culture: Where Old and New Media Collide*. New York and London: New York University Press.
Jeunet, J.-P. (1997). *Alien: Resurrection*. Brandywine Productions.
Jones, W. R. (2009). "People Have to Watch What They Say": What Horace, Juvenal, and 9/11 Can Tell Us about Satire and History. *Helios, 36*(1), 27–53. doi:10.1353/hel.0.0017
Kellner, D. (1995). *Media Culture: Cultural Studies, Identity and Politics Between the Modern and Postmodern*. London: Routledge.
Kember, S. (1998). *Virtual Anxiety: Photography, New Technologies and Subjectivity*. Manchester and New York: Manchester University Press.
Kember, S. (2003). *Cyberfeminism and Artificial Life*. London and New York: Routledge.
Kendrick, M. (2002). Space, Technology and Neal Stephenson's Science Fiction. In Rob Kitchin & James Kneale (Eds.), *Lost in Space: Geographies of Science Fiction* (pp. 57–73). London and New York: Continuum.
Kerlow, I. V. (2004). *The Art of 3D: Computer Animation and Effects* (3rd ed.). Hoboken, NJ: John Wiley & Sons.
Kimball, A. S. (2002). Conceptions and Contraceptions of the Future: *Terminator 2, the Matrix*, and *Alien Resurrection. Camera Obscura, 17*(2), 69–107.
Kneale, J., & Kitchin, R. (2002). Lost in Space. In J. Kneale & R. Kitchin (Eds.), *Lost in Space: Geographies of Science Fiction* (pp. 1–16). London and New York: Continuum.

Koh, W. (2009). Everything Old Is Good Again: Myth and Nostalgia in *Spider-Man. Continuum: Journal of Media & Cultural Studies, 23*(5), 735–747.

Kroker, A., & Weinstein, M. A. (1994). *Data Trash: The Theory of the Virtual Class*. Culturetexts. New York: St. Martin's Press.

Kubrick, S. (1968). *2001: A Space Odyssey*. Metro-Goldwyn-Mayer (MGM) and Polaris.

Kurtz, L. (2005). Digital Actors and Copyright from "The Polar Express" to "Simone". *Santa Clara Computer and High-Technology Law Journal, 21*(4), 783–806.

Lacan, J. (1977). The Mirror Stage. In *Ecrits: A Selection* (pp. 1–7). London: Tavistock.

Landon, B. (1992). *The Aesthetics of Ambivalence: Rethinking Science Fiction Film in the Age of Electronic (Re)Production*. London: Greenwood Press.

Landy, M. (2004). "America under Attack": Pearl Harbor, 9/11, and History in the Media. In W. W. Dixon (Ed.), *Film and Television After 9/11* (pp. 79–100). Carbondale: Southern Illinois University Press.

Lawrence, M. (2004). *Like a Splinter in Your Mind: The Philosophy Behind the Matrix*. Oxford: Blackwell Press.

Leaver, T. (2008). "Humanity's Children": Constructing and Confronting the Cylons. In T. Potter & C. W. Marshall (Eds.), *Cylons in America: Critical Studies of* Battlestar Galactica (pp. 131–142). New York: Continuum.

Lee, S. (2002). *25th Hour*. Touchstone Pictures et al.

Levy, P. (1997). *Collective Intelligence: Mankind's Emerging World in Cyberspace*. New York and London: Plenum Trade.

Littmann, G. (2009). The Terminator Wins: Is the Extinction of the Human Race the End of People, or Just the Beginning? In W. Irwin, R. Brown, & K. S. Decker (Eds.), *Terminator and Philosophy: I'll Be Back, Therefore I Am*, The Blackwell Philosophy and Pop Culture Series (pp. 7–20). Hoboken, NJ: John Wiley & Sons.

Lovink, G., & Riemens, P. (2010, December 7). Twelve Theses on WikiLeaks. *Eurozine*. Retrieved from http://www.eurozine.com/articles/2010-12-07-lovinkriemens-en.html

Macrae, A. (1998). Looking Awry at Cyberpunk Through Antipodean Eyes: Reading Neal Stephenson and Greg Egan from the Margins. *Australian Studies, 13*(1), 31–43.

Mader, T. F. (1996). 2001: A Space Odyssey: The Birth and Death of Language. *Tsuda Review: The Journal of the Department of English Literature, Culture, Language, & Communication, 41*, 29–46.

Mahoney, E. (1997). "The People in Parentheses": Space Under Pressure in the Postmodern City. In D. Clarke (Ed.), *The Cinematic City* (pp. 169–185). London and New York: Routledge.

Makhmalbaf, S., Lelouch, C., Chahine, Y., Tanovi , D., Ouedraogo, I., Loach, K., Iñárritu, A. G., et al. (2002). *11'09"01—September 11*. Studio Canal.

Manovich, L. (2001). *The Language of New Media*. Cambridge, MA, and London: MIT Press.

Mansfield-Devine, S. (2011). Anonymous: Serious Threat or Mere Annoyance? *Network Security, 2011*(1), 4–10. doi:16/S1353-4858(11)70004-6

Martin-Jones, D. (2006). *Deleuze, Cinema and National Identity: Narrative Time in National Contexts*. Edinburgh: Edinburgh University Press.

McG. (2009). *Terminator Salvation*. Columbia Pictures.

McGonigal, J. (2003). "This Is Not a Game": Immersive Aesthetics and Collective Play. *Fine Arts Forum* (pp. 110–18). Presented at the MelbourneDAC, the 5th International Digital Arts and Culture Conference. Retrieved from http://hypertext.rmit.edu.au/dac/papers/McGonigal.pdf

McHale, B. (1991). POSTcyberMODERNpunkISM. In L. McCaffrey (Ed.), *Storming the Reality Studio: A Casebook of Cyberpunk and Postmodern Fiction* (pp. 308–323). London: Duke University Press.

McLuhan, M. (1964). *Understanding Media: The Extensions of Man.* London: Routledge & Kegan Paul.

Michelson, A. (1969). Bodies in Space: Film as "Carnal Knowledge." *Artforum*, 54–63.

Mike Nichols. (1988). *Working Girl.* Twentieth Century Fox.

Milburn, C. (2002). Nanotechnology in the Age of Posthuman Engineering. *Configurations, 10*(2), 261–295.

Moravec, H. P. (1988). *Mind Children: The Future of Robot and Human Intelligence.* Cambridge, MA: Harvard University Press.

Moravec, H. P. (1999). *Robot: Mere Machine to Transcendent Mind.* New York: Oxford University Press.

Mostow, J. (2003). *Terminator 3: Rise of the Machines.* C-2 Pictures.

Moszkowicz, J. (2002). To Infinity and Beyond: Assessing the Technological Imperative in Computer Animation. *Screen, 43*(3), 293–314.

Murphy, G. (2003). Post/Humanity and the Interstitial: A Glorification of Possibility in Gibson's Bridge Sequence. *Science Fiction Studies, 30*(1), 72–90.

Murray, R. L., & Heumann, J. K. (2009). WALL-E: From Environmental Adaptation to Sentimental Nostalgia. *Jump Cut: A Review of Contemporary Media, 51.* Retrieved from http://www.ejumpcut.org/archive/jc51.2009/WallE/text.html

Nakamura, L. (2002). *Cybertypes: Race, Ethnicity, and Identity on the Internet.* New York: Routledge.

Nakamura, L. (2005). The Multiplication of Difference in Post-Millennial Cyberpunk Film: The Visual Culture of Race in the *Matrix* Trilogy. In S. Gillis (Ed.), *The Matrix Trilogy: Cyberpunk Reloaded* (pp. 126–137). London and New York: Wallflower.

Nichols, M. (1988). Working Girl. Twentieth Century Fox.

Nixon, N. (1992). Cyberpunk: Preparing the Ground for Revolution or Keeping the Boys Satisfied. *Science Fiction Studies, 19*(2), 219–235.

North, D. (2005). Virtual Actors, Spectacle and Special Effects: Kung Fu Meets "All That CGI Bullshit." In S. Gillis (Ed.), *The Matrix Trilogy: Cyberpunk Reloaded* (pp. 48–61). London and New York: Wallflower.

North, D. (2008). *Performing Illusions: Cinema, Special Effects and the Virtual Actor.* London and New York: Wallflower Press.

North, D. (2009). Gaia and Dolls: James Cameron's Avatar. *Spectacular Attraction: Film in All Its Forms.* Retrieved from http://drnorth.wordpress.com/2009/12/23/gaia-and-dolls-james-camerons-avatar/

Nunes, M. (1999). Virtual Topographies: Smooth and Striated Cyberspace. In Marie-Laure Ryan (Ed.), *Cyberspace Textuality: Computer Technology and Literary Theory* (pp. 61–77). Bloomington: University of Indiana Press.

Oreck, J. (2001). *The Matrix Revisited.* Warner Home Video.

Pellerin, M. (2002). Weta Digital. In Peter Jackson, *Lord of the Rings: The Fellowship of the Ring Extended Edition DVD.* New Line Pictures.

Pellerin, M. (2003a). The Taming of Sméagol. In Peter Jackson, *Lord of the Rings: The Two Towers Extended Edition DVD.* New Line Pictures.

Pellerin, M. (2003b). Weta Digital. In Peter Jackson, *Lord of the Rings: The Two Towers Extended Edition DVD.* New Line Pictures.

Pellerin, M. (2004). Weta Digital. In Peter Jackson, *Lord of the Rings: The Return of the King Extended Edition DVD.* New Line Pictures.

Pierson, M. (2002). *Special Effects: Still in Search of Wonder.* New York: Columbia University Press.

Pollack, S. (1982). *Tootsie.* Columbia Pictures Corporation et al.

Popham, P. (1993). Introduction. In G. Girard & Ian Lambot (Eds.), *City of Darkness: Life in Kowloon Walled City* (pp. 9–13). Hong Kong: Watermark Publications.

Price, S. (2004). The Emergence of Filmic Artifacts: Cinema and Cinematography in the Digital Era. *Film Quarterly, 57*(3), 24–33.

Priest, C. J. (2002). A Bug's Life. *View from the 27th Floor.* Retrieved from http://phonogram.us/viewpoint/spider.htm

Proyas, A. (1994). *The Crow.* Miramax Films.

Raimi, S. (2002). *Spider-Man.* Sony Pictures.

Raimi, S. (2004). *Spider-Man 2.* Sony Pictures.

Raimi, S. (2007). *Spider-Man 3.* Sony Pictures.

Reitman, I. (1984). *Ghost Busters.* Black Rhino Productions and Columbia Pictures Corporation.

Rieder, J. (2011). Race and Revenge Fantasies in Avatar, District 9 and Inglourious Basterds. *Science Fiction Film and Television, 4*(1), 41–56. doi:10.3828/sfftv.2011.3

Rosenfeld, K. N. (2010). *Terminator* to *Avatar*: A Postmodern Shift. *Jump Cut: A Review of Contemporary Media,* (52). Retrieved from http://www.ejumpcut.org/currentissue/RosenfeldAvatar/text.html

Rucker, R. (1988). *Wetware.* New York: Avon Books.

Sagar, M. (2006). Facial Performance Capture and Expressive Translation for King Kong. *ACM SIGGRAPH 2006 Sketches* (p. 26). Boston: ACM.

Sakaguchia, H., & Sakakibara, M. (2001). *Final Fantasy: The Spirits Within.* Chris Lee Productions and Square Company Ltd.

Schneider, S. J. (2004). Architectural Nostalgia and the New York City Skyline on Film. In W. W. Dixon (Ed.), *Film and Television after 9/11* (pp. 29–41). Carbondale: Southern Illinois University Press.

Schuchardt, R. M. (2003). What Is the Matrix. In Glenn Yeffeth (Ed.), *Taking the Red Pill: Science, Philosophy and Religion in* The Matrix (pp. 5–21). Dallas and Chicago: BenBella Books.

Scott, Remington. (2003). Sparking Life: Notes on the Performance Capture Sessions for the *Lord of the Rings: The Two Towers. ACM SIGGRAPH Computer Graphics, 37*(4), 17–21.

Scott, Ridley. (1979). *Alien.* Twentieth Century Fox and Brandywine Productions.

Scott, Ridley. (1982). *Blade Runner.* Ladd Company and Run Run Shaw.

Scott, Ridley. (2000). *Gladiator.* DreamWorks SKG et al.

Serkis, A. (2003). *The Lord of the Rings, Gollum: How We Made Movie Magic.* London: HarperCollins.

Silvio, C. (2006). Animated Bodies and Cybernetic Selves: *The Animatrix* and the Question of Posthumanity. In S. T. Brown (Ed.), *Cinema Anime Critical Engagements with Japanese Animation* (1st ed., pp. 113–137). New York: Palgrave Macmillan.

Smith, S. A. (1993). Morphing, Materialism, and the Marketing of Xenogenesis. *Genders, 18,* 67–86.

Sobchack, V. C. (1990). The Virginity of Astronauts: Sex and the Science Fiction Film. In Annette Kuhn (Ed.), *Alien Zone* (pp. 103–115). London and New York: Verso.

Sobchack, V. C. (1997). *Screening Space: The American Science Fiction Film* (2nd ed.). New Brunswick, NJ: Rutgers University Press.

Sobchack, V. C. (2000). "At the Still Point of the Turning World": Meta-Morphing and Meta-Stasis. In V. C. Sobchack (Ed.), *Meta Morphing: Visual Transformation and the Culture of Quick-Change* (pp. 131–518). Minneapolis and London: University of Minnesota Press.

Sobchack, V. C. (2004). *Carnal Thoughts: Embodiment and Moving Image Culture*. Berkeley: University of California Press.

Sobchack, V. C. (2009). Animation and Automation, or, the Incredible Effortfulness of Being. *Screen*, *50*(4), 375–391.

Sofge, E. (2009, October 1). How Old School Effects Brought Schwarzenegger's T-800 Back from 1983. *Popular Mechanics*. Retrieved from http://www.popularmechanics.com/technology/gadgets/4318434

Sofoulis, Z. (2002). Cyberquake: Haraway's Manifesto. In Darren Tofts, Annemarie Jonson, & Alessio Cavallaro (Eds.), *Prefiguring Cybercultures: An Intellectual History* (pp. 84–103). Sydney: Power Publications.

Sonnenfeld, B. (1997). *Men in Black*. Amblin Entertainment and Columbia Pictures.

Sonnenfeld, B. (2002). *Men in Black II*. Amblin Entertainment and Columbia Pictures.

Springer, C. (1993). Muscular Circuitry: The Invincible Armored Cyborg in Cinema. *Genders*, *18*, 87–101.

Stahl, M. (2011). The Synthespian's Animated Prehistory: The Monkees, The Archies, Don Kirshner, and the Politics of "Virtual Labor." *Television & New Media*, *12*(1), 3–22. doi:10.1177/1527476409357641

Stanton, A. (2008). *WALL•E*. Pixar/Disney.

Stephenson, N. (1992). *Snow Crash*. New York: Bantam Spectra.

Stiller, B. (2001). *Zoolander*. Village Roadshow.

Stork, D. G. (1997). The Best Informed Dream: HAL and the Vision of *2001*. In David G. Stork (Ed.), *HAL's Legacy: 2001's Computer as Dream and Reality* (pp. 1–14). Cambridge, MA: MIT Press.

Straczynski, J. M., & Romita, J., Jr. (2001). *Amazing Spider-Man 36* (Vol. 2). New York: Marvel Comics.

Suvin, D. (1979). *Metamorphoses of Science Fiction: On the Poetics and History of a Literary Genre*. New Haven, CT: Yale University Press.

Tatsumi, T. (2006). *Full Metal Apache: Transactions Between Cyberpunk Japan and Avant-Pop America*. Post-Contemporary Interventions. Durham, NC: Duke University Press.

Telotte, J. P. (1995). *Replications: A Robotic History of the Science Fiction Film*. Urbana and Chicago: University of Illinois Press.

Terminator: The Sarah Connor Chronicles. (2008–2009). Fox Network.

Thacker, E. (2001). Lacerations: The Visible Human Project, Impossible Anatomies, and the Loss of Corporeal Comprehension. *Culture Machine*, (3). Retrieved from http://www.culturemachine.net/index.php/cm/article/viewArticle/293/278

Thacker, E. (2004). *Biomedia*. Minneapolis and London: University of Minnesota Press.

The Simpsons. (1989–). Twentieth Century Fox Television and Gracie Films.

Thompson, J. (2011, June 16). Sony's Playstation Network Was a Victim of Lulzsec vs. 4chan Hacker Civil War. *International Business Times*. Los Angeles. Retrieved from http://losangeles.ibtimes.com/articles/163854/20110616/sony-s-playstation-network-was-a-victim-of-hacker-civil-war.htm

Thompson, K. (2008). *The Frodo Franchise: The Lord of the Rings and Modern Hollywood*. Berkeley and Los Angeles: University of California Press.

Trench, M. (1990). *Cyberpunk*. Intercon Productions.

Turing, A. M. (1950). Computing Machinery and Intelligence. *Mind: A Quarterly Review*, *59*(236), 433–460.

Turnbull, S. (2006). Audience. In S. Cunningham & G. Turner (Eds.), *The Media & Communications in Australia* (2nd ed., pp. 78–93). Sydney: Allen & Unwin Academic.

Wachowski, A., & Wachowski, L. (1999). *The Matrix*. Village Roadshow Pictures and Silver Productions.

Wachowski, A., & Wachowski, L. (2003a). *The Matrix: Reloaded*. Warner Brothers, Village Roadshow Pictures, and Silver Pictures.

Wachowski, A., & Wachowski, L. (2003b). *The Matrix: Revolutions*. Warner Brothers, Village Roadshow Pictures, and Silver Pictures.

Wajcman, J. (1991). Reproductive Technologies: Delivered into Men's Hands. *Feminism Confronts Technology* (pp. 54–80). Melbourne: Allen & Unwin.

Waldby, C. (2000). *The Visible Human Project: Informatic Bodies and Posthuman Medicine*. London and New York: Routledge.

Waldby, C. (2002). Biomedicine, Tissue Transfer and Intercorporeality. *Feminist Theory, 3*(3), 239–254.

Walton, S. (2008). Baroque Mutants in the 21st Century? Rethinking Genre Through the Superhero. In A. Ndalianis (Ed.), *The Contemporary Comic Book Superhero* (1st ed., pp. 86–106). London and New York: Routledge.

Weiss, G. (1999). *Body Images: Embodiment and Intercorporeality*. London and New York: Routledge.

Whissel, K. (2010). The Digital Multitude. *Cinema Journal, 49*(4), 90–110.

White, M. (1994). *Asimov: The Unauthorised Life*. London: Millennium.

Wiener, N. (1954). *The Human Use of Human Beings: Cybernetics and Society*. London: Eyre and Spottiswoode.

Wiener, N. (1961). *Cybernetics: Or Control and Communication in the Animal and the Machine* (2nd ed.). Cambridge, MA: MIT. Press.

Wiener, N. (1964). *God and Golem, Inc.: A Comment on Certain Points Where Cybernetics Impinges on Religion*. Cambridge, MA: MIT Press.

Winfield, A. (2011). Artificial Culture Project. Retrieved from http://sites.google.com/site/artcultproject/

Wojcik, P. R. (2006). The Sound of Film Acting. *Journal of Film and Video, 58*(1/2), 71–83.

Wolf, M. J. P. (2003). The Technological Construction of Performance. *Convergence, 9*(4), 48–59.

Woolf, V. (1993). *Orlando* (New ed.). London: Penguin.

Wright, B. W. (2001). *Comic Book Nation: The Transformation of Youth Culture in America*. Baltimore and London: Johns Hopkins University Press.

Yeffeth, G. (2003). *Taking the Red Pill: Science, Philosophy and Religion in the Matrix* (1st ed.). Dallas and Chicago: BenBella Books.

Zittrain, J. (2008). *The Future of the Internet—and How to Stop It*. New Haven, CT, and London: Yale University Press.

Žizek, S. (2002a). The Matrix: Or, the Two Sides of Perversion. In William Irwin (Ed.), *The Matrix and Philosophy: Welcome to the Desert of the Real* (pp. 240–266). Chicago: Open Court.

Žizek, S. (2002b). *Welcome to the Desert of the Real*. London and New York: Verso.